continued . . .

D0121925

Carpe Demon

"I LOVED *CARPE DEMON*! . . . It was great fun; wonderfully clever. Ninety-nine percent of the wives and moms in the country will identify with this heroine. I mean, like who *hasn't* had to battle demons between car pools and playdates?"

—Jayne Ann Krentz,
New York Times bestselling author of *White Lies*

"I welcome the novels that decide to be utterly over-the-top and imagine paranormal and superhero lives for their chick-lit heroines. Take *Carpe Demon* . . ." —*Detroit Free Press*

"This book, as crammed with events as any suburban mom's calendar, shows you what would happen if Buffy got married and kept her past a secret. It's a hoot."

—Charlaine Harris,
New York Times bestselling author of *Definitely Dead*

"What would happen if Buffy the Vampire Slayer got married, moved to the suburbs, and became a stay-at-home mom? She'd be a lot like Kate Connor, once a demon/vampire/zombie killer and now 'a glorified chauffeur for drill-team practice and Gymboree playdates' in San Diablo, California, that's what. But in Kenner's sprightly, fast-paced ode to kick-ass housewives, Kate finds herself battling evil once again. Readers will find spunky Kate hard not to root for in spheres both domestic and demonic."

—*Publishers Weekly*

"A+! This is a serious keeper—I am very ready for the next segment in Kate Connor's life!" —TheRomanceReadersConnection.com

"Smart, fast-paced, unique—a blend of sophistication and wit that has you laughing out loud."

—Christine Feehan,
#1 *New York Times* bestselling author of *Safe Harbor*

"Tongue-in-cheek . . . fast-pacing and in-your-face action. Give it a try. Kate's a fun character and keeps you on the edge of your seat." —SFReader.com

"Ms. Kenner has a style and delivery all her own . . . fun and innovative . . . [*Carpe Demon*] shouldn't be missed."

—FallenAngelReviews.com

"You're gonna love this book! A terrific summer read with lots of humor and crazy situations and action." —FreshFiction.com

"Kenner scores a direct hit with this offbeat and humorous adventure, which has an engaging cast of characters. Car pools and holy water make an unforgettable mix." —*Romantic Times*

Deja Demon

The Days and Nights of a Demon-Hunting Soccer Mom

Julie Kenner

BERKLEY BOOKS, NEW YORK

THE BERKLEY PUBLISHING GROUP
Published by the Penguin Group
Penguin Group (USA) Inc.
375 Hudson Street, New York, New York 10014, USA
Penguin Group (Canada), 90 Eglinton Avenue East, Suite 700, Toronto, Ontario M4P 2Y3, Canada (a division of Pearson Penguin Canada Inc.)
Penguin Books Ltd., 80 Strand, London WC2R 0RL, England
Penguin Group Ireland, 25 St. Stephen's Green, Dublin 2, Ireland (a division of Penguin Books Ltd.)
Penguin Group (Australia), 250 Camberwell Road, Camberwell, Victoria 3124, Australia (a division of Pearson Australia Group Pty. Ltd.)
Penguin Books India Pvt. Ltd., 11 Community Centre, Panchsheel Park, New Delhi—110 017, India
Penguin Group (NZ), 67 Apollo Drive, Rosedale, North Shore 0632, New Zealand (a division of Pearson New Zealand Ltd.)
Penguin Books (South Africa) (Pty.) Ltd., 24 Sturdee Avenue, Rosebank, Johannesburg 2196, South Africa

Penguin Books Ltd., Registered Offices: 80 Strand, London WC2R 0RL, England

This book is an original publication of The Berkley Publishing Group.

This is a work of fiction. Names, characters, places, and incidents either are the product of the author's imagination or are used fictitiously, and any resemblance to actual persons, living or dead, business establishments, events, or locales is entirely coincidental. The publisher does not have any control over and does not assume any responsibility for author or third-party websites or their content.

PRINTING HISTORY
Berkley trade paperback edition / July 2008

Library of Congress Cataloging-in-Publication Data

Kenner, Julie.
    Deja demon / Julie Kenner.—Berkley trade pbk. ed.
        p. cm.
    ISBN 978-0-425-22190-7
    1. Connor, Kate (Ficititious character)—Fiction. 2. Demonology—Fiction. 3. Mothers—Fiction. 4. Suburban life—California—Fiction. 5. Easter—Fiction. 6. Political campaigns—Fiction. I. Title.
    PS3611.E665D45 2008
    813'.6—dc22

                                                                                    2008004815

PRINTED IN THE UNITED STATES OF AMERICA

10 9 8 7 6 5 4 3 2 1

One

"Dammit, Kate. I thought you trusted me."

"Now really isn't the time for this discussion," I said, taking in all of the dark corners of the alley. For the last half hour, I'd had the uneasy feeling that we were being watched. But since we'd neither been attacked nor stumbled across an observer tucked into the shadows, my unease was beginning to feel a bit like paranoia.

I didn't like being paranoid. It made me crankier than my toddler when he missed a nap.

"Kate," Eric pressed, tapping the end of his cane impatiently on the asphalt.

I nailed him with my best glare of frustration. The one I'd been honing for close to fifteen years on our daughter, Allie. "Not now," I said. "Work, remember? Demons, boogeymen, creatures from hell?"

Eric raised his eyebrows, but I just smiled, secure in the knowledge that I was going to win this battle. Yes, I was avoiding the conversation. But I'd meant what I said. Now *really* wasn't the time.

"The alley's empty, Kate," Eric said, reasonably. "We haven't seen or heard anyone. Intuition's a great thing, but it's not going to jump out and attack us in the dark."

"You used to trust my intuition," I said.

"I still do. But you told me yourself you've encountered only a handful of demons in weeks. Call me crazy, but I think you're avoiding the subject."

"Hell yes, I'm avoiding it. Like I said, now isn't the time."

"Then when is the time, Kate?" he asked, his voice sharp, his temper peeking out around the edges. "We're here now. And it's not as if you're going to invite me into your kitchen to discuss this over a cup of coffee with you, Stuart, and the kids. So you tell me—when should we talk?"

"Don't be flip," I said, because Eric really wasn't playing fair. No. *David* wasn't playing fair. I couldn't let myself fall into the habit of calling him Eric. Not when only a few select people knew the truth.

The truth. Now there's a funny concept. Once upon a time, I thought truth was an easy thing. The sky is blue—true. The moon is made of green cheese—false. Evil walks among us—true. Dead husbands don't return to their wives and children in the bodies of other men. That one—surprise, surprise—turned out to be false. In my world, anyway.

At the moment, in fact, I was in a dark alley behind a popular San Diablo nightclub, arguing (or avoiding arguing) with *my* formerly dead husband who'd taken up residence in the body of a high school chemistry teacher named David Long. It probably goes without saying, but lately my life had gotten rather complicated.

My name is Kate Connor, and I'm a Level Five Demon Hunter with *Forza Scura,* having recently been promoted up a notch as the result of a horrific battle a few months prior from which I'd come out mostly unscathed. To be honest, the promotion came with no little bit of guilt, especially considering I'd done some things after that battle that weren't exactly worthy of the Vatican Seal of Approval. Like, for example, raising my first husband from the dead.

And then—for added measure—keeping that teensy little fact out of my postbattle debriefing.

Trust me when I say that resurrection is not a skill normally within a Hunter's repertoire. But I'd had the ability, and God help me, I used it. How could I not, with my daughter looking down at the father with whom she'd just been reunited? And, yes, with me desperate to save the man I'd once loved with all my heart and soul.

The only thing is, by using magic for such a damnably selfish purpose, I couldn't help but wonder if I hadn't tainted both our souls in the process. Not to mention complicated the hell out of my life.

"I'm sorry," David said. "I didn't mean to make light of everything you've been through. But this isn't only about you, Kate. Do you think it's been easy for me?"

I knew that it hadn't. "Sometimes. Maybe. I don't know." I tilted my head up and looked him in the eyes. "I think you're the one who got to go away for more than two months. Who got to sit and think and process everything that happened while I had to keep going on with life and dealing with a daughter who had her father back for about seven seconds, only to lose him again."

"Which is exactly why what I'm asking isn't unreasonable. A weekend, Katie. I'm only asking to spend a weekend with my daughter." His eyes met mine, and I saw the plea in them. "Is that so hard to understand?"

"No," I said. "Of course not. But it's complicated. And, dammit, Eric, you blindsided me. This night was supposed to be about hunting. Not custody arrangements." I winced, struck by the tone and meaning of my words. I never would have divorced Eric. *Never.* And yet for all practical purposes, it was as if we were divorced parents, our marriage having been abruptly terminated, but the issue of our daughter still hanging there between us.

"I can't risk hurting Stuart," I said, probably more coldly than I'd intended because my voice was flavored by guilt.

He looked at me for one long second, a muscle in his cheek

twitching. The mannerism surprised me and I looked away, confused. Eric had never had such an obvious tell. Which meant the gesture was pure David, and the fact that Eric and David were both the same and different struck me with such unexpected force that I stumbled on the sidewalk.

"How would I explain it to him, anyway?" I asked reasonably. "What possible excuse does a high school freshman have for spending the weekend with the chemistry teacher?"

"Maybe you should try the truth," David said. If he'd snapped the suggestion at me with a hint of sarcasm, I think I could have handled it. As it was, he spoke gently, as if he understood the power behind that word. *Truth.*

"I'm not telling Stuart about you," I said, with more force and determination than I actually felt. "I'm not telling him about any of this. *Forza.* My past. That I've come out of retirement. None of it. This isn't his life—it's not the life I have with him—and I don't want it to be."

Stuart hadn't married a woman who could eradicate a demon with the heel of a black leather pump or fling a steak knife at a hellhound and hit it dead center on the forehead. Instead, he'd married a woman who couldn't figure out how to force her self-cleaning oven to get with the program.

I'd kept the demon-chasing part of my life secret because it *was* a secret. No one outside *Forza* was supposed to know. And even after I'd come out of retirement to take care of the rapidly growing demon population in San Diablo, I still hadn't come clean with Stuart. Not because of the prohibition against revealing my identity, but because I didn't want my husband looking at me and seeing a girl other than the one he married.

Worse, I didn't want him to look and not like what he saw.

And though I might wish for my marriage to be a sanctuary wherein I never had to face my fears, more and more I realized that truth—that nasty demon—was barreling down on me. Soon, I knew, I would have to tell. Because as much as telling might drive us apart, maintaining secrets would eventually do that very same thing.

Knowing that fundamental fact was one thing. Having it forced upon me by the other man in my life was something entirely different.

"If he loves you," David said gently, "none of this will matter."

"*This*," I repeated. "There's that word again. You think it won't matter to him that I hunt demons? That I sneak out of the house at two A.M. and patrol the alleys and beaches armed with a blade and a bottle of holy water? Is that the *this* you're talking about, David?"

I took a step closer to him, my emotions a confused mix of anger, longing, and loss. "Or is there something else? Another *this*. You and me," I said, my voice catching in my throat. "You and Allie." I tilted my chin up and looked him straight in the eye. I saw my own pain reflected right back at me, and my voice faltered. "Those are complications Stuart surely didn't anticipate when he vowed before God to love me for better or for worse."

David winced, and I knew I'd struck a nerve. Eric had made the same vow, of course, but his was made null by the death of his body. That his soul had returned was, for me, both treasure and torment.

"But he *did* make the vow," David finally said, toying with his cane instead of looking at me directly. "If you love him, you have to have faith in him."

I pressed my fingers against the bridge of my nose, the gesture hiding the fact that I couldn't look at David. Not when all I would see was Eric.

"You told me you loved him," he pressed, this time meeting my eyes fully.

"I meant it," I said. And I had. I did. So help me, I loved my husband desperately.

The only trouble was, there were two men I loved. And two lives I couldn't reconcile.

I turned away and started walking toward the street and my car. I needed to clear my head, and if that meant taking the wimpy way out, then so be it.

I'd come here tonight not for the chance to spend some quality time with my recently returned-to-life dead husband, but because I anticipated the arrival of a newly formed demon. I'd assumed that David's motives were the same.

Not that I was naïve enough to think that the evening would pass entirely free of any discussion of our past relationship, but I truly wasn't expecting to be defending my decision not to tell Stuart. Or weighing the pros and cons of letting Allie do an overnighter with her previously dead father.

I stalked toward the main road, the sound of my own footsteps accompanied by the dull bass *thrum* from one of the nearby clubs. Then another set of footfalls sounded behind mine. I tensed, my training taking over even though I knew with near-absolute certainty that it was David behind me.

As I slowed, the *pad-thump* of his footsteps quickened. I took a deep breath to steel myself, then turned to face him. He paused, one hand clutching his cane, and although the faces were nothing alike, at that moment, it was Eric that I was seeing. Forget the face, forget the limp. The eyes belonged to Eric, and the apology I saw within melted my heart.

"I'm sorry," he said, and I thawed a little more.

"This isn't easy. We're both going to have to take it slow, you know? Be patient. And flexible."

The corner of his mouth quirked up. "Since when have you ever been patient?"

"Fair enough," I said wryly. The man really did know me too well. "The point is that we both have to make an effort."

"I know," he said, dropping all hint of teasing. "I would say that this isn't the way I wanted our lives to go, but I don't really think that needs to be said."

"No," I agreed. "With that, you have my full agreement. With a plan for visitation, though . . ." I trailed off with a shrug.

"This conversation isn't over."

"Only postponed. I know." I looked up at him, saw the doubt in his eyes. "Eric," I said softly. "I understand. So help me, I do. But like it or not, *I'm* the parent now. It's my decision to make, and I need to be certain I make the right one."

"You will," he said. "You always do."

His words, however innocent, reminded me of the intimacy we'd once shared. Once upon a time, Eric Crowe had known me better than anyone, and his faith in me had been as unshakeable as mine in him.

I brushed the comment away, feeling unreasonably twitchy. "I don't think Watson's going to show here tonight," I said, firmly shifting the subject away from my personal demons and onto the hellbound variety. "If he's out there, he's staying hidden."

"Still feeling like you're in the crosshairs?"

I considered the question. "No. I think we're all alone out here. If Watson was watching from the shadows, I think he's gone."

"You may be right," David said. "Want to do another pass just in case? Try another location?"

I hesitated, trying to decide on our best option. The morning paper had reported the near-death of Sammy Watson, one of the nightclub's bartenders. Sammy, it seemed, had been mugged in this very location. He was found unconscious and bleeding by a young couple who had wandered into the alley, apparently thinking that the stench of old french fries and rotting buffalo wings would add to the romantic allure of their evening. Instead of finding romance, they found a near-dead Sammy.

The article indicated that he'd been admitted to the hospital in critical condition. A nurse went on record that the staff had anticipated he'd be dead by morning, and they considered it their job to simply make him as comfortable as possible. Imagine their surprise when by morning Sammy appeared to be in perfect health, ready to whip out a few daiquiris and margaritas.

Because he was healthy enough to mix drinks, Sammy was released from the hospital, and the paper reported the tears of joy shed by his mother and girlfriend.

I felt a twinge of solidarity with those women. They'd thought they'd lost Sammy once, but he'd miraculously come back to them. Now, though, they were going to lose him again. I knew, because I was the one who was going to kill him.

Not him, actually. Sammy was already dead and gone. His body, however, was still fully functional, inhabited as it was by a demon. And since demons often returned to the place of their rising, tonight's alley patrol had seemed like a good plan at the time.

Now, at two-thirty in the morning, I was ready to hand Sammy his Get Out of Jail Free card.

"Maybe this one's got brains," David suggested. "Best way for him to stay in one piece is to avoid the local Hunter. At least until he's up to full strength."

"Hunters," I corrected.

David shook his head. "I'm not back on *Forza*'s payroll."

"But—"

He cut me off with a wave of his hand. "Not now. It's late, and we're both tired. And if we're giving up on Sammy, I think we should pack it in and get some sleep."

A queasy sense of guilt and fear snaked through me. "It's not—you didn't tell them about the Lazarus Bones, did you?"

He shook his head. "I made you a promise, Katie. Nothing would make me break that."

I nodded, mollified but still curious. "Then what—"

"Kate," he said firmly. "We'll talk about it later."

I didn't argue, mostly because it wouldn't have done any good. Eric, I'd recently learned, had many secrets. And though once upon a time I never would have believed it, now I knew that of all the people in his life, I was the one from whom he'd hidden the most.

David's continued status as a rogue Demon Hunter plagued me so much on the way home that I was forced—yes, *forced*—to drive through the twenty-four-hour McDonald's and down a large order of fries and a Diet Coke simply so that I'd have sufficient caloric energy to mentally process it all.

At least that's what I told myself as I slurped my soda and maneuvered my way down the deserted streets, stopping dutifully at all the flashing traffic signals even though there wasn't another car around for a hundred miles.

Part of the reason David had left for Italy a mere two days after the whole rising-from-the-dead thing was that he believed he owed *Forza* a debriefing. Essentially, David needed to lay out for *Forza* the full explanation of how Eric's soul had ended up in David's body, at least to the extent he could remember what happened. These things don't happen lightly, and we both knew that the *Forza* researchers were going to be all over it.

The other part of our adventure—the part where I used the dust from the Lazarus Bones to raise David from the dead—would also be of keen interest to *Forza.* I'd crossed a line when I'd made the split-second decision to resurrect David, utilizing the kind of magic I'd had no business playing with.

I'd do it again, though. I'm certain I would. But at the same time, I'd put my soul at risk that brisk January evening. Worse, I'd gambled with Eric's soul, too. Call me chicken, but I didn't want to hear the disappointment in Father Corletti's voice if I owned up to that.

Thinking of Father, I smiled and popped another french fry into my mouth. As the priest who headed up *Forza,* Father Corletti was like a parent to me. I'd been found as a child wandering the streets of Rome and had no solid memories of my own mother and father. It was Father Corletti who'd held my hand and read me bedtime stories. On my fourteenth birthday, he'd given me my very first stiletto (the knife, not the shoe). On my sixteenth, he'd given me a silver crucifix.

And it was Father Corletti who'd said yes when Eric asked for my hand in marriage.

David, of course, understood all that without my having

to explain, and it was he who'd suggested we keep the back-from-the-dead aspect of our most recent demonic battle secret. At the suggestion, I'd experienced a quick twinge of guilt. Lately, though, I'd become an expert at keeping secrets and suppressing guilt. If David was willing to keep silent, then so was I.

After all, even without the resurrection aspect, David's story was amazing. The kind of tale that the *Forza* researchers would transcribe by hand, then lock away in the restricted area of the Vatican library. In other words, Important Theological Stuff. So important, in fact, that I hadn't blanched when David told me about his planned departure, even though I knew Allie would be crushed to learn her newfound father was about to fly thousands of miles away.

As for me, I'll confess to being secretly glad that he was going away for a week or two. I didn't want him gone forever, not when I'd just gotten him back. But I couldn't help but crave a little space to process everything that had happened—from the demonic threat we'd managed to thwart, to the powerful magic I'd called on in order to keep Eric in this world with me for at least a little longer.

And to be honest, once she got over her initial disappointment, I think Allie was secretly glad her father was going away, too. As wonderful as Eric's return might be in theory, in reality, the situation required some major mental processing. It wasn't the kind of situation she could analyze for hours on end with her girlfriends. She couldn't go to the library and read a book on a similar subject. She couldn't do anything, really, except wait and process. In a way, David's departure was almost like a gift, and part of me couldn't help but wonder if he realized that, and if that knowledge didn't spur his departure.

I never expected him to stay gone as long as he did, though. What I'd anticipated to be a one- or two-week jaunt turned into almost three months, requiring David to take unpaid leave from his job at the high school, claiming he had to go to Europe to tend to an ill relative. And from the conversations during his scattered telephone calls to me and Allie, I got the impression that he fully intended to step back into his Demon Hunter role, possibly even abandoning his high school job all together.

So why was he still rogue? And why was he back to work at Coronado High?

My first guess came to me on the heels of guilt and fear—he'd confessed about the Lazarus Bones, and *Forza* had deemed his soul tainted and then soundly refused to allow him Hunter status. I shoved that proposition aside. If being resurrected by the bones had tainted his soul, then wielding them had surely seared mine, too. And I really didn't want to go there.

It wasn't merely blind denial that drove my hypothesis, though. It was trust. David made a promise. He told me that he'd honored that promise. And I wasn't inclined to doubt his words.

Which left open the question of why he hadn't been reinstated as a Hunter. I couldn't think of a single explanation, and I was still tossing possibilities around in my head as I pulled into our driveway.

I left the van in the driveway where I'd taken to parking it lately. *Forza* hadn't officially notified me that hell had frozen over, but I knew it anyway because Stuart had finally gotten around to fixing our creaky, slow, pathetic garage door (or, rather, he'd gotten around to hiring someone to do that very thing). But even though the glorious day had finally arrived, and the formerly painfully squeaky door now rose and fell with only the slightest whisper of noise, I still couldn't park the van in the garage. Why? Because I'd been so sure that my husband would procrastinate until after the election that I'd filled my half of the garage with various odds and ends I was collecting for a garage sale.

So much for having faith in my husband.

I took a quick sip of soda, shoved the last five fries into my mouth, then climbed out of the van. Then I scooted quickly to the far side of the house, bypassing the front door. The landing in front of the master bedroom has a dead-on view of the entrance hall, and the last thing I wanted was for Stuart to stumble out of bed and see me waltzing back into the house.

The night was dark, the sliver of moon hidden mostly by a blanket of clouds, and I clung to the thick shadows, hoping that no insomniac neighbors wondered what I was doing at this hour of the night.

Not that I was particularly worried about insomniac neighbors. Our neighborhood is about as suburban as they come, and with the exception of parties by a few of the teenagers, it's pretty much shut down after midnight.

Our yard is encircled by a wooden privacy fence with one gate on the side where we keep our trash cans and recycle bins. We used to keep it locked, but lately I didn't bother. I often needed to get inside in a hurry, and I'd discovered soon enough that if the demons wanted in, one little padlock wasn't going to keep them out.

Some might call that attitude pessimistic. I called it practical.

Out of habit, I did a quick sweep of the backyard, illuminating dark corners with the beam of my flashlight. I hadn't expected to find anything out of sorts, and reality matched my expectations. With any luck, Sammy Watson had decided to take a bus out of town, in which case he'd become someone else's problem and I could send him a gold-engraved note thanking him for freeing up a few hours of spare time on my behalf.

I slipped the flashlight back into my pocket as I moved from the gravel path onto our back porch. I found my house key in the back pocket of my jeans, and I pulled it out as I reached the door. French style, the door was made up of individual frames of glass, each of which displayed my reflection despite being smeared with the greasy fingerprints of my little boy. A forty-watt yellow bulb lit the back porch, preventing me from seeing inside, but reflecting back an image of the yard—and something gray and fast.

Without thinking, my knife was in my hand, and I sprang

off the porch and onto the gravel, craving the darkness to keep me covered. I let my eyes adjust without turning on the flashlight, and carefully examined the yard.

Nothing seemed out of the ordinary, but that hardly comforted me. *Something* had moved. And in my line of work, when *something* is something you can't easily see, that usually means that *something* is bad.

Though I'd already peered into the dark corners of the yard, I decided to go through the exercise again, this time getting more up close and personal with the shadows and crannies that seemed so familiar during the day and undeniably creepy at night. You might think that after years of fighting demons, I wouldn't be creeped out by the dark. You'd be wrong. I've probably got the willies worse than any five-year-old determined to keep the closet light on and not let fingers or toes dangle over the bed. Because unlike that five-year-old, who's seen only dust bunnies and stuffed animals, I've seen what's *really* hiding in the dark. And trust me when I say that it's not pretty.

Our yard is divided more or less into two parts, delineated by grass and gravel. The grass part is on the left, accentuated by a few fruit trees, some potted plants, and enough toys to supply half the children in a small developing country. The gravel is on the right, and on top of it we've got a plastic playscape for Timmy (that he's quickly outgrowing) and enough toys to supply the other half.

I checked the gravel side first, peering around the playscape, then under the storage shed that sits near the back of the graveled area. I found nothing of interest under there, just the cinder blocks that held the flooring up, a few rubber balls, and a Pyrex casserole that had been missing for more than a month.

All quiet, so I circumnavigated the shed, my feet crunching on the extra area of gravel we'd laid so that we'd have a shady place for Timmy's purple dinosaur sandbox. Lately, Dino was empty—my son interested more in tossing the sand around the yard than actually playing in it—but the lid was on. And though I didn't really expect a minuscule demon to be hiding in there, I popped the lid off with my foot, muscles tense and knife ready for action.

I terrorized a few pill bugs, a *Go, Diego, Go!* action figure, and a truly disgusting ancient racquetball, but otherwise all was well.

The area behind the shed is a haven for all our unsightly neglected stuff: bags of potting soil, loosely covered mounds of dirt and landscaping rocks, a rusty red wagon, and all the miscellaneous gardening tools that I intend to use but never quite get around to organizing. I inspected all of that detritus, found nothing, and moved on to the fence to check the narrow space into which we shoved rakes, shovels, and battered lawn chairs.

Once again, no demons.

I was beginning to think I'd been seeing things, and was tempted to pack it in. It had been a busy day, after all. I'd driven carpool, spent two hours doing laundry, wasted another two at the car dealership getting a tune-up and new tires, whiled away half an hour at Wal-Mart returning a bag of nighttime Pull-Ups I'd accidentally bought in the wrong size, and breezed through forty-five minutes chasing my toddler in the park. After all of that, I was bone-dead tired.

At the same time, I had a feeling I wasn't wallowing in paranoia. I'd felt eyes on me since the alley with David. And if I'd learned one thing in all my years, it was that Hunters are very rarely paranoid. Usually, there's a reason those little hairs on the back of your neck stand up.

With that axiom firmly in mind, I shone the light toward the few trees that dotted the other half of our lawn, checking first the ground and then tilting my head back to peer at the branches. Zilch.

Frowning, I stepped farther away from the shed and aimed my light at the roof, standing on my tiptoes as I tried to get a better look. Nada.

"Come out, come out, where ever you are," I called in a low whisper, more out of frustration than an expectation that any creature of the night would answer my call, and when I heard an answering *clack* in front of me, I almost jumped in surprise.

I arced my light down, illuminating the rickety potting bench behind the shed. I'd looked there already and seen nothing. Now the clay pots shifted, ever so slightly.

I took a firmer hold on my knife and stepped forward, silently at first as the grass crunched under my feet, then louder as I reached the gravel. I was close now, but still didn't see anything. Certainly not Sammy Watson.

With my heart pounding in my chest, I crossed the final five feet to the bench. As I did, one of the pots tumbled off and a gray blob leaped right at me. I thrust my stiletto forward, realized what I was seeing, and stopped myself an instant before mortally wounding Kabit, our big, gray, and apparently stupid, cat.

The cat, oblivious to having come within a hair's breadth of losing one of his nine lives, landed softly near my feet and began to twine through my legs, purring loudly.

I sagged with frustration and relief, then reached down and scooped him up. "Hey, dummy. I told you not to go out." The idiot cat had rocketed past me hours earlier as I'd sneaked outside to go meet David. A pampered fat cat, Kabit's delicate feline sensibilities weren't geared for sleeping under the stars.

"You could have been turned into a Kabit-kabob," I said. To which the little beast responded with a strangled hiss, his ears laid flat to show his utter contempt for such a suggestion. Or, more accurately, his total fear of the monster behind me.

Kabit's back claws ripped into my arms as he pushed off me even as I turned to face my attacker. Too late, though. Sammy Watson caught me midturn. A swift, hard blow to my arm released both the cat and my knife, and at the same time a steel blade pressed firmly against my throat, its presence quite sufficient to keep my feet planted firmly in place. "You die now, Hunter," Watson whispered as he grabbed my hair and yanked back, further exposing my throat to his blade. "Never will you wield the Sword of Caelum against my master!"

I didn't have time to think about my options; I could only react. I brought my left fist straight up between my own body and the demon, then slammed it down against the demon's knife arm just as his muscles tensed to slice my neck. The move was risky, but considering my predicament, I didn't much see a downside. Thankfully, the maneuver paid off— at least for the moment. The knife edge dragged along my skin, but didn't cut deep. I'd survive. Assuming, that is, that I could get myself untangled.

Easier said than done, though. The instant I'd slammed my fist against the demon, he'd released my hair, shifting his hold to around my waist and pulling me tight against him. Now he squeezed tighter. I gasped for breath, at the same time bringing my chin down to protect my vulnerable neck.

Apparently the demon wasn't dead set on seeing my blood spill from my veins. Any old death would be all right with him, and he caught my head in the crook of his arm. Having used that same maneuver, I knew what he was planning, and I didn't much like it. Get my head in a tight hold, twist, and voilà—one dead Demon Hunter.

Once again, a less-than-ideal outcome for me, and I was already fighting against it. I'd kicked out and around, slamming the heel of my shoe against his tender shin bone, then hooking my leg around his and tugging. The demon stumbled backwards and we both fell to the ground.

I gasped, the wind knocked out of me, and in that moment, Watson scrambled to right himself. He settled on top of me, his knife still clutched in his hand and my arms pinned uselessly to my sides, held tight by the demon's legs.

"Playtime is over, Hunter."

I strained against his hold on me, but it wasn't any use. My kicks met no resistance, and my arms were held fast. My blood pounded in my ears as his knife arced through the air. I was helpless, prayer my last and only defense.

The blade glinted in the moonlight as the point approached my breastbone. I sucked in air, instinctively pressing my back into the ground, trying to gain precious millimeters before the blade plunged into my heart.

I didn't want to die. But right then, I feared I wasn't going to be given much choice in the matter.

Time altered, the world moving at a painfully slow pace. The blade made contact with my shirt and continued down, the pain from the impact radiating out like a red stain. My life didn't flash before me, but my children's lives did. Hot tears flooded my eyes, and I cursed God for taking away my life. For letting evil get a foothold.

My scream was joined by a deep, guttural howl, and I realized two things at once: the pressure on my body had decreased, and something large and gray was attached to the demon's head.

Kabit.

I took advantage of the demon's distraction and burst upright, tugging my hand free and landing a solid punch under the beast's chin at the same time that I pulled my knees to my chest and then kicked up into his gut. His mouth snapped shut, cutting off the howl, and he fell backwards.

My brilliantly clever cat let out an earsplitting *yeeeooooowwwwl* and bounded away, digging his claws into the soft flesh of the demon's face and earning himself a month of tuna in the process.

The fact that Kabit was lazy, fat, and old—most definitely not an attack cat—didn't trouble me much. I take my miracles as they come, and this one had come in the nick of time.

As the demon swiped at his face, I leaped to my feet, looking around wildly for my knife or anything I could use as a weapon. I found one of Timmy's plastic shovels and lunged for it, breaking off the end so that when I stood upright, I was wielding a red plastic handle with a nasty sharp end. The kind of thing a child could put an eye out with. Or, for that matter, a Demon Hunter.

I considered throwing it, but ruled that out. I might be confident about the aerodynamic qualities of my own familiar knife. A plastic toy, not so much. The only way I could ensure a clean kill was to nail the bastard through the eye, up close and personal.

Not being a fool, the demon had turned and was now racing toward our back gate, weaving to avoid the plastic Tonka trucks and toddler garden tools that littered our yard. Not being hindered by such obstacles—I'm a pro at navigating around piles of LEGOs and miscellaneous Thomas the Tank pieces while carrying a hot roast and ordering children to wash up for dinner—I easily caught up to the beast.

I tackled him, knocking him off balance as he stumbled over the dinosaur sandbox that I'd left open. He landed with a thud, and I was right there on top of him in an instant, the plastic pressed against his eye. The slightest bit of upward movement, and this would be all over.

"Who sent you?" Sammy Watson was newly made; if he was going out of his way to attack me, it was on the orders of a demon higher up the food chain. "And what is the Sword of Heaven?" I demanded, having called upon my limited Latin resources to translate the blade's name.

"He comes again to face you," Watson replied, his voice almost singsong. "His wrath will multiply."

"Who?" I pressed. "Who is coming?"

The demon sneered. "He who seeks revenge. Who was thrust into cardinal fire. He will find his vengeance. And when vengeance combines with revenge, you and yours will die and hell on earth shall reign."

As that sounded like a less-than-ideal outcome, I pressed for more specifics.

His mouth split into a charming smile, complete with perfect teeth and twinkling eyes. Honestly, he must have made a killing as a bartender. "Secret," he said. "Can't share a secret."

"I've made demons tougher than you give up a few secrets," I said. "That's the beautiful thing about you bastards invading a human body. You get to experience all those lovely side benefits. Like excruciating pain."

"Do you wish for me to scream, Hunter?" he said, his words bold even though his eyes suggested that he was less than thrilled about my plan to torture the truth out of him. "Perhaps you desire your family to witness my demise."

"Perhaps I desire you to shut up until I'm ready for you to talk," I countered. I took my left hand off his throat barely long enough to snatch the ball out of the dinosaur and shove it into his mouth. My plan was to bind his hands and feet, then drag him behind the storage shed so that we were out of view of the bedroom window and the back patio. Once hidden, there were all sorts of ways I could make the demon talk, most involving a blade and holy water. And I *did* intend to get him talking. Clearly new trouble was brewing in San Diablo—and I needed all the information I could extract.

Carefully, I eased my weight off him, keeping my makeshift dagger at his eye. With my free hand, I grabbed one of his wrists and pulled it toward his back.

"Stand," I ordered, even as I eased to one side so that I could grab the knife that had fallen near him. I slid the eight-inch blade into the waistband of my jeans, then pushed him upright and edged behind him as he gained height. "Other hand," I said, "or this is over before it begins."

I held my breath, not knowing what he would do. If his orders were to kill me, he'd comply, waiting for the opportunity to try again. Otherwise, he might very well ignore my demands, knowing full well I'd shove my spike through his eye, releasing him back to the ether.

He eased his other hand around to his back, and I exhaled in victory. My original assessment was right—this was an assassination attempt, and he was going to cling to this form until I killed him, or until he killed me first.

"Walk," I said. I was close behind him, my left hand pressing against his crossed wrists, just below his shoulder blades. Since my right hand still held the stake against his eye, our progress was slow. But he moved, and I was willing to take this one step at a time.

After four small steps, he stopped. "Move," I insisted, but he just shook his head. *"Now.* Or I put a hole in that eye the size of California."

I heard a muffled word as the demon tried to respond from behind the ball I'd shoved in his mouth. "Dammit," I muttered. Whatever secrets this demon had would go unspoken until I removed the gag. But at the moment, freeing his mouth meant letting go of his arms or moving the spike away from his eye. Neither a desirable option.

So I punted. "Shut up and move," I insisted. "Once you're tied up all nice and cozy, you can talk all you want."

I shoved his wrists upward and felt the demon cringe in response to the pain that had to be shooting up his arms. Still, though, he didn't move other than to kick out, sending a spray of gravel shooting forward in the same direction from which I heard a familiar squeal of alarm.

Instinctively, I looked that way, then stiffened, terrorized by what I saw in the dim light of the moon—*Allie*, struggling against a demon who held her from behind, pinning her arms down at her sides. "I'm sorry," she whispered, as the cold hand of fear caught me around the heart and squeezed.

Two

Allie. I hesitated only a split second, but that was enough. The demon took the advantage, slamming its head back into my forehead, then dropping down. I dropped with it, then rolled clear, my concern no longer extracting information, but getting to my daughter. My demon, however, wasn't letting me go to her. It grabbed my legs and pulled me back.

I tucked in my legs and thrust out, managing to catch him in the gut as he was climbing to his feet. I glanced back over my shoulder, and the fear on Allie's face—not to mention her useless attempts to break free—bolstered me.

From my position on the ground, I propped myself up on one hand, kicked out a leg, and swung it into a crescent. I caught the demon midshin, sending him toppling. In seconds, I was on him, Timmy's shovel at the ready.

"Sorry, buddy," I said as I plunged the plastic into his eye. "Better luck next time."

I turned to race back to Allie, pulling the demon's knife out as I sprinted toward my daughter. The demon holding her didn't appear to have a weapon, and for that I was grateful. But Allie had been training diligently for the last two months, and I knew that if the creature had managed to get her in a stranglehold, he'd not only caught her by surprise, he was pretty damn strong.

He looked it, actually. Dressed like a ninja, he was clothed in black from head to foot. Even his face was covered, with slits only for his deep-set eyes, eerie in the weak moonlight.

I considered my options as I ran, not even conscious of what I was doing. I wanted to tackle them both, knocking Allie free and leaving me alone to pummel the demon. Normally I'd need a backup plan, as demons tend not to leave themselves open for direct attacks. This beast, however, seemed willing to do exactly that.

I kept expecting a change in his position. An arm moving to catch Allie around her neck. A knife displayed out of nowhere. Even a low voice sprouting some incoherent prophecy about swords and Hunters and the end of life as we know it.

I got none of that. Just my daughter looking scared and the demon looking . . . well, looking blank.

I lunged, then slammed the demon's blade straight into his buddy's eyeball, noting with some alarm how easily the blade went in, as if through nothing more substantial than pudding. With my other arm, I grabbed Allie by the shoulders and pulled her roughly out of the beast's grasp. "I'm sorry! I'm sorry!" she said as she crouched to one side.

I left the knife lodged in his eye, then leaped back, breathing hard and anticipating that little shimmer of demonic essence as the body sagged to the ground.

Too bad for me it didn't work that way.

Instead, jamming a sharp piece of metal through its eye only seemed to piss the creature off, a conclusion I very cleverly reached when it rushed me, arms outstretched, and then barreled right into me, toppling me over and grabbing me around the neck.

Beside me, Allie screamed, and I saw her clap her hand over her mouth and cast a quick glance back toward our still thankfully darkened house. Then she raced toward me even as I was scrabbling to grab hold of the knife still protruding from the zombie's eye.

That's what it was, of course—explaining the vacant expression, the fact that it survived a poke in the eye, and the oozy, decaying face. Frankly, it also explained the costume, because a rotting body can't wander the streets of suburbia without being noticed. Not even in California.

The zombie verdict also explained the lack of fight until I'd come near to taking it out. Zombies are controlled by a master. Once the master's out of commission, they exist in a pretty much mindless state, clinging fast to their last order, but not sure what they should do next, much less why they should do it.

Attack them, though, and they fight back. Self-preservation is a strong response all across the universe.

This zombie had no deficiencies in that area, either. He was determined not only to survive, but to make sure that his attacker didn't. Since that role fell on my shoulders, I was the one he was currently choking, the dead, cold flesh of his fingers tightening around my throat.

Have I mentioned that zombies are preternaturally strong? Even more so than demons in human form?

A rather inconvenient factoid under the circumstances, and I fought to stay conscious, willing my fingers to close around the handle of the knife. I tugged the blade out of his eye, realizing as I did that the pressure around my neck had decreased. Allie had jumped on her attacker from behind and was now jerking and yanking and kicking, all in an effort to get him off me.

It worked, too, because the creature lost his balance, his fingers loosening enough for me to break free. "Stand back," I said as I climbed to my feet. She did as I asked, and as the creature lunged for me once again, I caught it in the chest with a solid round kick, sending it toppling to the ground.

I didn't wait for it to react. I jumped on it, my knees on either side of its hips. And as its arms thrust up, trying to grab me, I plunged the knife down and through its abdomen, the eight-inch blade cutting easily through the soft flesh to lodge firmly in the gravel and hard-packed dirt of our yard.

The zombie flailed arms and legs, then grabbed for the knife.

"Dammit," I said, smacking his arms away. "Stop that."

It blinked stupidly, completely uninterested in minding. Beside me, Allie bounced up and down, all the while making little grunting noises.

"Are you okay?" I asked, shifting my position so that my feet were on one zombie hand and my own hands were holding down his other. He was strong, yes, but not unbeatable. And without leverage, he was going to have a hard time regaining the upper hand.

She nodded. "Yeah. Sure. No problem." She leaned closer, trying to get a look at the thing in the dark. "But shouldn't you cut off that arm or something?"

Exactly the response I didn't expect. "Excuse me?" I blurted.

"He's a zombie, right? So you kill 'em by cutting off their heads and arms and stuff, don't you?"

I squinted at her, bouncing a little as the zombie fought to get his limbs free. I smacked a flailing arm back down and readjusted my position. "Have you been in the attic? I thought we agreed you'd only read what I assigned or approved."

"I *have*," she said, standing taller and looking downright offended. "I totally swear."

"Then how—"

"Come on, Mom. It's not like I never watch cable."

"Cable?" I repeated, wondering what exactly they were airing on the Discovery Channel these days.

"Movies, Mom," she said, in such an exasperated tone that I had to assume she'd read my mind.

"Right. Of course." I considered for a second, quickly finding the flaw in her little speech. "Alison Crowe, you know perfectly well you aren't allowed to watch R-rated movies that Stuart or I haven't signed off on."

"Oh, come on! It's not like the movies are scarier than my life."

She had a point. I had absolutely no intention of letting her know that, but silently I had to admit that she had a point.

"Rules are rules, Allie."

Her shoulders slumped. "Whatever."

"Allie . . ."

"Yes, ma'am," she said, trying again.

"Better."

"So would you like to tell me when you've seen all of these zombie movies?"

"Um, Mom? Is this really the time?"

I indicated the zombie, more or less immobile beneath me. "I'm not going anywhere."

She hesitated, probably deciding if she should press the point. I put on my sternest mom face, though, and she relented.

"Bethany's," she said. "But I don't think they were R. Honest. She's got the Monster Channel in HD, which is totally cool, except that a lot of the movies are pretty lame." She frowned at the zombie. "For that matter, he's kinda lame."

"Trust me. We got lucky. These suckers are stronger than they look. You end up trapped in a cave with a hundred of these creatures, and they won't seem lame at all. Completely lacking in personality and pretty damn quiet, but not lame."

That seemed to sober her up. "So what do we do with him?"

I sighed. "Exactly what you said. Cut off their limbs."

"Cool!"

"*I'll* do it." R-rated life or not, I wasn't going to have my daughter dismember corpses, of either the totally dead or the living dead variety.

"Can I watch?"

I shook my head, wondering what had happened to my little girl who liked to put on ballerina tutus, flit around the living room, and insist that her life's blood was oozing out of her if she so much as stubbed a toe during her evening performance. Apparently she'd grown up. And gotten considerably less squeamish in the process.

"You can find me something more efficient to cut with," I said. "And fast."

She looked from me to the struggling zombie and then back to me again. "Right," she said with a firm nod. "Be right back." She hurried for the storage shed. Once upon a time, we'd kept it locked. Lately, though, we hadn't bothered. It's filled to the brim with stuff that we have no room for in the house. I've pretty much decided that if the thieves want to haul it away in the dead of night, they can have it.

Of course, if thieves can get in, so can other species of bad guys. "Allie!" I called out, suddenly fearful.

She turned, the door now wide open and my daughter unmolested. I exhaled in relief. "What?" she said.

"Nothing. Just . . . just thank you."

Her brows lifted in curiosity.

"For saving my butt back there. Tossing the cat was a stroke of brilliance."

The smile she flashed me was at least as broad as the grin from her second-grade class picture. "No problem, Mom. I think we make a pretty good team."

"Um . . . is it supposed to keep doing *that*?"

I looked down at the arm that was crawling toward me, powered by five determined fingers. I stepped out of the way and then stomped on the disgusting thing. "Unfortunately, yes. Hacking zombies apart only slows them down. It doesn't kill them."

"You have got to be kidding me!" Allie said, starting to sound a tad freaked out.

I had to laugh. She'd just spent the last fifteen minutes watching her mother whack the limbs off a zombie with a dull ax she found in the storage shed. And *now* she was freaking out.

"At least there's no blood," she said, her nose wrinkling as she scooted out of the way of the other spiderlike hand that was scrambling over the gravel toward her.

"Be careful around that thing," I warned. "It may look funny, but those hands are still deadly. It grabs hold of your ankle and climbs up to your neck, and I can't guarantee I'll be able to pry those fingers off."

"Right." She stomped down hard on it, and the hand flattened into the gravel. "So can it still talk?" She nodded toward the eyeless head that had lolled to one side, mouth moving and tongue wagging. Kabit, stupid cat that he is, trotted up and sniffed it, then batted at the nose with one curious paw.

"They can't talk, period," I said. "Dismembered or not."

"Oh." She glanced uneasily at it. "That's good."

"That pretty much sums up my feelings."

"So how do we kill it?"

"*We* don't," I said. "You need to get inside and get some sleep. As for why you were out here in the first place, I'll give you a pass for tonight since you saved my life. Tomorrow, though, I think we need to have a little talk."

"*Now* you're sending me inside? I already saw the über-gross part." Her forehead creased. "Didn't I?"

"Allie . . ."

"Mom, please? Please, please, pleeeeeze? I really, really want to help."

She got down on her knees, her hands clasped in front of her. When she did, of course, she released the squashed zombie hand, and I had to admit I was more than a little impressed with the lightning-quick reflexes that snatched the thing back as it tried to scurry away.

She wasn't queasy, she was determined, and I really did need the help.

I probably wasn't going to win Mother of the Year by letting my fourteen-year-old daughter help me clean up a dead demon and a dismembered zombie, but maybe I could write it down to mother-daughter bonding.

"Fine," I said. "You can stay. But that means you talk now. What were you doing in the yard at three in the morning?"

"Can't you tell me how we kill this guy first?"

"Allie," I said, edging toward my Wrath of Mom voice.

"Fine, fine. Whatever."

I twirled my hand, hopefully prompting forward motion in the confession department. At the same time, I picked up the ax again and prepared to hack off the fingers. I'd been serious in my admonition to Allie. And though I didn't relish more zombie mutilation, once I removed the fingers, the zombie would be more or less harmless.

Gross, but harmless.

"I overheard you on the phone," she said, as I brought the ax down, neatly removing two fingers in one blow.

I picked up the fingers and dropped them in an empty flowerpot, making a mental note to not forget they were there. Considering they weren't going to decay anymore, zombie fingers were never going to become the new rage in fertilizing products. "You did? When?"

"Well, I didn't exactly *hear* you. But early this morning, you got a call on your cell. And you looked at the number and then said you needed to get something out of your car to answer the question. And you told Stuart it had to do with an oil change or something."

"So?"

She rolled her eyes. "Like you could answer a question about an oil change."

The kid had a point. Put like that, it was a wonder Stuart hadn't picked up on my little game of smoke and mirrors.

"That still doesn't answer why you were in the backyard at three A.M."

"I figured it was Daddy on the phone," she said. She added a little shrug, shifting her weight a bit as she looked at the ground instead of at me. "He's been gone for so long and, well, you got that look on your face when you answered the phone."

"A look? What look?"

"Just . . . you know."

I had a feeling I did know, and decided not to press the point. I made a mental note to suppress any and all looks upon answering my cell phone. Especially if my husband happened to be in the room.

"So you figured it was David," I prompted, intentionally using his new name. "Then what?" I knew Allie understood intellectually that David couldn't slide back into the daddy role. Emotionally, though, I think she was still processing.

"That's all," she said, looking up to meet my eyes. I held her gaze, trying hard to project myself as the understanding mom. I knew this was hard on Allie—it was hard on me. More than that, though, I had no road map for helping her through this. We were both floundering, and the only thing that was going to get us through this was love and trust and faith that we'd come through unscathed.

"I watched from the front door while you talked," Allie continued. "But I couldn't hear anything. It's not like I was eavesdropping. Honest."

"I believe you," I said. "But?"

"But then I heard you go out in the middle of the night, and so I figured you guys must have planned to meet up somewhere. And that must mean that he was back. Here, I mean. In San Diablo."

"So that's it?" I asked gently.

"Yeah. Pretty much."

"And you came into the backyard to wait for me . . . why?"

"To find out if I was right," she said, her tone suggesting *duh* even if she didn't voice the word.

"Why not ask me in the morning?"

She tilted her head up to look at me. Her eyes glistened with tears, and my heart started to shatter. "Mom," she said. "He's my dad. How come he didn't call to talk to *me*?"

"Oh, baby," I said, my heart breaking. "It's not like that at all. Your father loves you desperately." I held out my arms, but she didn't come to me. Instead she let loose with a hysterical "*Aaaahhh.*"

She kicked, shaking her leg to try to release the hand that was making its way up her shin.

"Allie!" I abandoned my mutilated arm to rush toward my daughter and grab the runaway limb immediately below the wrist. "Pull," I yelled, even as I tugged from my end, my fingers prying at the dead fingers clutching my daughter's leg.

"*Mom,*" she wailed as the fingers clutched tighter. "It hurts."

"I know. I know. I'm sorry." I looked wildly around. I was managing to keep the thing from crawling up her leg, but I wasn't having any luck getting it off her. And those fingers were just going to get tighter and tighter.

"Okay," I said. "This way."

With me still holding the zombie limb, I scooted backwards toward the shed. "Did you see the pruning shears when you got the ax?"

She shook her leg, trying ineffectively to shake the thing off. "I think they're hanging just inside the door."

We maneuvered in that direction and with me still holding the zombie at bay—and Allie balancing on one foot so that I could reach inside without letting go of her new companion—I managed to grab the shears off the peg.

"Okay," I said. "Now hold still."

Her eyes widened. "This is so totally disgusting."

"Well, if it offends you, we could just leave it on. But people will ask questions. Especially at cheerleading. And I think it'll mess up your balance."

She scowled and rolled her eyes. "Just do it, already."

I opened the shears, then tried to pry a finger up to get the bottom blade underneath. No luck. I ended up cutting from the top, little by little, until I'd managed to slice off an entire finger.

It dropped harmlessly to the ground, and I went to work on the other four.

"This is absolutely the grossest thing ever," Allie said.

I tended to agree. "Just be glad there's no blood." I shot

her a wry look. "And when you're all grown up, I don't ever want to hear you say that we never did anything together when you were a kid."

"Ha, ha. Just get it off me, okay?"

"Working on it."

"What about the legs?"

"Not much they can do," I said, casting a sideways glance at a zombie foot that was tapping time, impatiently waiting to kick a little Demon Hunter ass. "With shoes on, they can't crawl. And so long as you don't get close—"

Allie held her hands up in a familiar surrender gesture. "Don't worry," she said as I finally snapped through the last digit. I get it." She looked around at our backyard, now more or less resembling the set of a horror movie. "What now?"

"Now we clean up." I stood up and wiped my hands on my jeans. I looked around the yard. "We need a box or something. Then we can take these things to Father Ben and let him deal with them."

"How?" Allie said. "You never told me how to kill them."

I frowned, because I'd been hoping she'd forget about that little detail.

"Mom," she said, her tone filled with teenage insistence. "I just had a zombie hand crawl up my leg. I think we've moved beyond protecting the teenager."

I wasn't entirely sure her logic was dead-on, but she was right about one thing: If there was one zombie, there were probably more. And I wanted my daughter paying attention to her surroundings—and not hanging out in our backyard at three A.M.

"Zombies die two ways. Either when they're completely incinerated—bones and all—or when their maker dies."

She turned around and stared pointedly at the dead demon by the sandbox.

"Yeah," I said. "That's what's bothering me."

"I don't get it. What?"

"He wasn't the zombie's maker."

"Okay, wait," she protested as she tossed the zombie's head into Timmy's Radio Flyer wagon. "You said earlier that the reason the zombie was just sort of standing there after you killed Dumbo over there was because he didn't know what to do once his master died."

"Exactly."

I watched her face, saw the flash of understanding as it all sank in. "So there's *another* demon running around? That dead one was his master, but somebody else was his maker?"

"That's my best guess."

She turned frantically, scoping out our yard and the darkness beyond.

"Don't worry," I said. "I don't think he's nearby." I had no idea where he was, but if he was sending newly formed demons to do his dirty work, he was probably laying low, ensuring that he didn't end up back in the ether before the Big Demonic Ritual went down. How did I know we were facing a Big Demonic Ritual?

Easy. Call it Kate's First Law of Demons: The level of demonic activity in a neighborhood is directly proportional to the number of domestic chores Kate must accomplish within a certain period of time. And it just so happened that I had only one week to pull together an amazing Easter fair for the neighborhood. I had no time to spare on Big Demonic Rituals. So, naturally, one had to be brewing. (And, yes, the cryptic comments about vengeance and revenge and mysterious swords were also a bit of a clue.)

Fortunately, David was back in town. He might be rogue—and I might be terribly curious as to why—but for better or for worse, he was still my partner.

Completely unaware of my internal meanderings, Allie's face scrunched up in a frown. "So, if the maker isn't nearby, where is he?"

"Staying safely away from the local Hunter, I'd think."

"Oh. Okay. So, um, the maker hires a master to boss the zombie around? Why can't the zombie just do whatever it wants?"

I had to laugh. "Zombies aren't demons themselves," I said. "Not like the ones you've seen inhabiting bodies or clawing their way out of portals to hell."

"There are *more?*" she asked, eyebrows riding high. "More kinds of demons?"

"You have no idea."

"Shit."

"Mmm," I said agreeably, ignoring the language faux pas that, under our new deal, should earn me one toilet-scrubbing credit, to be cashed in any time I wanted. "Here's the thing," I continued. "Only demons can make zombies. It's not common, and it requires the desecration of a holy relic. That's part of a Hunter's job, you know. Protecting relics and tracking down any demons that make it their business to steal or desecrate them."

"Okay. Got it." Her forehead creased. "So if zombies aren't demons, then what are they?"

"Real zombies are just . . . well, they're just animated flesh."

"I'm going to hate asking, but what did you mean by 'real' zombies?"

I glanced at my watch—ten past four. "We don't really have time for—" I stopped as light from my bedroom window flooded the backyard.

"Oh, shit!" Allie said.

"Allie . . ." I warned, but I shared the sentiment. Stuart, I realized, was awake.

Three

"*Kate!*" Stuart's voice called from the bedroom window.

I stiffened, my mind whirring as I ran through possible explanations for what Allie and I could possibly be doing with all these body parts. Not too surprisingly, none seemed particularly viable.

"Are you out there?" And then, more to himself, "Dammit, I can't see a bloody thing."

I exhaled, realizing that between the trees and the dark, we were essentially invisible.

I heard the window slam shut and reached out to grab Allie. "Quick! Hide the parts."

"Already on it!"

I turned to find her frantically tossing zombie bits into Timmy's dinosaur sandbox. Personally, I would have chosen the storage shed, but at least the kid thought fast on her feet.

"Good girl. You finish that, I'll take care of him." I trotted over and grabbed the dead demon by the ankles, then tugged and pulled until I got him behind the shed. I didn't have anything to cover him with, so I just pushed him as far under the gardening bench as I could manage.

The creak of the back door opening burst through the night like a shot. "Kate? Are you out here?"

I cringed, expecting him to focus a flashlight on us, but the light didn't come, and so I hurried toward Allie, my feet crunching on the gravel that surrounded the sandbox.

"Right here," I called brightly. "Hang on a sec!"

"What the hell are you doing?"

Allie tossed the last of the body parts into the dinosaur, and we both bent over to grab the lid, managing to bonk our heads in the process. "Ouch! Dammit!"

"Kate!"

I motioned for Allie to get the lid on the sandbox while I hurried toward Stuart, intercepting him before he stepped off the porch. "Right here," I said. "I'm here. I'm fine."

I stepped into the circle of light emitted by the back porch bulb and gave my husband an enthusiastic hug. "What on earth are you doing awake?" I asked, sounding oh-so-chipper, as if I'd merely gotten up early to enjoy the night air.

"I thought I heard someone scream," he said, his voice laced with controlled panic. "Are you okay? Why are you outside?"

"Uh—oh," I stammered, pulling back and looking out over the yard. As I'd hoped, everything beyond the patio was a dark blur; the only way Stuart would notice Allie or the body or, for that matter, the body parts, was if he decided to take that moment to catch up on yard work.

"Kate," he pressed, the panic edging out and anger edging in. I knew that transition intimately, having experienced it myself when the kids did something both stupid and dangerous. "What the hell is going on?"

"Nothing," I assured him. "I, you know, wanted some quiet time. In case you've forgotten, we have a toddler in the house."

"You have got to be kidding me," he said, his voice making perfectly clear he didn't find the joke funny at all. "It's the middle of the night—"

"It's getting close to dawn," I protested. "In L.A., people are already commuting to work."

He rubbed the bridge of his nose. "We don't live in Los Angeles, and that's not the point. I wake up, alone, and then hear a scream, and you're not willing to give me a straight answer? Forgive me if I'm a little worried. I think I've got every right to be."

"Stuart," I began, but I honestly didn't know where to go next.

"It's about me," a small voice said, filling the gap. I turned, startled, and saw Allie step into the light. "Mom's trying to protect me."

Stuart's jawline tightened. "From what, exactly?"

Her head hung low, and when she lifted it to look her stepfather in the eye, I saw a strength that no longer surprised me. "I snuck out of the house," Allie said. "And when Mom realized, we had a fight."

Stuart looked at me for confirmation, and I worked to erase the expression of bafflement and replace it with my best stern mommy expression. I waved a hand in Allie's direction, hopefully signaling permission for her to continue telling the story of her descent into teenage disobedience.

She took a deep breath, then looked at me for only a second before focusing on her toes. The position gave the impression of contrite submission, but I suspected she was afraid that she'd smile at me if our eyes met, proud of herself for saving my ass twice now. Once by tossing the cat, and again by conning my husband.

"I'm waiting, young lady," Stuart said.

"It's just that it's Friday night, you know? And Aunt Laura told Mindy that she could go, but I wanted to go, too."

"Go where?" Stuart asked.

"A party," Allie answered, without missing a beat. "At Zachary Tremont's house." Zachary Tremont is a senior and the quarterback. He's also the son of Horatio Tremont, a major movie star who divides his time between Los Angeles and San Diablo. The house is in a gated section of the town with access to a private beach. Horatio's parties are the kind that usually end up featured on such fabulous news venues as *Access Hollywood* and *Entertainment Tonight.* I could only assume Zachary intended to live up to Daddy's expectations.

"Mom said we couldn't go," Allie continued, shooting me a look of contempt that had me both mentally applauding her acting abilities and wallowing in an increased level of guilt. Not only was I lying to my husband on a regular basis, but now my daughter had joined the act, too.

For a brief instant, I considered coming clean right then and telling Stuart everything. But when I opened my mouth, I couldn't do it. There's a time for everything, and somehow, I didn't think this was the time for true confessions.

Or maybe I was just chicken.

At any rate, I heard myself saying, "The party was going to have alcohol. And I really don't think Zachary is a good influence." That, at least, was true. But on the whole, I wouldn't be winning the Spouse of the Year award.

"So you went anyway," Stuart said, finishing her story.

"No," Allie said. "But I was mad, you know? So I snuck out of the house to go spend the night at Mindy's after she got back, 'cause I wanted her to tell me about it. And when Mom realized I was gone—"

"You decided to scream at each other?"

"We saw a rat," I said, then decided that was the wrong thing to say. I had no interest in having exterminators sniffing around the house. What if I'd missed a finger? "Actually, I think it was a small coyote."

"When I was coming back," Allie said, joining in the improvisation. "'Cause Mom called Aunt Laura, and it was right before I came through the fence that we saw the thing."

Laura Dupont is my best friend, and her daughter Mindy is, conveniently enough, Allie's number one chum. To make things even cozier, our houses back up to each other, separated only by our fences and a utility easement.

"I get the picture," Stuart said. He reached for my hand, and I took it. "Rat or coyote, it's really not the issue. The point is that you disobeyed your mom and left this house without asking permission. You're grounded, young lady. The weekend and next week. After that, we'll negotiate Easter weekend. You understand?"

"Uh-huh," said Allie, even as I opened my mouth to protest.

"Maybe that's a little severe," I put in. "It's a vacation week. The cheerleaders have a fund-raiser planned, there are parties. Things she's been looking forward to."

"Which is exactly why she shouldn't be permitted to participate," Stuart said, as Allie shrugged noncommittally. "This isn't the first time you've done something like this, Alison," he added, turning back to my daughter.

About that, Stuart was right. The last time she'd sneaked out without permission, she'd been kidnapped and set up as the main attraction of a rather disgusting demonic ritual. This time, however, she hadn't disobeyed—not unless sitting outside in your own backyard waiting for news about your resurrected father counts as breaking curfew. I didn't think so, and my mommy guilt meter was off the charts.

I'd thought my days and nights had become complicated last summer when a demon had crashed through the breakfast room window. Trust me—back then, I didn't even know what complicated was.

"I don't know if—" I began, but Allie cut me off.

"It's okay. Stuart's right. It's cool." She looked at me. "Really."

"Inside," Stuart said, pointing toward the door. "And no sleeping in. Tomorrow's Saturday. You get up with the family. No lounging around just because you decided to go gallivanting around in the middle of the night."

"Yes, sir." She shot one last look at me, then skulked inside.

"You disagree?" Stuart asked, apparently reading my expression.

"No," I said. "But—"

"I love her, too, Kate," he said, reaching out to pull a piece of grass out of my hair. He twirled it absently in his fingers as I held my breath, wondering if he'd think to question how it got there. My husband, however, was too caught up with Allie to be concerned about me. "You can overrule me if you want—"

"No," I said. "It's okay." From what I could tell by reading my daughter's face, it *was* okay. A bit baffling from my perspective, but I could talk to her about that in the morning.

More important from an overall family point of view was Stuart's decision to step boldly into the teenage discipline abyss. By default more than design, I'd retained prime parental authority over Allie after Stuart and I had married. I'd be lying if I said that I hadn't greedily held that privilege close to my heart. Allie was mine, and sharing responsibility for major parental decisions would mean that Eric was truly gone.

But even while I'd clutched at the strings of my old life, I'd known it wasn't fair to Stuart. We were trying to carve out a family, and that can be tough when you're remolding one that had existed previously. Allie hadn't forgotten her father, and I didn't want her to. But those memories stacked up between her and Stuart, a towering gray wall that would forever keep them Alison and Stuart rather than father and daughter.

I didn't want Stuart to take Eric's place—even before I knew that Eric would return to claim that right himself, I hadn't wanted it. But I did want us to be a family. Allie loved Stuart, I knew that. But it's one thing to love a man who defers to your mother. It's something completely different to love and respect the man who can take away your freedom, not to mention your clothing budget for the year.

"It's hard," Stuart said, taking my hand and leading me to the porch swing. He pulled me down and hooked his arm over my shoulder. "What you have to do."

"What I have to do?" I repeated, hoping my voice sounded normal and he couldn't feel the tension I was fighting in my shoulders. "What are you talking about?"

"With Allie," he said, and I relaxed a little. "Keeping her

close, but giving her room to grow up. We've got more than a decade left with Timmy, but with Allie, you're right in the thick of it."

"*We're* in the thick of it," I corrected.

He looked at me, as if trying to see my thoughts. I looked back, hoping my face appeared unguarded and none of my secrets shone in my eyes. "You don't mind?"

"You're my husband. She's my daughter. What's to mind?" I stood up and held my hand out to him. "Trust me. If I disagree when you lay down the law, you'll be the first to know."

"Fair enough," he said, taking my hand as we walked to the door. He glanced at his watch. "It's not quite five. Not really worth getting up and dressed yet, and at the same time I'm not that keen on going back to sleep."

"You're not?" I said, amused. "I'm pretty sure we left Hi Ho! Cherry-O on the kitchen table. Maybe a quick game to lull you back to dreamland?"

"That would definitely lull me into oblivion," he conceded. "I was thinking of something not quite so G-rated."

"Hmmm," I said, pretending to consider. "It's a little late for a movie."

He took my hand and tugged me toward the stairs. "Come with me to my casting couch."

I laughed and followed, but at the foot of the stairs, I turned back, glancing toward our yard, currently doubling as a demon disposal.

"Kate?"

"Just thinking whether we locked the door," I lied as I considered my options. Plead a headache, and Stuart would stay up with me, rubbing my temples and providing hot tea. Plead exhaustion, and he'd tuck me into bed and snuggle close. And if I were to claim that I was frazzled by Allie's supposed misbehavior, he'd inevitably stay up with me to talk it through.

All of which meant that my options were pretty much limited to snuggling with my husband or confessing all and enlisting his help in hiding a body and boxing up various limbs.

In truth, the confessing all option was becoming more and more appealing. Eventually, I had to just bite the bullet and do that. But somehow four thirty in the morning didn't seem the right time. And to be completely truthful, considering the way Stuart's hand was rubbing the back of my neck and the way his lips were grazing the top of my ear, true confessions were the last thing on my mind.

We reached the top of the stairs just as a stream of light cut across the darkened hallway, accompanied by the squeal of hinges desperately in need of a shot of WD-40. A moment later, Eddie appeared, his hair shooting out in all directions and his eyes looking just as wild. Eddie's a former Demon Hunter who—as a result of a series of convoluted stories manufactured by yours truly—is now living in our guest room, with everyone in our household believing him to be Eric's great grandfather. Just another twist on our already convoluted family life.

"The devil himself better be in the living room," he said, giving the cord on his blue flannel robe a tug. "Can't think why else you'd all be making so much racket."

"Close," I said, keeping my smile bright even though I was less than thrilled with his choice of words. In my line of work, a reference to the devil himself could be quite literal.

"Allie and Kate saw a coyote," Stuart said helpfully.

Eddie let loose with a loud guffaw. "Hoo-boy. I'll bet they did. Gotta nip those suckers in the bud. Stab 'em with something nice and pointy. Make sure they don't come back again." He pointed a bony finger at Stuart. "That's the only way to take care of beasties like that."

"Thanks for the tip, Eddie," I said, keeping my voice calm even though I was seething. "We're going to bed, now."

"Sorry we woke you," Stuart said, aiming a look at me that suggested he was rethinking his decision to let Eddie live indefinitely in the guest room.

"Feel free to go outside and search for coyote carcasses,"

I said cheerily as we passed him on the landing. I punctuated my words with a significant look. With any luck, I wouldn't have to rely on postcoital demon carcass removal. Eddie would take the hint and handle that little chore for me.

Of course, the fact that Eddie yawned, turned around, and disappeared back into his room made me think that I really shouldn't bank on his help. I almost considered popping into Allie's room on the pretext of a kiss good-night and enlisting her to sneak down and take care of the damage, but I ruled that one out immediately. Killing demons and mutilating their slave labor together might be one for the memory book. Sending her out to dispose of the remains by herself though? That just didn't seem right.

"We should have brought a bottle of wine up with us," Stuart said, bringing me back to a much more pleasant reality.

"It's almost morning," I protested as I kicked off my shoes and climbed onto the bed next to him. If Eddie hadn't taken the hint, there was nothing I could do except sneak downstairs as soon as Stuart fell asleep again. "I could maybe handle a mimosa, but I'm thinking that wine isn't really my thing right now."

He pulled me close and started stroking my hair. "No? What is your thing?"

Ten seconds earlier, I probably could have come up with a response to that. Right then, though, my brain was turning to mush, the result of my husband's concentrated attention and my severe lack of sleep. "Um," I managed.

"My thoughts exactly," he said. He kissed me then, and I curled against him, feeling warm and safe and a million miles from the battle in the backyard only minutes before.

"Don't you have to get up at the crack of dawn?" I asked, which wasn't really a protest because to be honest I was starting to get with the program.

"I didn't even set the alarm clock," he said.

"What's wrong?" I asked, jarred out of my haze enough to sit up and twist around to look at him.

"Can't a man simply want to spend Saturday morning with his family?"

"A man can," I agreed. "Sure. But you're Stuart Connor, Candidate for Change, remember? And it's been months since you've gone to sleep without setting the alarm. Doesn't Clark need you at the office in the morning? The primary is practically nipping at your heels."

"True enough," Stuart said, then pressed a soft kiss to my forehead. "I told him I needed a few hours in the morning with my family."

"You did?" I felt warm and tingly all over, at least for the fifteen seconds before that feeling dissolved into cold, hard paranoia. "Why?"

It was a serious question, but my husband only laughed and drew me closer. "Kate," he murmured. And, suddenly, the idea of Stuart snuggled close without an alarm clock sounded perfectly appealing. I mean, honestly. Why question a good thing?

I didn't have an answer for that one, and so I let it ride, letting all of my worrisome thoughts drift away on a river of my husband's kisses.

In case you were wondering, it is remarkably hard to stay awake after sex. Especially the really nice kind of sex that leaves you all warm and languid and determined to cook your husband the best breakfast ever, despite your lack of culinary skills and your desire to never, ever leave your bed again.

I managed, though. The staying awake, that is. As Stuart rolled over, his arms clutching the pillow in that little-boy way he has, I forced my liquid limbs to push me upright. I sat there for a moment, watching the rise and fall of his chest in the dim glow of the single candle he'd lit on the bedside table. I blew it out, then slid out of bed and pulled on the clothes that had ended up in a heap on the floor.

A quick glance over my shoulder confirmed that Stuart was still down for the count, and based on past experience

I figured it was a safe bet that he wouldn't be waking up again for a while. And that was true even if a demon leaped out of the closet and attacked me right then.

Fortunately, I didn't have to put that theory to test, and I made it downstairs without waking my husband or tripping on a stray toy.

I went first to my purse and grabbed my cell phone to call David. Two rings, then straight to voice mail. "Hey," I said. "It's me. Our friend turned up last night after all, and he brought along a buddy. Everything's fine now, but they were spouting all sorts of nonsense about payback for stuff that happened in the past, so you ought to watch yourself. Plus, it turned into something of a party and I could use a hand cleaning up. So call me when you get this."

Hopefully he *would* call, and not simply show up. I had no idea what I'd say if he was here when Stuart woke up. Allie in the backyard made sense. The high school chemistry teacher? Not so much.

Still, as awkward as his showing up unannounced might be, at least it would be confirmation that he was alive and well. Considering our intertwined pasts, any demon seeking revenge against me was probably also interested in getting revenge on Eric, too. And for all I knew, Sammy's best demon buddy might have shown up at David's apartment about the same time I was shoving a stake through Sammy's eye.

I frowned, then called his cell one more time, this time stressing that he needed to call me the second he got the message. I forced myself not to grab my car keys and race out of the house. I was operating now off nothing but blind paranoia. For one thing, as far as I knew, most of the demon world had no idea that Eric had resurfaced in David's body. A few demons were privy, sure. But I didn't think that all of hell had yet got the message. And even if our former enemies were aware of his new identity, David knew how to take care of himself. I'd survived; I had no reason to think he wouldn't also.

Even so, if he didn't report by the time my household was awake and moving around, I'd drive over myself and check on him. Right now, though, I needed to make one more quick call before I checked on the beasties in my backyard.

This time, I dialed *Forza*. And once again, I got dumped into voice mail. Honestly, was I the only person right where I was supposed to be?

I left Father Corletti a detailed message of what had happened, focusing primarily on what the demon had said. Not only the reference to the mysterious Sword of Caelum, but also the bit about "he who seeks revenge" and who was "thrust into cardinal fire." And just for good measure, I threw in how vengeance would be combining with revenge.

To be honest, my call to Father Corletti was completely outside the bounds of protocol. I had an *alimentatore* in town, and Father Ben should have been my first call. But I felt justified in circumventing channels because it sounded like this attack was personal. And if it stemmed from a demon I'd encountered in my past, then contacting Father Corletti first made sense. He'd been there, after all, living those first years alongside Eric and me. Celebrating our victories and, yes, mourning our losses with us.

I hung up, then hurried outside, making use of the limited ambient light to navigate safe passage through the obstacle course that is our yard until I reached the shed. I opened the door and immediately saw the big, blue Rubbermaid tub I'd used to hold all the plastic Easter eggs, party favors, and other paraphernalia I'd collected for the upcoming Neighborhood Association Easter Fair. I'd tried keeping the stuff in cardboard boxes in the kitchen, but the lure was too much for Timmy, and I'd had to pry eggs and candy out of his disappointed little fingers one too many times.

The candy, of course, existed to fill the eggs. And that, unfortunately, was my job. And for no other reason than that I am an easily manipulated raving idiot.

Our house is in a planned subdivision and, like virtually every house in Southern California, we're part of a homeowners' association. And this year, the association is putting on an Easter fair, complete with Easter egg hunts, a moonwalk, a dunking booth, a bake sale, and, of course, the Easter Bunny.

One guess who got roped into organizing it all. What can I say? They asked me early one Saturday morning after I'd been out until four chasing down a teenager who'd been killed at a skateboarding competition and—you guessed it—revitalized as a demon. Him on a board and me on foot—it made for an exciting chase. Not to mention an exhausting one.

Was it any wonder I was in a groggy haze when Marybeth Allen, our association president, had called to rope me into the committee chair position?

Seriously, I should learn not to answer the phone.

I didn't want to dump all my Easter purchases out onto the dusty shed floor, so I grabbed one of the paper lawn bags Stuart keeps for clippings and transferred the contents of the tub into the sack. Tomorrow I could transfer everything back to the tub—after a good dosing with laundry soap, bleach, and Lysol.

Next, I headed toward the dinosaur and transferred the wiggling, jiggling, apparently very pissed-off limbs into the tub. The fingers were the worst. Like maggots, they inched along the bottom, glowing slightly in the dim light.

I slammed the lid on tight, then carried the tub back to the shed. Despite holding all the parts to build a complete zombie, the tub wasn't heavy. Zombies are odd creatures—no personality, no blood, next to no weight, and unimaginably strong.

The strong part of the equation could be rather unnerving. The featherweight characteristic, however, came in quite handy.

I slid the tub back into the shed, planning to move it to my car after Stuart left for the office. Then I'd take it to Father Ben at the cathedral. Father, I'm sure, would be thrilled to know that among his many exciting duties as my *alimentatore*, the disposal of zombie parts ranked high.

He'd already engaged in plenty of demon disposal, so this

new addition to his *Forza* résumé shouldn't be too much of a burden. And, hey, it was better than me dealing with it.

Speaking of demon disposal, I grabbed a tarp from one of the pegs right inside the shed door. Meant to cover piles of dirt during landscaping, I'd recently discovered that they make great covers for dead demons. That, frankly, is the key to running an efficient household—finding multiple uses for everyday items.

I headed around the shed, tarp in hand, planning to toss a cover over my dead demon. Unfortunately, I stumbled across a little flaw in that plan: I couldn't cover the demon with the tarp, primarily because there was no demon to cover.

Instead, I was looking at a big, empty space. A space where—less than an hour ago—I'd crammed a dead demon. Now there was nothing.

And I had no idea where he'd gone.

Four

By the time breakfast rolled around, I realized who must have moved my demon: *Eddie.*

That made perfect sense, of course. Unless he'd been sleepwalking, he had to realize what I'd been doing outside before Stuart's untimely interruption. And Eddie wasn't a stupid man; surely he'd picked up on the fact that I hadn't exactly been free to clean up my own mess.

My only question now was where had he hidden the body.

When I'd first started hunting, demon disposal wasn't an issue. Hunters were trained to exterminate the beasts, not clean up the mess left behind. We'd do our part, then call in a disposal team, a specially trained arm of *Forza* dedicated to making the empty demon shells disappear. Much like Roto-Rooter, one call did it all.

Because there were no disposal teams operating in California—much less San Diablo—I was pretty much on my own. Which meant that as soon as I retrieved the body Eddie had hidden, I needed to get it to Father Ben to hide. Either that or to David to work his high school chemistry magic on it—the details of which I hadn't yet brought myself to ask about.

First, though, I had to feed my tiny little eating machine. I'd been awakened at five forty-five (who needs sleep, really?) by a rousing chorus of "Mommy-mom! Mommy-mom! Mommy, Mommy, Mom," sung more or less to the tune of "Jingle Bells." Despite the little devil standing right at the side of our bed, Stuart managed to sleep through the concert. I, however, came immediately awake.

Now, my tiny tenor was perched precariously on his haunches at his place at the table, his high chair tucked forlornly in the corner next to a box full of empty egg cartons that I'd been collecting for months from all our neighbors.

I cast a look of despair toward the boxes. The neighborhood party was in exactly one week, and I hadn't exactly been stuffing Easter eggs with lightning speed. On the upside, Laura was coming over today to help with that very thing. On the downside, I now had more on my daily plate than preparations for a festival populated with—at a minimum—one hundred and twenty children and their various adult counterparts.

While I was feeling sorry for myself, Timmy was standing on his chair, one knee about to slide onto the table. He had his eye on the pepper shaker, and if he got there, the whole family would regret it.

"Bottom in your chair, young man," I said, moving to rescue the salt and pepper before heading back to the pantry. I opened the door—noting right away that there was no dead demon sprawled on the floor—then tried to divine something both delicious and nutritious to plunk in front of the kid for breakfast. Not managing that, I went the merely delicious route.

"Trix or Frosted Flakes," I said, holding up the only two cereal boxes I'd found in our mostly bare cupboard. I added yet another trip to the grocery store to my daily to-do list, right under "investigate Sword of Caelum," "find missing demon," and "dispose of body parts."

Honestly, I needed to break down and buy an organizer.

At the table, Timmy slid out of his chair and trotted to the refrigerator. He grabbed the handle on the freezer side and tugged, little arms straining. When the door finally popped open, he stepped back, eyes as wide as if he'd just discovered nirvana.

Too late, I realized what he was looking at.

I lunged to shut the door even as my toddler lunged to grab something. And despite all my Hunter training, he was faster. What can I say? A toddler on a mission for chocolate is not a creature to be toyed with.

He emerged from the freezer victorious, a packet of M&Ms in his hand and a huge grin on his face. I'm a sucker for frozen chocolate, and apparently the little devil had spied my secret stash.

"Chocolate!" he said victoriously, clutching the bag as he marched back to the table. "Mine!"

I intercepted, scooping the kid up in one arm. "Whoa there, little guy. That's not a Mommy-approved breakfast product."

"*Nooooooooooooooooooooooo!*" he wailed. "My candy! Mommy, I. Want. My. Candy!"

"I know you do, mister. But Mommy wants you to grow up healthy, okay?" Not that sugared cereal was *that* much better than M&Ms, but we all have our lines in the sand.

"No." His little forehead furrowed, and he frowned, putting on his best pout. The one that, in his almost three years of life, he'd learned worked best on Mommy. "No, no, no."

Not today, buddy.

"Sorry, kid. Between the two of us, I need it more."

He clutched the package tighter and turned his back to me.

"Timmy . . . What's the rule about arguing?"

He appeared to consider that one, and then he peered over his shoulder, his grin wide and toothy and positively adorable.

What can I say? The kid's gonna grow up to be a people pleaser.

"Please," he begged, drawing the word out and infusing it with a million kilowatts of whine. "Please, please, please?" His little hand went to his chest, rubbing the way he'd seen on *Signing Times*. That's what I get for plunking him down in front of educational programming: begging in two languages. If I let this go on much longer, I'd probably get a rousing *por favor* thrown into the mix, courtesy of *Dora the Explorer*.

"Ain't happening, kiddo," I said. "Cereal or toast. Your call."

He harrumphed—a habit he'd picked up recently, and for which I blamed Eddie—then wiggled in his chair, determinedly silent.

"Okay," I said, smiling as if I weren't at all irritated and liked nothing better than to negotiate breakfast in the morning. "I guess you're not eating today. Maybe lunch."

I moved quickly to snatch the candy packet, then turned and headed toward the pantry. One glance over my shoulder confirmed that he'd turned, too, and was eyeing me. Did I mean it? Would I really put up his cereal? Would the mean mommy really let the little boy starve?

Apparently she would, because I opened the pantry door and stepped inside. And no sooner had I done that than I heard shouts of "Tiger! Tiger! *Mommmmmmmy!* I want Tiger!" Because I speak fluent toddler, I shoved the Trix back onto the shelf and poured him a bowl of Frosted Flakes.

"Milk on the cereal?"

That question earned me an enthusiastic thumbs-down, and so I poured his morning milk into a glass and let him eat his cereal with his fingers, picking out each flake and crunching it noisily before finally swallowing when there was no crunch left.

While my little one chowed down, I stuck my head in the garage, half-expecting to find my late-night visitor propped up on the hood of Stuart's car.

Nothing. And just to be certain, I poked among the garage sale boxes that littered my old parking space, but all I found was bags of outgrown clothes; baby toys Tim had outgrown; boxes of VHS tapes we'd replaced with DVDs; two sets of dishes, each missing at least one part of a place setting; and boxes of other assorted family junk that I hoped would one day become some other poor sucker's family treasure.

By the time I came back into the kitchen, Allie had stumbled downstairs, looking about as bedraggled as I felt. She grunted something that I interpreted as a greeting, then opened the door to the refrigerator and shoved her head inside. I eyed the back of her head suspiciously. "You didn't go back outside last night, did you? Clean up the mess we left?"

She emerged with a strawberry yogurt in one hand and a string cheese in the other, her face an expression of utter disgust. "Eww! No, thank you."

Considering the condition of her bathtub and closet floor, the idea that she'd rushed to clean up probably was a bit optimistic.

"Had to make sure," I said, moving to the table to see how my youngest was getting on.

"Wait, wait," Allie called, kicking the refrigerator shut before trotting after me. The disgust on her face had evaporated, replaced by wide-eyed interest. "Do you mean they're *missing?*"

"Just the intact one. The other's now in a big plastic tub."

"But . . . but . . . where did it go?"

"I wish I knew." I also realized I hadn't told David about this newest twist in my demon drama.

"What's wrong?" Allie asked, and I realized I was frowning.

"Nothing," I said automatically. Then I decided that wasn't fair. "I called David last night to tell him about our adventure, and he hasn't called back."

"Oh." She took a bite of yogurt. "Are you worried?"

"No," I lied. "Of course not. He probably just hasn't checked his voice mail this morning."

"You don't think our visitor had a friend, do you?" she asked, now looking about as concerned as I felt.

The twist of worry in my stomach grew into a full-fledged Gordian knot and I pulled out my cell phone. Two rings, and I was dumped into voice mail. Again. "Dammit."

"Do you think . . . ?" She dragged her teeth on her lower lip, her face pinched.

"No," I said. "Of course not." Then, "But I'll run by his apartment real quick anyway. Just to update him."

"Not like you're worried," she said. "You're just bringing him up to speed. Right?"

"Absolutely."

She nodded, looking relieved that I was doing something. From my perspective, all I knew was that if something had happened to David, I needed to know about it. I needed to try to help. I needed to do something.

"What do I say to Stuart?" she asked, even as she tugged my laptop off the breakfast bar where I'd taken to keeping it, and hauled it to the breakfast table. I winced even though I knew in my heart she wouldn't drop it. The thing was still shiny and new, having come into my life only in the last thirty days. Allie had convinced me I needed the thing because sooner or later one of us would be so overwhelmed by the fascinating tidbits of demonic research we were stumbling across in cyberspace that we'd accidentally leave Stuart's computer on an incriminating page.

The logic, of course, was faulty, since there was no "we." I'm the complete opposite of a computer geek, and I still believe that Google is a fabulous toddler-age toy I've yet to find in the board game section at Target. In other words, I was never the one engaging in the research, and Allie was crafty enough to know how to delete histories and brownies and cookies or whatever, and all those other electronic clues.

Bottom line: My kid wanted a laptop to more-or-less call her own. And I'd indulged her.

And since she taught me how to use e-mail, I'll have to admit it doesn't suck.

"Mom! Hello? Quit worrying I'm going to drop it and answer the question. What do you want me to tell Stuart?"

I grimaced, because my daughter was becoming wiser with each passing day. And also because it really was a darn good question. I ran my fingers through my hair, considering even as I pulled my unwashed hair back into a ponytail with an old newspaper rubberband I saw lying on the counter. "Milk run," I said. It was the best that I could think of.

I grabbed my keys and my purse and headed for the door. I was stepping onto the front porch, my hand on the knob to pull it closed, when Allie pounded into the entrance hall.

"He answered! Just now. No idea why he didn't call, but he sent an e-mail."

Relief undulated through me, and I held on to the door-jamb, feeling a mixture of elation and nausea. "What did the message say?"

"He had to go to L.A., but he'll be back soon and he'll call you as soon as he can. And he said if you need backup, to call him. And to be safe. And," she added, with a bright smile, "he said to give me a kiss from him."

"That part's easy enough." I pressed a soft kiss to her cheek. "From your daddy."

"I'm glad he's not dead," she said, so matter-of-factly it made me cringe, as I remembered how common death was in my youth. We mourned, yes. But we never slowed down.

I shook off the melancholy. Allie was a long way from that life. A *very* long way if I had anything to say about it. Which, fortunately, I did.

"What do you think he's doing in Los Angeles?" she asked, as we moved back into the kitchen.

"No idea," I said, forcing my voice to sound unconcerned and uninterested. In truth, I was as curious as she was. He'd only come back into town yesterday. Why turn around so quickly and drive all the way down to L.A.? "Now that we know he's safe, I'm less concerned about his specific where-abouts than I am about a certain MIA demon."

"No kidding." She headed for the big picture window, presumably to make sure an army of demons wasn't about to come crashing through. She lifted her thumb to her mouth and began chewing on her cuticle. "So where do you think it could be?"

"My money's on Eddie."

"For what?" Stuart asked, dragging his fingers through his hair as he strode into the kitchen. He hooked his arm around my waist, pulled me close, and planted a kiss on my cheek. I was so distracted I barely noticed.

"Kate?" he repeated, as he released me and headed for the coffee maker. "Your money's on Eddie for what?"

"I—oh—you know. That he'll make some colorful joke in front of the kids at the festival next weekend, and all the neighborhood moms will shun me."

"Ah, is that all?" he said casually. "I thought maybe you were wondering where he hid the body."

Allie clapped her hand over her mouth in time to muffle a squeak, and I spilled the cup of coffee that Stuart passed to me.

"Ha-ha," I said, forcing a bit of mirth into my voice. "What a thing to say."

He grinned, clearly pleased with himself. "You're all so jumpy I figured murder and mayhem must be involved."

"Always is," said Eddie, shuffling into the kitchen and taking the seat across from Timmy, who immediately passed him a Frosted Flake. "So who died?" He looked at me. "That we don't already know about, I mean."

"We were just saying that if anyone knew where to hide a body it would be you," Stuart said, while I glared daggers at Eddie. "Former cop and all."

"Eh?"

"Your previous profession," Stuart said, pulling out the story I'd laid on him when I'd first brought Eddie home.

Eddie turned to me, peering at me over half-moon glasses. "He knows about that?"

"That you were a *cop*, Gramps," I said, as I grabbed the milk from the fridge and moved to fill up the cup of my toddler, who was now pounding his empty cup on the table and shouting repeatedly for "Mommy, milk! Mommy, milk!"

"A cop," he said with a snort. "I've watched those reality shows. They think they go after some bad characters? They ain't seen nothing 'til they've been trapped in a mausoleum with fifteen——"

"Waffles?" Allie blurted, holding up a box of Eggos she'd yanked from the freezer. I considered kissing her on the spot, then decided to take the more subtle approach and raise her allowance, applying it retroactively, all the way back to infancy.

"My head is swimming," said Stuart, shooting one final glance toward Eddie, and then shaking his head as if he'd just set aside a Sudoku puzzle that he was never going to work through. "So what fabulous plans do you have for this beautiful Saturday while I'm stuck in my office and Allie is under house arrest?"

He shot Allie a stern look as he spoke, and she held up her hands, each holding a waffle. "I didn't forget. Honest."

"Laura and Mindy are coming over, and the four of us girls are stuffing Easter eggs," I said, as Timmy dumped the dregs of his Frosted Flakes on the floor. "And cleaning."

"Great," Allie muttered behind me. "Grounded I can handle. Cleaning *and* grounded? Not so much."

"What'd the kid do?" Eddie asked. "Sneak out and get herself caught up in the middle of some bad-ass rumble?"

"What?" I said. "No. Of course not." Not exactly, anyway.

Eddie snorted. "Just thought. What with the scrape and all."

Stuart and I turned in unison to Allie, who automatically raised her hand to brush at her bangs. For the first time, I noticed the angry, red abrasion near her hairline.

"It's nothing," she said. "Doesn't hurt at all."

"I think we should clean the bathrooms before Laura gets here," I said brightly, before Stuart decided to ask me if I'd bodily wrestled my child to the ground as punishment for her supposed sneaking out. "You could join us, honey. I'm sure Clark understands the need for a candidate to have a sweet-smelling toilet."

"It's a nice offer," he said. "But I'll pass."

Of course I'd figured as much, but at least I'd distracted him away from Allie's face.

"Coffee for the road?" I asked, pulling his travel mug out of the cabinet. Not that I was trying to get rid of him or anything.

"Thanks," he said, then went over to get big, sloppy wet kisses from Timmy, our son's favorite kind. I poured coffee to the sound of slurpy kisses, then planted one of my own on Stuart's cheek as he came back to take the mug from me. At least, I tried to. He turned his head just in time, and ended up planting a knee-weakening kiss on me.

I swooned a little, and I'm pretty sure I moaned. What can I say? It's not every morning I'm greeted so enthusiastically.

"Um, hello?" Allie said. "There are children present."

I pulled away, and turned to her with what I'm sure was a googly-eyed smile. "You're right. We'll take this into the living room."

I grabbed Stuart's mug and walked him to the door, our arms intertwined. "I'd say I had a lovely night last night," he said. "Except that last night was this morning."

"You can say it anyway," I said, pressing the mug into his hand and reaching up to straighten his tie. "On a Saturday, no less. Before you became a man of the people, you used to go into the office in a faded Polo shirt."

"Oh, how the mighty have fallen," he said, making me smile. "Actually," he continued, "about that going-into-the-office thing. Didn't I tell you I wasn't heading straight out the door this morning?"

"You were serious?" I asked, feigning shock. "I assumed that was sweet talk to get me into bed."

"A little bit of that," Stuart confessed. "And a lot more truth."

"Oh," I said, and stopped moving slowly toward the doorway. "That's great."

Don't get me wrong—I love the idea of having Stuart

around more, especially on the weekends. But with a missing demon, I have to say he picked a crappy day to start playing the family man.

"I'm glad you think so," he said, taking my hand and tugging me back into the living room. "From the look on your face, I was beginning to think you were trying to get rid of me."

"Don't be silly," I said, managing to quash the nervous giggle that bubbled in my throat. "So, um, what exactly did you have in mind? In case you haven't noticed, the entire household is awake."

"Nothing that would trouble the natives," he said. "I only thought we could leave Allie to the slave labor, and you and I could sneak off for a bit. A quick drive, and then a movie. What do you say?"

What I wanted to say was that I was utterly flabbergasted. Stuart hadn't suggested a Saturday afternoon sneak-away since—well, not since he'd decided to run for office. "Photo op?" I queried. "Chance to show yourself as a man of the people? Random poll at the theater door?"

As soon as I said it, I wished I could take the words back. A flash of hurt crossed his face, quickly replaced by a pathetic smile. "I guess pretty much everything I suggest these days ties back to the campaign, doesn't it?"

"Oh, Stuart. I was only teasing. It's not—"

"But it is," he said.

I took his hands and looked into his eyes. "No," I said firmly. "It's not. I understand. You have a campaign to run. You've invested a lot of time and energy into this campaign, and you need to do everything to make it pay off. You'll make a great county attorney, and I don't resent the time away. Really." I crossed my heart. "I swear."

"All right," he said, and this time the smile seemed genuine. "But my offer still stands. I can carve out two hours to hold hands with my wife in a dark theater. And to be perfectly honest, I've even got a little ulterior motive going, too."

I cocked my head, trying unsuccessfully to read his mind.

"More ulterior than a dark movie theater and all the possibilities that lie therein?"

"Hold that thought," he said. "But I want to show you a house." He held up a hand before I could protest. "I know we're just thinking about it, but Bernie saw it come on the market, and he thought I might be interested."

Before Stuart went to work for the county attorney's office, he did real estate law exclusively, having put himself through law school by working part time as a real estate agent. Bernie was an investor he'd known for years, and he'd made a killing buying, fixing, and reselling houses in the older section of town. Lately, Bernie had been making noises about going into business with Stuart, and my husband had allowed himself to be bitten by the house-flipping bug.

Honestly, considering that San Diablo was becoming quite the haven for refugees from Los Angeles, the idea wasn't a bad one. And because Stuart knew that, the infection was spreading at a rapid pace.

"Don't you think you have enough on your plate?" I asked. "For that matter, are you allowed to do that kind of stuff and still be county attorney?"

"Don't worry about that, Kate. Legal training, remember? I've read all the rules and regs."

"It's an awfully big commitment," I said, thinking of the limited nest egg we had squirreled away. I had additional money, too—primarily my minuscule *Forza* salary—but Stuart didn't know about those resources, and I'd already decided to save that money exclusively for the kids' educations.

He took my hands. "It's an investment. And it's something we can do together."

I laughed. "Because I'm so good at laying tile."

He didn't laugh. "You're good at whatever you put your mind to. And the idea of working side by side with you . . ." He trailed off with a shrug. "I think we'd have fun."

"We probably would," I said, starting to feel bad about being so negative.

"So you'll look at it with me?"

"Okay," I conceded. "Set up a time."

"How about we go now? Then the movie?"

For a moment, I seriously considered that option. It had been months since I'd been to a movie, and the idea of sitting close and sharing a bucket of popcorn was appealing beyond all reason.

Then, of course, reality crashed down around me. Missing body. Squirming extraneous limbs. Sword of Caelum. Grounded Hunter-in-training. Hyperactive toddler.

Things to do, demons to kill. The usual Saturday morning rundown.

"Now won't work," I said, careening down a slippery slope of lies. "I already told Allie that we were going to be having a little talk this morning before Laura and Mindy get here. About boys and responsibility, the whole nine yards. Considering what happened last night, I don't know that we want that to wait. Do you?"

He immediately shook his head, looking so totally with that program that I had to plant my feet and smile through a tidal wave of guilt.

"How about this," he suggested. "The house now. Dinner and a movie later. I'd really like for you to see it during the day, and I'm booked solid tomorrow unless we can squeeze it in before mass."

I made a face. "Now you're not negotiating fairly." With two kids and a husband to get out the door on Sunday mornings, I considered myself lucky if we all managed to get to mass wearing something more appropriate than our pajamas.

"Thirty minutes," he said. "Max. And I'll let you pick the movie."

I cocked my head, thinking about everything I needed to do right then, the primary task being to find a missing demon.

At the same time, if Eddie had been responsible enough to hide the guy, then surely he'd be responsible enough to keep him safely tucked away until I returned. And if Eddie hadn't hid the body, then sitting at home for thirty minutes wasn't going to make the thing any easier to find. *That*, however, wasn't something I wanted to think about.

I drew in a deep breath and nodded. "All right," I said. "Thirty minutes." Because, really, how much trouble could a missing demon cause in a measly half hour?

Five

"The Greatwater mansion?" I asked, peering out the car's window at the once-stately mansion that had fallen into serious disrepair. "Wow. I figured you guys would start with something smaller."

"So did I," Stuart admitted, his voice laced with excitement. "But the price is right, and the potential profit is astronomical."

Built in the twenties, the place had been home to one of Hollywood's legendary silent-film producers. Or, rather, it had been one of his homes. Then as now, money flowed in Hollywood.

Over time, though, the house had changed hands and fallen into disrepair. The only house on that side of the street, the building sat back from the road behind what must have once been an impressive stone fence. Now the stone had crumbled, leaving a view of the equally ramshackle home and neglected yard.

I blinked, and had a vision of our savings spiraling down a whirlpool. In theory, I fully supported Stuart's decision to dabble in real estate. In practice, I was a fiscal wimp. "I guess there are tons of people in California who'd want a place like this," I said. "It's like a little slice of Hollywood."

"That's what Bernie and I are hoping. Want to see the inside?"

"Sure," I said. How could I say no when he looked so enthusiastic?

The house was even more magnificent up close, with intricate stonework and an attention to detail that you really don't see in modern houses. "Fabulous, isn't it?" Stuart asked as we approached the majestic front door. "Can't you see Timmy's trains all over the front porch?"

I laughed. "Don't even think about it. If you buy this house, you're buying to sell." Still, I had to silently acknowledge the appeal. The house had an old-world quality that reminded me of my youth, and I really could imagine Timmy's toys littering the front porch, and Allie's friends gathering in the front yard amid the hibiscus and birds of paradise. Even more, I could imagine Allie and me training in a closed-off wing, and I have to admit I secretly coveted the idea of having that much extra space. Room in the attic to seriously practice throwing a knife? What suburban mom doesn't want that for her daughter?

"How long has it been empty?" I asked as Stuart dialed a combination into a lockbox attached to the porch.

"Six months. But Emily Greatwater's been ill for years, which explains the condition it's fallen into."

He popped the key out of the lockbox and approached the front door, turning the knob first and finding it open. He pushed the door open, the creaking hinges singing out like something from an old Vincent Price movie.

He looked at me. "So much for the lockbox."

"No kidding." I followed him inside and found myself in a grand entrance hall, illuminated by a wash of light falling in from the floor-to-ceiling windows. But even the California sun couldn't erase the eerie quality of the room. Shadows fell across the marble floor, and cobwebs hung wide and across corners. The banister of the massive staircase, however, was dust free, as if a ghostly specter dragged a dainty hand-duster along when making its midnight rounds. The place was still furnished, and though most of the pieces were covered with white dropcloths, a few stately pieces had been uncovered, the intricate woodwork a perfect complement to the grand nature of the room.

A pile of rags lay abandoned in one corner, and that combined with the unlocked door made me wonder if this stately old place wasn't currently home for well-housed squatters.

"A lot of work," I said, heading down that slippery slope that would lead to breaking into our retirement account. "But this place really could be spectacular."

"Keep going," he said, indicating with his hand that I should head farther into the room. "From what Bernie tells me, it gets better."

I shot him a questioning look over my shoulder, but did as he asked and soon found myself at a fabulous set of french doors overlooking an ornate stone patio and, beyond that, what had to be an amazing view. I unlocked one of the doors and stepped onto the cracked stonework of a massive balcony extending out by at least twenty feet.

"Wow," I breathed. "It's like another room out here." With Stuart following, I led the way to the railing, and found myself gazing out at the reason people move to California. Lush green tapering off to tawny sand and beyond that—stretching for miles—the deep blue of the Pacific Ocean.

The house was nestled at the top of one of San Diablo's many hills. Not mountains, really, so much as attempts at mountains. As if the topography had tried to extend all the way to this part of the coast and simply couldn't bring itself to do it.

From this vantage point, we had a stellar view of another hill, this topped by the stunning beauty of St. Mary's Cathedral, a focal point for the entire town. That view was juxtaposed against the view of the San Diablo cemetery over which the house seemed to protrude. I looked down, saw the familiar Monroe family mausoleum, and found my breath catching in my throat. Eric was buried right next to Alexander Monroe, famous as the town's founder. Actually, the whole family was famous, from the patriarch Alexander to the freakish great-great-great et cetera grandson, Theophilus Monroe, who in the nineteen twenties had dabbled with psychics and ouija boards and ultimately left for Hollywood, where he set up a dubious career advising starlets out of their net worth. Apparently Theophilus was a bit of a bad apple who went out of his way to demonstrate that he didn't hold to his ancestor's pious ideals.

And it was only a few months ago that the Monroe mausoleum had played a role in raising David from the dead.

"Spectacular," I said, turning away and hoping Stuart wouldn't notice my reaction.

"I know, isn't it? I'm surprised there aren't rumors the place is haunted. Look there," he added, urging me to turn and look at a spiral staircase leading off the balcony and descending down to the cemetery. "For those romantic late-night strolls."

I conjured a smile. "Maybe we should come here tonight instead of the movie."

"Not on your life," Stuart countered. "I have very specific plans for tonight, and they require a darkened movie theater."

"Oh really? In that case, you better finish showing me around. I need to make a significant dent in my to-do list if you don't want me being a distracted date."

"I'll keep that in mind," he said as we headed back through the french doors. "So what do you think? Am I crazy?"

I looked around the huge room that must have once been spectacular. The potential was still there, but it was hiding under a million layers of grime and a thousand hours of repair. "I don't know how you think you can do it all," I said honestly. "Work. The campaign. The kids. If you think you can add flipping a house to the mix, I'm not going to argue. But I worry you might be overextending yourself a little bit."

Not that I wanted to tell Stuart at the moment, but I knew a little bit about piling one's personal plate too full.

"It's a concern," he said. "But I've been thinking what to do on that end as well." He reached over and squeezed my hand, his expression far away and a little devious. "I think I've got it all figured out."

"Yeah? So tell me."

He flashed an enigmatic grin. "Maybe tonight. Deep thinking requires popcorn."

"Hmmm," I said. "Methinks the man is keeping something from me."

"Never," he said, so sincerely that a knot of guilt twisted in my stomach. The same answer asked of me wouldn't generate nearly as earnest a response.

"Well, if your secret plan is to have me do all the work on your investment houses while you're out fighting for truth and justice, I think there's a fatal flaw in your plan."

"You wouldn't set aside your entire day to lay tile or texture drywall?"

"For you?" I teased, "of course. But you might not like the results. Remember the wallpaper in Allie's room?" I'd had the bright idea that I could handle wallpaper by myself. Let's just say I was wrong.

"Good point," he said.

I wanted to question him more about his secrets, but my cell phone rang and I automatically shoved my hand into my purse, my heart jumping in my chest as it did every time the phone rang and both kids weren't within shouting distance.

Italy.

I considered not answering, realized that would seem odd, and flipped the phone open.

"Hey!" I said brightly. "I'm so glad you called. I've been working on the Easter fair stuff all week, but I've still got a few details I need worked out." Am I a smooth liar or what? Honestly, it's remarkable how proficient I've become at the fine art of deceit.

At the other end of the phone, I heard a confused, "Katherine?" And then, in a flurry of rushed Italian, "Are you all right?"

"Of course this is an okay time," I said. "Hang on one second."

I flashed my husband my best overworked-mommy smile. "I'm sorry, but this committee-head thing is more complicated than it sounds. I know you want to look around, so you go wander. I'll just be a minute."

Fortunately, I was right. Stuart did want to check the place out, and he gave in to my suggestion without even the slightest protest. He headed to the kitchen, and I headed as far away from him as I could, moving up the marble staircase and then down a grand hallway until I found a wood-paneled room filled with furniture that would have made an *Antiques Roadshow* host swoon.

"Father," I whispered. "I'm sorry. I was with Stuart, and—"

"You must not worry, child," he said, switching to English for my benefit. "I understand."

"So what can you tell me? Who's after me?" I moved across the room and shut the door. If I knew Stuart, he was on his hands and knees investigating the plumbing. But even so, I didn't want to risk him searching me out and getting an earful. "And what's the Sword of Caelum?"

"I am afraid my conclusions are not good, Katherine. You have many enemies, including one from whom you pulled the key to invincibility at the last possible moment. It is he—the Destroyer—who is seeking his vengeance."

I shivered, fighting a whimper as memories flooded through me. My dorm-mate, Cami. The catacombs. And that mysterious ice-cold fire.

I'd been fifteen, newly partnered with Eric, and we had set out with five other teams into a crypt that snaked deep beneath the ancient city of Rome.

We'd come with a single purpose—to stop one of hell's vilest demons, Abaddon. He wasn't known as the Destroyer for nothing, and on that day, he'd been gearing up for a ritual that would allow him to walk the earth indefinitely in his true demonic state, corporeal and damned near indestructible. That kind of situation is what we in the demon-hunting biz like to call a Very Bad Thing.

As a general rule, demons don't often appear in their true form. Hollywood's representation of demons as snarling, scaly, fanged-and-yellow-eyed killing machines might be dead on the money, but it's not a form that a demon can sustain for any length of time outside hell.

As Level Two Demon Hunters with *Forza Scura*, a secret arm of the Vatican, we had the job of making sure this particular demon never got the chance to alter that status quo.

We won that day. But at a heavy price.

"Katherine?" Father said gently, his voice low and full of understanding. "You are still there?"

I blinked, forcing away the image of the demon slicing through Cami's neck, the way her head lolled forward in defeat. "Yes," I whispered. "I'm here."

"I am sorry to be the one to bring such memories to the forefront. But—"

"I need to know," I said, dully. "I have to know what I'm up against."

"There is power in your memories," he said. "Even the painful ones. I would not have you—" He cut off abruptly, and I heard the rattle of the phone as he shifted the handset in his hand, then muffled voices in the distance. "Katherine," he said, his voice sharp and curt as he came back on the line. "Forgive me. I will be but a moment."

"Yes, of course. All right." I drew in a breath, not certain I wanted to be quite so alone with my memories, but not willing to ask him to stay with me on the phone. I was no longer six, after all, and Father no longer tucked me in and promised I would be safe in my bed.

The truth was, I knew that I was never really safe. I think I'd known as much all my life, but that one basic truth had really hit home during that one mission. We'd lost ten Hunters on that vile day, and it was only by a miracle that Eric and I hadn't joined the body count. These weren't memories I wanted to revisit, and yet I couldn't prevent them. Everything came rushing back as I fell pell-mell into the past. The terror. The absolute certainty of knowing that we were going to die. That there was no way out.

But we *had* gotten out. We'd survived.

To this day, I didn't understand why.

The mission had started typically enough—creeping along the dark, dank catacombs, searching for a demonic lair. We'd separated from the others, each of the six teams traveling down different paths, looking for the secret entrance to Abaddon's ritual chamber. We carried our weapons and something else—a shard of the blooded stone of Golgotha. The relic—retrieved for this mission from the deepest recesses of the Vatican archives—had been broken into six pieces centuries before. For hundreds of years, each had lain innocuously beside its brothers in a velvet-lined box of carved ash.

According to centuries-old lore, brought together, the reconfigured blooded stone had the power to banish Abaddon to the darkest chambers of hell, foiling for eternity his efforts to find form. Assuming, of course, that we could get close enough to Abaddon to use them. After hours of creeping through the catacombs, I remember thinking that our chance might never come.

Like so many ancient catacombs, these had been crafted to house the dead in a time when cemeteries had overflowed and disease had oozed back toward the cities. The archways, walls, and ceiling were lined with skulls, femurs, and hip bones. A macabre piece of architecture, but practical at the time.

Together, Eric and I had followed one tunnel until it hit a

dead end, staying only one step ahead of a horde of approaching demons coming not for us, but to join Abaddon in his ritual. Their purpose didn't matter, though. If they stumbled across us on their way to their destination, the result would be the same, and any element of surprise we might take with us into the ritual chamber would be lost.

Trapped there, we danced the beams of our flashlights over the ancient bones as we frantically searched for a way out that didn't require us to go back the way we came. Louder and louder, the footsteps grew, and the intensity of our search ratcheted up until we finally located a skull embedded in the wall about five feet up from the ground. The bone had darkened, presumably from a combination of age and the soot from torches that had once been used by monks traveling these winding underground roads.

I could still remember how I peered closely at the mishmash of scrapes and gouges. Then, as if I were looking at one of those optical illusion drawings, the lines seemed to shift, all unnecessary marks fading into the background as the scratches formed a now-familiar pattern of interconnecting circles topped and underscored with wavy lines suggesting a hieroglyphic letter—the symbol of Abaddon.

But what to do with it?

Behind us, the demons drew closer, the light from their torches flickering in the tunnel and telegraphing their imminent arrival.

"Maybe it works like a doorknob," I said, shining my flashlight on a crusty sliver of metal that protruded from the nasal cavity of the nameless skull. I peered closer. A razor-sharp piece of iron had been embedded in the skull, set to protrude by about one centimeter. The crusty substance was—

"Ceremonial blood," Eric said, flicking a bit of the dried, red stain with the end of his dagger.

Behind us, the demon hordes continued to approach. We were in a room with no way out, trapped and waiting there, all nice and pretty like a little Hunter prize for the demonic masses. We needed out of that room, and as far as I could tell, the only way out was through that wall.

"Here goes nothing," I said, then slammed my left palm against the jagged piece of metal. I remember ignoring the way my palm burned and throbbed, interested only in the wall. I don't know what I'd expected to happen, but I had definitely expected something. All I got, though, was a big fat nothing.

"There's more," Eric had said. "An incantation, maybe."

"I could try 'pretty please,'" I said testily, "but I don't think it'll work."

Eric shot me a withering look. "Try pressing your palm against the mark."

I glanced at him, then quickly looked away, not wanting him to see my hesitation. I was being foolish and superstitious. I'd heard story after story about Demon Hunters in the throes of battle. I'd drafted fifty-page research papers on battle techniques. I'd read biographies of the most famous Hunters going back to the Middle Ages, even before.

And in all of that, the only time I ever got queasy was when a Hunter's soul was tainted. When faith faltered and a hint of darkness edged inside. That was the stuff of my nightmares, the images that had me waking up even before matins.

The thoughts that haunted me still today.

And even though I knew—really *knew*—that no demon was going to enter through my blood simply by touching the mark of the beast that I intended to battle, I couldn't stop the foolish, cold chill that ran through me.

Even so, I did it. I tempted fate, ignored my superstitions, and pressed my hand against the demon's mark.

All that—and not a damn thing happened. Except, of course, the demons drew closer.

We turned to fight, and it was only an afterthought that made me suggest that we try Eric's blood, too. I don't really know what I expected, but he sliced his palm as I had, then cupped it over the skull etched with the mark of the demon.

For a moment, nothing changed. Then a low groan split the silence, as if the world itself were being rent apart.

The wall was dissolving—the portal into the ritual chamber opening.

Not fast enough, however. Because before we could enter the chamber and stop Abaddon, we had to battle the approaching demonic minions. And that, I have to say, had been one hell of a fight. With two against dozens, we'd come near to being killed more times than I could count. More than that, we'd lost the stone when it had tumbled into a dark crevice that only moments before had swallowed a demon whole.

The loss of the demon had been a cause to celebrate. The loss of the stone? Not so much.

Though we'd lost our primary weapon, we were determined to soldier on, convinced by youth or hubris that we would somehow find a way to prevail. Fear and fury drove us, and somehow, we managed to battle our way through the now-open doorway. And the moment we stepped over the threshold, we were free. The demons didn't follow, instead waiting like lapdogs on the other side, watching for their master.

Watching and waiting for him to come and destroy us. Or, at least, to try.

Six

I shivered, standing by the window in that dimly lit room overlooking the San Diablo cemetery. I hugged myself, the walls of the Greatwater mansion seeming to press in against me as much as the memories.

I could still recall the damp chill that filled the air, along with the orange glow that permeated the cavernous room into which Eric and I had stepped. The glow came from seven pedestals that lined the circular room, each topped with a bowl of oil, burning bright. A huge brass urn stood in the center of room, with six heavy chains hanging immediately above it. Of the chains, four disappeared into the urn's depths. The last two hung about three inches above the lip of the vessel.

An ornate tapestry hung against the far wall, the intricate weaving depicting the serpent tempting Eve in the Garden of Eden. As I watched, the tapestry was ripped apart, the two halves flung aside by an invisible force to reveal Cami, naked and bound to a post. At her feet, nine huddled forms lay lifeless on the floor. Our friends and colleagues, now dead.

Cami looked up, saw us, and uttered a single word: *"Run!"*

And that was all she said. As I watched, horrified, a tall, skeleton-like man stepped from the shadows behind her, took a knife, and sliced through her jugular.

I reacted instinctively, as did Eric, and our knives flew across the room in tandem, each burying itself deep in the demon's eyes.

The body sagged to the floor, the demonic essence departing. I raced toward Cami, my face hot with tears, even as Eric called for me to stop. I clung to her body, still strapped to the post, but there was nothing I could do. She was dead, her blood staining her clothes, the stone floor, and me.

"Get away from her," Eric said, his voice as taut as a bow. "Right now."

I jumped back, but it was too late. Cami's arms broke their binds, then clutched me with superhuman strength. She moved away from the post, then slammed me against it, twisting my own arms behind me and binding me fast with the frayed ropes.

"No," Eric cried, racing forward. But Cami's body turned and held out a hand. That was all it took, and Eric went flying backwards. I'd never seen anything like that, and I gasped as he landed hard in front of the archway. Behind him, the demon horde cackled, but made no move to enter the room or attack.

"Oh yes," Cami said, her voice deep and unnatural. "In human form, the ritual has thus far endowed me with the ability to control the elements. In my own form, though, I will have so much more power."

She turned to me, then actually winked. "In other words, my pretty little one, you ain't seen nothing yet."

I struggled uselessly against my bindings, my eyes on Eric. He looked wild-eyed around the room, his gaze fierce, and I saw in his eyes an almost suicidal need to attack this demon, this thief who had taken our friends, and would soon take me. My hands were bound, so I couldn't flash any of our usual signals, but I blinked furiously, praying he was paying attention. Praying he realized the message I was sending in old Morse code. *Stop. Wait. Think.*

"Now, you two," Cami's body said, this time in her familiar voice, only slightly wetter because of the blood pouring out of her neck. A human could not have spoken at all. For that matter, most demons taking a human form couldn't manage. This demon, however . . .

I was beginning to learn that this demon was different from others I'd battled. And that realization sat hard in my gut, a heavy knot of fear.

"Welcome to our little party," the demon gurgled. "I'm so glad you could come. You're late, of course. Everyone else is all partied out."

She smiled at me as blood spurted from the wound in her neck.

"Don't look at me like that, my darling. I so hoped we could stay friends."

I turned my face away, disgusted when she drew her tongue down the side of my face and then laughed, the sound wet and gurgly.

"It's not Cami," Eric said, and though I *knew* that—I truly did—I still appreciated the reminder. It's one thing to understand how demons work. It's another to face their tricks and taunts up close and personal.

"Who are you?" I said. I feared I knew, but I wanted confirmation.

"I?" Cami asked, pointing to herself with an expression of utter innocence. "I am who you seek. Who you came to defeat." She smiled then, and my heart broke a little more. Cami was dead. My friend was gone. And this *thing* remained.

It was a crime. A horrific assault on Cami's body, but I reminded myself that it was *only* her body. Cami's soul had left as soon as death had taken her. At the same time, Abaddon had slipped from the ether into her still form, filling her limbs once again with life.

A puddle of blood pooled at her feet, and I knew the body would be useless to the demon soon. Demons invaded the dead—it was their most common modus operandi. But where the human's death was caused by a mortal wound, the demon's squatter's rights lasted only as long as the body itself could remain alive. Here, with nothing to stanch the flow, Abaddon would be kicked back to the ether once sufficient blood drained from Cami's body.

Somehow, the short duration of Abaddon's lease on Cami's body didn't make me feel any better.

"Do not mourn, little one," Abaddon sneered. "I think perhaps your Cami would have liked it this way, sharing her body with me even for so fleeting an instant. Surely she did not have faith enough to keep me from taking refuge within these long, lithe limbs." He stroked her body as he talked, moving his hands as if Cami were pleasuring herself. "Nor, for that matter, did any of your ilk."

"Bastard," I said.

"Cami's faith was strong," Eric said, his voice loud and firm, yet clearly meant for me. A demon can't possess the body of the faithful. As the human soul leaves the body, it *fights*. And those with faith have the strength to ward off the evil. "If her faith wavered at the end, that only means she's human."

"It means she was stupid," Abaddon said. "Foolish and unprepared, not to mention uninformed. Much like you two," he added in a sickly polite voice that seemed to come not from Cami but from the room itself.

In front of us, Abaddon pressed his hand against Cami's jugular, temporarily stanching the flow of blood. As he did, I saw what he held there—the shard of the Golgotha stone.

I whipped around, my gaze going first to the chains overhanging the urn and then to Eric, his expression as confused as I felt. His eyes still searched the room, though, and I realized he'd gotten my earlier message. He was waiting and watching, searching for a way out of this mess.

I hoped he found it soon. Not only was I out of ideas, but

even if I had a brilliant one, I wasn't exactly in a position to implement it.

"You really must insist that your researchers do a better job," Abaddon said, continuing to speak in that haughty, affected tone. "You're right, boy. Her faith never wavered."

The demon took a step closer, eyes fixed on mine. "Does that make you feel better?" Abaddon said, now in Cami's voice, the tone simpering. "Make you feel all safe and secure knowing Cami kept her *faith* until the end? Faith in what, Kate? Oh, yes, I know your name. Katherine Andrews, so eager. So ambitious. Will you retain your faith when I slit your throat? And I *will* kill you. You know you have no chance. What use can faith possibly be against me when I have command of all the dark power of the occult? Forces powerful enough to circumvent faith and find a stronghold in your young, lithe limbs."

"The Golgotha stone," I said. "*Forza* was wrong. It doesn't prevent your ritual—"

"Oh, no, child. Your pitiful leaders were right. The blooded stone of Golgotha earns both my respect and my fear. But Kate, my darling little poppet, neither you nor yours have the stone. *This* stone," he said, holding the shard high above his head, "has no name. How fortunate I learned of its existence. How fortunate it came into the light so that I could draw it back with me into the dark."

The demon spread his arms wide, as if inviting me close for a hug. I managed to hurl a wad of spit right at the demon's feet.

"So sullen," the demon said, again in Cami's voice. "Katie, I thought we were friends. Best buddies."

She moved away, finally reaching the urn. She released her hold on the wound in her neck, and allowed Cami's blood to spill into the vessel. Then she slipped the shard into the last link of the fifth chain. Once it was secured, she gave the chain a tug and it slowly descended until the stone was no longer visible.

"Five stones to raise me," Cami said, her eyes turning black.

"Six to bind me. The blood of three vestal virgins, flowing but not alive, to protect me." Her smile was white, and I flashed on a memory of Cami, laughing in flannel pajamas as she stood at the sink next to mine and dutifully brushed her teeth every night. I blinked back an unwelcome rush of tears and reminded myself to focus. Somehow, I'd stop this demon. And I'd do it for Cami.

"You know your Roman history, don't you, Katie? You, who've grown up in this ancient city? There are no vestals left, of course, but I have found a worthy substitute. For what were the vestals but secret-keepers? And what females now, within the seven hills of Rome, still keep such weighty and clandestine confidences?"

I knew the answer, of course. As a Demon Hunter, my very life was a secret. As for the rest—

"And you are, of course, pure. Like my host and the young Greta? Your male cohorts I assume are pure as well, but since history requires a female . . ." The demon trailed off, then approached me. Cami's body was slowing down, becoming paler. I tried not to think about that. On the one hand, the departure of the demon would be good news for me. At least until one of those demons beyond the gates rushed in, overpowered Eric, and slit my throat.

The demon leaned closer, bathing me in its rancid breath. "So tell me—just between us girls—are you still capable of serving Vesta? Or would you have been buried alive for betraying your vows?"

I didn't answer, but I didn't have to. I was only fifteen years old and Catholic. Raised not only in the Church but in the Vatican itself, my only father figure a priest. The answer was obvious, and the demon knew it.

"And Katie makes three," the Cami-demon said. "Now *where is the stone?*"

"Gone," I said, silently thankful we'd dropped the damn thing. Not such a bad move after all. "You should have told your thugs not to attack us."

For an instant, I saw a flash of the true demon inside—red

eyes and bulging skin, as if thick spines were about to burst forth. Then she gave a shake of her head, and everything settled into place, her smile so friendly and her eyes so bright that my heart skipped a little. *This* was Cami. Except, of course, it wasn't.

"Not to worry, little ones." She turned, then faced Eric. I struggled against my bonds, terrified of what she might do to him. But my worry was unfounded. With one wave of her hand, she swept him aside, as if an invisible hand had picked him up and pitched him like a dirty sock against the far wall. He crashed there, smashing against one of the pedestals and sending it tumbling. Oil spread on the ground, still burning, so that it looked as if we were already walking through hell's fiery landscape.

But it was what I saw when I looked back at Abaddon that really had me cringing. He held Cami's hand outstretched in front of him. In the archway, the demons dropped to their knees, their murmured chants now rising to full-bodied voices. An eerie light seemed to fill the chamber through which we'd entered, and after a moment, I saw a shadow in the distance. I squinted, trying to figure out what was happening.

And then I saw it. The stone, brought up from the depths of the pit. Now it floated through the air, drawn mystically to Cami's outstretched hand.

I shivered, my mind racing as I cut a glance toward Eric. He winced, shifting his position to a crouch, ready to take the first possible moment and spring. He looked at me, his eyes burning, and I knew he wanted to go for it right then. I shook my head, hoping he understood. Attack her now, and he'd surely die. The battle was a loser even with weapons. With only my knife, Eric would be dead meat in no time.

No, the time to fight was coming, much as I wasn't crazy about the details of the window of opportunity. Abaddon had to leave Cami's body and enter mine—that much, she'd made clear. The time to attack was in those few brief moments before I died, thus saving the world and saving my life. All in all, a nifty result.

I only hoped Eric could make that window.

With the stone in hand, the Cami-demon came toward me, her walk a bit wobbly. Her skin was so pale she seemed translucent. She held the stone out, and try as I might, I couldn't break my bonds and knock the treacherous impostor out of her hand.

"Now, Kate. There's no point in fighting. All I ask is that you do me one teensy little favor." And then she shoved the stone into my mouth, pushing it so far back I almost gagged. "Safe keeping," she said. "Wouldn't want you not touching it when the ritual words are spoken. That," she added, "wouldn't do at all."

And with that, she collapsed to the ground, the last drop of life having stained the stone floor.

I wanted to mourn for Cami, but there wasn't time. With Abaddon back to being incorporeal, someone had to come perform this big-deal ritual. Which, translated, meant that someone had to come kill me.

My best guess was that it was going to be one of the hundreds of demons now bursting through the archway like a swarm of hornets. The swarm parted, half heading toward Eric, the other half forming a circle around me.

One tall demon with midnight-black hair stepped out of the group and walked toward me. He looked up at the ceiling, which seemed to pulsate with an odd glow. *Abaddon*, I realized. The demon's essence hung suspended somewhere between the ether and our world, caught by the power of the still-unfinished ritual.

The demon in front of me, I knew, had come to bring that act to a close.

He moved toward me, and I thrashed uselessly, the stone making it impossible for me to even scream out for Eric, who I desperately hoped was still alive. I could no longer see him, but I pinned my hope on the fact that the demons were still clustered there, going after something. Surely if he were dead, they would have joined their cohorts in the circle.

The demon pressed his thumbnail against his cheek, then

rent his flesh, drawing blood. Then he reached for my forehead. And though I tried desperately to sink into the wooden post behind me, he managed to paint a bloody mark on my head.

He stepped back several paces, then kneeled, his head lowered so that I couldn't hear his words. Panic gripped me. I had a feeling this wasn't going to be a lengthy incantation. Worse, I suspected it culminated with slitting my throat.

I tried to scream for Eric, but I couldn't get past the stone in my mouth. I tried to break my bindings, but they were too tight. In other words, I was pretty much screwed as the demon lifted his head, flashed a grin filled with rotten teeth, and then marched toward me, the knife held high with an air of ceremony.

He muttered an incantation as he walked, a mix of Latin, Akkadian, and Hebrew, from what little I could hear. I heard him call various demons by name and swear allegiance. And as he stepped up behind me, I heard a reference to blood, bile, and "the blackness into which our sacrifice would fall."

From the corner of my eye, I saw him lift the knife. Instinctively—cowardly—I closed my eyes, my thoughts focused on Eric and God and the life I was leaving behind. I forced myself not to think of the vile thing that would soon fill my body, choosing instead to remember all the good I'd done in my short tenure as a full-fledged Hunter.

I tensed, expecting the sting of the blade across my neck. Anticipating the nothingness to follow.

But oblivion didn't come. Instead, I heard a high-pitched *whzzz* and then a *thud* as the demon hit the ground. I opened my eyes to find the demon at my feet. Across the room, I saw Eric on the ground, one arm outstretched. I realized he must have burst through the horde of demons, flinging himself onto the ground and into the burning oil even as he'd let fly the dagger that had saved me.

Now his shirt smoldered as hidden demons pulled at his legs, dragging him through the hot oil and back into their close. His face was a bloody, bruised mess, and I wanted to cry out in desperation and frustration.

With one hand, he clawed at the floor, but his other hand was clenched tightly closed. He lifted his face to me and our eyes met. "Do you trust me?" he called.

Always, I screamed in my head. Unable to speak, I nodded.

As I watched, baffled, he unclenched his hand, and I saw that it was filled with ash. He drew in a breath, then blew out violently, sending the ash into the hot oil spreading across the floor, a small blue flame dancing gleefully atop it.

Immediately, the blue flame erupted and waves of deep red flames followed the path of the oil, reaching high toward the chamber's ceiling and eviscerating everything in its path—demons, pedestals, and, I feared, Eric.

That fear, thank God, was unfounded. As the living, lurching flame turned the demon horde to dust, Eric lunged forward into the center of the room, away from the flame snaking around the perimeter.

He raced to me, breathing hard and unsteady on his wounded leg. With one quick motion, he snatched his knife out of the fallen demon's eye. In seconds, I was free, and I ripped the stone from my mouth and tossed it into the moving flame.

"What the hell did you do?"

"I don't know exactly," he said.

I stared at him. "You don't know?"

"Later," he said. "Right now, let's survive."

"Good plan," I said. "How?" I looked around, quickly realizing that the situation was more dire than I'd anticipated. The fire that surrounded us was now arcing up, forming a canopy over our heads. It burned wildly hot, destroying everything it touched, including the ceiling. Rock and mortar dripped down on us like molten lava, and in the center of it all, I saw a shimmer that I knew had to be the essence of Abaddon, writhing as if in agony.

That, I figured, was good. If we were going to die a fiery death, at least we were taking one demon down with us.

"I love you," I said to Eric, as the circumference of fire tightened around us.

"I know you do," he said. "But this isn't over yet."

"Are you nuts?" I retorted as the fire seemed to sniff us out, a living thing seeking new prey. Through the shimmer of heated air, I could see the archway, through which lay the safety of that first chamber. There was, however, no way from here to there.

"Every thing around us is ashes," I pointed out. "Burned to a crisp in milliseconds. I'm all for optimism, but that's taking it a little too far."

"We're going through," he said, pointing to the doorway. "Run. Don't stop. And don't look back."

I took an involuntary step to the side, away from him. "We can't. There's no way we'll—"

"You said you trusted me," he reminded me, taking my hand and tugging me back toward him. And toward the flames. "Didn't you mean it?"

"I meant it," I said, realizing even as I said the words just how much I meant them. "I do trust you." No matter how absurd—no matter how terrifying—I knew that I would follow Eric anywhere.

Even into the fires of hell.

"Katherine? I am so sorry. Forgive my rudeness, but I have been dealing with many fires these past few days, and—"

"Fires?" Father's soft voice pulled me from my memory, and I blinked, almost surprised to find myself unscathed and no longer wrapped in those queer flames. "Oh. Right." I re-wound his words. "No, no. That's fine. I, um, I had a lot to think about."

"Yes," he said, and I could imagine him nodding. "I imagine that you would."

"Are you sure?" I asked Father, my voice little more than a whisper. "Are you absolutely positive it's Abaddon?"

"As sure as I can be without Abaddon himself speaking his name. But the demonic attacker's pronouncement suggests no other conclusion."

"Why?"

"Cardinal fire," he said, as if that explained everything.

To him, it probably did. To me, not so much.

"The ash that Eric tossed into the burning oil," he explained after I expressed my cluelessness. "It created cardinal fire. That is, of course, how you escaped even as the demons and their lair were eviscerated."

"I figured out the escape part," I said. "After all, I was there." After we'd raced unscathed through the fire, Eric confessed that he'd had no idea what the ash would do, or whether we could survive. But he'd trusted our *alimentatore,* who had given the ash to him with instructions to use it only in the direst of emergencies. "It's this 'cardinal fire' stuff that is news to me."

"It is the ash of an alleged heretic wrongly burned, who forgave his accuser, the Church, and the cardinal who ordered his death at the very moment the flames consumed him. The ash is extremely rare . . . and also extremely dangerous. Wilson provided it to Eric without *Forza*'s approval or authorization," he added, referring to our very first *alimentatore,* Wilson Endicott. "Fortunately, no harm befell you."

"Just the opposite, I'd say," feeling a bit testy. "That fire is what saved our lives. If you're saying we shouldn't have had it—"

"I am saying that cardinal fire is inherently dangerous to some. It is not a thing to be trifled with."

"Dangerous how?" I knew Wilson, trusted him completely. He would never have intentionally put me or Eric in harm's way.

"Katherine," Father said gently, "we face new problems today. I tell you this only because it is the reference to cardinal fire that makes clear the enemy you face today."

"Right," I said, duly chastised. I needed to keep my head in today's game and not preoccupied with twenty-year-old battles and their enigmatic consequences. "So why now? He hasn't only recently regained his strength, has he? Did this cardinal fire put him that long out of commission?"

"We do not believe so," Father said. "Our understanding is that the fire either cleans an area of an obvious demonic presence and destroys its temple and talismans, or it reveals a hidden presence so that the presence can be battled and defeated. But as demons do not exist in our world, the victory is temporary only, sending the demons back to the ether until they are able to once again get a toehold in our world. Unlike what you have experienced in the past, cardinal fire does not trap a demon in any sort of talisman."

"Which takes us right back to my question. If Abaddon wanted revenge, why wait so long? Why come after me now? And why me? Why not Eric, too?"

"The answer, it would seem, lies in the Sword of Caelum."

That, at least, was an answer I'd expected. After all, the Watson demon had made a big deal of the sword thing. "Okay. But what *is* the Sword of Caelum?" A *thump* echoed in the hallway and I inhaled sharply, suddenly fearful I wasn't alone.

"Katherine?"

"One second." I eased across the room and opened the door, peering out down the long hallway. "Stuart?" I called.

A pause, and then his answer drifted up. "Are you looking for me?"

"I heard something," I explained. "Just making sure you're okay." Not the entire truth, but workable.

"Fine," he assured me. "There's air in the pipes. Made a hell of a racket thumping around when I turned the water back on."

"Okay, cool. I'm going to keep investigating up here." I stuck my head back in the warm wooden room and shut the door, cutting off his answer, but not too worried that he'd be offended. If he was actually going through the motion of inspecting the plumbing, I could probably stay on the phone for an hour and he'd never notice I was missing.

"Sorry, Father," I said, getting back to the nitty-gritty. "Go on."

"Ah," he said. "Of course." He cleared his throat, and I could hear the rustle of paper as he looked at his notes. Even in his late seventies, the man had an enviable memory, and I knew he didn't need to rely on his jottings. Having them there was merely a comfort, and I smiled a little as I pictured him sitting behind his simple oak desk, a portrait of the pope on the wall behind him.

"Most believe that the Sword of Caelum does not really exist," he began.

"Is that a fact? The demon I met last night seems to think it does."

"A rumor only," Father Corletti said. "Mist and magic. For centuries, there have been stories about the Sword of Heaven, brought down by the Archangel Michael to aid the worthy in the battle against evil. Most believe it is the equivalent of a fairy tale for demons. A story told to frighten, with no substance behind the words."

"And you believe that?"

"I cannot say with any certainty whether it does or does not exist. If the demons believe that it does, and believe that you wield it, that is enough to put you in danger. And, perhaps, to give you an advantage."

"The danger I get. The advantage, not so much."

"I understand. But Katherine, if the sword does exist, it would be a miraculous thing indeed. Charged with the power to strike down a particular high demon when wielded by the prophesized one whose familial blood burned in the flame that forged the blade."

I ran that through my head twice and couldn't make it compute. "Come again? Did you say a *particular* demon? And what's that about the forging?"

"According to legend, the sword has the power to strike down—and prevent from ever rising again—the kith and kin of one particular demon named during the ceremony that blessed the blade."

"Abaddon?"

"That is certainly my assumption."

"And he thinks I'm the one who can wield it."

"Apparently so."

"Why?"

"That, I do not know. For that matter, we do not even know for certain that the sword exists. The full legend instructs that a knight—his name long lost to history—struck down the demon Themoratep in the year 504 B.C. That was the first use of the sword, which was then reforged, its blade primed for a new owner and a new victim."

"That's an awful lot of detail for a legend," I said.

"I agree. And it is those details that suggest the truth behind the legend. It is also interesting that we have historical artifacts referencing Themoratep. But all predate the birth of Christ by more than five hundred years."

"You believe this," I said, certain I was reading him right. "This isn't smoke and mirrors to you."

"No, Katherine. It is not."

"But why would Abaddon think I know anything about this sword?"

"That, I cannot say. The tales consistently reference a prophecy. The naming of the Sword Keeper. The one individual who will be born to wield the sword and strike the demon down in his true form, never to rise again."

"Oh." I thought about that. "Familial blood," I said. "You mentioned familial blood earlier, right? Does that mean my mom or dad would have been a Sword Keeper, too?" I kept my voice steady as I asked the question. To be honest, I rarely thought about my parents. But there were times when I wondered who they were—and why they had left me.

"I do not believe so," he said gently. "As I have said, my limited research suggests that the Sword Keeper is the subject of a prophecy. More, the Keeper will be within the bloodline of he who reforged the sword after it slayed the last demon. But there is only one Keeper. Should he or she fail, the demon's life will go on, and the sword will become useless unless reforged again by one with the power to do so."

"In other words, if anyone is going to destroy Abaddon, it

has to be me." I frowned, feeling a bit like Atlas with the world on my shoulders.

"If you are the Keeper, then yes. That is so."

"And if I fail? Who has the power to reforge the sword?"

"That, we do not know."

"Sounds like we don't know a lot," I said, testily.

"I am afraid that is true," he agreed.

"And what we *do* know doesn't make any sense," I said, still not liking this whole scenario.

"Myths and legends often don't make sense, my child. You know that."

"No, from a practical point of view. Why would the archangel bother to bring down a sword that does something I can already do?" Strike down a demon in human form, and his essence goes back to ether to wait for another body to invade. But on the rare occasion when a demon shows his true scaly, snarling, icky self, then he's actually vulnerable to attack. It's *hard* to kill him, sure. But if you manage, then it's a done deal. That demon's not going to be bothering anyone anymore. Ever.

"So what makes this blade so special?" I pressed. "I mean, my knives are perfectly capable of slicing onions as well as demons, and they didn't have to be forged in any special fire." Though I did take out a demon once with a Ginsu knife. Right after Eric and I were married. I hated mucking up the knife, but the fight was fast and clean.

"Yes," he said, chuckling. "But how many true onions have you diced in your career?"

"Ah," I said, deflating a bit. The answer, of course, was none. "What can I say? They're crafty little buggers."

"Indeed. And not only does the sword have the power to slice through their armor like a hot knife through butter, but you also missed a key point of the myth as I relayed it earlier."

"Kith and kin," I said.

"Therein lies the true beauty of the sword. And also the reason that most believe its existence to be myth."

"I'm not following."

"Strike down the demon, and you strike down his inner-most circle as well."

"Whoa." I stumbled a little, then settled myself in one of the high-backed leather chairs. Father Corletti was right—that was big news. Demons weren't exactly social creatures, but they were hierarchical. And I never seemed to stumble across one but to find out that he was working for another one. If this sword was real, then like the little tailor who swatted flies, I could take out seven—or more—with one blow.

And how sweet would that be?

"So Abaddon thinks I'm this Keeper person?"

"It would appear to be so."

"Am I?"

"That is not a question to which I have an answer. None within *Forza* have heard the prophecy. Few believe the sword is even real. But if the demons believe it is you, then it may be so."

"And Abaddon's minions are trying to take care of me," I said. "End my involvement before I can do the same for their boss—and for them, too."

"That would seem to be their plan."

"Considering I don't know where this thing is, I'm think-ing I got a raw deal."

On the other side of the world, Father Corletti chuckled. "Ah, my dear, what else is new?"

I had to laugh, too. Not because of the situation, but be-cause Father Corletti was right.

"Be careful, Katherine," he said, all humor now gone from his voice. "I do not wish to lose you."

I reached up to finger the silver crucifix he'd given me so many years ago. "I'm not too keen on that outcome, either," I said. "I love you. I'll call soon."

I hung up, an odd combination of frustration and senti-mentality coursing through me. His actual information was not particularly useful. Yes, I now knew the legend.

But considering I neither had this mythical sword nor knew where to start looking for it, having the fairy tale at my fingertips was cold comfort.

Even so, simply talking to Father made me feel better, as if he were reaching across the miles to give me a much-needed hug.

I brushed my thumb under my now-damp lashes, feeling foolish but unable to escape the simple, basic truth: I missed Father. I missed having *a* father. And in the absence of a true parental figure, I'd clung first to Father Corletti and then later to Eric, letting those men in my life fill the empty spaces in my heart.

I liked to think that somewhere along the way I'd grown up a bit, that I'd come at my marriage with Stuart from a slightly different angle. But I wasn't entirely certain it was true. In the end, I'm not even sure it mattered. Not anymore. I had kids of my own now. And ultimately, the past isn't important. All that matters is the future.

I looked around the room, smiling a little. My husband was downstairs putting every ounce of himself into our future—his campaign, this idea of flipping houses. I'd had two good men in my life, and I was surrounded by people who loved me. As life circumstances went, I really couldn't complain. Bitch about having no idea what prophecy I was supposed to fulfill—sure. But complain? No way.

Not exactly a life-altering moment, but I will say that my perspective shifted slightly. And if Stuart wanted to take a risk with our future on this house, then why shouldn't he? I took a risk with our future every night I went out to hunt. At least he was doing me the courtesy of telling me the truth.

I closed my hand around the brass knob, then gave a tug, preparing to go tell him that very thing. Instead, I found myself face to face with a grime-covered demon, complete with rotted teeth, rancid breath, and denim overalls so filthy they would have stood upright even without the demon inside.

And, yes, I was certain it was a demon and not a zombie, because it opened its mouth and ordered me to die.

Being the obstinate sort, I decided not to take its suggestion. Instead, I jammed my finger forward, aiming for its eye. The demon turned my attack to its advantage by grabbing my finger and bending it backwards. The bone snapped, and I cried out, the pain shooting through me so fast and hot I was certain I couldn't have only injured a finger, because how could pain so large originate with such a tiny body part?

"*Kate?* Are you okay?"

"Fine," I yelled, even as I twisted my body around to keep my wrist from breaking like my finger. With my back to the demon, I kicked up, my heel connecting smartly with his groin. Not as sensitive a place for a demon as it was for a man, but the blow still held enough force to knock him off me. And as soon as my arm was free, I whipped around, my crescent kick catching him in the jaw and sending him stumbling backwards out of the room.

I forced my pain beneath the surface, ready to finish this off. I wasn't given the pleasure, however, because my cowardly foe turned tail and ran, heading down the stairs where he would, undoubtedly, collide with my husband, who surely hadn't believed my lame "fine" only moments before.

Needless to say, I ran after him.

"Who the hell—" I heard Stuart cry out, and then as I rounded the bend in the stair I saw the demon thrust out an arm and send Stuart hurtling to the ground.

"Stuart!"

"Kate! Are you okay?" To my amazement, he was already back on his feet and racing toward the door after the guy.

"*Don't,*" I called. "He's drugged up or something. He could kill you."

At the doorway, Stuart halted, and I saw the demon plow through the front yard, then turn and race down the street. My feet itched to go after him, and from the way Stuart was swaying from side to side, I could tell he wanted to as well.

Fortunately, he turned and looked at me. Or, rather, not so fortunately, because I must have looked a mess. He took the stairs three at a time and was at my side when my knees went wobbly as my adrenaline rush faded.

"What the *hell* did he do to you?" Stuart demanded, turning toward the doorway as if he could tractor-beam the creature back by the force of his will.

"Wasn't him," I lied. "He must be a squatter, and he scared me. I tripped and smashed my hand against something." I winced. "I think it's broken."

He pulled me close, our embrace a bit awkward because of my finger hanging out there. "You had me worried," he said gently. "If something happened to you . . ."

"I'm fine," I said, pulling back and forcing a smile.

He grimaced. "Uh-huh. Come on. Let's get you to the ER and have that X-rayed."

I wanted to protest that I didn't have time for the ER, but I didn't. He was right. As inconvenient as it might be, the finger was broken, and I needed a splint. And about the only upside of *that* was that if I requested the metal kind, it ought to slide quite nicely into a demon's eye. How's that for finding the silver lining? Because no matter what, I intended to track down my derelict friend and finish our business.

I just had to work it into my schedule somewhere.

Seven

"You're serious?" I demanded, pointing my newly splinted finger at Eddie for what had to be the forty-seventh time. "You really didn't move the body?"

I'd been back from the hospital for all of twenty minutes. Stuart had dropped me and my Vicodin prescription off, kissed me soundly, then headed to the office. I'd hurried inside, frantic to check up on Allie (who'd been allowed to babysit her brother despite the presence of demons in the neighborhood only after I'd confirmed that Eddie was awake and Laura was only a phone call away). I also wanted to fire off an e-mail to David, filling him in on the padre's information and letting him know about my most recent demon encounter. They were, it seemed, coming out of the woodwork as fast as they were disappearing.

Eddie swallowed his mouthful of SpaghettiOs. "You go deaf during the night, girlie?" he asked, his speech muffled by the fact that his teeth happened to be sitting beside his glass of milk. "I said I didn't, and I meant it. You wanted me on body patrol, you should have told me."

"I was with Stuart," I pointed out, my voice rising with exasperation.

Eddie just shrugged. "Man's got a good strong back. You shoulda got him to cart your dead demon away."

"Dead demon!" Timmy shouted, from where he'd plunked himself down on the floor and was now channeling the genius who'd first conceived "Jingle Bells." "Dead de-mon! Dead de-mon! Dead, dead de-de-*mon!*" I keep one cabinet door free of any child safety latches, freeing the kid up to start a band with whatever pots and pans happen to be under there. Today, he'd found a beat-up saucepan and a wooden spoon, and I silently swore to rearrange my shelves. Plastic, I think, was destined for that cabinet.

"That's a great song, sweetie," I said, trying for loving and nurturing, but probably hitting somewhere closer to frazzled and freaked out. "Maybe you could sing it a little softer?"

"Mom," Allie said urgently. "You don't think Stuart—"

"No way," I said emphatically. "Stuart puts up with a lot, but finding a dead body in the backyard? I'm absolutely convinced he'd mention that to me."

"That pansy boy? He'd have the cops here before you could say *plea bargain*."

I had to admit Eddie was right. About the police, that is. Not about the pansy-boy thing.

"Maybe Daddy?" Allie suggested.

"David? Absolutely not. If he'd been here last night, he would have helped. Not stood back and waited to move the body. For that matter, why wouldn't he have said something in the e-mail?"

Allie grimaced. "Maybe he saw me and didn't want to deal. Maybe *that's* why he went to L.A. To look at apartments or something."

I pressed my uninjured index finger to my temple and looked at her. "Allie, sweetheart, you're going a little crazy with the imagination, okay?"

"But—"

"But nothing. Your father wants nothing more than to

spend time with you. But sometimes adults have to take care of adult things first. Trust me. You two are going to spend time together. But it's complicated."

"Because Stuart doesn't know."

"Pretty much," I agreed.

She made a face. "So I'm being punished because *you're* keeping secrets."

Pretty much, I thought. But this time I didn't say it. She may be right, but smart-mouthing wasn't allowed. "Maybe Stuart had the right idea grounding you," I said.

"Sorry, Mom."

She looked appropriately contrite, so I decided to let it drop. "The bottom line is that we're still missing a body and we don't have any idea who moved it."

"Well, someone must have," Allie said. She frowned for a second, then looked up at me, eyes bright. "Maybe the demon who broke your finger," she suggested.

She'd been riveted when I'd relayed the story about encountering the demon in the Greatwater mansion. I'd fudged the details a bit, as I hadn't wanted to relay my conversation with Father Corletti, at least not until I had a chance to first discuss it with David. Not that my omission mattered to my daughter. One demon attack was enough to keep her occupied.

"He could have hauled his friend away, right?" she continued, warming to the theory. "Maybe he was even in our yard last night."

I looked at Eddie, then shrugged. As theories go, it wasn't bad. "Could be," I said. "I doubt it was in the yard, but I suppose it's possible that my scuzzy demon carted Sammy Watson away. But why leave the bits and pieces behind?"

"I don't know," Allie said. "I can't, like, think of *everything*. But someone must have taken it away. I mean, it's not like the demon could stand up and walk away on its own." Her eyes widened as she looked from me to Eddie. "Could it?"

"Of course not," I said automatically. "I've explained how all this works. Stab through the eye, the demon is released, and that's the end of that. All you've got left is a dead body and a demon floating around in the ether. They're essentially useless if they're incorporeal. And dead bodies don't get up and walk away. Do they?" I demanded, turning to Eddie for confirmation.

"Eh," he said with a noncommittal shrug. "You been around as long as me, you've seen pretty much everything."

I gaped at him. "Are we talking metaphorically here? Or have you actually seen an eviscerated demon get up and walk again."

"Couldn't it be a zombie?" Allie asked. Which, under the circumstances, was a damn good question.

"Phhhhbt," Eddie said. "Not damn likely. You got any idea how rare zombies are? Ain't like all that crap they got coming out of Hollywood. Demon's got to put together a whole big production to raise a zombie, and most of 'em don't bother. Too obvious. And unless they got a solid chance at getting a foothold, demons'd rather lay low."

"A foothold?" Allie asked, looking both perplexed and scared.

"Yeah, you know," he said, waving a wild hand as if he were stirring up trouble. "End of Days, Armaggedon, judgment day. Whatever the hell you want to call it, it's *hell* that's the key part of the equation."

"Thank you," I said, keying off Allie's stricken face. "Thanks so much."

"Eh, yank up your big-girl panties. I told ya it's rare. Ain't gonna do it unless there's something fierce brewing. So it ain't like we're looking the Apocalypse in the face or anything."

"Eddie," I said, hooking my arm around Allie's shoulder and pulling her tight. "There's a butchered zombie in the storage shed."

"Oh." I watched as Eddie's face went through a range of permutations, ending on mildly befuddled. "Well, ain't that a pisser."

"To say the very least," I said.

"So, is this, like, the end of the world?" Allie asked. "I mean, you guys have to tell me the truth. 'Cause if it's all over, I'm *so* not studying this semester."

The joke was lame, and I could hear the fear underneath.

"Eddie's exaggerating," I said. "As usual."

"Hmmph," he said. "Mighta overstated a little bit. But the bottom line's the same. You got a demon running around making zombies, then you got a demon that's up to something."

As consoling speeches went, it wasn't the best I'd ever heard, but it did seem to make Allie feel better. At the moment, that was all I really cared about.

"But what's it up to?" Allie asked, and I realized for the first time that she hadn't overheard the demon's mysterious meanderings about me and the Sword of Caelum, or that business about revenge. Good. I might have decided to let her start training, but that didn't mean I wanted her jumping feet first into every demonic mystery. Not, at least, until I had a better idea of what was going on.

"And what's the difference between real zombies and fake zombies?" she continued. "You promised last night you'd tell me."

"Fake zombies?" Eddie asked.

"Her words, not mine," I said. Then to Allie, "You promised yesterday afternoon you'd clean your bathroom, but you haven't gotten around to that yet."

"*Mo*-ther!"

"Just teasing. Hang on a second and let me get your brother settled. Then between Eddie and me maybe we can give you an education in the undead, and figure out what to do with the body bits in the shed."

She didn't look thrilled with the delay, but considering Timmy had slid off his chair and padded over to me, and was now tugging on my shirt and begging for *Curious George* in a stage whisper, I think she knew she had no choice.

"You're gonna have to do the explaining yourself," Eddie said, while I scrolled through the TiVo menu, looking for an episode of the PBS program he hadn't seen eight dozen times.

My toddler is a creature of repetition. He'd watched and abandoned *Dora*, *The Wiggles*, and *Clifford the Big Red Dog*. Occasionally he'd revisit them for nostalgia purposes, but for the most part, he'd moved on. A little monkey and a man in a yellow hat were his latest obsession. Stuart and I were taking bets over what would follow when poor George was pushed out of the number one position.

"What?" I said, cursing my remote as it skipped right over Timmy's program and pulled up an old *Law & Order* instead.

"I said you're on your own with the zombies."

"Where are you going?" I wrestled the remote control into submission, did a little cheer, and settled Timmy on the couch.

"Library," he said. "I wasted enough time this morning being your relief babysitter." He tapped his watch. "I gotta hustle if I want to hit the library before lunch."

"I've got a bucket of body parts to deal with and you're leaving to go peruse the stacks?"

"Hell no," he said. "I'm leaving you to go flirt with the librarian." He managed a sloppy wink. "Tammy's working today. Damn fine woman, Tammy."

"I'm sure," I said. "But—"

"Mom! What about the zombies?"

I took a deep breath for patience, then nodded at Eddie. "Fine. Go. Abandon me in my time of crisis."

He snorted. "How long have I lived here now? You got the cojones to handle yourself in a crisis. You got your blind sides, girlie, but you still got a couple of nice big ones."

I grimaced. "Thanks. I think." Not that I didn't appreciate the vote of confidence, however poorly phrased, but that didn't mean I was going to jump for joy when my potential help decided to hit the road.

"Tell you what," he said. "I'm feeling magnanimous today. I ain't gonna move any bodies. But if you need me, you call me." A wide grin split his craggy face. "Sounds like a country song," he said, and he headed toward the door humming an off-key tune.

"Great. Thanks. Thanks so much." He wasn't listening, of course. He was already heading out the front door, getting ready to walk the six blocks to our neighborhood library branch.

Feeling somewhat abandoned, I returned to the kitchen to face my daughter's interrogation.

"You promised," she said without preamble. "Zombies. Go on. Tell me everything."

I had to laugh at her enthusiasm, and I was just about to do exactly that, when a dull *thud* at the back door made us both jump. I gave myself a mental shake and calmed down. I'm trained to deal with things that go bump in the night, and I can handle things that go bump in the daytime, too. For another, even if the demon carcass had returned, he wasn't going to be polite enough to knock.

"It's nothing," I assured Allie.

She looked ready to argue the point, when Laura's voice filtered through the closed door. "Kate! Get a move on before I drop all of this."

I rushed to the back door and found my best friend hidden behind a Rubbermaid tub topped with a cardboard box overflowing with pink and green plastic baskets, shredded plastic grass, and cheap plastic toys. The thudding came from the pale-pink Keds she'd banged against the bottom of my door.

"Do I even want to know what you did to your finger?" she asked, by way of preamble.

"Do I even want to know what you're bringing into my house?" I retorted.

"I found the greatest stuff at Big Lots," she said. "Seventy-five percent off."

"But we already have a ton of stuff."

"Kate," she said in her most serious voice. "*Seventy-five percent off.*"

"Right. Got it." Laura is an extreme shopper. And where

sales are concerned, it's best to stand back and let her do her thing.

"The finger?" she pressed, resting her load on the arm of one of my chairs.

"Pissed off a demon," I admitted. "Then didn't move fast enough."

"Isn't that always the way?" she said, but I noticed that she seemed slightly paler as she said it.

"Don't worry. It doesn't even hurt anymore."

"Because you're a kick-ass Demon Hunter immune to pain?"

"That and the Vicodin." The comment didn't earn me as much of a smile as I was expecting. "I'm fine, Laura," I said. "Trust me. Of all the injuries I've had over the years, this one is nothing."

"But it's the first real injury I've seen. To you, I mean. You're like the superhero here, you know? *My* wrist might get smashed up, but superheroes aren't supposed to break."

I nodded, acutely aware of my decision not to tell her about David's death-by-demon only mere months ago. "Sorry to burst the bubble," I said. "But I'm really okay." I peered at her. "Are you?"

"Yeah," she said, then frowned, her forehead creasing. She nodded, firm and resolute. "Yes. Absolutely. I'm fine. Chickenshit, but fine."

"Fair enough." I nodded toward the junk she'd schlepped to my house. "Can I help?"

"With that finger?" She made a face, then passed me the bag filled with Easter grass.

"Thanks. Your confidence in my skills while wounded is enlightening."

"Save your strength for the demons," she said, then hoisted her bin and headed toward the kitchen.

"Good advice," I said, tagging after. "Wish I'd followed it. I wouldn't be heading up an Easter fair committee. It's positively surreal that I volunteered to do this. And I really can't believe you're joining in the madness."

"It's fun," she said, completely sincerely. She plunked her load down by one of the kitchen chairs, then picked up one of the Easter baskets. "See? Once we tie little bows on each handle and shove some grass inside, these will make fabulous goody baskets for the kids. All they have to do is take one, then run madly around the park looking for eggs."

How could I argue with logic like that?

"Besides," she continued. "I have to help. It's part of the sidekick oath. Whither you go, I must follow."

"I'll keep that in mind the next time I'm forced to take Timmy grocery shopping," I said. "Seriously, though. Thanks. There's no way I'd manage all of this on my own, and with you channeling Martha Stewart I feel like I have professional help."

"One," she said, heading toward my coffee maker, "I don't need to channel Martha. I'm glorious in my own right, and damn good in the kitchen."

"That you are," I confirmed. "Been reading self-help books again?"

"Every night," she said. "And two, I don't mind helping at all. It keeps my mind off Paul and the countdown to freedom. And three, you are a committee head, Kate. You're supposed to delegate. I shouldn't be the only slave labor on your rolls."

I shrugged. "It's easier to do it myself."

She lifted an eyebrow, and I immediately backtracked.

"Fair enough. It's easier to have *you* do it for me. See? I *am* delegating."

"And so did I," she said.

I squinted at her. "Come again?"

"Monday," she said. "The committee is descending on your house to help us stuff the eggs and make ice cream sandwiches and cupcakes."

I stared at her as if she'd grown two heads. "Wait. What? You've got people coming over here in just three days? When am I supposed to clean? Have you seen my living room?"

"Yes. This weekend. It's fine. And it's in *two* days. Today is Saturday."

I shook my head. "Right. I'm still in Friday mode." I shot

her a glare. "That's twenty-four hours less than I had three seconds ago."

"See?" she said, wiping Frosted Flakes off Timmy's abandoned chair before taking a seat. "That's why I take on these little projects. The cries of gratitude from my adoring public."

"Mom's worried the committee will get zombiefied," Allie offered. She'd pulled herself up to the kitchen counter and was sitting there now, kicking her legs on the cabinet doors.

"Zombiefied?" Laura repeated.

"Allie," I warned.

"Well, you are."

"Not the zombies," I clarified. "Your heels. And no, I'm not. Zombies I can handle. Ten women in my kitchen?" I shivered and turned back to Laura. "Did I piss you off somehow?"

"*Zombies*," she said again, completely unrepentant on the committee thing.

I gave up. "Allie and I were in the middle of a little chat on zombies when you arrived."

"Of course you were," Laura said. "That's why I come here. The calm, sane conversation."

Despite herself, Allie grinned. "But we can talk now, right? Where's Mindy?"

As far as I knew, Allie had kept her promise not to tell her best friend about my secret identity or about Allie's training. If Mindy joined us, we'd have to move on to other scintillating topics. Like whether to use green grass in the green baskets or go hog wild and use pink.

"Her dad called as I was leaving. She'll be over soon, though."

"Good," Allie said, but whether to Mindy's short absence or anticipated arrival, I wasn't sure, and I felt an unpleasant little twist in my heart. Mindy was Allie's best friend, the two of them having survived junior high and the beginning of high school, different activities, and a rather nasty bout of competitiveness early in the school year. Having weathered the storm, I hated to think that it might be my Big Secret that would end up pulling them apart.

Allie pulled her feet up and hugged her knees. I cleared my throat loudly and pointed, and she immediately hopped off the counter and moved to the red retro step stool. She propped her chin on her fist and regarded Laura. "Did you see a body on your way over?"

Laura shifted her attention from me to Allie and then back to me again. "Uh, no. Should I have?"

"We're missing one," I said.

"It's always something."

"Isn't it just," I agreed, then gave her a quick rundown on last night and this morning, conveniently leaving out the part about the sword.

"That is absolutely disgusting," Laura said. "It could be anywhere."

"It's just a body now, Laura."

"That doesn't make it any less disgusting if it turns up in my flower garden."

"The odds against it migrating to your flowers are astronomical," I assured her.

"Yeah," Allie said. "Instead it's just gonna go knock on your front door."

"Very nice," said Laura. "But so far, my house has been perfectly demon free, and—" She cut herself off, looking from Allie to me. "She's not kidding, is she?"

"Well, I don't think you need to worry about the demon knocking on your door," I said.

"So glad to hear it," she said with a wry expression. She plucked a basket out of the cardboard box, then reached down to open the tub next to her chair with her free hand. "But why all the talk of zombies?"

"Allie thinks there's a very good chance that our missing body has been turned into a zombie."

"In any other family, I'd say your kid had a great imagination." And then, without any warning at all, Laura leaped from her chair and screamed.

Eight

"*Aaaaah!*" Laura cried, her chair tumbling as she scrambled backwards, her finger pointing down toward the tub.

I looked, saw what she was pointing at, and burst out laughing.

"What in heaven's name is *that?*"

"That's our zombie," Allie said brightly.

"That's *my* tub. I can't believe you brought in the tub from the shed," I said, trying very hard not to shake, I was laughing so hard. "You should have said something."

"We're using body parts for the party?" Laura asked, her voice rising.

"I needed the tub," I explained. "The candy and eggs and stuff are in a lawn bag now."

"You *needed* the tub," she said, taking a tentative step closer to the tub. "Is that a finger?"

"What happened? What happened?" Timmy yelled, racing into the kitchen toward us. "Mommy screamed?"

"No, sweetie, that would be Aunt Laura."

"Thanks," she said.

"The hand almost climbed up my leg," Allie said, with

oodles of enthusiasm, even as her little brother peered into the tub with ghoulish glee.

The blood drained from Laura's face, and she looked at me for confirmation.

"You have to hack them up," I said. "It stops them, but it doesn't kill them."

"Oooh! Wormies," Timmy said, then leaned into the tub and snatched a finger.

We all leaped toward him. "No, no," I said. "That's not for you, buddy."

"*Mine!*" he cried, dancing away from me, holding the finger high. It wriggled and squirmed, but was generally harmless. "Mine, mine, mine!" He started marching around the kitchen table, finger held high.

Intellectually, I knew I should go after him and wrest it from his hot little hand. Instead, all I wanted to do was run for the video camera.

"So, will you tell me already?" Allie begged, hopping off the stool and following her brother. "About the real and fake ones? Mindy's gonna be here soon, and unless you guys say I can tell her everything . . ." She trailed off, looking from me to Laura hopefully. Apparently her blatant omission from her best friend had been on her mind lately, too.

I let Laura field that one, not only because she was in charge where Mindy was concerned, but also because I was still savoring Timmy's delighted march with the displaced finger.

For a moment, Laura looked like she was considering the possibility of telling Mindy. Then she shook her head. "I'm sorry, Al. But Mindy's got a lot going on right now. I don't think we need to add demons to the mix."

"Demons are better than divorce," Allie said, and although I know she didn't mean her words to sting, I saw the way Laura cringed. "Oh, gosh. I'm sorry. I didn't mean—"

"It's okay, sweetie," Laura said as Timmy turned one hundred and eighty degrees and launched himself at Allie. "To be honest, I wish Mindy didn't have to put up with that, either."

"Ah-ha!" Allie said, catching Timmy around the waist and holding him upside down. "I got you!"

Timmy squealed, absolutely delighted with this turn of events.

"Two swings," Allie said. "Then I want the wiggly toy. Deal?"

"Deal!"

She hauled him upside down to the living room, and I didn't have to be able to see to know she was holding his thighs and swinging him between her own before tossing him on the couch. The toss, in reality, was more of a gentle placement, but Timmy loved it just the same.

Meanwhile, Kabit padded over, lifted himself onto his haunches, and hissed at the contents of the tub.

"You said it, kitty," Laura said. "Yuck."

"Okay," Allie said, coming back into the room with the zombie's index finger held daintily between her own finger and thumb. "That worked, and he's happily back in monkey land."

"You win the good big sister of the year award," I said as she tossed the finger back into the tub.

"Lucky me. So will you tell me now? The real zombie/fake zombie thing?"

"There are fake zombies?" Laura asked. "Like what I buy at Hobby Lobby for Halloween?"

"Not exactly," I said. I took a step backwards so I could see into the living room. Sure enough, Timmy was camped out too close to the television watching George wheel around his apartment with a cast on his leg, and Mindy was nowhere near the back door. In other words, the coast was clear.

"Real zombies," I began, "are just animated flesh. Like this guy," I added, nodding to the tub.

"Since you can't kill them," Allie told Laura, "you have to hack them up. But they don't bleed."

"That's really good to know," Laura said, looking like she might throw up.

"The trouble with those zombies from a demon's perspective is that they're a whole lot of trouble to make," I added.

"It involves the desecration of holy relics," Allie chimed in, proving once and for all that she *can* pay attention, and that there was absolutely no reason for the C she got in American history last semester.

"Exactly," I said. "And they don't blend in particularly well, either, you know?"

I pulled out one of the kitchen chairs for Allie and motioned for her to sit. As long as I had a captive audience, I might as well put them to work.

"Why *do* the demons want them?" Allie asked as I put one of Laura's baskets in front of her, then motioned to the Easter grass and ribbons.

I plunked a purple basket down in front of me and reached for the green grass. With my finger, I could easily fill baskets with grass. Tying gorgeous ribbons on the handles? Maybe not so much.

I shoved a handful of grass in and considered Allie's question. "Cheap labor, more or less. Send out an automaton to maim and kill, and you don't risk getting nailed through the eye."

"But the *demon* attacked you," Allie said. "Not the zombie."

"I know," I said. "That's definitely strange."

"The missing demon?" Laura asked. Her forehead crinkled. "You have a demon and a zombie, right?"

"Right," I said, thankful that Laura had subtly shifted the conversation, because I hadn't told Allie the entire truth. Since zombies can't talk—and since my demon felt compelled to chitchat about the Sword of Caelum and revenge and other nasty stuff—it made sense that it was a demon who'd jumped me.

"So those are the real ones," Laura said. "And that's what we've got here?"

"Exactly."

"And the, um, *parts*? You had to hack it up because . . . ?"

"You saw the way it was wiggling in Timmy's hand. The parts don't have to be attached to the body to move around."

"When the hand grabbed my leg, Mom had to cut its fingers off with the pruning shears."

"And you thought you'd never get any use out of those gardening tools."

"I love it when my tools multitask," I admitted, grimacing a little when my stomach growled. My handful of M&Ms for breakfast hadn't really hit the spot, and although I knew I should have something more substantial, at the moment all I really wanted was the sugar rush so easily supplied by my freezer.

I gave in, getting up and grabbing a bag of sugary goodness from the freezer. What can I say? I'm a weak woman.

"Okay, so back up," Laura said, reaching out her hand for a helping of candy. "Why is that zombie real? I mean, other than the fact that squirming body parts is about as real as reality gets?"

"They're the definition of zombie," I explained. "The folklore. The movies about the creepy brain-eating creatures that roam through the night with their arms outstretched."

"*Ewww*," Allie said. "I forgot about the brain-eating part."

"They don't really do that," I said. "They're nothing but moving flesh. They don't have to eat. All they do is exist, and even then only to serve their master."

"But back to the real thing," Laura urged. "What exactly is an unreal zombie?"

I had to put that answer on hold for a moment, because my son—apparently smelling chocolate—came charging into the kitchen. "Candy, Mommy! I want candy!"

"It's only fair," Allie said.

"Thanks for the advice, Mom," I retorted. "But he just had breakfast."

"Um, that was two hours ago, remember? And I'm pretty sure he ingested a grand total of ten flakes, then smashed the rest on the table and wiped them onto the floor."

"I'm still thinking that's not the best argument for chocolate. Scrambled eggs or a peanut butter sandwich, maybe. But chocolate?"

She cocked her head. "What did *you* have for lunch?"

"I'm not a little kid," I said, then watched her face as she tried to decide whether I was in a good enough mood to parry if she lobbed back with a fancy retort.

Apparently, I didn't look that chipper, because she backed off, becoming suddenly interested in tying her shoe.

Good call.

"Mine!" Timmy hollered, his hand reaching up and wriggling blindly on the tabletop as he searched for candy. "Party candy, Mommy! Want. My. Party. Candy!"

"It is absolutely your party candy," I said, sweeping the candy back a good six inches even as I decided not to bother correcting him about the "my" party thing. Why not let him think Mom threw him a party and invited the entire neighborhood? "That's why you have to wait for the party. It wouldn't be any fun if party day came and there was no candy, would it?"

He climbed up in a chair, eyeing the candy now on the far side of the table and very much out of reach. "Want candy," he said, in the tiniest voice.

"Timmy . . ."

That did it. His face fell, overwhelmed by this ultimate betrayal by the mother who loved him. His lower lip started to quiver, and I was done for.

I told myself I gave in so that I could finish my zombie spiel before Mindy arrived. In reality, I was suckered by the pouty lips and long lashes of a tousled-haired little boy.

After a bit of toddler negotiation, which consisted of me telling him he could have two M&Ms and him insisting he wanted ten, we finally settled on five counted out slowly into his greedy little palm.

"Anyway," I said, as soon as Timmy was settled again, "the other kind of zombie isn't just animated flesh. It's really a demon. Instead of moving into a newly dead body, he sets up shop in a body that's been down for the count for a while."

"I thought they had to do it right after you died," Allie

said, the area above her nose pulling into a little V as she mentally skimmed all the Hunter texts I'd assigned her over the last few months. "The soul slips out, and they slip in."

"Right," I said. "That's the entry portal. Miss that, and they're out of luck." They're out of luck, too, if the body belonged to a person with faith. Those souls go out kicking and screaming, protecting their earthly host from the indignity of becoming a shell for a demon. "But if they wait until the body starts to decay . . ." I trailed off with a shrug. "To be honest, I don't really understand it. I only know that about the time the ick factor sets in, so can the demon."

"To *any* body?" Allie asked.

"Pretty much," I said.

"But they don't do it very much," Allie said. "How come?"

I shrugged. "Demons want to be human. They covet our form. They covet our ability to touch, to feel. The carnal aspects of being human. Plus, they want to blend in."

"And Danny Demon walking down the street decomposing isn't going to get to experience all the perks that go with being human?" Laura asked.

"Exactly. Not to mention that demons rarely *only* want to be human. They've got bigger end-of-the-world type plans. And it's hard to be subtle when there are maggots poking out of your eye sockets."

Allie grimaced, an M&M pausing on the way to her mouth.

I fought a smile. "Squeamish?"

"I *so* am not," she said, then shoved three candies into her mouth and chewed vigorously.

Another light rap on the door, followed by, "Allie? Aunt Kate? Can I come in?"

"We're in the kitchen, sweetie," Laura called.

Allie stood up as Mindy walked in. "We're going upstairs, okay?" She aimed a pointed look at me. "Anything interesting happens and you totally have to tell me."

"What's going to happen?" Mindy asked.

"Oh." For a moment, Allie looked completely befuddled. "Mom's arguing with Stuart."

"Lucky you," Mindy said, rolling her eyes and pointedly *not* looking at Laura.

"Not that kind of fight," Allie said as they left the breakfast area. "Mom wants to put a swimming pool in the backyard, and Stuart thinks—"

I couldn't hear what Stuart thought, but I had to admit that a pool didn't sound like a half-bad idea. "I could infuse the thing with holy water and have my own backyard demon trap," I said to Laura.

"You're thinking about getting a pool?"

"I am now. Wasn't ten minutes ago. The kid does think on her feet well. Any chance Mindy bought it?"

"This time, maybe. Whether she'll keep on buying it . . ." Laura shrugged. "One of these days, I'll either decide it's okay to tell her, or we'll find out that she's known all along, and she and Allie are better at keeping secrets than we thought."

She had a point. I grabbed the coffeepot and refilled both our mugs.

"Speaking of secrets," she said. "Why didn't you tell her that the missing demon can't be a zombie?"

I looked at her, impressed. "Aren't you the good little pupil?"

"Perfect attendance for all of first grade," she confirmed.

"After that?"

She shook her head. "Bad. Very bad. Never got the attendance award again."

"I can tell it's scarred you."

"For life," she said. "Seriously, why didn't you tell her?"

"She'll figure it out on her own if she thinks about it," I said. "But in the meantime, I don't really want her wondering what kind of creatures were creeping around our backyard in the wee hours of the morning." Because Laura was right, of course. The demon had originally entered Sammy's body when the "portal" was open, and by the time I stabbed it in the eye and sent the demon rushing toward hell or the ether or its local demon hangout, the portal had closed and no new demon could move in.

But the body was still fresh and new. Not the least bit decayed. All nice and tidy. Which meant it wasn't yet ripe for a zombie takeover.

And that, of course, meant that our demon hadn't gotten up and walked away. Someone had moved the body.

My fourteen-year-old may have definitely clued in to the whole "a Hunter's life is a dangerous life" thing, but that didn't mean I felt the need to exaggerate the lesson.

"There's more I didn't tell her," I confessed.

"Oh?"

"Revenge, vengeance, and the Sword of Caelum," I said.

"Gesundheit."

"Very funny. You know that's supposed to keep a demon from flying up your nose, right?"

She lifted an eyebrow.

"No, seriously. It means 'bless you' or 'good health' or something. And people used to think that when you sneezed it gave a demon the opportunity to shoot up your nose."

"So they said 'bless you' to keep the demon out."

"Exactly."

She pondered that for a moment. "But *can* demons fly up your nose?"

"Not that I know of," I said, then paused, considering the question more thoroughly. "But I do remember reading about an exorcist during the Roman conquest of Judea. In front of the emperor, he pulled a demon through a man's nostril."

"Not only is that absolutely disgusting," Laura said, "but I'm completely impressed that you remembered it. I thought you said you were more interested in fighting than in reading."

"I was," I admitted. "But that didn't mean I was exempt from the schoolwork part. And even in the realm of demon lore, that one's just ooky enough to stick in your memory."

She grimaced, then rubbed a hand under her nose. I laughed, catching my own hand rising to do the same thing.

"Okay, but we got totally sidetracked. What's the Sword of Caelum?"

"The Sword of Heaven, if you translate from the Latin. Other than that, I have absolutely no idea," I admitted. "But apparently the demons aren't about to let me wield it."

"Oh, one of those," Laura said.

"One of what?"

"A cryptic comment. Demons make a lot of them."

I couldn't argue with that. "This time, I actually have a little more information," I admitted. I relayed what Father Corletti had told me, filling her in on the salient points about my past encounter with Abaddon so that the full story would make sense.

"Well, hell," she said.

"That pretty much sums it up," I agreed. "I was perfectly content taking out the stray demon here and there. I absolutely don't need another demon out there who thinks that I need to be eradicated from the face of the earth. I mean, I've got a party to plan."

"That too," Laura said loyally. "But what I meant was that it doesn't sound like there's much for me to do. Your peeps in Rome have already done all the research for you."

"My peeps?" I repeated, amused. "And no, believe me. There's a ton for you to do. Nobody in Rome can find anything about this supposed prophecy. But it must be out there. I mean, the demons must have some reason for thinking I'm their girl, right?"

"In other words," she said, "I still have tons of research to do. Can't *anything* in this business be simple?"

"Apparently not," I said, fighting a grin. In truth, I wasn't overly confident that Laura would find the answer hidden deep within the bowels of the Internet, especially considering that a whole gaggle of *Forza* researchers hadn't managed as much. But stranger things had happened. Besides, Laura is the only woman I know who can find anything—*anything*—on sale somewhere in cyberspace. How many Vatican priests could locate a pair of vintage Chanel sunglasses half a continent away, haggle down to seventy percent off, and get the seller to kick in free shipping? I'm thinking none.

And if I could put that talent to work for me, so much the better.

Besides, I knew she wanted to help. And, frankly, I craved the solidarity.

She cocked her head, looking at me. "What are you grinning about?"

"I was trying to remember what you and I talked about before I got back in the game."

"The PTA," she began, counting on her fingers. "Bake sales, how to find fast and easy recipes, our husbands' careers, our children's grades, whether we needed to trade in for a bigger car, whether we were going to let our daughters get their driver's licenses at sixteen, whether we were going to let our daughters date at sixteen. Or wear makeup at sixteen. Or—"

"Fair enough," I said. "I remember. And you seem to remember in detail." I paused, not sure I wanted to ask the next question. "Do you miss it? Not having, well, *that* as the focal point of our morning?" I pointed to the blue tub, once again with a full cadre of zombie parts.

"Are you kidding?" she said. "Life is so much more interesting now."

"And dangerous," I pointed out.

"There is that," she admitted. "But Kate, you already know my answer. It's the same for me as it is for you."

"It is?" I'd been trained from childhood to be a Hunter. It was in my blood, in my life. And though I'd lived a few years as a normal mom in a normal family in a normal town, that didn't mean the real me hadn't been hiding under the surface. Clearly it had, because now that I was out of retirement, this wasn't a life I wanted to give up. The job was too important. And, yes, I enjoyed the thrill.

"Paul and I got married right out of high school," she began. "And I stayed at home and eventually we had a little girl, and life was good. I worked hard on the house. I did all the right things with Mindy's schools. I was an active mom, a supportive wife. I did absolutely everything I could to build up this marriage for us. You know?"

I nodded, not at all sure where she was going with this.

"And then one day I find out the bastard's been having an affair. I've put my heart and soul into a marriage that's been an illusion all along. It wasn't real because it was one-sided."

"I'm not—"

She held up a hand. "What you do—what I do when I help you—it's important. As important as it gets. And that's not something I can have an illusion about, you know? I was fooling myself with Paul—or he was fooling me—but not this. Not now. We're fighting evil. The Big Bad. And when you get right down to it, I think that's pretty damn amazing." She shot me a smile, her cheeks slightly flushed. "So, no. I don't miss it. Besides," she added with a nod to my Easter-paraphernalia-covered table, "if you think that the PTA and the kids and volunteer bake sales aren't on our radar anymore, then you need to crawl out of your hole. Because I'll research for you until the wee hours of the morning. But I am *not* stuffing Easter eggs all by myself."

"Fair enough," I said, a little humbled that she did get it. For better or for worse, we were in this together, and for all the right reasons. "Let's decorate ten of these baskets and then I'll turn you loose to figure out this sword thing."

"It's a plan," she said, reaching for a spool of silver ribbon. "What are you going to do about that guy?" she asked, pointing to our dismembered friend.

"The cathedral. Where else? In fact, I should probably go now, just in case Stuart decides to come home for lunch or something." I gave her the lowdown on my husband's recent burst of togetherness—our romantic interlude this morning, his invitation to a movie, and our quick trip to scope out the mansion.

"Not very Stuart-like," she said. "At least not since the campaign started."

"I know," I said. "Nerves? Election jitters?"

"I'm voting for guilt or worry," Laura announced.

"About what?"

"About spending so much time away from you," she said. "That's the guilt part."

"And the worry?"

She shrugged and reached for a blue M&M. "Maybe he's picking up on the fact that you're keeping secrets."

"It's probably nothing," I said, more to convince myself than her. "Why does it have to be one or the other? I mean, he *is* my husband, and he *does* love me."

"And he so often invites you to movies in the middle of the day, right?"

"Oh, hell," I said. "It's gotta be the guilt thing, right? I mean, I'm careful. He can't have a clue. Can he?"

"You need to tell him," Laura said, and not for the first time.

"I know," I said. "And I plan to. I just don't know when."

"Figure it out," she said. "Or else it's gonna come back to bite you on the butt."

I nodded. I'd figured out on my own that my butt was in danger. But that didn't mean I'd figured out the best way to handle it.

I pointed to the zombie. "Right now, I'm going to worry about him. You'll stay and watch the kids?"

"Of course."

I grabbed the tub and hefted it. "Catch the door for me?"

"I can't believe I picked up a tub filled with an entire body. I actually went to the gym twice last week," she added wryly. "I guess those damn workouts are paying off."

"That's just the nature of zombies," I said. "Extremely light. Extremely strong."

"Nature or not, it's still pretty funky."

"The situation is funky," I corrected. "And I might be a bit skewed in my opinion by the fact that I've had to haul several dead demons to the cathedral over the past few months. But to me, the fact that the zombie is light and easily portable isn't funky, it's a perk."

"Can't argue with that," she said, propping the front door open with her foot, then grabbing my keys off the entryway table.

She followed me down the sidewalk to the driveway, then opened the rear of the Odyssey. The tub slid easily in, and I closed the back door. If only I'd known back when we bought this thing how useful it was going to be for hauling around monsters and demons.

As I turned back around, Eddie strolled up the driveway. "Hold up a minute there, girlie."

"I thought you were at the library."

"Was," he said in a hushed tone. "Now I'm watching our mysterious stranger."

"What mysterious stranger?" Laura asked, her voice normal.

"Hush, woman! Don't you know they sometimes got extra-keen hearing?"

Laura's mouth curved into a little frown. "Actually, I didn't know that."

"Who?" I asked, before we could get off on a tangent. The question, though, wasn't necessary. A simple glance across the street, and I knew exactly who Eddie was talking about. A tall, lanky man in ill-fitting clothes, with dark hair and an olive complexion.

"Demon?" I asked.

"Could be. Noticed him when I was leaving," Eddie said. "Kinda creeping around. Don't live on this street or yours," he said, pointing to Laura. "Got a nose for these things. Can't stay alive long as I have without being able to sniff out trouble."

"So you've stayed here watching him?" I prompted.

"Hell, no," Eddie said. "I went to the library. Told you I thought Tammy was working."

"But I thought you said you knew he was trouble," Laura said.

"That's what you got this one for," Eddie said, hooking a thumb at me.

I caught Laura's eye and gave the slightest shake of my head. With Eddie, it was best not to pursue these things.

"So what brought you back?" I asked.

"Schedule got changed, so Tammy's not on today after all. Talked to Imogene for a bit, but she's a fruity old bat, and I couldn't see much use to hang around the library, so I headed on back—"

"—and our friend is still here," I finished.

"Like I said. Suspicious."

"So what do we do?" Laura asked.

"Oh, that one's easy," Eddie said. "We kill the bastard."

Nine

I grabbed hold of Eddie's elbow, tugging him back. Our interloper might be a demon, sure. He might also be lost, visiting friends, or just plain nosy. Irritating and rude, maybe, but not necessarily demonic. "How about we try something a little less dramatic," I suggested.

"Eh? Like what?"

"Something radical and unexpected," I said. "Like asking him what he's doing."

He snorted. "Well, sure. If you're gonna be all pansy-ass about it."

I caught Laura's eye, and for a moment I feared for her safety. She was laughing so hard, I was certain she would fall to the ground and bang her head on the cement.

"Wait here," I said to both of them.

The mysterious stranger glanced toward us once while we were talking, but when I turned my head in his direction, he was studiously looking everywhere but at my house. And the instant I stepped into the street, he started walking down the sidewalk. Definitely suspicious. I crossed at a diagonal, reaching into my purse for the pump bottle of hair spray I'd cleaned out and filled with holy water. I sprayed a bit on both palms, then replaced the bottle and closed my hand around my knife, keeping the blade concealed inside my bag.

Mystery man walked faster, and I hurried to catch up, finally intercepting him in front of Wanda Abernathy's house.

"Hi," I said, sticking my hand out and trying to look like a friendly—if pushy—suburban mom. "I noticed you looked a little lost, and I thought maybe I could help."

"I . . . oh. Yes." He took my hand, and there was no sizzling, popping, or burning. In the demon-hunting world, that's a good thing. I still didn't know who the stranger was, but at least I knew he wasn't a demon.

"You are most kind," he said with a hint of Eastern European accent. Prague, maybe? I couldn't be sure. "But I am not lost."

"Deidre? Is that you, honey?"

I turned and found Mrs. Abernathy standing in her doorway holding an umbrella and a can of Lysol. "It's me, Kate. From across the street. Sorry if we're bothering you."

"Is he a friend of yours, dear? Because I was just about to call the police. I can't abide loitering. Too many people loitering in my yard lately. Hiding in the bushes. Creeping up the steps. Unacceptable. Simply unacceptable!"

"He's not a friend, and I was just explaining that to him."

"Yes, I am not loitering," he said. He turned to Mrs. Abernathy. "I am not bad man."

She squinted at him through Coke-bottle glasses, then lifted her chin and turned her inspection toward me. "How is your committee coming, dear? Deidre is bringing the grandbabies, you know. Tucker is so excited about the Easter Bunny."

"Um," I said, not as easily convinced as Mrs. Abernathy that our neighborhood stranger wasn't a bad man. "It's going great, but right now . . ." I trailed off, indicating the stranger.

"Oh, yes, of course. You take care of it, Carla, dear." She waggled a finger at me. "Always a pleasure to see you again."

"You better get on inside now," I said gently. I pointed toward her umbrella. "It's going to rain, and you don't want to get wet."

"Oh yes. Yes." She closed the umbrella, then shuffled backwards. I took a deep breath, hating how helpless I always felt after talking with Wanda, and irritated with her daughter for not pushing harder to get the elderly woman into Coastal Mists or some other assisted-living facility.

At the moment, though, Mrs. Abernathy wasn't my prime concern. In front of me, the stranger was rummaging in a battered leather messenger bag. I tensed, my hand tightening around my knife in anticipation of an attack.

None came. Instead, he handed me a colorful flyer with *CARNIVAL* written across the top in beautifully skilled calligraphy. "We are near the boardwalk. Much fun for the family. You will come, yes?"

"Ah," I said. "Well, it certainly looks—"

"You will come." He gave a firm nod of his head, as if that were the end of that.

Since I wasn't inclined to argue the point, I shifted gears. "So you've been passing out flyers? How come you've been so long in this spot?"

"I eat my lunch," he said, then rummaged again, this time coming up with a crumpled paper bag. He held it open to me, revealing a banana peel, an empty bottle of water, and the crust of a sandwich of dubious innards. "Is okay?" he asked.

"Sure thing," I said, with what I hoped was a cheery smile. "You go right on delivering your flyers."

"Thank you, miss. Thank you." He backed a few steps away, first yanking off his hat to hold it at his chest, as if he were a poor peasant and I the generous landowner who'd just granted him a new cow. After a few yards, during which I feared he'd topple backwards, he turned and hurried down the block, this time with his nose in the direction he was traveling.

I watched him go, then went back across the street to my

driveway. I handed the flyer to Eddie and watched while he read it.

"Damn demons come up with cleverer and cleverer cover stories every day," he said.

"He wasn't a demon. I had holy water on my hand. And his breath smelled perfectly fine."

Eddie snorted, looked at me, then shook his head as if I'd failed him utterly. "Got the cojones, maybe. But you're still a damn sight naïve."

"Slow down around this curve!" Laura said, her voice a little frantic. Eddie had volunteered to stay with the kids—a miracle as far as I was concerned—and although he wasn't my top choice of a sitter for Timmy, the kids had survived the morning without injury or a total nervous breakdown, so I figured we were safe.

Now, Laura was clutching the handhold above the passenger door, her body twisted so she could look toward the back of the van.

"I'm only going twenty-five," I said. "What's with you and the speed today?" Earlier, she'd warned me I was going far too fast over a speed bump. I'd been going just shy of seven miles an hour.

"*That*," she said, pointing to the back of the van where the tub was sliding around. "What if the lid pops off? What if we're trapped in the van with those parts?"

I hid my smile. "For one, I don't think we'd be trapped. This thing's got a remarkable number of doors. And two, I hacked all the fingers off the hands. At worst, we'd have ten little worms squirming around the van. Gross, but not really a threat."

She scrunched her face up. "I'm overreacting, aren't I?"

"Not to the situation," I said. "I don't think it's possible to overreact to zombies in the backyard. Teeny-tiny zombie parts trapped in a tub, though . . ."

"Overreaction," she said. "I get it." She tilted her head to the side. "Okay, here's something I don't get. The Lazarus Bones."

Cold, guilty fingers scurried up my spine. "Oh," I said, stupidly. I hadn't told her about what happened with David, and the only other people who knew were Allie, Eddie, and David himself. And though Eddie was the wild card of the bunch, I still didn't believe any of them had shared my secret.

I'm honestly not sure why I hadn't told Laura what happened with David. I'd told her right away, after I'd learned that David was really Eric, but the fact that I'd raised David from the dead hadn't been as easy to reveal. I'm not sure why. She's my best friend, and I'd told her about broken rules before, but this rule . . .

This rule was different. It wasn't like running a red light, or even like telling her what I did for *Forza* despite my secrecy oath. No, by bringing David back from the dead, I'd broken God's rules. Worse, I'd played God. And I feared that my selfishness had scarred not only my own soul, but David's, too. And that kind of fear I held close to my heart, hiding it behind an emotional wall of regret and desperation.

Even so, I think that under other circumstances, I would have finally broken down and told Laura the truth. She was, after all, my best friend, and keeping secrets from her ripped me in a way that caused almost physical pain. But Laura had lost her husband. Her high school sweetheart. The man she'd believed she would grow old with.

I, however . . .

I was now both cursed and blessed with the two men in my life whom I loved more than anything. And to tell that to Laura now seemed too much like twisting the knife deeper into her already broken heart.

I swallowed. "So, um, what about the Lazarus Bones?"

"Not them so much as Goramesh," Laura continued, oblivious to my internal meanderings. "You know, when he came here to find the bones? He wanted to raise a whole army of the undead, right? I mean, wasn't that the point of all that?"

"Absolutely." The High Demon Goramesh had come to San Diablo at the end of last summer, shattering forever my illusion that my hometown was a demon-free zone and jump-starting my return to active duty with *Forza*. "So what don't you get?"

"But why did he bother? I mean, if they can make zombies any old time."

"Not any time," I clarified. "It's a big deal."

"But so was stealing the Lazarus Bones," she countered. "So what was the advantage?"

"Camouflage," I said. "Remember back when Eddie told us how the Lazarus Bones worked? The bones restore the body back to its physical state at the time of death."

"Right, right," she said, obviously remembering the key points from last summer. "So the army of the undead would look like you or me instead of something out of *Night of the Living Dead*."

"Exactly. And since the bodies would have a demon in them—and not merely animated flesh—they'd blend in easily. Unless someone notices their really gross breath or happens to spill a vial of holy water on them."

"Oh, wow," Laura said. "That's something I never really thought of before."

"What?" I asked, taking my eyes off the road to look at her.

"How much they blend in," she explained. "I pretty much picture you fighting them, getting rid of them, and that being that. But what about the ones you don't know about? I mean, he could be one," she said, pointing out the window at a well-hued pedestrian. "Or they could be my waiter. Or my doctor." Her lip curled. "It's really not one of my happier thoughts."

"Especially since you're dating your doctor," I added.

"I can assure you his breath is perfectly fine," she said, her expression prim. "But you know what I mean, right?"

I nodded; I did know. I'd learned that lesson a long, long time ago. "There's always been evil in the world, Laura," I said. "All that's changed is that you know about one more package."

"Somehow," she retorted, "that doesn't make me feel better."

I had forgotten that this was the Saturday before Palm Sunday, and we found Father Ben with the bishop in a flurry of preparations, surrounded by a half dozen deacons, liturgical ministers, and church volunteers.

Father Ben was head to head with Delores, the volunteer coordinator, going over something on a clipboard. He glanced up, and I managed a friendly little wave that I hope conveyed that we hadn't dropped by merely for a social call.

He finished up, then hurried to us. "Kate, is this an official visit? This isn't a very good time."

"I know. I'm sorry. But yeah. It's a business call."

He cast a glance over his shoulder toward the bishop, confirming that the other man was busy with two of the deacons. Then Father Ben pressed a hand on my shoulder and eased me out into the foyer, Laura tagging along behind. "What's happened?" he asked in a low whisper.

I gave him the quick rundown, skimming over the fact that I had circumvented his authority to go to Father Corletti at the outset. It was a point that Father Ben picked up on right away—and about which he didn't seem to care. There's another reason I really like that man.

"Hopefully *Forza* will be able to provide more information," he said when I was done. "The Sword of Caelum certainly isn't anything within my expertise." He tilted his head and lifted one shoulder, the effect mildly self-deprecating. "Not too unusual, though. I'm still new at this."

"But getting more knowledgeable by the day. And how better to become even more of an expert than by cross-referencing all of my old reports. Maybe somewhere along the line some demon made a reference to this prophecy. I wouldn't have understood it at the time, but I reported everything every demon said word for word."

"That's a really good idea," Laura said.

"It's worth a shot, anyway. Right?" I asked Ben. It was a long shot, but it was also the only thing I could think of. Considering the information from Father Corletti, I had a feeling only a limited few within the demon population knew about the prophecy. So the odds that a demon had relayed a clue to me were slim. Still, we had to look. And it probably made more sense than plugging "Kate Connor prophecy Sword Caelum" into Google. *That* really was a long shot.

Beside me, Laura shifted. "I guess that means I'm out of a job?"

"You have tenure," I promised.

"And I can certainly use assistance," Ben said. "Particularly this week." He looked solemnly at me. "Kate, I'm sorry, but finding time is going to be difficult."

"I know," I said. "But—"

"I will do everything I can," Father Ben assured me. "And Laura will assist me, I'm certain."

"Absolutely," Laura agreed. "It will be a relief to know what I'm looking at rather than slogging blindly through cyberspace. Do you already have Kate's old reports?"

"Most of them have been shipped here," Father said. "As her new *alimentatore*, it is one of my duties to review and analyze past reports, and to summarize and index them if that hasn't already been done."

"Lucky you," Laura said. "But it does sound like that's the way to go. I'm totally your girl for helping."

"Wonderful," Father Ben said. "Now if you'll—"

"Hang on a second," I cut in. "I'm not sure that Larua going through those reports is the best idea. There are things in those files—"

"Don't worry," she said, picking up on my concern. "Nothing will surprise me. Truly."

I considered arguing but held my tongue. She'd be surprised, I knew. Even after all the things she'd seen, when she read the reports of my youth, I knew that she'd be very, very surprised.

"Father Ben!" Delores's shrill voice carried all the way to our far corner of the foyer. "Yoo-hoo! The bishop needs you again."

"Of course," he said, turning. "Tell him I'll only be a moment. Ladies," he said, turning back to us. "I'll be in touch shortly."

He took a step away, and I instinctively reached for him even as Laura called out, "Wait!"

He stopped and faced us, and I saw the panic on his face. "There's more?"

"Um, yeah." I licked my lips. "We need to get a package into the crypts. Can we go around back without being noticed?"

"The demon's body?" His forehead creased. "I thought you said it was missing."

"Not the demon. The zombie."

"Animated body parts?" His voice echoed through the foyer, and he looked around, making sure no one had overheard. He leaned close and lowered his voice again. "Kate, you can't be serious."

I goggled at him because, of course, I was completely serious. When he didn't immediately break into a smile and assure me he was teasing, I got a little concerned. For months now, we'd been hiding the bodies of dead demons in the crypts below the cathedral. It wasn't the best solution, but it was better than leaving San Diablo strewn with the bodies of newly vacated demon hosts. Especially since local law enforcement tended to get antsy when they stumbled across dead bodies.

"Kate," Father Ben said, filling the gap left by my extremely loud silence. "A dead body is one thing. But animated body parts? What if someone heard them scratching around in there? What if those fingers managed to scrape away some mortar and get out?"

"But . . . but . . ." That was all I could come up with, because Father Ben had raised some valid concerns.

"But that means Kate will still have a tub of body parts in the back of her car," Laura volunteered.

"Yes!" I said, jumping all over that. "What if Stuart opens it?"

"I think we'd all like to see the expression on Stuart's face if that happened," Father Ben said, earning a laugh from Laura and a glare from me.

"Can't you call a funeral home or something? Arrange to cremate the parts?"

"And I'm sure that would raise no questions whatsoever," he countered. And then, before I had a chance to think up a clever retort, he added, "I think the most practical thing to do is take your tub to David to work his chemical magic."

I sighed, because of course I'd already thought of that. "He's in Los Angeles," I said, my voice sounding remarkably like Allie's when she didn't want to clean her room.

"He'll be back this afternoon," he said, making me wonder even more why David had gone to L.A. "It won't kill you to hang onto the zombie for a few more hours."

I made a face. Considering the zombie was in pieces, he was technically right. Still, this was the undead we were talking about. And I'd learned never to take anything for granted.

Twenty minutes later I pulled into my driveway with a tub of zombie parts still in the back of my car. I'd called David twice from the road, but each time, I'd been dumped straight into voice mail. Rather irritating, actually, because he'd told me to call if I needed him.

As soon as I stepped through the front door, I was assaulted by my teenage daughter, who pretty much launched herself at me from the across the room.

"Mom! You have *so* got to say yes!"

"Mommy! Mommy! Mommy!" Timmy shouted, coming up fast behind his sister. "Wanna go! Wanna go!"

I had no idea what they were talking about, but since they

obviously weren't terrified, I figured our corner of the world wasn't coming to an end, no zombies had entered the scene, the downstairs was demon free, and Allie hadn't stumbled across a spider.

"What are we talking about?" I asked, looking sideways to Laura, who now had her own fourteen-year-old beggar clinging leechlike to her waist. "Do you know?"

"No clue," she said. "But I'm not complaining. I haven't been hugged this tight since Thanksgiving."

"What am I supposed to say yes to?" I asked Allie, scooping up Timmy and trying to hold a wriggling mass of giggling boy.

"The carnival! Eddie brought home a flyer. It's at the beach, on the boardwalk. You *have* to let me go. Please, Mom? You or Aunt Laura can drive us and pick us up later? *Pleeeeeeze.* Everyone's going to be there. I just know it."

In my arms, Timmy picked up the chant, bouncing and shrieking "We wanna go!" at the top of his lungs, even though he clearly had no idea what a carnival was or why he would want to go.

"Allie! Allie!" I shouted, trying to be heard above my son. "You're grounded, remember?"

"Well, yeah. But it wasn't like I—"

"And I would have been happy to point that out to Stuart last night. But you said you were okay with it. And now it's a little too late for me to come to your rescue."

"But it's a *carnival*. I didn't know there was going to be a carnival. Please? You can drop me off during the day, and Stuart doesn't even have to know."

I frowned, because as unfair as her punishment was, I couldn't get behind the lie-to-my-husband plan. Ironic, I suppose, considering that lately I'd been lying to him on a pretty much daily basis.

At the same time, my Mom radar had perked up at her plea that *everyone* would be there. In Allie-speak, that meant boys. And I hadn't heard her mention boys in months. Not since she'd started holing herself up with my books and weapons.

If my kiddo was looking to trade a level of studiousness for a bit of boy-craziness, I have to admit I was all for that. From a theoretical, hand-holding-only, absolutely-no-unchaperoned-dates-or-unsupervised-alone-time sort of way.

"Please, Mom. Pretty please?"

I looked at Laura, still attached to Mindy. "What do you think?"

"I'm totally caving," she admitted. "But my spousal problem is slightly different from yours."

"Come on, Aunt Kate," Mindy said. "It won't be any fun if Allie's not there, too."

"Let me think about it," I said. "I haven't even put my purse down, and I need to try to get David on the phone again." With any luck, he'd left Los Angeles and was heading back. If I caught him in his car, he could swing by, pick up the tub, and remove Mr. Zombie from my life.

Allie's eyes perked up at the mention of her father. "How about if you guys come, too?" she said, her desperation to hang out with her father clearly reflected in the fact that she was offering to publicly attend a carnival with her mother. "It would be totally fun to see Mr. Long again," she added, cutting a glance toward Mindy. I gave her brownie points for being careful.

I avoided the issue, easing my way toward the kitchen with Timmy balanced on my hip. Obviously I'd been an idiot to mention David, but at the same time, I didn't really want to keep them apart. They both needed and wanted time together. The tricky part was making sure that desire didn't further complicate our lives.

And that, I realized, was pretty damn selfish of me.

I grabbed the handset and was about to give his number one more try, when it rang. I looked at Caller ID—*David*.

"Speak of the devil," I said. "Are you back?"

I expected an answer, but all I got was a laugh.

"What?" I demanded.

"Kate," he said gently. "Aren't you the one who keeps reminding me we aren't married anymore?"

"Right," I said, feeling my cheeks heat and quashing an unwelcome wave of jealousy as I imagined him walking down the Santa Monica Pier with a bikini-clad blonde. I shoved the image aside and told myself I was being ridiculous. "It's just that you said to call if I needed you and—"

"Was there another attack?" he asked, his voice sharp with worry. "Are the kids okay? Are you?"

"We're fine," I assured him, feeling guilty now because his concern was so genuine. "But I have loads of news, not to mention a tub full of zom—" I cut myself off sharply, realizing Mindy was still lurking about. "Um, a tub of stuff I really need you to work your magic on."

"Demon carcass."

"Along those lines, yeah."

"But you're not going to tell me what."

"Can't," I said. "It's crazy busy here what with Allie and Mindy running around and Laura helping me with the committee and—"

"Mindy," he said. "I got it."

"So you can help me?"

"For you, Katie? Anything."

I laughed. A nice sentiment, but considering we were talking about melting down a body in acid, it was hardly a moment worthy of a greeting card.

"When can we do it?" I asked.

"Not today. I'm still in Los Angeles."

"Oh?" I hoped I sounded casual. "Father Ben said you'd be back this afternoon."

"Yeah," David said. "That's what I'd thought. Turned out it's taking longer."

"Oh." I cleared my throat. "So, what are you doing down there, anyway?"

"Just some research," he said vaguely. "But I'll be back tomorrow."

"Morning?" I asked, hopefully. Honestly, the sooner I

passed my unwanted passenger off to him, the better I'd feel.

"Probably about ten."

Beside me, Allie bounced up and down, mouthing "carnival" and making hand motions that I assumed were supposed to mimic a Ferris wheel.

"So I'll come by your apartment after mass," I said, turning my body sideways to my daughter. I wasn't prepared to commit to a carnival with David. About that, I needed a bit more thought.

"*Mom!* The carnival! Ask him about the carnival."

I gave her a sharp look, but it was too late. I heard David's low chuckle in my ear. "Is that Allie? Tell her I'm game."

"I'm not sure that's—"

"It looks like fun. I passed it on my way out of town this morning. I was thinking maybe we could all go together tomorrow. Or if it makes you more comfortable, we could go apart and coincidentally bump into each other there."

I glanced over at Allie, who was looking at me with puppy-dog eyes. I had no idea if she could hear David's half of the conversation, or if she was simply wishing. Either way, the kid was desperate.

My shoulders sagged with inevitable acquiescence.

"What about the tub of stuff?"

"Bring it along," he said. "We can shove it in my trunk, and I'll take it home and take care of it."

"You sure you don't mind?"

"Kate," he said, his voice low and soft. "It's never a burden to help you. I want to see you. I *need* to see you. And I'm desperate to see my daughter."

How could I argue with that?

"All right," I said, mentally running down my Stuart-related options. Most likely, he'd be working tomorrow. The primary was drawing closer and closer, and he was going to be losing a few hours tonight, what with our date. "One o'clock," I finally said. "We'll come home to change after mass, then head straight for the beach."

"Great," he said. "And Kate?"

"Yes?" I whispered, my insides fluttering from the tone of his voice.

"I—never mind. It's nothing. I'll see you tomorrow."

I love you, too, I thought. But all I said was good-bye.

Ten

"Champagne or a Shiraz?" Stuart asked, setting aside the wine list.

"Champagne?" I squinted at him, distracted from my current occupation of watching a suspicious black-haired septuagenarian two tables away. Not only had the waiter's expression when he bent in to take an order suggested that the elderly woman's breath was a far cry from minty-fresh, but the lady had—literally—not taken her eyes off me. A little fact that was both suspicious and irritating since although I desperately wanted to know what the demon population was up to, I wanted this night with my husband with an equal degree of desperation.

"Champagne," Stuart repeated. "A sparkling wine produced originally in France and often used for celebratory occasions. I'm sure you're familiar with it."

"Right. Champagne. Sorry." Reluctantly, I stopped watching my potential demon and focused instead on my husband across the candlelit table. "Maybe we better go with the Shiraz. I don't think I dressed for champagne."

The corner of his grin quirked up, revealing a familiar

dimple even as his slow gaze looked me up and down, the heat in his eyes when they finally settled on mine unmistakable.

"Champagne it is, then," he said.

"Right," I said, wondering if I was blushing. He was making me feel all tingly; I might as well have the drink to match.

He signaled to the waiter, who'd been hiding in the shadows near a table occupied by a gorgeous woman in a bloodred dress who looked less than excited with her companion. She wasn't even trying to make eye contact with him, instead looking everywhere around the restaurant but at her date.

The waiter glided up to our table in that five-star way that excellent waiters have. After putting in an order for a duck quesadilla appetizer and a particularly fancy bottle of bubbly, Stuart reached across the table for my hand, then kissed my injured finger. "How's it feeling?"

"Don't even worry about it," I said. "I have a very high pain tolerance."

His brows lifted. "I seem to recall a very loud demand for an epidural, followed by a rather colorful death threat."

"There's pain," I said. "And then there's *pain.*"

"Ahhh," he said, whereas a woman would have been in total and immediate solidarity with me.

"Despite the splint, are you having a good time?"

"You're kidding, right? I'm having a fabulous time." When Stuart had suggested dinner and a movie, I'd expected a salad or a burger at our favorite diner near the beach. To end up here at Emeralds, the most hoity-toity restaurant in all of San Diablo, was more than a little surprising.

"You seem a little distracted," he said, and I realized I was staring at my demon-lady again.

"Sorry, sorry," I said, forcing myself to concentrate. As it was, I was being ridiculous. Just because a creepy old lady was staring at me didn't mean the minions of hell had descended on one of San Diablo's premier dining establishments. "I thought I saw someone I knew, and I can't remember her name. It's driving me crazy."

The corner of his mouth twitched. "Driving?"

"Have it your way," I said. "I'm already a crazy person."

"But you're my crazy person."

"Yup. You're stuck with me."

"I'm sorry about the reservation mix-up."

"Stuart . . ." I trailed off with a shake of my head and a squeeze of his fingers. "We had a drink in the bar. That was hardly a faux pas."

He kissed the tips of my fingers, sending electric sparks shooting all the way down to my toes. "I know. But I want tonight to be perfect. We so rarely have date night lately that I can't bear the thought of something going awry."

I laughed. "We have a teenager and a toddler. I think we're supposed to assume things will go awry for at least fifteen more years."

"And after that we're free? The yoke of parenthood seems looser already."

"Not free, just further removed."

"So instead of going home for the children's emergencies we'll have to drive to a dorm. Or fly."

"Bite your tongue," I said. *"Drive.* Preferably without actually leaving the county." Last month, Allie and I had gone to a college fair at the high school. And although Allie had been totally nonchalant about the whole thing, I'd spent the evening on the couch, nursing a glass of wine and trying to concentrate on the latest issue of *Real Simple.* That, I'd thought, seemed safer than contemplating my baby leaving me in less than four years time.

"You," I said, pointing an accusing finger at Stuart. "You are so not supposed to torment me about the kids leaving until Allie turns sixteen." That was my magic number, primarily because I figured it would take me a full two years to really get used to the idea.

"Sorry," he said, though the twitch at the corner of his mouth suggested that he wasn't sorry at all. "At any rate, I'm glad we're finally seated. And with champagne," he added, with a nod to the returning waiter.

The waiter—who couldn't have been much more than twenty-one—opened the bottle with a perfected ease, then poured two glasses without dribbling a drop, thoroughly putting me to shame. As soon as he'd faded back into the shadows, Stuart lifted his glass. "To us."

"To us," I agreed, then took a sip, letting the bubbles fizz in my nose. "So is there a reason for all this? Buttering me up about the house?"

"The thought had crossed my mind," he said. "But no. No ulterior motives whatsoever."

"Really?" I asked, undoubtedly sounding a little more than dubious.

"Can't a man take his wife out to a fabulous restaurant? Does there have to be a reason?"

I cocked my head to one side, looking at him. "There doesn't *have* to be . . ."

"No ulterior motive," he said. "Nothing more than I love you and I want to spend time with you. We don't even have to talk about the campaign or the house if you don't want to."

I laughed. "You're serious."

"Absolutely. I know you've gotten the short end of the campaign stick."

"No, I didn't. I got the best part."

He laughed. "An empty house without your husband channel surfing all weekend?"

"Nah," I said, teasing. "That's merely a perk." I leaned back in my chair and looked at him, suddenly sappy and sentimental. "The best part is that I've got you."

He laughed. "Now who's got an ulterior motive?"

"Well, it's understandable," I deadpanned. "Did you see that dessert cart?"

"Good point," he said, the flecks of gold in his irises shining in the candlelight. I had a sudden flash of an image—those eyes shining from a candidate poster, his classic jawline and once-broken nose giving him a rugged, honest appearance.

Right then, I knew with absolute certainty that my

husband was going to win the election. How could he not? He was brilliant, dedicated, and definitely designed for television.

"What?" he said, buttering a slice of the crusty French bread.

"Just thinking how lucky I am."

"Are you?" he asked.

I blinked, thrown a bit by his tone. We'd shifted gears somewhere without my noticing. No longer teasing, Stuart seemed more than interested; he seemed concerned.

"Of course," I assured him, dropping my bread to reach for his hand. "What do you think?"

"Lately—" He broke off with a shrug and a shake of his head. "Never mind."

"No, wait. What were you going to say?" I was talking through a lump in my throat, afraid my world was about to cave in around me.

"We've both been busy lately," he said. "I don't want us to be so busy apart that we forget to be together."

"Never," I said, feeling guiltier by the second. Yes, he'd been absent a lot, but if he was feeling any distance in our marriage, that wasn't something I could lay at his feet. The responsibility was all mine, and I knew that I needed to tell him the truth. Waiting wasn't going to make it easier. If anything, it was going to keep getting harder and harder.

I stifled a sigh, instead lifting my glass and polishing off the remaining champagne.

The corner of Stuart's mouth curved up. "Thirsty?"

"Enjoying the fizz," I said. "And a champagne buzz never hurt anyone."

Across the room, the black-eyed woman grabbed her purse and stood up, her eyes still glued to me.

I took a deep breath. "Stuart, there's something—"

"*You*," the woman hissed, a bony finger pointed right at me. "I thought so."

She nodded, beady black eyes taking in me, my husband, and the surroundings. Then she shoved her hand into her purse. "I must go," she said, then moved on without waiting for my reply.

"Wow," Stuart said, his expression somewhere between amused and horrified. "She certainly seems to know you."

"I think I'll go see if I can remember where we met," I said, sliding out of my seat and grabbing my own purse.

"Hurry back," he said. "I plan on getting you drunk and having my way with you, and I can't do that if you're holed away in the ladies' room."

I lifted an eyebrow. "Is that your plan? I'll definitely hurry, then." I blew him a kiss and headed for the restroom.

I'd been to Emeralds once before, and I remembered the ladies' room as a kind of shrine to all things feminine. The restaurant itself was housed in a remodeled Victorian, and the powder room had been constructed by knocking down a wall and combining the existing bathroom with an airy sitting room lined on one side with windows overlooking the restaurant's private garden and then, beyond that, the beach.

This "lobby" area included plush chairs and every toiletry known to woman. Forget your mascara? Your hair spray? Your deodorant? Not to worry! They had it for you here!

At the moment, the cavernous lounge area was empty. Good for me, because I really didn't need an audience of primping women while I had my little chat with my best new demon buddy, who I assumed had headed all the way back, presumably lying in wait for yours truly.

The stalls and sinks were farther in, through a set of swinging café doors, and it was to those doors I headed, heels clattering on the hardwood floor. Sure enough, the moment I pushed through the doors, she stepped out from the first stall.

"You are here," she said, in that low, gravelly voice. "I am so glad we finally meet."

"*Enough.*" I'd been off my guard in my own yard and nearly got myself and my daughter killed. This time, I was playing offense, and hard. I lunged before she could, grabbing her around the neck from behind and holding with just enough force to make it clear that I would snap her neck if I had to. That wouldn't do much to a demon except slow her reaction time, but *that* would give me enough of an opening to get something nice and sharp through her eye. Something like, oh, the stiletto I'd pulled from my purse as I'd entered the room and now held tight in my free hand.

"The Sword of Caelum," I said. "Talk. And talk now."

Or, at least, I tried to say all that. Unfortunately, I was drowned out by the pitiful wail of her scream and then the deep tremors in her body as she held back terrified sobs.

And that, frankly, was not computing.

"Who are you?" I demanded, completely confused. "How do you know me? Why were you watching me? And what—"

"I—I—I—mogene," she finally managed. "Imogene Gunderson."

I let my arm relax slightly. There was something familiar about that name. I shifted around until I was in front of her, the knife a visible warning of what would happen if she did the wrong thing. Then I reached into my purse for my hair spray bottle of holy water and zapped her in the face.

Not a thing happened.

And that's when I remembered. *The library.*

Oh, shit.

I let go and jumped back, as if the weight of my guilt alone would give her the strength to lash out and send me crashing through the wall. "Mrs. Gunderson," I said, surprised the old lady hadn't died of a heart attack right then and there. "I'm so sorry. I thought you were a de— um, a desperate person I've been having some trouble with. A stalker. You know. Weird."

She looked at me, her shaky hands smoothing her clothes as her eyes stayed fixed on my knife. "I think I know weird when I see it."

I shoved the knife into my purse. "Honestly, I'm just . . . I don't know . . . there really isn't anything to . . ." I tossed my hands up, then tossed them up again. "Here," I said reaching for her. "Let's get you sitting down."

But she was already halfway to the swinging door, hugging the wall to stay as far away from me as possible. "Eddie said you were odd, but I had no idea. No idea at all," she repeated, then backed out of the toilet area and into the lounge.

I stayed behind, flabbergasted that I could have made such a mistake, and rather irritated that Eddie was running around town telling perfect strangers that I'm strange.

The good news, of course, was that I didn't have to kill anything. Always a plus when you're in a public place with nowhere to hide the body.

I gave Mrs. Gunderson enough time to pull herself together and leave, and then I followed suit, heading into the lounge area. There I caught a glimpse of my reflection and backtracked. This was a hot date, after all. A few girlified touch-ups were required.

I leaned in and inspected the damage. For the most part, my makeup hadn't sloughed off, which was remarkable considering that the typical time that cosmetics took to vanish from my face was roughly seven-point-five minutes. A few strands of hair had sprung free of the clip I'd used to secure the pile on my head. The curl had held, though—thanks to about a gallon of extra-hold hair spray—so the effect was still cute. Maybe even a little sexy.

I cocked my head, then made a little moue, drifting a bit in the fantasy that I was a sexy young thing instead of a mom of two. Not that I'm complaining. I have, after all, finally gotten back into a size eight. Hunting demons does great things for your muscle tone.

I scoped out the supply of free cosmetics, then reached for a mascara sample. A tiny little bottle with a tiny little brush, it was about the cutest thing ever, and the perfect souvenir for Allie.

For that matter, it was too cute to pass up at the moment, so after I dropped one into my purse for my daughter, I snagged another for myself, then popped it out of its personal plastic wrap. For a restaurant so concerned about making sure the patrons stayed well coiffed, they hadn't given much thought to the lighting, and I was in an awkward on-my-toes-and-trying-to-get-close-enough-to-the-mirror-to-see position when the woman in red from the next table over sashayed in.

She looked down her nose at me, then went to the next sink over, looking me up and down before focusing on her own reflection in the mirror. Considering the way her expression changed from disgust to pleased, I had to assume she liked what she saw.

In fairness, I can't say I blamed her. She looked like a celebrity up from Los Angeles to party on our pristine beaches. About the only thing that marred the image at all was her perfume, which had been poured on way too heavily, probably courtesy of a personal shopper who'd told her what to buy, but not how much of it to wear.

Thankfully, she finished up at the sink before I did, then turned to leave. The air cleared, and I realized I could breathe again, the overwhelming scent of lilac and vanilla giving way to something significantly more subtle, if less pleasant.

I realized where that foul odor came from a split second before she moved, and didn't even have time to curse my stupidity. Because I didn't have a weapon handy, I whipped around with the mascara wand as my only line of defense between me and the stacked, blond demon, thrusting it toward her big blue eyes.

Realizing she'd lost the element of surprise, she abandoned all efforts at subtlety and leaped at me, dodging my tiny cosmetic weapon.

"You cannot be permitted to wield the sword," she shouted as I skipped sideways, escaping her grasp by millimeters. "He who shall become The One will see you die."

"Yeah?" I cleverly retorted, yanking the hem of her skirt to knock her off balance even as I kicked out and got her in the gut. "Abaddon?" I demanded, pressing her back against the wall between the sink and toilet areas. I held the wand at her eye, certain she knew that this time I wouldn't miss. "I stopped him from becoming super-dude once before. I think I can handle it again."

"*Carmela*," she hissed, which really wasn't the response I'd been expecting. "Come, Carmela," she repeated even as the window behind us shattered in an explosion of glass. I ducked, yanking down the demon even as I turned my face from the flying shards, silently cursing what I saw out of the corner of my eye—a zombie, standing rough and ready amid the broken glass.

"For crying out loud!" I shouted without thinking. "Enough with the freaking zombies!" Which probably wasn't the most professional of responses, but it summarized my feelings quite accurately.

At the same time, the demon shifted, trying to get out from under my hold. I wasn't having any of *that*, though, and about the same time the zombie made the final leap across the room to grab at the back of my shirt and pull me off her master, I thrust the mascara wand deep into the demon's eye.

The maneuver had the side benefit of stopping the now-masterless zombie in her tracks, who stood there, her viselike hand still clutching my shoulder, completely befuddled. She'd clearly been told to assist the master, and now that the master was gone, she was confused about what exactly she was supposed to do.

To be honest, she wasn't the only one.

I was held fast by a rather oozy-looking, scraggle-haired zombie who would undoubtedly fight me if I tried to get free, then shift into self-preservation mode when I defended myself. And we were both trapped beside the dead body of a beautiful Emeralds customer. Not to mention, my husband was probably beginning to wonder how long a simple trip to the ladies' room could take.

I had no good options, and so I twisted around and down, surprising the zombie, whose fingers were suddenly grasping only air. As for me, I'd danced a good two feet away, glass crunching under my shoes. And, miracle of miracles, the zombie wasn't coming after me.

Okay, this was good. Maybe I could make this work after all.

First thing, I headed toward the main door, prepared to flip the lock. Only there wasn't a lock. *Great.*

In lieu of a lock, I shoved one of the plush chairs in front of the door. So far I'd been extremely lucky that no one had tried to join our little ladies' lounge party. That luck couldn't hold out indefinitely, though, and I wanted to be prepared for the inevitable party crasher. I wasn't sure what I would say if someone tried to get in, but I told myself I thought well on my feet and something brilliant would come.

Next, I grabbed a bottle of hand lotion from the toiletry basket. I took a couple of paper towels and used those as a barrier between my hands and the lady in red's ankles. Then I pulled her into the handicapped stall and rubbed her all over with a paper towel soaked in hand lotion that, I hoped, would sufficiently mess up any fingerprints I'd left on the body.

I locked the door from the inside, crawled under, and headed back to my zombie. With any luck, I could get Father Ben to come retrieve the body, maybe pretending she was a drunken parishioner desperately in need of confession. It was the best I could come up with, and I was once again struck by the fact that my job was so much easier when I had a disposal team at my beck and call.

The zombie was another problem all together, and unless I was prepared to enter into an all-out fight, there wasn't a damn thing I could do but shove the chair aside, exit the ladies' room, and leave her standing there alone. The trouble with *that*, of course, was that sooner or later, someone would eventually come into the powder room, take one look at Carmela, realize she wasn't a woman but a monster, and try to do something about that, and Emeralds would have a full-blown horror movie on its hands.

Granted, most people aren't inclined to leap to the monster conclusion, but even if they assumed she was merely ill and tried to help her, the moment they tried to move her or—God forbid—do any sort of medical test, the zombie would interpret the actions as hostile and transform from a clueless, confused blob to a preternaturally strong killing machine whose only purpose was to ensure its survival. A great plot for an action movie, maybe; not so terrific for the people of San Diablo.

And all the responsibility would be on my shoulders.

Which, of course, meant that I had to make the first move. I had to get the zombie back out through the hole in the window, find something with which to hack her up (or use the knife in my purse, however impractical), hide the pieces, and get back before my husband started to really worry.

No problem, right?

I mentally inventoried the contents of my purse, cursing myself for not carrying a scythe. Or, for that matter, a really sharp razor.

Still, you work with what you got. Isn't that the sign of a true professional? I took my knife in one hand and my house keys in the other. Then I leaped across the room, surprising the zombie even as I prayed my aim was good.

It was; that's the benefit of a stationary target. I thrust my keys into her right eye and the knife into the left, a maneuver which had two outcomes: One, my foe was now blind. Two, my foe was now really, *really* ticked off.

And because Carmela wasn't the least bit worried about attracting unwanted attention, she flailed around the room, crashing into lamps and overturning chairs and generally making a huge nuisance as she tried to find me. The point of *that*, of course, would be so that she could rip my horrible little head off.

Hopefully, that plan wouldn't be coming to fruition.

At the same time, I couldn't simply keep my distance and let her destroy the room. I needed to catch her, drag her out the hole in the window and off to someplace remotely private, and then start whacking off limbs.

The scenario put a serious damper on my evening out

with Stuart, but, again, that's what happens when you have a demanding job.

"Okay, Carmela," I said. "It's time for you and me to rumble."

At the sound of my voice, she turned and attacked, racing blindly to where I stood. I grabbed an outstretched arm and the waistband of her pants and flung her toward the window. Because she was light, she practically soared through the air, then smashed down on the sill, a few jagged pieces of glass slicing through soft flesh and trapping her there as she kicked and struggled. Thank goodness she couldn't scream.

"Off we go," I said, hurrying to grab her by the ankles. My plan was to flip her over and out, then climb out behind her. I was *not* expecting someone to help me by grabbing her hands and tugging from the other side. I let out a short yelp, realized David must have returned to town early, and exhaled loudly.

When I peered out, though, I saw the man from my street. The one who'd shoved the carnival flyer at me.

"You?"

"Me. I am Dukkar," he added, with a friendly little nod. Then he gave the zombie a firm tug, and it dropped to the ground. As it began to push its way up, Dukkar picked up a machete and whacked off the right arm. He stepped hard on the chest and repeated the process with the left.

Right then and there, I decided Dukkar was my new best friend. He, at least, was smart enough to travel with a serious cutting blade.

"You go," he said, looking up at my undoubtedly flabbergasted face. "You go back to your husband."

No, no, no. Not without some answers. Like who he was, how he knew about zombies, and what the hell he was doing outside the ladies' room of Emeralds.

"You go now," he said, ignoring all of the questions I fired off to him. "I clean up mess. The zombie. The demon."

"You know about the demon, too?"

"I know you must be careful. Only you can wield the sword. You must be protected."

"Whoa," I said, my voice sharp and my interest very much piqued. "Answers. *Now.* Like how you know about the sword. And more important, how you know about me."

His eyes widened and I had the distinct impression that he believed he'd said too much.

Too bad.

"I'm not going anywhere until I get some answers," I countered as he hacked off a leg.

Naturally, that's when the door to the ladies' room slammed open. Or, rather, tried to slam open. The force of the door moved the chair about four inches, then stopped. I held my breath, then felt every drop of blood drain from my body as I heard the voice calling, "Kate? Kate, what the hell are you doing?"

I turned and saw myself reflected in the mirror, along with Stuart's face peeking in through the crack. And if I could see him, he could surely see me.

Damn.

I climbed back inside. "Long story," I said.

"Open the door."

"Um." I glanced toward the window and realized he couldn't have seen any of the zombie or the carnival man. "Right. Sure."

I shoved the chair aside, then hustled out, tugging the door firmly shut behind me.

"Dear God, Kate. What the hell were you doing in there? That old lady came barreling out with a completely freaked expression on her face, and I kept expecting you to follow, but—"

"Counseling," I said, which was the first and only thing that popped into my mind. I took his hand and started leading him back toward our table, wanting to get as far away from the ladies' room and *that* particular explosion as possible.

"Excuse me?"

"There was this girl in there. Troubled teen. Pregnant. That's why she shoved the chair in front of the door. Afraid her parents would walk in," I said, spinning lies with the same ease with which I could spin a dagger. "But I think she freaked Mrs. Gunderson out a little."

"The old lady?"

"Right. She left. I stayed behind to help."

We'd reached our table now, and I realized with a start how long I'd been gone. The duck appetizer was ice cold, with Stuart having not taken a single bite, waiting instead for me to join him. "Oh, Stuart. I'm so sorry. And now we'll miss the movie."

"You don't have to be sorry," he said. "And the movie is totally in your hands. We can stay and have dinner, or we can leave and go to the theater."

"Leave," I said, clinging to the offer like a life raft. Because at the moment, I wanted more than anything to get out of that restaurant. I checked my watch. "You pay the bill and I'll go get the car from the valet."

He blinked, a bit startled by my snap decision, then nodded. I hurried outside, afraid that any minute the maitre d' would hurry after me, overflowing with questions about the broken glass, the body in the handicapped stall, and what sort of nonsense crazy Mrs. Gunderson was spouting.

Fortunately, I managed to avoid all that, and the valet trotted off with our keys and ticket at the same time Stuart stepped outside to join me. He eyed me quizzically, and though my instinct was to say, "What?" I kept my mouth shut. At the moment, probably best not to hear exactly what he had in mind.

Turned out, though, that Stuart didn't need my opening to get the conversation going. "You're a good woman, Kate," he said.

"I . . . thank you," I said, surprised.

"Is the girl better?"

I thought of the dead demon and the dismembered zombie, both of whom were hopefully being dealt with by my new best friend. "Yeah. I think she's going to be just fine."

"I'm glad," he said. "But Kate? You don't have to save the world."

"I don't?" I asked, wishing desperately that he were right.

"Sometimes it's okay to back off," he said, as I moved closer to my husband, now looking at me with soft, generous eyes. "You do too much. The house. The kids. Committees. PTA. And I bet you do stuff I don't even know about."

Wasn't that the truth?

He was looking pointedly at me, as if he expected me to fill in the blanks with everything else I had on my plate. I didn't. Instead, I managed a weak, noncommittal smile.

After a second he sighed. "The point is, taking up lay counseling in restaurant bathrooms is probably too big a commitment."

"I know. Truly. And I'm so sorry. I messed up our whole evening, and I know dinner would have been fabulous."

There was an uncomfortable beat during which I was afraid he'd suggest we return to the restaurant and wait for the movie to come out on DVD. Then it passed, and all he said was, "A dinner of popcorn and hot dogs will be fabulous, too, as long as I've got you next to me."

"Always," I said, as love and guilt and a dozen other confused emotions jostled for position inside me.

"And I hope this isn't a movie you care too much about," he added with fire in his eyes.

"What do you mean?" I asked, as our car turned into the circular driveway.

He smiled enigmatically, then pulled me close and planted a long, sensual, knee-numbing kiss on me, right there for all the world to see. A kiss so hard and deep that I didn't need to ask the question again, because I knew exactly what he meant. If I wanted to actually watch the movie, I'd have to wait for the DVD. Tonight was all about my husband, a dark theater, and the very back row.

Eleven

"Mommy, Mommy, Mommy." Beside me, Timmy bounced on the kneeler, making the pew in front of us shake and probably annoying the people sitting there who were—thankfully—either too polite or too reverent to turn around and glare.

"Timmy, hush." I closed my eyes and counted to ten. I'd had a rather late—and enjoyable—night, then lounged comfortably in bed until I'd realized that it wasn't Saturday but Sunday. That realization had been like a dose of cold water on my slightly hungover, sleep-deprived head, and I'd managed to stir up even more of a headache rushing around getting everyone ready for church. Now my poor abused cerebrum felt near to exploding, and my son's chatter wasn't helping.

"Mommy, *look*. Look what I make!" He shoved a palm frond into my face and, since I had no choice, I looked. "Very nice. Now shhhh!"

Sunday mass is usually a more relaxing event, because St. Mary's is one of a few Catholic churches that actually has a nursery for the little ones. During Holy Week, however, the nursery is closed. This makes absolutely no sense to me since the little buggers are used to being coddled, played with, and sung to for an hour each Sunday. They're not used to sitting still and listening quietly to the readings, the homily, and the rest of the service.

Today, though, he was seated between me and Allie. He'd done remarkably well, but that was in large part due to the fact that I came to mass armed with a tote bag filled with surprises. Silly Putty, crayons, a coloring book, a picture book about mass, and the significantly less pious picture books of *Blue's Clues* and *Dora the Explorer*. I also brought two bags of Goldfish crackers.

Considering we still had about ten minutes of mass to go, I clearly hadn't stocked up enough.

A quick tug at my skirt. "Can we go? Please, Mommy? Wanna go *now*."

Frankly, at the moment, so did I.

Stuart leaned forward and told him to be quiet, as if I hadn't already tried the direct approach forty-seven times already. I refrained from giving him a dirty look. This was church, after all.

Instead, I rummaged in my purse until I found my compact mirror. "Soon," I said, shoving it into his hands. "In the meantime, here." If I was lucky, by the time he bored of the mirror, it would be time for communion and he'd be entertained by walking down the aisle with his arms crossed for the blessing.

As it turned out, I was dead on the money, the mirror losing its fascination factor right when it was our turn to head to the communion rail. The novelty of our walk, however, didn't last, and Timmy spent the bishop's final prayer sitting on the kneeler and pretending to read the hymnal, flipping so noisily through the pages I feared for rips, and Allie's high-pitched whispers of "Timmy! Stop it already," really not helping.

As for me, I decided to let it slide. A ripped hymnal I could replace. At least he wasn't whining.

As soon as the service was over, I gave him a little shove and he happily followed at Stuart's heels. "Great service, Father,"

Stuart said, shaking the bishop's hand at the door before moving down the sidewalk to mingle and schmooze. With the primary barreling down on him, mingling and schmoozing was becoming an almost daily activity.

"Kate," the bishop said, turning to me. "So good to see you. And you, too," he added, ruffling Timmy's hair.

"I wanna go to the park," Timmy announced, pointing due east past the parking lot. There was nothing to see from the cathedral parking lot, but if you knew what you were doing, you could walk down the hill, follow a few winding trails to a clearing, and find a little brook with a broken-down playscape. Not church property, but somehow, all of the kids knew it was there, even the little ones.

The bishop laughed. "That's between you and your mom, kiddo."

"Is it open again?" We didn't go often, but on occasion we'd bypass the cathedral swingset and trek down there after mass. For the last few months, though, the area had been roped off with the type of orange net used to surround construction sites. I wasn't about to schlep all the way down there only to find out the area was still closed off.

"I've been told that the playscape is back in business as of last week," the Bishop said. "I'm not sure of the ETA for the rest of the area."

"Repairs?"

"An archaeological dig, actually. After the last heavy rains, some of the creek bed eroded away and revealed some remains."

"Human?"

The bishop shook his head. "Animal. Though there were artifacts as well. Tribal rituals, we assume from centuries past. The museum took over the site and is cataloging everything. I expect we'll be able to view the finds in a year or so."

"Cool," Allie said.

"*Mommy*," Timmy howled, not interested in archaeology at all. "I. Want. Playground!"

"Carnival, kiddo. Today's the carnival. But maybe next time."

"I enjoyed the homily, Father," Allie said, stepping up to fill the conversational gap.

"Thank you, Alison," the Bishop said.

"I didn't see Father Ben," Allie said. "Is he here?"

Lately, Allie had been meeting with Father Ben every Sunday, returning books she borrowed and taking new ones the padre had already reviewed and I'd approved. The kid was way more interested in the more bookish aspects of demon hunting than I'd ever been. Clearly she took after her father.

"I'm afraid he had to go out to the desert. Father Caleb at Holy Trinity became ill, and Father Ben is celebrating the mass with the parish today. Perhaps I can help you?" the bishop added. "Or Delores?"

Allie shook her head. "No thanks. I was just wondering."

She stepped toward me, and the bishop turned to greet the family behind us. "Bummer," she said.

"I've got plenty for you to read. And I'm pretty sure you have a history paper due after the break. Maybe you should work on that instead of memorizing demon facts."

She rolled her eyes. "Mother. I can do both, you know."

"I know you can," I said. "I'm just not sure you will."

Across the parking lot, I saw David looking at us from beside his car. I hadn't seen him at mass, but considering the crowd on Palm Sunday, that was hardly surprising.

As I tilted my head in acknowledgment, Allie noticed and looked from him to me. "Can I ride with David to the carnival?" she asked.

"No," I said, as Stuart walked up to us. "Because you're not going. Remember?"

"But—*Oh*. Right."

"Heading home?" Stuart asked, pressing a kiss to my cheek.

"That's the plan." Which, technically, was true, as there was no way I was heading to the carnival without changing clothes and feeding Timmy. Practically, though, I wanted to get to the carnival as quickly as possible, because I was hoping to find Dukkar, my zombie-hacking, demon-hiding buddy from the restaurant. I figured the odds were good, considering he'd handed me a carnival flyer during our first meeting. True, he could have been carrying it as a prop, but I couldn't help but recall the intensity in his eyes when he'd insisted I visit the carnival.

So visit I would, and now I was excited about it for reasons other than the cotton candy.

"Have a good day," Stuart said, leaning in to give me a kiss that was a bit more passionate than the circumstances or the surroundings would suggest. I didn't usually swoon on the sidewalk in front of the cathedral, but with kisses like that, I might be starting. "I'll see you tonight."

"I hope that's a promise," I countered.

"Definitely."

"Can we *go*?" Allie said, though whether she was exasperated by the public displays of affection between Stuart and me or frustrated by the fact that I wasn't with her father, I couldn't tell. And, honestly, right then I didn't want to know.

"Yes," I said. "Absolutely." We'd come in two cars, and as Stuart headed toward the Infiniti, I ushered Allie and Timmy toward the Odyssey.

"Kate! Kate!" I'd stepped from the sidewalk to the parking lot, and now I turned to find Delores Sykes, the cathedral's volunteer coordinator, hurrying toward me.

"Hi, Delores."

"So good to see you," she said. "And look at you!" she added, grabbing Allie around the shoulders and hugging tight. "You've grown a foot in the last two weeks, I just know you have."

Allie managed a weak smile, then grabbed Timmy's hand. "I'll go strap him in his car seat," she said in her most helpful voice, and I jealously watched her go.

"I know I haven't been in to work on the archives in a while," I began. "But—"

"Oh, no, no," she said. "Don't worry about that. I know you have your hands full with a teenager and a little one."

"Oh. Thanks." I wasn't sure what else to say. Usually Delores was hitting me up to spend more time in the cathedral archives, reviewing the boxes and boxes of materials that were left to the Church, organizing donation lists, and forwarding anything that looked to be of genuine historic interest on to the professional archivists. It was a project I'd been roped into months ago, and though I couldn't complain too loudly—the things I'd learned down in the basement archives had actually helped me save the world—it still wasn't a job I relished. The room was musty and dim, and the boxes tended to be filled with bugs.

Gross and tedious. Not a stellar combination.

"I was actually hoping to see if you could squeeze out one or two hours to help organize a special luncheon next month in honor of Saint Maedhog."

"Who?"

"Saint Maedhog, dear," she repeated, as if that would suddenly make him spring to mind. "His feast day is in early April."

"Oh." I frowned, confused. "I . . . has the cathedral always done Feast Day luncheons?" This was a new animal to me. And considering every day was the feast day for some saint, I feared I was about to land deep in a never-ending pool of volunteer work.

"Oh, no, dear. This is going to be a special fund-raiser for the restoration fund." The cathedral had been in renovations for what seemed like eternity, with most services being held in the bishop's hall. Easter week was an exception, and it had been nice to be back in the beautiful sanctuary. If Delores's volunteer project would get us back in there permanently that much sooner, I was all for it. More, I was feeling the tug of hypocrisy if I refused to help.

"What do you need me to do?"

"Nothing terribly complicated. Invitations, refreshments.

Things like that. We'll work it out at the first committee meeting. Okay?"

"Sure," I said, conjuring a smile. "Sounds great."

"I knew I could count on you, Kate," she said.

"So why this saint?" I asked before she could hurry away. "Did someone simply want to do an April function?"

"Oh, no, dear. It's because of Father Ben, of course. He's going to be our luncheon speaker."

I swiped my hand over my head. Her words were going past me without making any sort of connection at all.

"Oh, goodness. You and he have become such good friends I just assumed you knew. Saint Maedhog is one of Father Ben's ancestors."

"Wow," I said. "I had no idea. It's like a brush with fame."

"I suppose it is," Delores said, leaning in closer. "But between you and me, I met Sean Connery once. He's no saint, but honey, that's *my* idea of a brush with fame."

I grinned. I understood completely.

As it was, it took us only forty minutes to make it home, change, and get back to the beach. It took another twenty minutes after that to find a parking space, inconveniently located five blocks away in the center of the Old Town shopping district.

Since I figured Timmy's little legs wouldn't last that long, I hauled the umbrella stroller out from behind the Rubbermaid container of zombie parts, parked the kid in it, and the five of us started walking. Well, the four females did, anyway. My little man sat comfortably in his stroller and immediately fell asleep, clearly worn out by working so hard to behave in church. I pushed slowly, both because I didn't want to wake him and because I wanted Laura and myself to follow about a block behind Allie and Mindy.

"You're digging yourself in deeper and deeper," she said, nodding toward Allie.

"I know, I know. But I really couldn't leave her at home. She's dying to spend some time with her father, and it's hard to comply with a grounding for an offense she didn't commit in the first place."

"Then you should have—"

"Told Stuart. Yes, I know."

"Or at least told him that you were lifting the punishment for the afternoon so that you could enjoy the carnival with your kid."

"You're really impossible when you're right. You know that, don't you?"

"Of course." We walked in silence for a few moments. "Speaking of being right," she finally said. "What are you doing about the bigger picture?"

"As in, have I revealed all to Stuart? Believe it or not, I almost did last night. But we got a little sidetracked."

"The demon and the zombie," she said, because, of course, I'd already told her the whole story. "And you think they're trying to kill you so that you won't have the chance to use this sword thing?"

"That's my best guess."

"See, I'm thinking that would have been a really nice segue into telling Stuart."

"Yes, but then I would have missed out on making out like a teenager in the back of a movie theater."

"Excuse me?"

Okay, so I hadn't told her the *whole* story.

She cleared her throat.

I looked at her sideways. "What?"

She twirled her hand, urging me to talk. "Come on, Kate. You can't drop a bomb like a movie make-out session and then not follow through. I don't have the rule book with me, but I'm certain that violates at least ten different regulations regarding the handling of gossip within a friendship."

I laughed. "Okay, fair enough. Let's just say that Stuart was more attentive last night than he has been in quite a while. At the restaurant, at the movie, and after we got home."

"How nice for you," she said, her eyebrows rising as her mouth twitched with the makings of a smile.

"Very," I agreed.

"Really?" she asked, quirking a brow. "Even if all this attention is because he's picking up on your vibe?"

"I have a vibe?"

"Your dead ex-husband has come back to life. You're sneaking around behind your current husband's back to see your ex. We've talked about this, Kate. Yeah. You have a vibe. Stuart's probably completely freaking out about the state of your marriage. Tell the man the truth."

She was right, of course. Fancy dinners, sweet words, and movie make-out sessions weren't par for our usual course. Adding a little spark to a marriage was one thing. But in this case, I saw the motive behind setting the fire.

"It *is* Eric we're talking about," Laura said gently. "Does Stuart have reason to be worried?"

"No!" I said, the answer coming before I could fully think about it. "I mean, of course not. Stuart's my husband. I love him."

I would never do anything with David, but that didn't change how I felt. David was Eric. And I loved Eric. And the fact that I was married to another man couldn't ever change that.

"You love David, too," she said, pretty much reading my mind. "And he's your husband as well. Or, sort of, anyway."

I made a face, not sure I wanted to get into that theological kerfuffle. So far, I'd hesitated asking Father Corletti's opinion on the status of my marriage. I knew the answer as far as the State of California was concerned. As for the state of my soul, the question remained. Did I have one husband? Or did I have two?

"I'll talk to him Wednesday night," I said.

"Got a hole in your calendar and looking to plan a few fun-filled few hours?"

"Cute. No, tomorrow he has the morning show at one of the network's affiliates, and then he's flying to Sacramento and won't be back until Tuesday morning. Then that night is the dinner party at our house. And I can't see telling him before a TV appearance or a campaign party."

"I see your point. 'Hey, honey. I hunt demons in my spare time. Think I can help you round up the bad guys once you're in office?'" She shook her head. "Definitely not the right approach."

I rolled my eyes. "Wednesday," I said. "Come hell or high water, I'm telling him Wednesday."

Laura grimaced. "The way things are going, my money's on hell."

Twelve

"You're sure this is a good idea?" I asked Laura as I shelled out twenty-five dollars to buy Allie a wristband that would allow her to go on all the rides without tickets.

"Trust me," Laura said. She pointed to a spider-looking ride in which the passengers lay on their stomachs and were whirled around in midair. "As many times as they're going to want to go into the fun house or ride that spinning, whirling death thing, we'll be glad we coughed up the money for the all-included price."

"I bow to your shopping savvy," I said, having learned long ago not to argue with Laura where the value of a dollar is concerned.

"Where's Daddy?" Allie asked as the ticket-booth man strapped the band to her wrist.

I cringed, but Mindy was one booth over, busily fidgeting with her own band.

"David, sweetie. You need to remember to call him David."

"Right. Sorry. I know that. Really I do."

"And the answer is, I don't know. He's got to be around here somewhere."

We both craned our necks, trying unsuccessfully to find the man. The parking lot for the boardwalk and beach was crammed full of carnival rides, tents, ticket booths, and snack shacks. Among all these temporary structures, so many people moved in thick throngs that you would have thought no one in San Diablo had ever been to a carnival before.

"We're *never* going to find him," Allie said, sliding into a whininess I hadn't heard from her for at least several glorious weeks.

"I promise we will," I said. "Until we do, why don't you and Mindy go enjoy the carnival? I paid for that wristband—I at least want you to get some use out of it."

She aimed a sour expression my direction, but eventually nodded. "Okay, but if you find him, it totally qualifies as an emergency and you *have* to call my cell phone. Promise?"

"Cross my heart."

" 'Kay. I'm gonna see if Mindy wants to ride that thing," she added, pointing to the spiderlike machine that Laura had tagged right away.

"Fine," I said. "Go. I'll be here with my feet safely on the ground."

She gave a disgusted little shake of her head. "Jeez, Mom. You're such a wimp."

Laura laughed as she and Mindy hurried off. "And just like that, you're reduced to the level of us plebeians."

"I scream when I find a bug in the bathroom, too," I said.

"Oh, how the mighty have fallen."

"Hang on," I said, twisting quickly to look behind me.

"What?"

I scoured the area around us, seeing no one out of the ordinary. "Paranoia, I think." But I wasn't entirely sure that was the case. I distinctly remembered that odd sensation of being watched in the alley on David's first night back. Then again in my own backyard, and that on a night when a demon's body had gone missing. (And as far as I could tell, had thankfully stayed missing, not turning up in Dumpsters or ditches or other places that might cause the police to ask all those irritating questions.)

Now the feeling was back, this time in broad daylight. My only suspect was Dukkar, but he was nowhere to be seen.

"I know that look, Kate," Laura said.

"Goose bumps," I said. "Like someone's watching me."

"Maybe it's David," she suggested. "Or our carnival flyer friend."

"Maybe," I said. "Come on. Let's either find David or get something cold to drink."

"Do carnivals sell wine coolers?" she asked, heading into the thick of things.

"I don't know. But I think it's high time we find out."

As it turns out, this carnival did, which made it a high-class operation in both my and Laura's estimation.

We were on our second bottled cooler when Timmy decided he'd had enough of that napping thing and woke with a start and a definite opinion as to where we should go next.

"Nemo! Mommy, Mommy, look! Nemo!"

Sure enough, one of the game booths was strung with clown fish and other denizens of the sea. Not the Disney licensed version, but my little boy didn't care.

"Want out!" he said, leaning forward and straining against the strap on his stroller. "I want a Nemo!"

I didn't bother to explain to him that getting out of the stroller wasn't actually going to get him much closer to holding a Nemo in his hot little hands, but I did release him. He raced pell-mell to the edge of the game, then reached up, as if by the sheer force of his desire he could will one of those fishies to drop down into his hands.

"Gotta play the game, little guy," the carny said. I cocked my head, considering the carny and, more important, wondering if he knew who I was. If he was one of the ones who'd been watching me.

"Mommy, please? I want Nemo." He rubbed his chest and pouted his lips and looked so dang cute I had to give in.

"How much?"

"Three for five," the carny said, pointing to the darts that lined the railing. The idea was to toss them and pop the balloons. I hesitated to ask how many pops it took to earn a Nemo.

"Five tries," I said to Timmy. "But there's no guarantee you'll win."

"Ten." He held up two hands, all five fingers splayed out.

"Yay, you! What a good counter. But, no. Five tries."

"Seven!" One hand disappeared behind his back.

"Five."

"Three, Mommy! Three, three, three!"

"Sweetie," I said. "Five is more than three."

I'm not entirely sure he believed me, but he finally let loose with an "Okay, Mommy," which I swear had exactly the same tonal quality as his sister's famous *whatever.*

"So here's the way the game is played, little man," the carny said, leaning over the counter to pick my son up and plunk him on the thick railing. "You take this dart—hold it carefully—and you toss it at that wall. Aim high, boy. You pop one, you get a prize. More you pop, bigger the prize. Got it?"

Timmy gave a thumbs-up and looked at me for assurance. "Have at it, kiddo."

He picked up a dart, the carny stepped out of the line of fire, and away the thing flew.

Surprisingly, it actually made it to the wall. The point didn't hit a balloon, but I was pretty darned impressed that my little boy managed to send a dart flying that far.

"Second time's a charm, little man," the carny said, handing him a bright yellow dart.

As it turns out, it was. The carny gave him a few pointers and he popped balloons with darts two and three. Four went wild, but he popped another with five. Not a bad average, all in all.

"Good job, boy. You get any of the prizes along the pole. Take your pick, little dude."

The carny had a big wide grin, obviously assuming Timmy would be thrilled. I knew better. There was no Nemo on the pole. All the Nemos were strung across the top of the booth.

"Nemo!" Timmy said.

"Can't do that, dude. But this fishy here's real cute." He pointed to a yellow fish with bulging blue eyes.

"Ne. Mo." Timmy put his little fists on his hips and stomped his foot. "Want Nemo!"

"Calm down, sweetie," I said, hauling him off the railing and plunking him on the ground beside me.

The second I did, the tears started, and I was forced to face that most delicate of mommy moments: Explain to my child that you don't always get what you want, or win him the damned fish.

Call me a wimp, but I chose the fish.

"How many balloons to win Nemo?" I asked.

"Fifteen," he said. "In a row."

I looked at Laura, who shrugged. "Don't look at me. I couldn't do better than Timmy."

"Here." I passed him nine dollars. "Let's go."

"Little boy's gonna be awfully disappointed if you don't get him a Nemo," the carny said. "I can sell one to you for thirty."

"I think not."

"You got a husband around here? Maybe he ought to give it a whirl."

Not only was he now pissing me off, but I decided that he couldn't possibly have been surreptitiously watching me if he was that clueless. I pointed to the railing. "The darts, please."

He sighed, low and deep, as if it pained him to see an innocent female like me embarrass myself in front of my little boy.

And, to be honest, with so much riding on my performance—winning a fish for Timmy and impressing the chauvinist carny—I was probably more nervous tossing that first dart than I'd ever been in combat with a demon.

Pop!

"Score one for the little lady," the carny said, causing Laura to slap her hand over her mouth to keep from laughing.

That broke the ice, though, and I fired off the remaining fourteen darts in quick succession. I aimed my most feminine smile at the carny, then pointed to Nemo. To his credit, he didn't say a word, just passed it to me and watched as I passed it to my little boy.

"Thank you, Mommy."

"Any time, kiddo," I said, pushing the stroller back into the throng.

"Show-off," Laura said from beside me.

"Maybe," I said. "But at least I've still got it."

"So does your daughter," Laura said. "Look."

I followed the direction of her outstretched finger and found Allie across the makeshift walkway. David was by her side, and they were huddled close together, her father showing her how to properly hold the pellet gun that would take out the metal duck targets.

"She nailed two in a row," Laura said. "Not sure what he thinks he's telling her. Seems to me the kid's got it down."

As I watched, Allie planted her feet, aimed, and pulled the trigger three times in quick succession. Three duckies fell back, the pellets having hit them dead center.

I smiled, a wave of mommy pride cresting inside me.

"I don't see Mindy," Laura said.

"With friends, probably. I bet Allie peeled away from the group when she saw David."

"Lucky for Allie. I'm sure she wanted to spend time alone with David. It can't be easy keeping secrets from your best friend."

"It's not," I said, speaking from experience. I'd tried keeping my secrets from Laura, but I hadn't been too successful. In truth, I'm glad she found out. I wasn't entirely sure I'd want to do what I did without Laura having my back, keeping me sane and helping me when my demon-hunting life infiltrated on the mommy part of the equation.

As we watched, Allie tilted her head back and laughed, then bounced up and down like a little girl, clearly delighted with something her father had said to her. I pressed my lips together and blinked, determined not to cry. What was there to cry about right then, anyway? My kid was happy, and surely that was a good thing.

"You know what I don't get," I said. "Why she wasn't more upset about Stuart grounding her. If it hadn't been for seeing David at this carnival, I think she would have been perfectly content to spend all of spring break hanging out in the house." And that, frankly, wasn't my daughter. Or at least, it hadn't been until she'd learned about my secret life. With that knowledge under her belt, she'd morphed into a study bug. And while I liked the academic bent in theory, in practice it made me a little nervous. Allie was either becoming less like the daughter I knew . . . or she was hiding something from me. And I can't say I was comfortable with either option.

"Mindy's going to be at her dad's most of this week," Laura said. "Maybe Allie figured it was a good time to hang out and download her music. Maybe even study."

"The only thing that kid studies lately is demons. But as far as I know, there's no demonology course offered at the high school. If there is, I think she'll get an A."

"It's just the newness of it," Laura said, catching on to my worried undertone. "She wants to impress David. And you, too," she added in a rush.

"I know," I said, hoping she was right. "But it's spring break. I figured she'd want to go to the beach. Do all those car washes with the cheerleaders," I continued, as Laura looked at me with the oddest expression. "Beg to go to parties for the football players."

Laura's brow furrowed, but she didn't say anything.

"What?" I demanded.

"Kate, didn't Allie tell you? She quit cheerleading."

"*What?*"

"Mindy told me a day or so ago. I assumed you knew."

I hadn't known, and the fact that Allie would do something so major without either telling me or consulting me knocked me more than a little off balance.

Fortunately, I didn't have time to brood, as the subject of my angst soon appeared at my side, her face bright and happy and her father in tow.

"Did you see me? I got all the ducks. I totally kicked ducky butt!"

"Allie!" I said, but through laughter.

"Sorry, but I did. Didn't I Da—David?"

"You were great," he said, giving her shoulders a little squeeze.

"David," I warned, aiming a glance at his arm around our daughter's shoulder. It was one thing for him to hug Allie in private, but I'd already seen two of her teachers and at least fifteen kids from her class wander by. Let a rumor mill like high school get wind of inappropriate touching from a teacher, and we'd all be facing a lot of questions and accusations that we really didn't want to deal with.

"Right," David said, sliding his arm off and stepping a respectable distance away, both hands balanced on the head of his cane. "So where's the zombie?"

"My car," I said, lifting my eyebrow. "How'd you know?"

"You had the word half out before you remembered Mindy was in the room."

I frowned. Hopefully Mindy wasn't as clever at interpretation as David. "You ready?"

"I don't have to come, do I?" Allie asked.

"You can do whatever you want," I said. "Just don't leave the carnival area."

"Over there," she said. "I saw Charlie over by the Tilt-A-Whirl."

"Do you have money?"

"Ten bucks," she said.

"Be good. Keep your phone on."

She gave me a salute. "Yes ma'am. If anyone messes with me, I'll get 'em in the gut with a round kick. 'Kay?"

I looked at David and rolled my eyes. "A bit overeager."

"Just a bit," he agreed, his voice tinged with laughter.

"You guys go on ahead," Laura said. "I'll watch Timmy."

I aimed a grateful look in her direction, and from the answering incline of her head, I'm sure she understood the message. The toddler-free chance to talk with my first husband. I definitely owed her one.

"She's thrilled to be spending time with you," I said as we walked across the Pacific Coast Highway.

"The feeling is mutual." He turned to me. "Have you thought any more about a weekend?"

"Honestly, I haven't." I held up a hand before he could protest. "And I don't want to even mention the possibility to Allie until I figure out what I'm going to say to Stuart."

"Kate—"

"I'm not trying to be difficult. I promise. Your time with Allie is way up there on my priority list, but we agreed that I'm calling the shots here."

"I think 'agreed' may be stretching it a bit."

I glared at him.

He held up his hands. "At the very least, I thought you'd come up with a game plan or two."

"I know," I said, feeling guilty. "And I will. But it's been kind of busy lately."

He stopped on the sidewalk, his cane in one hand, and his free hand taking my elbow and pulling me to a halt beside him. "So what's going on, Kate?"

I hesitated only a second, then told him the full story that, so far, he'd gotten only in cryptic bits and pieces. "Allie knows most of it, of course, since she was there. But she didn't overhear the demon talking about the Sword of Caelum. And that's not something I want her to know. Not yet, anyway. And I haven't told her that we're pretty sure Abaddon is behind the attacks on me."

"You're in danger, Kate. She has a right to know."

"No." I shook my head, adamant. "You weren't there, night and day, when I told her the truth about me. She thought it was cool, but she was worried, too. Worried that hunting demons might kill me the same way it had killed her father." I glanced up at him and saw him nod in understanding. "It's one thing for her to know I'm out there, fighting the good fight. I can't avoid that. But I don't see any reason to announce to my fourteen-year-old that I'm a specific target for some bad-ass demon holding a twenty-year-old grudge."

"Doesn't sound like it's a grudge. It sounds like Abaddon's got another plan for invincibility and he thinks you and this sword could muck up the works."

"I know," I said. "Too bad I don't have the sword. I'd put it to serious good use." I looked him in the eye. "Right now, though, I don't think Allie needs to know."

"She can handle more than you give her credit for."

"I give her full credit," I said. "But I'm her mom. It's my job to protect her. It's what parents do, or have you forgotten how you spent four entire weeks researching the safest car seat?"

His eyes crinkled, laughing at the memory. "Fair enough."

I caved a little, too. "I'm not saying I'm never going to tell her, but I'd like to have a little bit more solid understanding of what's going on. What's this prophecy that names me? And what exactly is Abaddon up to? The demon in the red dress called him The One. But The One what?"

"Is Laura looking into it?"

I nodded. "Hopefully she'll figure something out soon. But don't sidetrack me. I want an agreement from you about Allie."

"Do I have a choice?"

"I'm sorry. But this is hard enough without micromanaging parenting. I'm the one on deck. As far as everyone else in the world is concerned, you're her teacher, not her father. And as much as you might think that sucks, that's just the way it is."

"What about you?" he said, his eyes looking straight into my heart.

My breath hitched. "What about me?"

"Do you think it sucks?"

I hesitated, not sure if I should tell the truth and feel disloyal to my husband, or craft a lie and hurt the first man I ever loved. I settled on truth. Sometimes, it's just easier. "Yeah," I said. "It does suck. But Eric, that doesn't mean . . . you have to understand that I have a good life now. A good man who loves me, and a little boy who means the world to me. I'm not going to—"

"I know," he said. "I know exactly what you're going to say."

"And you understand?"

"As much as you understand my wanting to spend time with Allie. Just because I get it, doesn't mean I'll do it."

"I'm sorry," I said, emotions swirling like flies. "I am. But sometimes—"

"What?"

I couldn't look at him. "It's nothing." Which, of course, was a lie.

He laughed. "That's what you used to say when you were mad at me."

I looked up at him, surprised he'd figured that out.

"Good Lord, you're *mad* at me?"

"Not really," I rushed to reassure him. "It's just that . . ."

"What?"

"I don't know. Maybe I do feel a little mad at you sometimes."

"For what?"

I shrugged. "For coming back, I think." I tilted my head up, forcing myself to look at him, to see that flash of pain cut across his eyes. "For wanting a piece of your life back, and at the same time for confusing the hell out of me."

I blinked, setting free a tear that had been clinging to my lashes. It trickled down my cheek until David's thumb caught it at the side of my mouth.

"I love you," I said, my words little more than a whisper. "I've always loved you. But I love Stuart, too. I really do. And this is killing me. It's killing Allie. And I hate myself for thinking it, but sometimes I wonder if—"

I broke off, looking over his shoulder at a nearby storefront, unable to say the words or look him in the face.

"If you should have let me stay dead?"

He'd always been able to finish my sentences, but that was one I wished he'd never uttered. Even so, I couldn't deny the truth. "I'm sorry."

"Don't be. Of course you're confused. Hell, I'm confused and I'm not being pulled in different directions. You have a new life, Kate. I respect that. But I want to find a way in, at least a little." He ran his hands through his hair, and I had the feeling he wanted to say more. That he just plain *wanted* more.

Then again, why wouldn't he? I'd gained a new husband, a new child, and a new life. Eric had lost everything.

"I don't know," he said. "Maybe I should move. Back to L.A. Even Rome. Allie could come visit. If you're not willing to tell Stuart the truth, we could make something up. Stuart knows you grew up there, right? Surely we could come up with a plan."

"I don't want that," I whispered. I didn't want Allie to go overseas without me. And as selfish and complicated as it might be, I didn't want David that far away.

"Good." He tilted my head up so that I had no choice but to look in his eyes. "I don't want it either, Katie. But I'm fighting. I want it known for the record that every day I'm here—every moment I'm around you—I'm fighting my way through my own particular hell."

I shivered, his words making me unreasonably uneasy. But I saw nothing there other than love, concern, and a desperate longing.

"I know," I said, my eyes welling. "And I'll understand if you have to leave. But I'm saying it for the record, too, and no matter how complicated it makes things. I don't want you to go. Now that you're back, I don't want you to leave me again. I know that makes me selfish, and it probably makes me a terrible wife. But it's how I feel. I love you. I want you. And if I'm going to fight anything," I admitted, feeling my cheeks burn despite the cool ocean breeze, "it's the temptation to do something about that. Because, David," I said, "that's one line I'll never cross."

"I know," he said, leaning close and letting his voice fall to a low, passion-filled whisper. "But I'm not as strong as you, Katie. I never have been. So don't expect me to make the same promise. I won't. For that matter, I won't even try."

I shivered, fighting the urge to let him take me in his arms. To kiss me and let me lose myself in memories. I wished desperately that I could segregate my life—this piece here, that piece there. To keep it separate and neat and clean.

I couldn't, though. And I wouldn't risk what I already had.

"The body," I said, stepping away from him and clicking the button to unlock the van. "It's in that tub right there."

"Right," he said, following my lead to drop the subject like an extremely hot potato. He handed me his cane, then hefted the tub, and as he did I heard little scratching noises, like fingernails scraping against plastic. For the record, I really despise zombies.

"I'm one block over," David said.

"Should we drive?" I asked, looking pointedly at the cane I was holding.

His brows rose. "You've seen me fight, Kate. It helps, but I can manage without it."

"Right. Of course." Eric had had a high tolerance for pain, too. Of course, I didn't know how well that translated now that he was in another man's body. For a moment, I considered asking, then decided that was one of those questions best left for another day.

"Walk with me?" he asked, stepping off the curb.

I hesitated, debating whether that was the best idea under the circumstances.

"I promise to be a complete gentleman," he said. "No attacks upon your virtue at all."

I looked at him dubiously, and he laughed.

"Come on, Kate. Don't you trust me?"

"That's the trouble," I teased. "I trust you too much."

"Ah, but you have the cane. You can gut me if I step out of line," he added, referring to the sword hidden inside the innocent-looking crutch.

"True enough," I said, then fell in step beside him, grateful that he understood enough to tease me. Not that I expected any different. Eric had been my best friend as much as my husband and lover. Of all the people in the world, he knew me better than anyone.

"Have you taken Allie patrolling yet?" he asked.

I looked up, startled. "No, and I don't plan to. She's only fourteen."

His brows lifted and the corner of his mouth twitched.

"Fourteen, not raised in *Forza*, and with about five seconds of training under her belt. No. I haven't taken her patrolling."

"And yet she's still battling demons," he said, looking pointedly at the tub.

"Technically, that's a zombie."

"She's ready, Kate. And she can use the experience. Let me take her out one night. Hell, let *us* take her out one night."

"Absolutely not," I said, in the same tone I use when the kids beg for snacks before dinner. "Not happening, don't ask me again."

"I'm her father, Kate."

"Eric," I said, a warning in my voice. "I mean it. She doesn't patrol. Not now. Not with me. Not with you." I looked him in the eye. "You weren't talking with her about patrolling when you two were shooting ducks back there, were you?"

"She's ready, Kate."

"Answer the question, *David*."

He drew in a breath, a muscle in his jaw twitching. "No," he said. "We weren't talking about patrolling."

"Good," I said. "Because she's not going." I shot a sideways glance his direction and saw him stiffen, his shoulders tight with irritation or anger.

I told myself not to take it personally. Why wouldn't he be ticked? I'd just vetoed him, after all. One more reminder that he's not part of the decision-making process anymore. It's all on me now, no matter how hard that might be—for me and for David.

"David, look," I said, wanting to make peace. "I'm not saying no forever. Just for now. She needs to train more. Become more comfortable with her skills. It's one thing to throw a cat in her own backyard. It's something completely different to walk into harm's way in a dark alley."

"Right. You're right."

The words were agreeable, but the tension I felt wasn't.

"You're mad."

"I'm not mad," he said. "I'm preoccupied."

"With Allie."

"With whatever's watching us," he retorted, his voice dropping to a whisper. "Remember the night in the alley?"

"And earlier today," I said. "On the carnival grounds. See anything?"

"No, and it's possible there's nothing to see. I've felt eyes on me since we left your car."

He turned, whipping around so fast the body parts in the tub slammed against the inside, then scrambled and slithered again, the bits and pieces all stirred up.

"Nothing," he said. "I'm not liking this."

"I'm not much liking it, either," I said, now also feeling watched, though whether my feeling was genuine or a reflection of his I really couldn't tell. "Let's drop this off and get back. I want to check on the kids."

By the time we reached his car, secured the tub in the trunk, and headed back down the street toward the beach, the creepy sensation had dissipated. "Maybe we were imagining it," I suggested.

"If it were Laura, I'd believe that. Us? We've been trained

to tell the difference between real and paranoia. Which means the odds are good there really are things hiding in the shadows keeping tabs on us."

The man had a point.

"They seem to have backed off for now, anyway."

"Probably watching to see where I have this Sword of Caelum thing hidden."

"Too bad you don't have it. A sword that can strike down a demon and his cohorts forever would be pretty damn useful."

"So would cardinal fire," I said.

David stopped short. "Pardon?"

"The stuff you had when we fought Abaddon. That was the hell fire Sammy Watson was talking about."

"I know," David said. "But why do you want cardinal fire now?"

"Well, duh. You saw what it did. A whole army of demons, and *poof.* They were gone."

He started walking again, his body stiff. "It's dangerous stuff. Wilson didn't tell me how dangerous when he gave it to me."

"So Father Corletti said," I admitted. "But I really don't see how. The only ones who got hurt were the demons."

"I risked our lives, Katie," he said. "And I didn't even know it. I would never have intentionally put you in harm's way, and yet——" He cut himself off with a shake of the head.

"Hey, it's okay. Twenty years later and going strong."

I got a smile, but not as big as what I was trying for. "As I understand it, the danger is twofold. Yes, you destroy the demons who are already out, corporeal, and attacking you. But if there's a hidden demon—in a talisman, say—all the fire does is destroy the shell. It makes the hidden demon vulnerable. Reveals it, if you will. But it doesn't destroy it. So if you had a bad-ass demon trapped in a stone, for example, you could accidentally release it with cardinal fire."

"That wouldn't be good," I said, thinking of the bad-ass demon we'd recently seen released from a stone.

"The other risk is more personal. It's purity. We survived

because our faith and our bodies were pure." He looked at me and licked his lips. "We wouldn't survive another trip through the fire."

"Oh." I thought about that. "Wow," I said, as the implications truly struck home. If Abaddon had been wrong—if I hadn't been the vestal virgin he'd sought—I would have burned to death with Eric at my side.

The possibility made me shiver.

"You okay?"

"Just remembering," I admitted. "Abaddon. I can't say I ever thought I'd be tangling with him again."

"Me neither."

"That actually raises an interesting question," I said. "Why come play in my backyard?"

"Come again?"

"Well, if the prophecy is that I can kill him, why not simply stay away? I mean, it's pretty common knowledge I'm not globe-trotting these days. San Diablo is my turf. So if Abaddon thinks I can kill him, why not simply stay on the other side of the earth? Why come here?"

"You don't know that he has," David reminded me. "Minions, yes. Abaddon, no."

"Fair enough. But it's still a big deal to send his minions. Why bother? Why not simply torment the rest of the globe and leave my few square miles alone?"

"That's actually a really good point. Why are the demons suddenly so concerned about this thing? You're probably the most stagnant Hunter in *Forza*."

"Thanks a lot."

"You know what I mean. But the demons aren't stupid, and they know it, too."

"Which means for some reason, Abaddon is planning to make a trip here," I said. "Or else he's already here."

"Revenge?" David asked.

"So Sammy Watson said, but I don't believe it. Why wait more than two decades for revenge?"

"No idea. But he's definitely planning something, and his minions are trying to clear a path for him."

"By taking me out. Always nice to be the center of attention."

"You always were such a diva," he said, then ducked as I smacked him, because "diva" was about as far away from my personality as "lustrous and manageable" was from my hair.

"At least we know where to focus our research. Maybe we can figure out what's so special about right here, right now that it would draw a demon with a death mark. Figure out what Abaddon's planning on doing here, and we'll be one step ahead of him."

"Worth a shot," David said, then caught me eyeing him. "What?"

"Nothing. Only how nice it was to be back in the groove, bouncing ideas off you." I licked my lips, afraid I was revealing too much, but at the same time knowing that this was Eric I was talking about. And there really was nothing about me he didn't already know. "I've missed that. I've missed you."

"Me too," he said, his tone more than his words underscoring the depth of feeling.

We walked a few more moments in comfortable silence before he nodded to a small Italian café. "Remember when we ate there?"

"How could I forget? That was the first time we ever hired a babysitter. You were so nervous."

"Me?" he countered. "You were the one who kept calling the house every twenty minutes."

"Only because I knew you wanted me to."

"I remember the dinner was delicious," he said, reaching out to take my hand.

"Not as delicious as dessert," I said. And then, realizing that what had come out of my mouth qualified as blatant, unadulterated flirting, I tugged my hand away. "Um, anyway. It was a great evening."

"Yeah," he said, his warm eyes skimming over me. "It was."

We'd reached the highway again, the carnival spread out on the parking lot across from us. "I should go find Allie," I said as we crossed the street. "Rescue Laura from my hyperactive toddler."

"Probably be the nice thing to do," he agreed. "But I've got eight tickets burning a hole in my pocket, and that fun house right there takes four to enter."

"Really? That's very interesting news."

"Remember when we brought Allie to a carnival? What was she? Seven?"

"And she threw up in the Tilt-A-Whirl? Believe me, I remember."

"Come on," he said, nodding toward the fun house. "Laura will survive for three more minutes. Trust me. It'll be fun."

I hesitated only a second, telling myself that the kids weren't around, and it did seem like fun. And, truth be told, I wasn't ready to leave Eric—*David*—yet.

"One time through," I said. "But if anything scary jumps out at me, you're in for it, buster."

He gave his tickets to a leather-faced old man in a blue apron, then ushered me to go ahead. At first, the fun house seemed less than accurately named. The floor moved ever so slightly, and the trick mirrors on the walls were so dirty it really didn't much matter if your body was shortened or elongated.

As I rounded the corner to the next section, I aimed one of those looks at David. The kind that asks without words, *What the heck were you thinking?*

He shrugged, then laughed, and I laughed, too. Lame as it was, it was still fun.

And, in fact, there was significantly more fun in the next section of the fun house. This part—which had a squishy floor and purple lighting—was lined with trick mirrors so that you had to tread carefully if you wanted to find your way to the exit. And each time you took a wrong turn, you stepped on a siren, which announced your mistake to every-one else in the house.

Behind me, David stepped on two sirens, while I man-aged to get through with none. Frankly, I think he did it on purpose, as he was laughing a heck of a lot harder than I was, and I knew perfectly well that he'd been trained better than that to watch reflections and see the patterns in mazes.

"It's a *fun* house, Katie," he said, taking my hand and urg-ing me into the spinning tube that we had to run through if we were going to make it to the other side without falling. "Not one of *Forza*'s skill tests."

I managed a *hmmph*ing sound—courtesy of Eddie—but was laughing by the time we reached the end of the tube. "Uh-oh," I said, pointing to the black curtain in front of us. "A haunted section?"

"You better go first. I'm scared."

"Yeah, right," I said, but I pushed past him through the curtain and into a near pitch-black room. So far, that was about the only thing remarkable about the room. And as I'd done dark before, I was less than impressed.

Then the floor began to move.

It rolled, a thick layer of carpet and foam laid over tubes that rose and fell as you tried to walk—*try* being the opera-tive word, because with the very first undulation I toppled sideways and landed, laughing, in David's arms.

"Okay," I said. "This is getting better."

"Much," he agreed, his voice low and his breath steamy.

I was pressed hard against him, the movement of the floor working against me as it pushed me even closer to his body. He'd grabbed me right below the waist when I'd fallen, and now his hands drifted down, cupping my rear.

"Eric," I whispered, then, "*No.* David, no."

But all he said was, "Yes." And as the word died on his lips, his mouth closed over mine with such passion and des-peration that it drowned out everything except the beating of my own heart.

I didn't want to kiss him back, so help me, I didn't. But where Eric is concerned, there's a limit to my strength, and it took every ounce of resolve in my body to press my hands against his chest and break free of his hold.

"I'm sorry," I whispered, swallowing my words more than saying them. I stumbled forward, not caring anymore if he was following and not paying attention to the rest of the fun house.

When I reached the end, I pushed my way past the black strands of plastic that hung like retro beads from the ceiling, then found myself blinking in the bright sunlight.

Damn him.

And damn me, too. For liking the way he felt and for thinking that it was okay to go down memory lane like that. Especially after he'd warned me. Because he had. *I'm not as strong as you, Katie,* he'd said. *I never have been.*

He'd warned me, and I'd listened. But I still hadn't heard.

I turned, realizing he was probably about to exit the fun house, too, and right then I'd had my fill of David. I hurried around the contraption and lost myself in the crowd and my thoughts. I knew I should be looking for my family, but I needed a few minutes to myself, and so I bought a soda, then walked aimlessly, taking in the sounds and smells of the carnival.

After twenty minutes or so, I realized I needed to get with the program, and I looked around to get my bearings. I found myself standing in front of a nomadic-style tent that looked like something straight from the Old Testament. An old woman stood in the doorway, barefoot, her face craggy from age and exposure. She wore a peasant-style blouse, a colorful skirt of flowing, gauzy material, at least five gold chains around her waist, and one huge, gaudy necklace from which dangled a truly ugly amulet with two intertwined lines intersecting a circle. She looked like a gypsy, and that, along with her European accent, had me slowing down and paying attention.

"Come in," she said, her red fingernails beckoning me closer. "Come and hear your fortune, little one."

"I'm not sure I want to know my fortune."

She chuckled. "Ah, an honest answer. Better than the excuse I usually get."

"What's that?" I asked, interested despite myself.

Her face scrunched up and she spoke in a whine. "Can't stop. In such a hurry." She looked me dead in the eye. "They never are, you know. The ones who say so. Not like you."

I swallowed, my mouth suddenly dry. "What do you mean?"

One shoulder lifted in a grand shrug. "Eh. Always in a hurry, you are. It hangs on you, you know."

I slowed, looking at her, something about the self-assured tone of her voice making me wary. "What does?"

"That need. That pressure. Off to fight the beast again. Isn't that right, dearie?" she asked, with the same sweetness that I imagined of the witch who invited in Hansel and Gretel.

My hand slid into my purse, my fingers finding my knife. "You seem to think you know a lot about me."

Her gaze dipped down, skipped over my purse, then rose back to my face. She held my gaze for one beat, two. Then she waved a hand toward a weather-beaten sign above the entrance to the tent. "Fortune-teller," she said. "I see all. And you wear your personal demons on your sleeve."

"Who are you?"

"Me? I am no one special. Merely someone who watches. Someone who learns. Someone who tells."

"Have you been watching me?" I took a step closer, my posture aggressive as I sniffed her breath and looked in her tent. Her tent was empty. Her breath, normal.

Not that that was a foolproof test, of course, but coupled with the small crucifix I now saw tucked into the indentation of her neck, I'd be willing to lay odds against demon.

"I watch what is in front of me. What I see, though, it troubles me."

"Yeah, well, some of what I see troubles me, too."

"It would," she said, with a knowing nod. "How could it not? You opened the door to the darkness—you walked right through it."

I shivered, a cold chill passing over me. "What are you talking about?" I asked, though I feared I knew perfectly well. How she knew about the Lazarus Bones, though . . . That, I didn't know.

"The darkness, dearie. You felt it, yes? All around you. Pushing. Pulling." Her eyes met mine, flat and terrifying. "The darkness won. Don't let it win again."

"Who the hell are you? Why have you been watching me?"

"*Kate.*"

I turned, sucking in air as I saw Stuart amid a throng of people, his long steps carrying him right to me.

I turned to look back, but the woman had slipped into her tent, uninterested in either my questions or my husband.

"Stuart!" I said, trying for bright and cheery. "What are you doing here?" I managed a smile, but at the same time I scanned the crowd, looking for my daughter.

"Publicity photos. Someone suggested some pictures at the carnival would be good for the campaign, and Clark jumped all over that. So here I am."

"Here you are," I repeated.

"What are *you* doing here?"

"Oh, well, you know. Laura suggested it, and I thought Timmy would get a kick out of it. So, you know. We came." I shrugged helplessly, my wobbly smile fading as I saw a familiar face in the crowd behind him. I reached for his arm, planning to pull him into the fortune-teller's tent, but it was too late. Allie burst through through the crowd, a teddy bear clutched in one hand and David's elbow tight in the other.

"Mom! Mom! Look what Da—"

Stuart turned at the sound of her voice, and Allie's eyes went wide.

"What I won," she finished lamely.

David, apparently sensing blood, broke free, then peeled off to the right, letting the crowd swallow him whole and leaving me alone to handle damage control.

Honestly, sometimes it sucks being me.

Thirteen

There are times when I wish that Stuart were the yelling type. Yelling, I could handle. I could glare and say that nobody talks to me in that tone, no matter how upset they are. I could yell back. I could flounce out of the room, insisting that I wouldn't return until he calmed down. (The only problem with that plan being that I've never really been the flouncing type.)

Stuart, however, wasn't yelling. For the last three hours, in fact, he'd barely spoken a word, and the words he had spoken were utterly, remarkably, damnably civil.

Yet another reason he'd win the election. The man knows how to control his emotions. That was for damn sure.

The same could not be said for me.

I fidgeted. I twisted. I started conversational threads that hung out there, finally dying a slow, painful death from lack of fertilization.

Mostly, I spun the little arrow on Hi Ho! Cherry-O and plucked cherries from a paper tree. It wasn't cathartic, but it was safe.

"My turn!" Timmy said, then flicked the arrow so hard

that all our cherries shifted on our trees, as if an earthquake had hit our orchard. "Two!" he said, holding up two chubby fingers.

"Good boy." I pointed to the game board. "So what do you do?"

"Pick two cherries," he said, then proceeded to dump four into his little yellow bucket.

"Not four, squirt," Allie said. She'd managed not to look Stuart in the eye since the carnival, a feat that had required no small amount of physical contortions. Now she was concentrating on her little brother, her back turned oh-so-casually toward her stepdad.

"Two," she said. She held up two fingers to illustrate. "Put two back."

Timmy's face scrunched up. "But I wanna win."

I looked over at Stuart. This was the part where we usually shared a knowing grin. But he wasn't looking my way. Instead, he was looking at the back of Allie's head with a mixture of confusion and pain that about ripped my heart in two.

I think it might have been easier if Stuart had demanded to know what the hell was going on. If he'd pulled me and Allie aside at the carnival and given us both no end of grief. Frankly, he had the right.

He hadn't done that, though.

Instead, he'd looked at each of us in turn and then said he'd see us at home. He'd left, leaving me to wallow in guilt and Allie on the verge of tears.

Laura and I had spent most of the ride home assuring Allie that none of this was her fault. That I'd chosen to let her out of her punishment, and that it was me Stuart was mad at. By the time we got home, she seemed less on the verge of tears, but stiffer around Stuart than I'd ever seen her.

As for me, I pretty much wanted to throw up. I'd wanted to help the relationship between my daughter and her father, but the way I'd gone about it had put a huge dent in her relationship with her stepfather, the man whose house she shared, and who'd put up with the onset of puberty right along with me.

I didn't want to hurt either of the men in my life, but to be honest, both of them had to take a backseat to my daughter. Right now, though, I didn't have a clue how to make Allie feel better. All I knew was that I'd blown it and that somehow, someway, I had to make it right.

On the game table, Timmy was still clutching desperately the two cherries he didn't want to let go.

"Go on, Timmy," I said gently. "Put them back on the tree. You can get them on the next spin."

He pooched out his lower lip, but complied, and I considered that a step up from last week, when he'd tossed the game board across the room.

What can I say? The kid likes to win.

Fortunately for family peace, he actually did win this game, spinning all the right spins and pulling cherries off the tree while Allie, Stuart, and I were plagued with birds, dogs, and spilled buckets.

"I win! I win!" He jumped off his chair and marched around the kitchen, his bare feet making smacking sounds on the tile floor as he headed for his cabinet. He yanked out a cookie sheet and banged on it in time to his delirious cries of victory.

"No!" Allie shouted. "Make the little beast stop. He's too loud. Too loud." She ran forward and scooped him up, swinging boy and cookie sheet high as they both laughed. "If I let you down, will you be quiet?"

"No!"

"If I let you down, will you be quiet?"

"No!"

"If I give you candy, will you be quiet?"

"Allie!"

"Yes!"

"Deal." She set him on the floor, then shrugged at me. "A girl's gotta do what a girl's gotta do."

As she stole a packet of M&Ms from my freezer stash, I looked sideways at Stuart, happy to see that he was smiling.

"Look, Daddy," Timmy said, running to show his father this amazing, forbidden, bedtime prize. "Want one?"

"Yeah, sport," Stuart said, pulling Timmy into a bear hug. "I think I do."

He held his son tight, and I had to look away, afraid if I watched the two of them any longer I'd start crying.

Apparently, Allie felt the same way, because she stood there behind Timmy, then whispered, "I'm sorry, Stuart. I'm really, really sorry."

My heart twisted, knowing that she wouldn't be apologizing for anything if she hadn't saved my life Friday night, and I debated the wisdom of revealing all to Stuart right then. I'd told Laura why I wanted to wait until Wednesday, and those reasons were all still sound. Still, some of the variables had changed, and maybe now was the time to come clean.

I didn't have a chance. Before I could get my thoughts in order, Stuart gestured for her to come to him. As Timmy clung to him like a little monkey, he took one of her hands. "I'm sorry, too. Let's chalk it up to adolescence and overreactive parenting, okay?"

"Okay," Allie said, but I could tell she didn't really understand.

"I mean I'm ungrounding you, Allie."

"You are?"

"Yeah, kiddo. I am." He looked at me—really looked at me for the first time that night. "Okay?"

"Sure," I said, sounding as baffled as Allie looked.

"Okay, then." He stood up, holding Timmy close to his chest. "My night to bathe the rugrat," he said without being reminded. He headed into the living room, Timmy squirming and giggling in his daddy's arms.

Allie looked at me, her eyes wide and her face pale. Then she took off running after them. At the table, I closed my eyes, listening to the sound of my family.

I heard a loud sniffle, then the clomp, clomp of my daughter barreling up the stairs. A few moments later, I heard Stuart's more regulated footfalls, then the squeal of pipes as the water in the kids' bathroom began to run.

I sat a moment longer, nursing a now-cold cup of coffee. Then I stood up and started to clean the kitchen.

Honestly, it wasn't one of our more stellar attempts at family night, but we'd survived. And I think that meant a lot.

Stuart was sitting on the closed toilet and drying off Timmy when I stepped inside, then leaned against the doorjamb and watched the two men in my household. Stuart looked up and smiled at me, his hands full of a wriggling, giggling little boy, and something in his expression told me that all was forgiven.

I swallowed a throat full of tears, certain I'd gotten better than I deserved in this man. Hell, in this marriage. And definitely with my kids.

"Kate?"

"Sorry," I said, wiping my eyes. "You're a great daddy." I shrugged. "That's all."

"And that makes you cry?"

"Tonight, I think pretty much anything is going to make me cry."

He pulled the Nemo towel off Timmy, then gave his bare bottom a swat. "Go put on a nighttime Pull-Up, okay?"

Timmy gave a thumbs-up and hurried naked from the bathroom. Inevitably, I'd find twenty-seven Pull-Ups scattered across his floor five minutes from now, but in the moment the sacrifice seemed well worth it.

"Come here," he said, and I came. He settled me on his lap, and I balanced my feet on the edge of the tub, one arm around his neck and my face pressed against his shoulder. "Did I do the right thing?" he asked.

I leaned back so I could look him in the eye. "What do you mean?"

"With Allie. Dropping the grounding."

"Absolutely," I said. "And I'm sorry."

He shook his head, exhaling loudly. "I don't need to hear 'I'm sorry.' I want to hear that you love me."

"Of course," I said hugging him tight. "Desperately."

"That's enough for now."

"No, it's not," I said, leaning back in his arms and searching his face. "I should have told you. I shouldn't have just taken her to the carnival. I should have called you. Discussed it with you. Argued with you that night you grounded her in the first place. But I should never have taken her like I did. Even if you hadn't found out, it wasn't fair to you. I undermined your authority, and there's no reason on earth that justifies doing that." The words poured out, and I meant every word I said. I'd blown it on this one, and now my whole family was paying the price. It was, I knew, time to fess up. "I'm sorry, Stuart. I'm so, so sorry, and I owe you one whopper of an explanation."

"Just tell me one thing. Is our marriage in trouble?"

"No," I said fiercely, the answer both true and automatic. Yes, I loved David or, at least, I loved the man he used to be. But my marriage was solid.

"Then there's nothing else to talk about."

"But . . ."

He put a finger on my lip, then shook his head. "I don't want to hear anything else. Please, Kate. Right now, I only want to hold you close. At least for the next five seconds before Timmy comes looking for us? Can you give me that? Just you and me tonight and no justifications or explanations filling up the space between us?"

I hesitated only a nanosecond, his wishes warring with my need to ease my own guilt. "Yes," I said, snuggling close. "Of course I can."

I woke up at six A.M. to the clock radio blaring, then sat bold upright, frantic that I hadn't yet been to the grocery store for the dinner party that night.

That panic lasted about forty-seven seconds, and then I remembered that it was—thankfully—only Monday. I had more than twenty-four hours to worry about the dinner party. Today, I only had to worry about the committee members who were coming to work on the Easter party.

I made a mental note to thank Laura again for inviting everyone to descend on my house, and to subtly suggest that the next time she thinks a group project is a good idea she ought to hold it in her own living room.

I rubbed my face with the palm of my hands, listened gratefully to the still-silent baby monitor, and plotted ways to kill Stuart for setting the alarm so early.

Then I remembered.

I lunged for the remote and clicked the TV on just in time. Sure enough, there was my honey, all decked out in his best suit and tie, chatting with the morning-show host about the details of his campaign platform.

After his five-minute interview was over, I clicked pause on the TiVo control and let Stuart's image fill the screen as I got dressed. Ask me about the details he'd discussed during the interview, and I doubt I could repeat even one. But I was certain that the polished, articulate man I saw on television was sure to draw voters by the droves.

Honestly, I couldn't have been more proud. And the real upside? I was awake a full hour before I'd planned to get up. On a normal day, that would be grounds for divorce. Today, I was happy to have the extra time. With any luck, I could rid the couch of Cheerios, peel a few gummy bears off the bookshelf, suck a few dust bunnies into the vacuum, and still shower and change before the neighborhood hordes descended on my front stoop. And, honestly, who doesn't want to spend her morning couch diving for loose change and Cheerios?

I'd already found sixty-seven cents, two dice, and a Candy Land game piece by the time Allie stumbled downstairs, blinking and tugging her robe tight around her, and looking even more comatose than she usually does in the mornings.

"Help yourself to breakfast," I said. "I'm going to go wake up the Timster."

On a normal day, we'd be dressed and out of the house

already. This was spring break, though. So while Allie vegetated on the couch watching scintillating morning programs, I started to clean the kitchen, stopping only when I heard signs of life coming from Timmy's room. I headed up that way, tossing off the suggestion to Allie that perhaps she might want to finish wiping down the counters in the kitchen while I got her brother dressed, but I wasn't taking bets that she'd actually do it. So imagine my surprise when I came downstairs to find her breakfast dishes put away, the dishwasher loaded and turned on, and the counters sparkling.

It was, I thought, shaping up to be an amazing day.

That's when the phone rang and suddenly I was thrust into a hell the likes of which I'd never experienced in all my demon-hunting days: finding a replacement Easter Bunny less than a week before the big day.

"No, an Easter Bunny," I said into the phone, trying to communicate the direness of my need to the guy at the other end. As soon as my bunny had bagged, I'd let my fingers do the walking, turning up absolutely nothing useful. Desperate, I'd called a temp agency. "Do you guys have any Easter Bunnies who can work this coming Saturday?"

"Lady, we send out professional temps. You want a bunny, you'll have to call for an acting gig."

All well and good, but that was what I'd tried to do in the first place. The phone book, however, wasn't my friend.

"We really need to drag you into the twenty-first century, Mom," Allie said from her perch on the couch. She pointed to my laptop, now sitting forlornly on the breakfast bar. "The Internet."

Now I'm not nearly as techno-savvy as Laura or my daughter, but I can handle Google. And though I didn't find anything promising in San Diablo or Santa Barbara, I found a couple of agencies in the L.A. area that seemed amenable to sending their actors up the coast for worthy gigs.

And, really, what could be more worthy than making small children happy at Easter?

"I certainly understand your dilemma," the manager at one such agency said, "but in case you hadn't noticed, it's the Monday before Easter. We're all out of bunnies."

No problem. After all, I had eight more agencies on my list to try. Unfortunately, all eight said essentially the same thing. Rough translation: Lady, are you insane?

Great. Just great.

"Any luck?" Allie asked, following me as I headed toward the kitchen to refill my coffee, sit at the table, and eat frozen M&Ms for breakfast.

"Lots," I said. "All of it bad."

She took the seat across from me and snagged a brown M&M.

"Anything you want to tell me?" I asked, thinking about the candy and, more specifically, about the many times she'd complained that if she ate one more piece of candy she'd burst out of her cheerleading uniform. Patently untrue, but definitely fourteen.

Her eyes widened in a classic deer-in-the-headlights manner, and then a wash of something that could only be described as guilt painted her face. "Um, no?"

"Uh-huh," I said. "Tell me another one. Seriously, Al. Why didn't you tell me you'd dropped out of cheerleading?"

Her shoulders sagged and she closed her eyes. "Oh, right. I should have," she rambled, sounding completely relieved to finally have it out there on the table. "Absolutely. I'm sorry. Totally."

"So why'd you do it? I thought you loved cheerleading."

She lifted on shoulder, then let it fall again. "Dunno. I guess with all the demon stuff it just didn't seem important anymore."

"But sweetie, it's part of high school, part of growing up. And you were having fun."

"I guess."

I leaned back in my chair, not sure where to go from there. "I don't know, Al. I wish you'd asked me before you dropped off the team. Cheerleading is the kind of thing I missed out on by not going to high school, and looking back, I wish I'd had the chance to do something like that."

"Do you really?"

I considered the question, wanting to give my daughter an honest answer. "Sometimes," I said. "Most of the time I'm content, but that's because my life was my life." So much for deep philosophy. "My point is that I'm not going to stand back and regret the way I grew up. But that doesn't mean I don't want more for my kids. That I don't want *normal* for my kids."

"But I'm not you, Mom," she said, slapping me without even meaning to. "And besides, I've done the cheerleading thing. So I can mark it down, and if my kids ever ask, I can say I was a cheerleader. Right?"

How could I argue with that?

"So what are your plans for the day?" I asked, shifting away from the deep mother/daughter discussions. "Hanging with Mindy?"

"She's in L.A. today, remember? With her dad."

"Right. I forgot. We should make a trip to L.A. soon," I said. "A girls' day out."

"Really? That would be so cool."

"You'd like that?" I asked, probably sounding completely desperate for reassurance that my teenager still wanted some closeness with her mom.

"Totally," she said, beaming. After a moment, the beam turned to a frown. "So is that what's gonna happen with me?" she asked.

I didn't follow.

"Getting shuffled between you and Daddy," she explained. "Mindy hates it, but her parents hate each other. At least you and Daddy still love each other, even if you're not supposed to," she added, her words like a knife blade twisting in my heart.

"Allie . . ." I trailed off, not even sure where to begin.

"No, it's okay. I get it. Daddy died. It's not a divorce, so it's not the same."

"It's not," I agreed. "But that doesn't mean it's not hard. Your father's here now, but he's—"

"Not exactly my dad? Yeah, I kind of get that."

I pressed my lips together, not sure where to go from here. "Do you want me to talk to Laura again? Maybe if you could talk about this with Mindy, it might help."

She shook her head and sighed. "It's not talking I need," she said. "Honest. And even if it were, how big a jerk would I be to shove my dad in Mindy's face right when hers is packing up with his new fiancée and moving to L.A.?"

The kid had a point. I'd certainly had similar thoughts about sharing all of my secrets with Laura.

"The only thing I really want is to spend time with Daddy."

"I know. And we'll figure that out soon. But we—"

"He wants to spend time with me, too," she said, her chin rising and her voice a little too sharp.

"You talked to him about that?" If David was airing our parental laundry, I was going to do way more damage to him than any zombie ever would.

"Um, no," she said, clearly covering for her dad. "I mean, nothing specific. Just that he liked hanging with me at the carnival."

Secrets. I took a sip of my coffee and looked at my daughter's face. Years ago, I could read every emotion. Now she was keeping secrets and I no longer knew the language of her eyes, her smile. That loss made a little hollow part in my stomach, and what made it worse was knowing that the secrets had gotten bigger and more closely held since her father had returned.

His death had brought Allie and me close together, closer, I think, than a lot of moms and daughters. Now I feared that his return was driving us apart, and I wasn't sure what to do about that. I didn't want to lose my daughter. Didn't want to lose the closeness and the relationship we'd once had.

And I didn't want to resent David for taking that away from me.

Because the truth was, no matter how much I'd loved

Eric, if I had to choose between husband and child, I would choose my kids, no doubt in my mind. With David, I'd brought him back. *I'd* made the choice and done the deed. And how painfully ironic would it be to find out that by giving my daughter back her father, I'd managed to push her away from me?

"So back to my question—now that you're ungrounded and unencumbered by cheerleading obligations, what were you thinking about doing today?"

"I thought I'd hang with you," she said, which had the immediate effect of soothing my tattered mommy ego.

"Yeah? Today is egg-stuffing day."

"Oh." Her expression was not one of overwhelming excitement.

"Not what you had in mind?"

"I was hoping for something more meaty. Like maybe training in the backyard with the crossbow?"

"Maybe later," I said. "Somehow the middle of day doesn't seem like the best choice for crossbow training."

"We've done it before," she protested.

"Yes, but I'm thinking that the backyard three hours before the hordes are supposed to descend on our house may not be the most prudent choice."

She kicked back in her chair. "Whatever."

"That was your only idea? Crossbows?"

"I could go to Cutter's and spar," she suggested, referring to our martial arts instructor. "You have to be in top-notch shape to be a Hunter. It's really all about the reflexes," she added seriously.

"Is that a fact?"

"Definitely," she said, so seriously I had to look away to hide my smile. Apparently my assumption had been right: David and Allie had been deep in hunting-related conversations at the carnival.

"You're right, of course," I said. "But you can't go to the studio today."

"But Mom! That's so totally unfair. I'm on break. It's not like—"

"It's closed, remember?"

"Oh." She thought about that. "Right. I forgot. He's in New York at some tournament. So what about me doing some research? I could help with that, right? I know Aunt Laura's on the Internet and all, but would it hurt to have me looking, too?"

"For what?" I asked. "Zombie info?" I thought about my conversation with David—about how there must be something big brewing in San Diablo if a demon marked for death at my hand had decided to send his minions here to take care of me. "I've actually got a better idea. How about you look into—"

"The Sword of Caelum?" she asked, bouncing a little on the seat cushion. "If it's really some über-cool tool that lets you whack out demons with a single blow, then I think we really need to be focusing on where it might be. I mean, maybe we'll have to go to Rome. Or Argentina. Or, or," she added excitedly, "maybe it's frozen in a glacier. Like at the end of *Frankenstein*. I mean, that's where folks send things they don't want found in this world, right? And Abaddon obviously doesn't know it's lost if he's worried about you having it. So if we figured out where it had been hidden, we could—"

"Allie!" I said, holding up a hand to cut her off. "Slow down there, kid."

She looked up at me with wide, eager eyes, and I didn't have the heart to tell her that her biological father was now in So. Much. Trouble.

"Mom?"

"Sure, honey. You go ahead and research the sword. You find anything interesting—anything at all—you let me know."

"Will do," she said, standing up and firing off a little salute. She looked so full of purpose and importance I couldn't help but smile, not to mention feel a little guilty for not already suggesting she get busy on the research. I also made a mental note to run up into the attic and get some of my old *Forza* mission reports out of my hunting trunk. Even if they didn't help with her research, I knew they'd be the kind of thing Allie would like to read through.

She grabbed my computer and headed for the stairs, pausing only once to look back at me. "Mom?"

"Hmm?"

"How come you didn't tell me? What the demon in the backyard said, I mean."

A dozen lies flitted through my head, but I ended up landing on the truth. "Because I didn't want you to worry about me, baby."

"But Mom," she said, with the slightest hint of a shadow in her eyes. "I do that anyway."

Fourteen

When I was fifteen, Eric and I found a demon's lair and stopped the creature from becoming both corporeal and invincible.

When I was sixteen, I located a nest of vampires in Prague and took them out with the help of a local schoolteacher and a handy-dandy blowtorch.

When I was nineteen, I heard rumors that a succubus was preying on Swiss men. Eric and I investigated, took the bitch out, and still had time to ski the Alps before reporting for duty back at the Vatican the next Monday.

With a résumé like that, you might think that I could tackle any task, handle any emergency, totally hold it together in a time of crisis.

Apparently not. Because this damn bunny fiasco had pretty much put me under the table.

"No, no, no," I said into the phone, enunciating as clearly as possible. "It really needs to be a bunny. Who's ever heard of the Easter chicken?"

"Makes sense to me," the guy at the other end of the phone said. "Ya got eggs, doncha? So why wouldn't you have a chicken?"

I extricated myself from that conversation as quickly as possible, then immediately dialed Laura. Not for moral support. Not for suggestions. But for that most basic of primal needs—*whining*.

"It will all work out," she assured me. "Honest. These things always do."

"*How*? How do they work out? Timmy is convinced this party is all about him, I have a swarm of women descending on my house in three hours, demons are trying to kill me—which wouldn't be unusual except that they now have zombie cohorts, and unless I think of a solution fast, the kids are going to be getting baskets for the egg hunt handed to them by Freddy the Easter Chicken. Honest, Laura, I really don't see it getting better any time soon."

"Stuart," she said.

"Pardon?"

"Stuart is the answer to your prayers."

I held the phone away from my head and stared at it, as if somehow she would be able to sense my disbelief through the phone wires. "I love the man, don't get me wrong. And there have been times when I've thought that very thing. But if you think that Stuart is going to step up to the plate and spend hours on the phone locating an Easter Bunny for me, then you obviously haven't been spending time with the same man I married."

"Not finding," Laura said. "*Being*."

"Huh?"

"A costume, Kate."

"There are no costumes. There are no actors. There is a complete moratorium in the world on bunnies." I could hear my voice rising to a hysterical pitch. Zombie parts on my kitchen floor, no big deal. But toss me into a domestic crisis, and you'd think the world was coming to an end. Clearly, I needed to get a grip.

"Just leave it to me," she said.

"You're kidding, right?"

"Nope, totally serious. You concentrate on saving the

world. I'll concentrate on the bunny suit. It's my little contri-
bution to the fate of humanity. Besides," she added wryly,
"with Mindy gone, the house is empty, and I'm all alone with
my soon-to-be-divorced thoughts. Trust me. It's better that I
keep myself occupied."

"Fair enough," I said, because I'd be a fool to say anything
else. "But what exactly are you planning?"

"You'll see," she said, and as she did, I was almost positive
I heard a smile in her voice. And for some reason, that—more
than demons, more than zombies, more than freaky mystical
swords—made me very, very nervous.

Three hours later, I was on the floor in the playroom letting
Timmy use me as a highway for his trucks when I heard a
pounding on the back door. I left the kiddo to his trucks and
his Duplo blocks, stuck my head in Allie's room and asked
her to keep an eye on her brother, then trotted down the
stairs to find my soon-to-be-no-longer best friend standing at
the door clutching an in-progress bunny costume.

"Don't look at me like that," she said, holding up her free
hand. "You don't have to wear it. You just have to try it on so
that I can make adjustments."

"I'm not even close to Stuart's size," I protested, as she had
me pull on the pants she'd pinned together out of fuzzy gray
material. "How'd you do this so fast, anyway?"

"Honey, while you were gallivanting around the streets of
Rome, some of us were forced to learn how to sew and cook.
I may not be a total domestic goddess, but I've been making
Mindy's Halloween costumes for the last thirteen years."

"But it's only been three hours."

She waved a hand, indicating that was nothing. "Please.
Do you know how many times Mindy changed her mind
about her costume at the last minute? If I can turn a princess
into a penguin in one afternoon, I think I can manage to pull
together a rabbit costume from a pattern in three hours."

She had a point. And although I'd done the same for

Allie, our situations weren't exactly equivalent. When my six-year-old daughter decided that she didn't want to be a princess but instead wanted to be an octopus, I convinced her that because it was Halloween, she needed to be the ghost of an octopus. One white sheet, two holes, and a few snips of the scissors to make eight tentacles, and I was done.

And that's about as domestic as my personal goddess ever gets.

"Okay," Laura said, inserting another pin. "I think this is good. Now I need you to put on the top. I'm just checking the shape," she added when I protested.

I wasn't at all convinced, but I trusted her, then shimmied into the getup, careful to avoid the pins. Essentially, I was wearing a big gray hoodie. Later, I assumed, she'd add the ears, the cotton tail, and whatever other accoutrements this season's fashionable Easter Bunny was wearing. At the moment, though, I looked like something Kabit coughed up, big and gray and slightly fuzzy.

Naturally, the doorbell rang.

"Don't move. I'll get it."

Laura disappeared into my entrance hall, then returned almost immediately trailed by Marissa Cartwright and her hyperspoiled daughter Danielle. Behind them came Fran, her daughter Elena, and Betsy Muldrow from two streets over. Not the entire gang, but a darn good start.

"We'll be starting in the kitchen, of course," Marissa said, giving me a look that suggested that if I dared to argue, I was stupider than I looked. And considering I was wearing a bunny suit, I imagined I looked pretty stupid.

"Where else?" I said, my smile so forced it hurt.

A loud guffaw sounded from the top of the stairs and I looked up to see Eddie staring at my outfit.

"It's a costume," I said. "Not an evening formal."

"I ain't saying a word," he said, clomping down the stairs. He took a look around at all the women. "You girls working on that Easter party today?"

"Want to help?"

"Rather stick pins in my eyes," he said, a sentiment I understood completely. He turned around and headed back up the stairs, exactly the way he'd come, muttering something about his room, cable, and escaping a tornado of estrogen.

I watched him go, wondering how painfully he'd kill me if I sent all the kids upstairs to the playroom and then begged him to help Allie with child care.

Probably very, very painfully.

A timid knock sounded at the front door and I turned, momentarily distracted from my thoughts of tormenting Eddie. "Hello?" I peered into the foyer, saw Wanda Abernathy, and waved at her to come in.

"Lovely outfit, dear," she said sincerely.

"Thanks." I turned away and rolled my eyes at Laura. Apparently my fragile neighbor was now a comedian. "Are you on the committee?"

Wanda blinked at me. "Committee? Where do I sign up?"

"Never mind. I'll take care of it for you." I took her hand and led her to the living room. She might be a character, but she'd just saved Eddie's butt and he didn't even know it. Plus, the neighborhood kids loved her, primarily because she would sit on her front porch and wave to every child who passed, whether taking his first steps or zipping by on a souped-up skateboard.

Marissa shifted her weight from foot to foot, already antsy with all this wasted time.

"Fran and Betsy, you two come with me. Wanda, stay with Kate and get the kids organized." Marissa nailed me with an eagle-eyed glare. "Timmy is around today, isn't he? I brought Danielle with me because I assumed there would be social interaction."

She glanced sideways at Elena, who, apparently, wasn't sufficiently social to meet Marissa's demanding standards. Across the room, Fran met my eyes, and I didn't have to be psychic to understand exactly what she was thinking. For about five minutes last fall, we'd all ignored Marissa's stormtrooper-like approach to life. After all, she'd been traumatized by the fact that both our teenage daughters had been kidnapped and terrorized by teenage boys dabbling in some pretty bad stuff. (Okay, let's be honest: They'd been kidnapped and terrorized by demons, but Marissa and the rest of the committee members didn't have access to that pertinent piece of information. And though Allie remembered, Marissa's daughter JoAnn still had a blissful case of limited amnesia.)

At any rate, especially considering the guilt I feel whenever anything demonic touches one of my friends (or, in Marissa's case, acquaintances), I'd been especially conciliatory. But this was Marissa we were talking about, and it hadn't taken too long for her rough edges to slice right through my good humor.

In other words, I was back to hating the bi—

"Mom!" Allie called down the stairs. "Timmy wants to bring his train stuff down and I really don't want to carry it. Do I have to?"

Marissa sniffed. "I don't think Danielle would be interested in playing with trains. We're trying to promote her femininity."

I kept my mouth shut and concentrated on climbing out of the bunny suit without sticking myself with one of Laura's pins. "It's fine, Al. Just bring Timmy. We'll distract him down here."

"Maybe you could put something educational on television?" Marissa suggested. "I think Danielle's a little beyond Timmy in her stages of play."

A hand closed over my shoulder—and I decided I should probably be grateful to Laura for holding me back. The crypts might provide an excellent hiding place for demonic bodies, but I had a feeling Father Ben would frown if I shoved Marissa's moldy carcass in there.

"Television is out of the question," Wanda said. "I haven't liked a single show since *The Waltons*." She nodded firmly to the kids. "We'll play games," she announced, patting Danielle on the back even as she urged Timmy to come over from the staircase on which he was now cowering. He liked Danielle about as much as I liked Marissa. For that matter, I wasn't crazy about Danielle, either. She whined, griped, kicked, and bit. And on top of that, she invariably stole Boo Bear and forced Timmy into a near nervous breakdown. I try to be understanding and blame it on her mother, but when a pigtailed little tart is tormenting my baby, I don't much care if she's over forty or under four.

This time—yay me—I'd gotten smart and shoved the bear on the top shelf of Timmy's closet to be retrieved after the meeting broke up. In the meantime, though, Timmy looked like he'd been kicked in the stomach, being forced to endure the presence of his dreaded enemy without his absolute best buddy.

"I'll play, too," Allie said. "How about Candy Land?"

Timmy—being well-mannered and generally a pleasure to be around—bounced up and down, enthusiastically approving the choice.

Danielle—being the spawn of Satan (and I should know)—scowled and insisted on Lucky Ducks.

Elena—being pleasant and having a nonneurotic mother—smiled and clapped at every potential game presented to the group.

"Can't do the ducks," I said. "No batteries." And I didn't really want to listen to the quacking of a dozen ducks as they went around and around in a tiny circle.

"Candy's bad for you," Danielle announced, pushing Candy Land away with the tip of her finger, as if it were a sticky, twice-licked lollipop.

"Pretend candy's just fine," I said, undoubtedly setting Marissa's parenting back a solid nine months. Bummer.

I'm probably a horrible person for not having more sympathy for Marissa, but the truth is I hadn't liked the woman before her daughter was almost eviscerated by a demon, and I didn't like her now.

What can I say? At least I'm consistent.

My general disdain for Marissa was soon dissipated by the steady stream of women who flowed into the house over the next half hour. Soon, my kitchen was full of at least a dozen women all standing around, drinking coffee, gossiping, and doing nothing productive whatsoever.

"I brought champagne and orange juice," Candace Pritchard said. "That should make the work less tedious." Which, I thought, it would if we could finally get to the working part of the equation.

"Ladies! Ladies!" I began, trying to get their attention so that we could get moving with the projects and I wasn't forced to face a future with a dozen women living in my house. Not that anyone was paying attention to me.

A shrill wolf whistle cut through the din, and I looked over at Laura and smiled gratefully. With Laura playing the role of general, we eventually got everyone split into three groups—eggs, cookies, and baskets. I ended up in the egg group, which meant I sat at my table with three other woman and filled approximately seven million eggshells (give or take) with confetti, then glued little squares of tissue paper on top to hold the confetti in until that glorious moment when the egg was smashed over someone else's head. With my still-splinted finger, I was the slowest in the group, but considering I'd opened my house for the festivities, I didn't feel too guilty.

Laura and I had set up a card table with four chairs next to my regular table, and Marissa and her crew camped there, decorating the baskets Laura had brought.

Laura herself was working with three other women in my kitchen to make large chocolate chip cookies, which, once cooled, would become the outsides of ice cream sandwiches.

About half an hour into it, we'd actually made some serious progress, and by the time Wanda wandered into the kitchen to announce that she was completely worn out and going home, we were well over halfway done.

"Thanks so much for playing with the kids," I said, walking her to the door. "It was a big help."

"I know, dear," she said, patting my hand.

"Do you need help getting home?" She seemed pale and a little unsteady.

"No, no," she said. "I'm tired, not feeble."

"All right then," I said, but I stood at my front door and watched her walk home, just in case.

Her departure left Allie in charge of the little ones, but she seemed to be doing okay, and I returned to the kitchen. All in all, I have to confess that my urge to kill Laura for setting this up had faded. The whole day was actually kind of fun, even though the more mimosas we had the less work we got done, trading productivity for stories about our kids' antics and our husbands' cluelessness.

"Mommy! Mommy! Mommy!" Timmy's voice rang out through the house, loud and accusatory. I hurried into the living room, all set to witness one of little Danielle's moments of meanness. Instead, she was playing quite nicely on the floor with a coloring book and crayons.

"What?"

"Upstairs," he said. "Up. Stairs."

I looked to Allie, who shrugged. "I told him we're playing downstairs."

Timmy stamped a small foot. "Not playing. Miss Wanda go upstairs."

"Oh, sweetie, Miss Wanda went home. She wasn't feeling good and—"

I was interrupted by Eddie's howl of frustration, underscored by Timmy's determined shake of his head. "Right," I said. "I'll check it out."

I took the stairs two at a time and found Wanda with her hand on the door to the attic. "Wanda?"

She turned around, eyes wild. A second passed, then another. "The bathroom?"

Eddie tromped into the hallway. "Crazy old bat scared me to death poking her head in my room."

I glanced down the hall and saw that the door to my bedroom was open, though I was certain I'd closed it. "Wanda, honey, you went home, remember?"

She reached out for the attic door again. "I'm looking for the bathroom," she said stubbornly

"Right. Come on, then. I'll help you find it." I took her arm, surprised by the initial resistance before she relaxed and let me lead her toward the stairwell.

"Aw, hell," Eddie said. "I'll take her back." I goggled at him, amazed. On the whole, Eddie wasn't known for his sympathetic disposition.

He snorted. "Too many damn women in this house. I'll take her home, then walk to the library. Got a date tonight, anyway. Taking Tammy out for dinner." He winked at me. "With any luck, you won't be seeing me until tomorrow."

I forced a smile, quite certain that was more information about Eddie's private life than I really needed. "Tell Mrs. Gunderson I'm really, really sorry." I'd told him my tale of woe early that morning, expecting him to apologize for suggesting to all of the library workers that I was more than a little strange. To say that Eddie was unrepentant would be an understatement.

He waved a hand. "Don't worry about it. Probably the most exciting thing's happened to her in months."

I wasn't sure I wanted to be Mrs. Gunderson's most exciting thing, but considering Eddie had volunteered to take care of Wanda, I was keeping my mouth shut.

He led her back downstairs, and I aimed myself back toward the kitchen, where Marissa and Laura were cutting thin slabs of ice cream to press between two of the now-cooled cookies. "The kids are going to love those," I said. "For that matter, so would I."

"Ah-ah," Laura warned. "Can I trust these in your freezer, or do I have to take them home with me?"

I crossed my heart. "Promise," I said as I settled back in beside the table.

"So whatever happened to your self-defense class?" Betsy

asked. I'd bumped into her at Cutter's studio one day. Her thirteen-year-old daughter Alicia takes classes with him, and the girl had seen me spar. Rather than make up a complicated story, I'd made up a simple one, telling her I'd been practicing martial arts for years and trained with Cutter to keep my skills up. One thing had led to another and before I knew it, I'd suggested teaching a self-defense class to the neighborhood women. Considering the beasties that showed up in my neighborhood—often drawn here because of me—I figured it was the least I could do.

"I honestly haven't thought much more about it," I admitted. "I'm happy to do it, and I guess we could rent space at the clubhouse or use Cutter's studio. But do you really think anyone would sign up?"

Betsy looked at me like I was nuts. "Are you kidding? I'd sign up in a heartbeat."

"Me, too," chimed in Candace.

"You know I would," said Laura.

I glanced at Marissa, who turned and leaned against the counter as if considering both me and the proposition. "I'm in, too," she said. "I mean, it's a crazy world, out there. Anything that helps me protect my kids, and I'm jumping all over it."

She caught my eye, and I nodded. Maybe Marissa and I had more in common than I thought.

Fifteen

I spent the rest of Monday recovering from my mimosa head-ache, vegging with my kids, and trying to ignore how empty the house felt without Stuart. And, for that matter, without Eddie, who I could only assume really had gotten lucky.

Timmy and Allie and I played endless games of Scrabble (our version of it, anyway, as Timmy makes whatever combi-nation of letters he wants and gets points simply for naming the letter), then Tim and I settled in to watch *The Incredibles*, a movie currently high on Timmy's list of favorites.

To my surprise, Allie watched with us, even offering to make the popcorn. All in all, a lovely afternoon and evening, even if I made no progress whatsoever toward figuring out what the local demon population was up to.

Of course, I paid the price on Tuesday when I woke up to the realization that I should have spent Monday evening at the grocery store. I sat bolt upright in bed, jerked awake by the inescapable fact that I had T minus eleven hours and counting to Stuart's dinner party. And I really wasn't ready.

I considered taking Timmy to KidSpace, then remem-bered that they were closed for spring break, an anomaly that caused me no end of confusion. Wouldn't parents forced to work while their kids are in school need day care even more urgently during the breaks?

At any rate, it was just as well. Considering that the local demon population had shifted into overdrive, I preferred to have the kids nearby.

"Couldn't we have stayed home?" Allie moaned, not nearly as won over by the proximity thing as I was. She slunk down in her seat and did a good imitation of a rag doll with serious depression issues. "I can babysit Timmy long enough for you to go to the store. We've got locks and alarms, and I'm dead-on with a knife these days."

"This isn't about demons," I lied. "Can't I have some to-getherness?"

She looked sideways at me, and I started to regret the to-getherness thing. "Togetherness" at the grocery store usually transformed my normally well-behaved children into a tiny whirling dervish and a taller morbid teenager with the atti-tude of a death row inmate marching to the gas chamber.

Lucky me.

"So what have you learned about the sword?" I asked, hoping to bump her mood up a notch. Mine had already el-evated simply because of the mostly empty state of the park-ing lot. I got a prime parking space and, with any luck, the traffic in the aisles would be thin.

"Not much," she said.

"How about this enemy of mine who wants to become The One?"

"Same answer," she admitted, pulling out a shopping cart shaped like a blue race car and holding it steady while I strapped in her brother. "I've been reading through those re-ports you gave me, and you've got a buttload of enemies out there in demonland."

"Allie."

"Well, you do."

"Language."

"All I said was 'butt.' "

I aimed the mommy look at her, and she grimaced.

"Sorry. You have a whole bunch of enemies out there. Better?"

"Much," I said, though I silently conceded that "buttload" more accurately conveyed the scope of the situation.

"Anyway, it doesn't matter because it could be any one of them. I mean, all the bigwig demons seem to want to be super-demon-dude, you know?"

I did indeed.

"Well, keep at it," I said. "Maybe something will jump out at you."

"Hopefully not a demon," she said, then laughed at her own joke.

I fought my own grin and realized with a start that I was enjoying having my daughter follow in my footsteps. The insight gave me pause. I'd always told myself I wanted my kids to have a normal life. So why was I suddenly cultivating my teenage daughter's desire to get out there and fight the good fight? Was I being a good mom, factoring in my child's wants and desires while still trying to keep some semblance of control to keep her safe? Or was I being selfish, reveling in her desire to be like me and wanting to increase the bonds that tied us together?

I didn't know, and I can't say I much liked the question. At the end of the day, all I knew was that I wanted my kids safe and warm and alive. But with every day I allowed Allie to train to hunt demons, wasn't I taking a giant step backwards? Because no matter how much I told myself that she was only doing research, safely ensconced in her bedroom at home, the deep, dark truth was that a day would come when that wouldn't be enough. And on that day, she'd either listen to me or defy me, just like any normal teenager.

Unlike any normal teenager, though, defiance in the demon-hunting world could mean death. And that wasn't an endgame I even wanted to think about.

"Mom? Hello? Earth to Mom."

I jerked myself back to the present. "Sorry. What?"

"Shopping, remember? I asked if we needed veggies."

I shook my head. "Nope."

Her eyes widened. "So what are you feeding these people? Chef Boyardee?"

"Same idea, different class," I admitted. I'd told Stuart he could host a dinner party at the house, and I even said I'd cook, an activity that required all of my concentration to come out even remotely edible.

Because lately my concentration had been divided, I'd decided to take the easy way out. And that meant aiming the shopping cart to the specialty foods section. More expensive, but as they say in the commercials, I'm worth it. A sentiment I'm sure Stuart would agree with if he understood that his choice was between edible and delicious on the one hand and shoe-leather meat with squishy vegetables on the other.

The specialty counter was blissfully free, and as I ran through my menu choices with the girl behind the counter, Allie amused Timmy by pretending to be a traffic cop while he spun the steering wheel in his cart like a wild thing. Hopefully he'd give that up sometime between now and age sixteen. Either that, or I'd have to face the harsh reality that my little tyke was going to be driving in NASCAR.

"Okay," I said, once I'd filled the cart with an assortment of foil-covered trays and pans. "A few more things and then we're on our way home."

I stood there a second to get my bearings, and as I did, the phone rang. I checked the Caller ID then flipped the phone open. "Insanity central."

"You must be at the grocery store," Stuart said. "I tried home first and no one was there."

"Really? I expected Eddie home by now. He has more stamina than I give him credit for."

"Where is he?"

"Hot date last night," I said, and Stuart chuckled.

"I've got to give the man his props," my husband said. "He constantly surprises me."

"Doesn't he just. So what's up?" I asked, switching gears.

"Are you at the airport? I saw you on television yesterday morning. I'd say you have the female vote locked up."

"Good to know," he said. "And no, I'm still up north."

The cold chill of panic settled over me. "Could you repeat that?"

"Don't panic," he said.

"Too late," I countered. "You promised you'd be home in plenty of time to help."

"Kate, I don't have wings. They canceled the flight."

"Shit," I said, with absolutely no remorse about cursing in front of the kids.

"I'll be home by six forty-five. I swear."

"Oh, good," I said. "A whole fifteen minutes before people are scheduled to arrive. And here I thought I'd be doing the whole thing without you."

"I love you," he said.

"You better." I made kiss-kiss noises, then signed off, my mood deteriorating rapidly. The kids, perhaps sensing the approaching storm, stayed remarkably quiet as I steered the cart to the alcohol aisle. I wanted to stock up. Because believe me, as soon as the first guest arrived, I was making myself a cocktail.

After filling the cart with vodka, gin, wine, beer, and an assortment of mixers, I went searching for treats for the munchkin, planning ahead for the inevitable child bribery it would take to get dinner pulled together without ripping out all my hair.

"Cheddar Bunnies!" Timmy yelled, breaking his vow of ritual silence as we turned down the cookie and cracker aisle. "Please! Please! Cheddar Bunnies and round crackers!"

Round crackers were Ritz, and because I could justify buying those by also buying something to top them with (which would also reduce my guilt level as I would have "cooked" an appetizer), I agreed.

I tossed the crackers and the bunnies in the cart, then ran down my mental inventory. It was a safe bet we were out of milk, so I told Allie to hold the fort with her brother while

I scurried over to the dairy aisle to grab a gallon, all the while praying that Timmy wouldn't throw a fit.

No such luck.

I returned to hear my son's loud, indignant cry of "No, no, no! *Mommy!* Stinky! Stinky! Stop! Stop!"

I didn't have a clue what could possibly be stinky, but as I was sure the other store patrons weren't interested in hearing about Timmy's olfactory issues, I hurried the rest of the way into the aisle, my pace increasing exponentially when I heard Allie's sharp, panicked cry of *"Mom!"*

I raced around the corner, coming to a screeching halt when I saw Wanda Abernathy—no longer looking pale and feeble—standing right behind my son with a barbecue fork, courtesy of the accessories aisle, its tines pressed tight against my little boy's throat. A wave of nausea crashed over me, both from the danger to my son and from the fact that mere hours ago, this woman had been in my house. Had been alive and human and having fun with my children.

Allie stood stock-still about four feet away, obviously not sure what to do. Her eyes caught mine, and when she blinked, I saw a tear trickle slowly down her cheek.

It will be okay. No matter what, I was determined that this demon bitch wasn't hurting Timmy. No matter what, *that* wasn't happening.

I needed to do something fast, though. Right then, we were the only people in the aisle. If someone joined us, I didn't want to think what Wanda would do.

"Give me the sword and the boy lives," she said, in a sickly sweet version of Wanda's voice. "For the time being, anyway."

"What makes you think I have it?"

"You are the one. The prophecy foretells and the signs bring certainty. He comes, and the path must be cleared." She smiled then, the way Wanda had when she saw a child on the street. "Give us the sword or the boy dies. The choice is yours." She turned, looking hard at Allie. "The girl, too, though her death will come slowly. Painfully. One strip of skin at a time."

The blood drained from Allie's face, and I fought the instinct to go to her and pull her close. "Keep your filthy hands off my children."

"Give me the sword and I will," she said, Wanda's voice so sweet and clear it made me want to cry.

I looked at Timmy, so vulnerable. I don't think he would have been scared were it not for the stricken expressions on the faces of his mom and sister. But that was enough, and he was sitting perfectly still, tears streaming down his face.

Then again, maybe he did understand the danger; I'd never once seen Timmy sit still.

"All right," I said, getting more and more afraid that someone would soon join us.

"Mom!"

I held up a hand. "No. It's just the sword. It doesn't matter if they have it. I've stopped demons without an enchanted sword a hundred times over. I can do it again, I'm sure."

"But you—"

"I've made my decision, Allie," I said sharply. "I'm not risking your brother or you."

She pressed her lips together meekly, then looked down at the floor, presumably to hide her expression—finally!—of comprehension.

As for me, I looked at Wanda. "It's in my car. Seemed safer than keeping it in the house. That's what you were looking for, wasn't it? Not the bathroom."

"Clever girl," she said, as my heart squeezed tight. I understood everything now. Wanda's comments about being watched. Her ill health at my house. And her fumbling attempts to search for the bedroom.

Wanda had been in the demons' sights. They'd needed someone who could get close to me, not so much to fight, but to search. And when Wanda had passed away in her home after leaving my house—whether naturally or with a demonic push—a demon had stepped into the void, then returned, determined to find the sword that was supposedly hidden in my house.

"We go now," the abomination said, and I swear I hated the demons even more for violating the physical shell of that sweet old woman.

My keys were in my pocket, but I considered reaching into my purse for my knife. I could do it—I knew I could. But with Timmy right there, I didn't dare.

"Get it yourself," I said, tossing the keys in Wanda's general direction. And as Allie gaped at me, I said a silent prayer that she'd get with the program. With Eric, I wouldn't have worried. But though Allie might be his daughter, she was a long way from being my partner.

The demon reached up, taking a step back as she grabbed for the keys. As she did, I lunged for the cart, yanking hard and sending it rolling toward me.

Allie, bless her, got into the game, knocking Wanda's teeth out (literally) with a well-placed crescent kick that sent teeth and keys skidding down the aisle, ending up underneath a section of metal shelving.

Not to be outdone, I grabbed a bottle of vodka out of the cart, took aim, and hurled it at Wanda's head. It hit with a satisfying *thwack*, then shattered on the concrete floor.

That's when I really did reach for the knife, my hand closing around it before I realized that a body in the grocery store would cause more problems than it solved.

Wanda, realizing she'd lost her advantage, took off running. Allie started after her, but I lunged forward and caught her sleeve. "No. Let her go."

"But she—and Timmy—and—and—"

"I know," I said, rushing to unstrap Timmy and cuddle him close. "But let her go."

About that time, a guy wearing a red shirt with the store logo emblazoned on the breast pocket came tearing around the aisle, skidding to a stop when he saw the smashed bottle of vodka. "They said they heard shouts two aisles over."

"Some crazy lady tried to kidnap my brother," Allie improvised. "She was completely freaked out. And when we wouldn't let her take Timmy, she tossed a bottle of vodka at us."

"No kidding?" The kid looked to me for confirmation and I nodded. "Are you okay?"

We assured him that we were, and while the kid called for cleanup on aisle four, we beat a hasty retreat, pausing only long enough for Allie to lie on her belly and retrieve my keys.

Ten minutes and several hundred dollars later, we were all huddled in the van, now missing a front windshield because Wanda had apparently taken me at my word. Since the destruction of my vehicle had started happening on a more or less regular basis, I had my AAA card ready, along with the number of a local car rental place.

"Do you think she's coming again?" Allie said, once we were settled in the rental.

"Probably," I admitted. As long as the demons thought I had this sword, they were going to keep on coming. Unfortunately, they'd figured out—rightly—that the best way to get to me was to go through my children.

"That was *Mrs. Abernathy*," Allie said. "We knew her. Mindy and I used to play at her house." She pressed her lips together, her face tight.

"I know, baby."

"They can't do that. They shouldn't be able to do that. She was nice. She wasn't evil or mean or crazy."

"No," I agreed. "She wasn't."

"I'm gonna be sick," Allie said, looking a little green as she clapped her hand over her mouth. She wasn't, though, and after a moment, she took her hand away and looked at me with sad, serious eyes. "It just keeps getting realer and realer."

"Yeah," I said, stroking her hair and looking into her eyes. "Are you gonna be okay?"

She nodded, a little tentatively. "It's never going to stop, is it? Even if we get Mrs. Abernathy, I mean. It just keeps going and going."

"We will get her," I said. "And as for the other, that's the nature of evil. It's a rough wake-up call, I know."

"We can't stop, either, can we?"

"You can stop anytime you want to, baby."

She turned and looked wistfully back at the grocery store, then twisted in her seat to look at Timmy, who'd fallen asleep in his car seat. "No," she said finally. "I don't think I can."

"Eddie?" I called, as I trundled into the house, my arms full of grocery bags. "Can you give us a hand and I'll fill you in on the latest?" In addition to the news about Wanda, I wanted him on board with my car rental cover story—a fender bender in the grocery store parking lot.

No answer.

I grimaced, having a hard time reconciling Eddie with a wild night of dating.

"Mom," Allie said, her voice so tense and sharp that I grabbed a steak knife out of the block on the counter before turning to her. *"Mrs. Abernathy,"* she said, her face pale and her lips tight. "He walked her home last night. Remember?"

I did remember, and I was kicking myself for not remembering earlier. "Call David and tell him to meet me at her house," I said, then realized there was no way I was leaving her and Timmy alone, even to make a phone call. Not with Wanda wandering the streets. "Never mind. Call Laura." I grabbed the phone from her and did that instead, as Allie gaped at me.

No answer.

"Dammit!"

"Mom!" Allie said, heading toward the door. "Eddie! Come on!"

I hesitated. I didn't know what I was going to find at Wanda's, and I didn't want the kids with me when I found it. But at the same time, this could be a ruse of some sort. And if I left the kids alone—even with the alarm turned on and

Allie with her knife—I'd never forgive myself if something should happen.

"Dammit, dammit, dammit!" I hurried toward the door, swinging Timmy up to my hip as I passed by. "You stay right by me," I said to Allie, my voice firm. "Stray one inch—do one thing out of line—and you don't train for a month. You understand?"

She nodded, wide-eyed and serious. "I got it."

"Then come on."

We raced across the street, cutting diagonally to Wanda's house. I pounded on the front door, got no answer, then moved around to the back to repeat the process. Allie shadowed me, peering through windows and calling out for Eddie.

Nothing.

"Mom! Do something!"

My sentiments exactly, and without even worrying if the neighbors were watching, I slammed my purse through the window next to her back door. I reached inside, flipped the lock, and two seconds later we were inside.

"Bad Mommy," Timmy said. "You broke it."

"Sorry, kiddo. I had to. Now *shhh*. Mommy wants to listen."

I signaled to Allie to hold his hand and to follow, and she nodded, one hand clutching a steak knife, the other her brother's tiny hand.

As far as I could tell, no one was home. There were no signs of life, and the more rooms we investigated, the more worried I became.

"Maybe he really is with Tammy," Allie suggested, her own expression reflecting my fear.

I pulled out my cell phone and called the library, then asked to speak to Tammy. "This is Kate Connor," I said, after she came on the line. "I was wondering if Eddie was with you."

"Why no," she said. "He missed our date yesterday and—"

I hung up. Rude, but I've never been at my best when I'm frantic.

Allie's chin trembled. "Gramps isn't—"

"We're not thinking the worst until we have to," I said. "Do you understand?"

She nodded, then picked up Timmy and clung to him the same way she used to clutch her rag dolls.

"Come on."

"Where?"

"Once more through the house," I said, aiming straight for the closet under the stairs.

Wanda Abernathy, I soon learned, hung on to a lot of junk. But though I found everything from boxes of costume jewelry to bags of flyswatters, I didn't see any signs of Eddie. Not in the closets, not under the beds, not shoved into cabinets. Neither our search nor our calls turned up any sign of the man.

"The attic," I said to Allie, who'd been following on my heels like a puppy, her desperation as acute as my own. I tossed her my phone. "And call David after all. We need the help."

She nodded, her face still ashen, but her eyes alert and determined. As we hurried into the garage, she dialed while I tugged at the string to extend the ladder. It dropped down and I climbed up, clapping my hand over my mouth in defense against the dust and bits of insulation that fell on top of me. But though I crawled along the beams to every corner of the house, I still didn't find Eddie, and so help me, I was beginning to lose hope.

"He wasn't there," she said. "I left a message." Her expression began to crumble. "What are we going to do?"

"Keep looking," I said. "There has to be some—did you hear that?" I cocked my head to the side, looking around the garage.

"The car! Mom, he's trapped in the car!"

The only trouble with that theory was that Wanda drove a teeny-tiny hatchback, and I'd already peered inside when we'd entered the garage. Still, Allie was right. I could hear a faint thumping, and it sounded like it was coming from the car.

"Doesn't make sense," I said, opening the doors and crawling through the well-kept little vehicle. *"Eddie?* Can you hear me?"

"Gramps!" Timmy hollered. "Grampa! Grampa!"

"Gramps!" Allie added. "Are you in here?"

Another thump, and—yes—it was definitely coming from the car.

"Mom!" Allie said, on her belly on the garage floor with her brother right beside her. "Look!"

I bent down and saw what she was looking at—a thin line in the concrete with a tiny metal ring on one end.

"A crawl space," I said. "Come on."

I wasn't crazy about the whole neighborhood seeing us, but we didn't have a choice. We got Wanda's car into neutral, then eased the vehicle back into the driveway. Then we shut the garage door again. Nothing suspicious about a car parked in a driveway, right?

As Allie worked the garage door controls, I slid open the crawl space hatch, then looked down to find Eddie bound and gagged, with barely enough room to kick out. He'd managed, though, and it was his kicks that had finally alerted us to his presence.

I jumped down into the crawl space, alarmed by how blurry everything seemed before I realized I was crying.

"I'd give you grief about those pansy-ass tears," he said as I yanked off his gag, "if I weren't so damn happy to see you."

For a moment, I couldn't speak. Then Allie jumped down beside him and threw her arms around him so tightly, I felt the first hint of a smile through the tears. Above us, Timmy peered in, and I held up my arms, swinging him down to join the reunion with us.

"God, Gramps!" Allie cried. "We were so scared!"

"Not me," he said, squeezing her back. "I knew you'd find me."

The words were sincere, without a hint of Eddie's usual

curmudgeonly flair. And that, more than anything, told me just how scared he'd really been.

"Come on," I said, slicing through the rope that bound his wrists and ankles. "Let's get you out of here."

"What happened?" Allie asked, helping him up from the other side.

I climbed out first, then grabbed Timmy after Allie held him up for me. We found a step stool, then dropped it down to Allie so that Eddie wouldn't have to do acrobatics to get out.

"Got me right after I walked her home. Asked me to come in and check on something for her. Didn't think nothing of it and now I'm feeling like a damn fool, that's for sure."

"You and me both," I said, giving him a hand on the final step.

"Was the chewing gum that did it," he said. "Cinnamon. Didn't even smell a hint of that demon stench."

I didn't even have that excuse, because I hadn't noticed the gum. I *had* noticed her wandering my halls, but it was *Wanda*. Crazy, eccentric Wanda. People I knew didn't get turned into demons. It simply didn't happen.

Except it did.

For that matter, it had happened more times than I liked to admit, and I could still remember with perfect clarity the very first time that the body of someone I cared about had been breached. The way that Cami's body had mimicked the way she'd been in life, as if deliberately taunting me by tugging at my memory.

"We let our guard down," I said, hugging Timmy close. "And we shouldn't have."

"Good news is she's the only one they got," Eddie said, straightening slowly, the hours in cramped conditions taking their toll. "Least for the time being."

"What do you mean?"

"Heard her talking to herself. Either that or to her master. Don't know. All I know is that I overheard some damn fine intelligence."

"What?" Allie said, practically bouncing.

"Until Wanda went and had herself a heart attack, they were fresh out of bodies. The bimbo you got in the ladies' room was the last minion in San Diablo."

"But that's not right," I said. "There's that scuzzy guy that did this to me." I held up my finger for illustration. "Believe me, I'm looking forward to taking him out."

"Daddy already did," Allie said, and a few seconds later, her cheeks burned bright red.

"He did?"

"Well, um, that's what he told me."

"Good for lover-boy," Eddie said. "And it means I'm right. Wanda's the last. For now."

"That's good," I said, still surprised Eric hadn't mentioned Scuzzy's death to me.

"It's very good," Eddie countered. "Because whatever they're up to requires corporeal assistance. We kill off Wanda, and we may be able to stop them in their tracks."

"Too bad we don't know what that is," I said wryly.

"Can't help you there," Eddie admitted. "But I know this mysterious sword is a big honking problem for the demons. They're convinced you have it and that you're gonna bring some bad-ass demon down with it."

"Abaddon."

"Suppose so," he said. "And the fact that they think you have the sword is the only reason I'm alive to tell you this."

"A hostage," Allie said, her voice flooded with awe.

"Smart kid," Eddie retorted. "Now get me home. I want to change and go to the library. See if any of lover-boy's books got a mention of anything that might help."

During our life together in San Diablo, Eric had worked as a rare-books librarian, filling the library with unique and curious finds.

"Now?" I asked. "Eddie, you've been trapped underground for an entire day. You should rest. Drink water. Then rest some more."

He snorted. "Been sleeping for hours. Now I'm ready to

nail a few demon bastards to the wall." He illustrated the desire with a solid one-two punch, then a forward kick that knocked him sideways and into Allie, who managed to steady him.

"I don't know . . ." The one-hundred-eighty-degree flip from disinterest to a desire to castrate every demon in a fifty-mile radius was totally understandable. But desire wasn't worth a lot if he was going to get himself killed.

"What if you get light-headed?"

"I'll drink water."

"What if you pass out?"

"I'll take the youngster with me."

"Not with Wanda loose out there and pissed off, you won't. What if you ran into her?"

For that one, he didn't have a snappy retort.

"I'll think of something," he finally said.

"At least rest for half an hour," I begged, leading us all through Wanda's house and back across the street toward home. Allie's hand was clutched tight in Eddie's, and my arms were tight around Timmy clinging to my chest like a monkey.

"Half an hour," he said as I stuck my key in the door. "You want to stuff me full of food and water, you do it now," he said. " 'Cause when that timer goes off, I'm out of here."

"Fair enough," I said, pushing the door open to reveal Wanda Abernathy standing in the middle of my hallway, a crossbow aimed at my chest and a toothless grin on her wrinkled face.

Sixteen

"Holy crap!" Eddie said, rolling to one side with Allie even as I shoved Timmy to the ground, the arrow from the crossbow zipping out our open front door to embed in the kumquat tree growing in the front yard.

"You cannot stop him," Wanda said. "He will rise, and in rising, The One will have revenge. The One will have vengeance. And you and yours will surely fall as he rises, becoming whole and one through the becoming."

"What the hell does that *mean*?" Allie called, even as I whipped out with my purse, holding the handle as the bag caught Wanda at the ankles, sending her tumbling.

"Right now," I said, "you're the only one who's falling."

"Yes!" Allie said, scrambling forward and grabbing my keys off the floor where they'd fallen.

"Whoa there, missy," Eddie said, holding her back by the tail of her shirt even as Wanda was climbing to her feet, swinging the heavy wooden crossbow like a battle-ax.

"Bad lady!" Timmy said. "Bad, bad lady!"

"Damn straight," Eddie said. He grabbed one of the arrows off the floor and lunged forward.

"Eddie," I called, but it was too late. He was already there, and he was pissed. And though Wanda tried to put up a fight, it was no use. Eddie was a raging ball of fury.

Allie and I rushed forward to help, but it wasn't necessary. Eddie lashed forward with the arrow, sliding it deep into Wanda's eye even as I turned Timmy toward me, pressing his face to my chest.

"The bitch is dead," Eddie said. "About damn time."

No kidding, I thought, hugging my baby close.

I checked the clock: only two forty-five.

This was turning out to be a very, very long day.

Allie peeled back a foil corner and peered at the cannelloni inside. "Is it still good?" she asked, her nose crinkling.

With barely more than four hours until the hordes descended, those were exactly the kinds of questions I didn't need. "Of course they're still good. Why wouldn't they be?"

"Duh. They sat in the car while we went off and did . . . you know. Do you know how much bacteria can grow on food?"

"No, and neither do you," I said. "I saw the grade you got in biology."

She gave the meal another look of total disdain. "Well, *I'm* not eating it."

"No one asked you to," I said curtly. "And there is absolutely nothing wrong with the food."

"You'll feel pretty stupid when all of Stuart's contributors are dead of food poisoning."

"Go," I said, thrusting my finger out toward the living room. "Play with your brother. Clean your room. Read a book. Just leave. Now."

She complied, but a whispered *"salmonella"* drifted back toward me.

Teenagers.

Still . . .

I grabbed my laptop off the counter and moved it to the

table. As soon as the machine was awake, I navigated to Google and did a search for *food*, *car*, and *salmonella*. The results were less than illuminating, particularly as I saw nothing relevant right off the bat.

Not being the kind to poke around the Internet, I decided to approach the question the old-fashioned way. I called Laura.

"You're fine," she said after I'd explained the situation. "I swear you won't kill anyone. At least, not anyone human. What you do after the party I'm not responsible for."

"Very funny," I countered, as Allie wandered back into the kitchen, heading for the refrigerator, with Timmy trailing behind her, holding his sippy cup out like little Oliver begging for more.

"Need any help?" Laura asked.

"Believe it or not, I think I've got it under control."

"Really?"

"No," I admitted, holding Tim's cup while Allie filled it with milk. "But you've got a date with a doctor tonight, and I'm not about to beg you to come help me instead of primping."

"You're a good friend," Laura said, and I laughed, the sound cut off by Allie's own hysterical cackle. I looked over to find her not at the refrigerator returning the milk, but in front of my laptop.

"Ha!" she said. "You did believe me."

"I have to go," I said to Laura, who was savvy enough to have figured out what was going on, and was trying to smother her own hysterical giggles.

"You are *so* busted," Allie said, pointing to my very pathetic attempt at searching Google.

"Busted!" Timmy mimicked.

"Maybe," I conceded. "But I was right." I waved at the stacks of pans. "Totally edible."

She made a face, but didn't argue. Instead, she turned back to the computer, presumably looking for evidence to shore up her point of view.

"Give it up, Al," I said. "Come help me move all this stuff to my own pans. I want it to look like I've been slaving for hours."

"Um, I don't think so," she retorted, staring down her nose at me. "If you're gonna lie to Stuart about where his dinner came from, I'm *so* not helping."

If only that were all I'd been lying to Stuart about.

Short of grounding her again or bribing her with something on the level of a new car (or her very own crossbow), I couldn't see my way clear to persuade her to dish out cannelloni. Fortunately, it was the actual preparation of food that had me mostly stymied. Pretend preparation? That one I could handle all on my own.

"You got an e-mail," Allie said from her perch at the table. "Can I open it?"

"Who's it from?"

She clicked a few buttons, then looked up at me, eyes wide. "Father Corletti."

I debated making her leave so that I could read the e-mail in private, then decided to throw caution to the wind. She already knew I had raised her father from the dead; what could she possibly learn from Father Corletti that would be worse than that?

"It's a big document," she said, after I'd given permission and she'd clicked on it. "Hang on, I take it back. It's a picture."

"Of what?" I asked, transferring the rest of the entrée and putting the whole pan in the refrigerator. I'd put the reheating instructions in my purse somewhere. As long as I could find them, this dinner party thing would be moving in the right direction.

"Hang on. Oh. Look. It's the cover of some book."

"That's it?" I moved to peer over her shoulder, but the picture was gone, replaced by the text of the e-mail.

"He says they're scanning in the book for you and he'll send along a translation, too, since he knows your Akkadian is rusty."

She twisted around to look at me. "You can read Akkadian?"

"According to Father, I can't," I said, squinting at the screen. "So the cover of the book shows the symbol of the ancient tribe that forged the original sword." I made a face. "Somehow, I don't think they were native to San Diablo."

"So?"

"So what is Abaddon doing here? Why come if he thinks I'm waiting here, all ready with some magic sword to strike him down?"

She thought about that for a moment. "The beaches? With a name like San Diablo, we're probably a fine travel destination for your higher class of demon."

I smacked the back of her head with the dishrag I'd been carrying. "Open the photo and quit being a goof," I said.

"Yes, ma'am."

She clicked, but the photograph must have been huge, because it took forever to appear on my screen, loading one line at a time from the top down. "I thought you said we had high-speed Internet."

"Mother . . ."

I shut up, shamed by my utter lack of technological know-how, and started to go over every countertop with 409 instead. Timmy, bored, headed back into the living room to play with his train.

"Here we go," Allie said, and I immediately abandoned cleaning (any excuse) and headed back to the computer to examine the photograph of the illustrated book cover—an intricate line drawing of two hands holding a circle bisected by two intertwined lines.

My breath caught in my throat—I'd seen that symbol before.

"So what're we looking at?" Eddie asked, shuffling into the room, his hair damp and his face shaved.

"Mom got a picture from Father Corletti. All about the

tribe that forged the sword. But it doesn't look like anything helpful," she added, clearly disappointed.

I, however, had to disagree. "That symbol," I said, tapping the screen. "I know it."

"You do?" Allie asked, whipping around to see if I was serious. I was. Deadly serious.

"The fortune-teller at the carnival," I said. "She was wearing an amulet around her neck. *That* amulet," I added.

"Well, come on!" Allie said, jumping up.

"No, no, no," I said. "This isn't a family affair." It was one thing for Allie to be caught unexpectedly in the middle of a fight and to hold her own. It was something else entirely to walk headfirst *into* the fight. And believe me, I was expecting a fight.

"But Mom!"

"Dammit, Allie. I said no. Besides, I need you to stay here and research. This is the first solid clue we've gotten."

She made a snorting noise. "Like I'm gonna find anything useful on the Internet. I don't even know what words to punch into the search."

"Bet your daddy stocked that library with lots of picture books," Eddie said. "I'm heading that way. Why don't you come with me?"

She crossed her arms over her chest, sullen. "I'd rather go see the carnival lady. I bet Daddy wouldn't make me sit back and do research. He'd let me be in the field."

I opened my mouth, hoping a brilliant retort would fly out, but Eddie got there first.

"That demon-bitch smack you on the head and loosen your brains there, girlie? You know how many demons are out there? More than you'd ever be able to take down in the field. You want to be on the front lines and actually win, you got to know how to get the advantage. And how do you think you do that?"

"Research," Allie said, her voice small. "But isn't that what Mom's doing with the carnival lady? Asking questions and stuff like that?"

Smart girl.

Eddie tilted his head sideways and squinted at her. "Nice try, kid. But what do you think your mom's gonna do if that nice lady with the necklace ain't willing to talk?"

"Kick her ass?" Allie said, and Eddie snorted.

"I think that about sums it up."

"I'm not exactly Dirty Harry," I said.

"Who?" Allie said, making me feel a million years old. "And anyway, you're Kim Possible," she said, referring to the heroine in one Timmy's favorite shows. And one of my guilty pleasures.

I took being compared to a Disney cartoon heroine in the spirit it was given and told her thank you. Then I grabbed Eddie by the elbow and steered him to the living room. "I'm not sure this is such a good idea," I said, bending over to roll a stray train back to Timmy. "I mean you two going out. Especially after—well, you know."

"The girl wants to do something, Kate. And after that old bitch shoved me under her floor, you better believe I do, too."

"But—"

He held up a hand, his eyes more serious than I could remember seeing. "You can't keep her inside forever, Kate. And as long as you're in this business, she's gonna be in some danger. Hell, as long as you're alive. Seems to me the first time demons came knocking in San Diablo you weren't in business anymore, were you?"

"No, but Eddie, they kidnapped you. This is more than just a vague threat."

"That's exactly what it is right now," he said. " 'Cause for the moment at least, we got an advantage. There ain't no demons out there to nab her. Not till someone dies and some new beastie steps in."

"Could have happened already," I said, though in truth I doubted it. Not only did a demon have to be paying attention in order to make that moment-of-death portal, but the deceased also had to be of dubious faith. True, a lot of demons are out there roaming the streets, but it wasn't as if they were springing up as fast as dandelions in April.

"Decision is yours, girlie, but I'd give the kid some room. She's almost fifteen. How deep was the shit you waded into at that age?"

A lot deeper than anything we'd seen in San Diablo so far. Not that I acknowledged that out loud.

"We're gonna have crossbows in our backpacks, holy water in our sports bottles, and knives up our sleeves. Nothing's taking us down."

"That's not a promise you can make," I said, but the fight had gone out of my voice. The truth was, if she was in danger, she was in danger anywhere, including at home. And with Eddie, she was that much safer.

"I love the girl, Kate," he said. "I'd die before I'd let anything happen to her."

"I know." I drew in a deep breath. "Allie," I called. "Can you come here a sec?"

It took less than a sec for her to arrive at my side. "I can go?"

"With Eddie, never leaving his sight, and fully armed. I don't give a flip what signs the library might have about no weapons. You fill your backpack up, and you carry a bottle full of holy water. Anything weird at all, and you call me. Understand?"

"Yes, ma'am," she said, her expression stern, serious, and studious. She couldn't maintain it, though. About a second later, she tossed her arms around me. "Thanks, Mom. We're going to figure this out, I promise. And whatever Abaddon is up to, we're going to nail his sorry ass to the wall."

"Good girl," I said. "That's exactly the kind of attitude that keeps a Hunter alive."

"Am I a Hunter?"

I met Eddie's eyes, then shook my head. "No," I said

truthfully. "But as much as I might wish a different life on you, I think you're well on your way."

The satisfied smile that touched her lips told me I'd said the right thing. *Said,* maybe. The big question was whether I'd *done* the right thing.

And that was a question to which I really didn't have an answer.

While they packed up and headed out, I tried to make some slight progress on cleaning and dinner, wanting to take advantage of the relative silence while Timmy was occupied. But honestly I was too distracted. And although a wave of adrenaline from my supreme dinner-party phobia *should* have kicked in, so far my body was having none of it.

Apparently I'd made the right decision to buy the food premade, because I was clearly incapable of doing anything more involved today than putting food on a dish. And even that wasn't happening particularly artfully.

The phone rang, and I jumped for it, exhaling in relief when I saw that it was David and not Allie or Eddie.

"What the hell's going on?" he asked, frantic. "Is Eddie okay? Is Allie?"

"We're all fine," I said, bringing him up to date, as Allie's message at Wanda's house had been less than complete. "I let her go with Eddie to the library to research. That's okay, right? Do you think any of the books you brought into the collection will help?"

"Nothing jumps to mind," he said, "but I was bringing in everything I could get my hands on. I've got a pretty decent collection of materials over here, too," he said. "They can come here next if they don't find anything at the library."

"So I didn't screw up sending her to the library? I'm not hopelessly endangering her? I'm not a horrible mother?"

"You're a wonderful mother," he said, the softness in his voice affecting me like a caress. "And no, you didn't screw up at all."

"Thanks," I said, and for the first time since Allie and Eddie had left the house, I relaxed, having shifted a tiny bit of the weight of the world to David's shoulders. "Listen," I went on. "I've learned more." I started to fill him in on the amulet, and was just up to the part about the gypsy lady at the carnival when David's phone clattered to the ground.

"*Goddammit,*" he yelled, and then I heard nothing else except the sound of a struggle, cursing, and breaking glass.

"Eric!" I screamed. "Shit, shit, shit! I'm coming."

I raced into the living room and pulled a screaming, whiny toddler away from miles of train track. Said boy wasn't happy about the situation, and his screams of displeasure more than matched what I'd just heard over the phone from David.

Dammit, dammit, dammit.

I grabbed my keys from the hall table, flung open the front door, and screamed as a dirty, decaying, grime-covered zombie leaped on top of me, sending both Timmy and me tumbling to the ground. I rolled over on top of it, all the while yelling for Timmy to run, then pounded my fist into its face. "I. Do. Not. Have. Time. For. This." With each word, I pounded harder, releasing all of my fear and frustration onto my undead, animated corpse of an attacker.

Then, for good measure and because it's the smart thing to do with zombies, I stuck my splint through one eye and then through the other. After all, a blind zombie is a more easily controlled zombie—albeit more pissed off as well.

I grabbed Timmy and scurried into the kitchen even as the zombie stumbled to its feet, knocking down the table in the entrance way in the process. I dropped the kid on the floor, then grabbed the huge knife that Laura had insisted I buy—"it's great for cutting meat"—and raced back to the front of the house, carrying the knife by the handle with the blade exposed in exactly the manner I'd told Timmy to never, ever do with knives or scissors or anything sharp.

The zombie still had his ears attached, and he heard me coming. He lashed out and I slammed the knife down, managing to hack his hand off at the wrist so that it hung on by only a tiny bit of sinew. I made a mental note to thank Laura, then started whacking away like a madwoman, slicing at everything that moved, and doing my damnedest to get the creature down on the ground so I could manage some serious limb removal.

How I managed is a blur, but I know I fueled each thrust of the knife with a guttural yell. "You." *Hack.* "Are keeping." *Chop.* "Me." *Whack.* "From." *Pound.* "My *husband*." *Blam!*

Technically *first* husband, but why split hairs with a zombie?

At the end of the zombie massacre I found myself splayed out on the floor of the entrance hall, body parts squirming around me, and several new and unique scuff marks on the tile. Hopefully Stuart wouldn't notice.

After catching my breath, I ran around the house grabbing up body parts and tossing them in a laundry basket. Then I dumped the whole mess in the oven. What can I say? It was the only place I could think of that was safe. No way was Stuart going to come home and decide to whip up a hot apple strudel. Trust me on that one.

The zombie taken care of, I scooped up Timmy and raced out the door, cursing Abaddon, zombies, and hell in general.

With fumbling fingers, I got Timmy strapped in, then fired the ignition, gunned the rental, and peeled backward out of our driveway, mowing over the garbage cans by the curb in the process.

Shit.

Not that I was worried about the garbage. I was too busy worrying about David and trying to concentrate on driving despite the fact that I was terrified I'd arrive to find him dead.

"Don't you *dare* die on me, Eric Crowe. Not again. Don't you *dare*."

I looked both ways at the main intersection, but didn't bother to stop for the light. Instead, I gunned it, skidding around the corner so fast the inside of my van could have doubled for an amusement park ride. Or maybe not so amusing considering the way Timmy was howling.

"I'm sorry, I'm sorry, baby. I'm sorry." I repeated it over and over, unable to slow down and comfort my sobbing baby boy, and knowing that my own agitation was surely contributing to his desperate, heart-wrenching cries.

As I raced down the streets, I fumbled for my cell phone and called Allie. She answered on the first ring, which sent relief flooding through me. "Be careful," I demanded. "A zombie just attacked me, and if there's a zombie, then—"

"There's a demon controlling it," she finished. "Wow. Okay. We'll be on guard."

"And stay together. Don't you dare leave Eddie's side."

"Yes, ma'am."

In truth, the demon was probably nowhere near the library. Instead, he was probably near the beach, attacking David. I decided to leave out that little factoid, though. Better that Allie stay on her guard and not worry about her father.

After extracting a dozen more promises to be safe and watchful, I clicked off and returned all my attention to the road, banging the heel of my hand against the steering wheel when traffic slowed to a crawl.

In fact, traffic was so horrible that by the time I reached David's apartment near the beach I felt like sobbing right along with Timmy. I careened into the parking lot, then nearly collapsed with relief when I saw David stumble out of his second-story apartment, still in the throes of a cold, hard rage.

He saw me, and the violent lines of his face softened, his eyes shifting from the illusion of endless black back to the familiar silver-gray.

I gripped the steering wheel, almost afraid that what I saw wasn't real. But then he looked down at me from above. *I'm okay*, he mouthed, and my tears started in earnest all over again.

"Kate," he said, as soon as he'd reached me. "Kate, it's okay. I'm okay."

"You son of a bitch," I cried, pounding ineffectually on his chest. "You scared me to death."

His mouth quirked into an all-too-familiar smile. "And here I thought maybe you didn't care anymore."

"Don't even joke about that," I said, cupping my hand to my palm, simply because I needed reassurance he was still there. "You know it isn't true."

"I do know," he said, his eyes clouded with something I didn't recognize. "Sometimes that's the only thing that keeps me going."

I wanted to reach out, to hold him, but in the backseat, Timmy squirmed, a subtle reminder that I'd given my heart to another man. "Mommy?" my little guy called out softly, as if he were afraid if he talked too loud, his crazy mommy would gun the car engine again and go plowing through the streets of San Diablo.

I turned and gave him a smile. "You're being great, sweetie. I think I see a packet of Goldfish crackers in your future."

"Fishies?"

"For good boys? Absolutely."

"Yay!" The tears evaporated and the stricken expression disappeared. Life, it seemed, was easier at almost three. At almost forty? I had problems that cheesy baked crackers really couldn't fix.

I unbuckled myself and slipped out of the car, then stood in the open doorway, now on more even ground. It was an illusion, of course. My emotions could slip away with Eric at any moment, without any warning. But somehow being eye to eye, rather than seated and vulnerable, gave me a psychological advantage. I figured I needed it.

"What happened?"

"I almost killed him," Eric said, his voice flat. "I actually almost killed the son of a bitch. The little bastard attacked me and I wanted to take him out so badly, it was as if the emotion were a fire inside me."

Clearly, the demon had pissed him off more than I would have expected from an attack. What I didn't understand was why. "You're *supposed* to want to kill the demons," I said. "That's kind of our whole raison d'etre."

"Not a demon," he said. "I almost killed a human. And I did it," he added, looking me straight in the eye, "because the greasy little bastard tried to kill me first."

"Maybe your attacker was a pet?" I asked once we were in the car and speeding toward the carnival grounds to look for the gypsy lady with the Sword of Caelum amulet. "Working for Abaddon?" Demons use humans all the time, so the question wasn't off the wall.

"Not a pet," David said, his voice hard and angry.

"Dammit, talk to me. Why would a human attack you if he wasn't working for the demons?"

"I don't know," he said, but the words lacked conviction and I caught the way he tapped his cane on the floor of the car, as if his mind were only half with me.

"Eric," I said softly, a slow panic building. "What's going on? Is this about the Lazarus Bones?" The possibility ratcheted my fear into overdrive. Had someone learned of what happened and decided that David was an abomination? But how? And would they seek to punish me, too, as the hand that brought him back?

We drove in silence the rest of the way to the carnival grounds, me lost in guilt and fear, and David quietly staring out the window, his thoughts clearly far away.

We parked illegally along the shoulder of PCH, then marched the short distance to the gypsy lady's tent, me carrying my son clutched in my arms, and David and I both praying that the woman was still there.

She was.

"You," she said, looking up from where she sat behind a table draped with silk scarves and topped with a crystal ball on a small gold stand. Her gaze cut sharply to the left, focusing on David, who'd stepped inside right after me. "And I see you have brought a friend."

"Who are you?" I demanded, shifting Timmy to one hip so I could reach in my purse for my knife. "And don't lie. I want to know about the Sword of Caelum."

"I know nothing about a sword, Kate," the woman said, her words firm and her eyes fixed on my face.

I lifted my chin, wary. "Then tell me what you do know. Other than my name, that is."

"I know him," she said, pointing an accusing finger over my shoulder even as I heard David's sharp intake of breath.

I whipped around to find a bruised and bloodied Dukkar behind David, the sharp edge of a knife pressed right against his jugular.

"His name is Eric Crowe," the woman continued. "And the blackness clings to him like night."

Seventeen

Her words stung, but that didn't slow me down. I dumped Timmy on the ground, then launched myself across the tent, yanking the old lady around and getting my arm across her neck.

"Mommy!" Timmy screamed.

"It's okay, honey. Mommy's only playing." To the woman, though, my words held a stronger tone. "I don't normally kill humans," I whispered into her ear. "But today I'll make an exception. Let him go."

"I would willingly die to ensure that the vile beast does not live," the woman said, which wasn't particularly encouraging.

Still, her companion didn't have the same fortitude, and I saw the hesitation in his eye and saw the tension in his knife arm ease. David must have felt it, because he shifted slightly, then brought his elbow back and into his captor's gut. It was a risky move—one that could easily have gotten him killed—and I shoved my own captive forward, hoping that by knocking her to the ground, I'd distract the man even more.

David anticipated my maneuver, and as soon as I gave the woman a shove, I saw him thrust his body backwards, knocking down his already unsteady captor. Meanwhile, I stepped in front of Timmy, protecting him in case the old lady got any ideas.

David had already burst into motion, yanking the sword hidden in his cane free and jamming the tip up against the battered man's neck, even as his foot came down hard on the man's rib cage.

I grabbed Timmy's hand, tugging him along with me as I retrieved the man's knife from the ground, and then I bent down and pressed it to his throat as David took a step back. That close, I could see even more clearly the damage David had done to this man after Dukkar had attacked him in the apartment. His face was swollen and purple, his lip split, and chunks of hair were missing.

I winced, but forced myself not to feel sympathy. *He'd* attacked David, after all.

David helped me yank the man to his feet, and we stood there together. Me with one hand holding my son and the other with a blade at the ready. David set to defend us with his cane.

"Talk," I said, as David took Timmy's hand and pulled him back, letting me focus entirely on my hostage and the woman with whom I was bargaining. "I haven't got the slightest problem killing a demon's pet."

"Pet?" Timmy repeated, and I forced myself to tune out my toddler. Undoubtedly this entire incident would result in years of therapy down the road, but at the moment there wasn't much I could do about that. As long as I got us all out of here alive, I'd consider the afternoon a success.

"No problem killing a demon's pet?" the woman repeated, her eyes not on me, but on David. "Is that a fact?"

"Don't even think about playing that game," I said.

"You trust him?" she asked, eyes narrowed at me. "That one with the stench of evil upon him?"

"Shut up," I said, my voice low and dangerous. "This isn't about him, it's about you. It's about the sword. And it's about who the hell you people are."

"We are like you," she said in a low, even tone. "At least, we are like what we believed you to be."

"And what's that?"

"A Hunter, of course. One who seeks out and destroys evil no matter where it might breed. A different method, perhaps, but the results will prove the same."

"What method?" I demanded.

"Release Dukkar," she said. "Release him, send that one out of the tent, and we will talk together."

"David stays," I countered. "And I'm not taking this knife off his neck until I like what I hear." I shot a sideways glance to David, who nodded, but his stormy eyes never left the woman's face.

Something was going on under the surface, and I didn't know what. All I knew was that these freaks were my only lead on what the demons had planned, and there was no way I was backing off from my advantage.

"What method?" I asked again.

"We wait for the one," she said. "We wait. We watch. We see."

"The one?"

She inclined her head. "One who needs our assistance. Dukkar provided such aid at Emeralds, did he not?"

"He did," I admitted, though grudgingly. "But he was only there in the first place because you people have been following me around. Watching me."

"We watch you still," she said. "And we see much."

"What?" I demanded, surly because we were getting nowhere. "What do you see?"

"You," she said. "You are unsure. Remorseful. It clings to you, a sour stench infiltrating your very essence. Trust your instincts, Kate. You know that you are right."

"All I know is that you're not telling me a damn thing," I said. "What do you know about the Sword of Caelum?"

"I know only what I have heard and seen."

"From me," I said.

"From the one you killed," she said. "Thoughts linger. They cling. And it is the way of my kind to read the essence left behind."

"English, please."

"She's saying she's psychic," David said. And what I thought was interesting was that he didn't say she was full of crap.

"*Enough,*" I said, as irritated by the direction of my thoughts as I was with this crazy woman. "What are you talking about? Who did I kill?"

"The demon, of course. The one called Watson."

And that was when the light dawned. "*You* took the body," I said, even as Timmy started to hum his dead-demon "Jingle Bells" tune.

"It was necessary in order to gain the insight. They come, and the window to stop them closes with each passing moment."

I made a face. "Woulda been nice if you could've taken the hacked-up zombie, too."

"The zombie was useless. There is no essence. No spirit force to linger and read."

"All right," I said. "You've caught my attention. What did Watson have to tell you?"

"Vengeance," she said. "Revenge. Both against you and yours."

"*Bzzzt!*" I said, impersonating a game show buzzer and making my son laugh. "Thanks for playing, but that's old news. Watson told me as much himself. Why don't you try telling me *who* is coming."

"He who destroys," she said. "He who decimates. Once defeated, but not suppressed."

"You're not exactly batting a thousand today. Also old news," I said. We'd figured out that Abaddon the Destroyer was coming days ago.

"He comes," she said, swaying on her feet, her voice taking

on an ominous singsong tone. "He comes with his brethren to strike us down. To prevail over what has been written and turn prophecy into folly."

I opened my mouth to tell her to cut the bullshit, but then David's hand closed on my shoulder. "No," he whispered. "Look at her face."

I looked, and saw that he was right. As nutty as our gypsy lady might be, she also seemed to have fallen into a full-blown trance.

"In the shadow of the Lord," she continued, as the man to whose throat I held a knife crossed himself. "As day falls into night. The desecration of the hallowed eve when the sanctified blood has flowed. On that eve shall it flow first. And one shall augment the other and the prophecy shall be no more." Her eyes popped open, bloodshot and swollen. She opened her mouth as if to speak, said nothing, then collapsed in a heap on the ground.

"What the—?"

"She recalled the demon's essence," my captive said. "It is exhausting to be defiled in such manner, the edges of her mind touching something even as minuscule as the remnants of thought. She will rest now."

"But what about the sword?" I asked, keeping the knife point on his neck. "She has the amulet."

His mouth curved into an ironic smile. "The design of the necklace is quite common. An ancestral symbol, yes. But also a decorative item." He waved a hand to encompass the Bedouin-style tent, like something out of *Lawrence of Arabia*. "It is all trappings, yes? Designed to entice those who seek into the tent."

"Seek what?"

His shoulders lifted in a deep shrug. "That depends on the person. What do you seek, Kate Connor?"

"I already told you that. I'm looking for the sword. A sword that can wipe out demons. A sword forged in ancient times by a tribe that wore that symbol."

"I am sorry our information disappoints," he said, bowing his head in apology despite the blade I still held (albeit with considerable lackluster) at his throat. "But I have no more help to offer you."

He took a step back, and I let my knife hand drop. We were done here.

"Go now, and you may leave this tent without incident. Stay, and I cannot guarantee that either of you will survive."

Big talk considering I was the one with a knife, but I wasn't inclined to argue the point. The time for demons was over. I had a small child to comfort and a dinner to prepare.

"I don't think I've ever seen you that still," I said to David when we were back on the road. Timmy had fallen asleep in the car seat, and though I'd started the drive in silence, I couldn't keep it up. "For that matter, I've never seen you that quiet." I wanted to say more, but the words wouldn't come, and my own hesitancy scared me. This was David, after all. No, this was *Eric*. The man with whom I'd shared all my secrets.

Now, though, my nerves were frazzled and shot. For months, I'd feared I'd somehow tainted his soul by playing God with the Lazarus Bones. Now, it seemed, I had confirmation in the frantic ramblings of a crazy gypsy woman.

"Not too much I could say to those people," David said. "Silence seemed the best plan."

"You could have told them they were wrong," I said, my voice low and my eyes on the road.

"I could have," he said. "And I'm sure they would have believed me." He paused, waiting for me to look at him, I'm sure, but I couldn't do it. Not when I knew he'd see doubt in my eyes.

After a moment, he sighed. "Kate, they didn't trust me. You needed information. I was completely out of the equation.

Forcing my way into the scenario would have made things worse. Not better. At least now you know something."

"Do I?" I said, thinking more about the woman's accusations than her revelation of Watson's talkative essence. "I'm not sure that's information I want to have."

I clenched my hands on the steering wheel and looked straight ahead, hoping my thoughts didn't show on my face. I should have known better.

"Katie," he said, his voice so gentle I couldn't help the tears that spilled from my eyes.

"I did something, didn't I? I did something to you when I brought you back and you've been afraid to tell me. Or else you don't know. Either way, oh God, Eric. I'm so sorry."

I sniffled, then wiped the tears with the back of my hand.

"Pull over, Katie. Pull the van over, okay?"

I nodded, snuffling, then did as he said. As soon as I'd shifted into park, he moved from his seat toward me, lifting me easily and settling himself underneath me. I didn't protest. Far from it, I welcomed his touch. I needed to feel him, to know that he felt strong and solid and good. To know that I hadn't tainted him so badly that the sin rubbed off from the slightest contact.

"What have I done to you?" I whispered, my face pressed against his chest. "I was so selfish, so stupid."

"*No*," he said. "You didn't do anything to me. Nothing, Kate. *Nothing.*"

"Then why—"

"How the hell do I know?" he said sharply. "Do you know that lady? Do you know Dukkar? Because I don't, and they don't know us, either. Yes, you used the Lazarus Bones. Yes, you were probably weak and selfish. But Kate, sweetheart, why on earth would that taint my soul?"

"I don't know," I admitted. "But we're not talking about earthly things."

"Do you trust me?"

I pressed my lips together, hesitating only a second, but it was enough. He noticed.

"Yes," I hurried to say. "Yes, of course I do." I meant it, too. I truly did. But in that brief hesitation, I wondered if I'd lost some of *his* trust.

"Then believe this," he said. "You did nothing to me. The Lazarus Bones did nothing to me. You hold no responsibility for the fate of my soul. I swear."

"Eric . . ." I pushed back, my hands on his chest as I searched his eyes.

"I'm the same man you married, Kate. I promise."

I let that soak in, liking the sound of it, even though I knew it wasn't true. "You once told me you weren't," I reminded him.

A hint of a smile flickered over his mouth. "The shell has changed," he admitted. "The rest is the same." He closed his eyes, his body tense. "If you think it's not hard . . . knowing you've moved on, and I'm stuck, an outsider in my wife's life. You think you harmed me by bringing me back? You didn't. Not any more than you harm me each day by going about your life. Because it's hard, Katie. It's so God-damned hard."

"I know it is," I said, barely able to find my voice. I wanted to say more, but there was nothing else to say. Our life was what it was. Words of comfort wouldn't change anything, and words of love would only make the chasm between us harder to tolerate.

"Drive, Kate," David said, sliding out from under me. "That life you have needs you."

"David," I said, stung by his harsh tone.

"I'm sorry." He strapped himself back into the passenger seat and held up his hands. "Honestly. I'm sorry. But like I said—it's hard."

I bit back a retort. He already knew it was hard for me, too, and we'd been over that ground ad nauseam. The bottom line was that he was right. At the moment, a looming dinner party took precedence over any domestic problems I might be having with my first husband.

"About that," I said. "I kind of need a little favor."

"Oh?"

"Casual dinner party. Political chitchat. Not the kind of thing you want interrupted by stray body parts."

"And you're worried about body parts because?"

"I had a visitor right after you called. And since I was in a hurry to get to you, I more or less dumped the parts in the oven."

His mouth twitched. "More or less?"

"Okay. More."

"Frankly, this changes my whole perspective."

I looked at him out of the corner of my eye, suspicious. "What?"

"Your dinner party," he said. "I'm thinking I'd just as soon avoid a dinner where the food's been cooked up close and personal with body parts."

"Hmmmph," I retorted. "I'll have you know that is absolutely not the case. Gelson's is cooking, not me."

He laughed. "Now *that* is the Kate I remember. And here I thought old Stuart had domesticated you."

"Not a chance," I said, fighting my own smile.

We swung by his apartment so he could get his car, then headed in convoy formation to my house, arriving right as Eddie and Allie were coming up the sidewalk. Allie picked up her pace, then flung herself into David's arms the moment he stepped out of the car.

I cringed as I unstrapped Timmy from the car seat, then glanced around to see if any of our neighbors were watching—especially neighbors with high school students who knew full well that David was the chemistry teacher and not the uncle I was so tempted to fabricate.

"Come on, guys," I said, putting my sleepy son down on the driveway. I waved my hands to herd the crowd toward the door. "Let's get inside and you can tell us what you learned."

Allie pulled away with a frown. "Nothing," she said. "All sorts of stuff about Abaddon, but nothing we didn't already know. He has a history of seeking an invincible form on this earth. Never achieved it—duh. Tends to forge alliances with other demons, which I guess is kinda rare."

"Demons aren't exactly buddy-buddy types," David acknowledged. "So that's something."

"Except here, his allegiances are all lower demons or animated body parts. Good information," I told Allie. "But not—"

"The answer. Yeah. I know. It sucks."

Eddie snorted. "Gal seems to think she's gonna find all the answers in one trip to the library."

"Doesn't work that way, kiddo," David said, swinging his arm around her shoulder even as he hoisted Timmy up on his hip. "Wish it did."

"Did you used to do lots of research?"

"Are you kidding? Why do you think the library has all those books? Your mom liked to jump in and kick some butt. Me, I'd step back and learn all the facts first."

"Oh, thanks a lot," I said, unlocking the front door and pushing it open for the troops. "You make me sound like Lara Croft or something."

"No way, Mom," Allie said. "She always did *tons* of research first."

I grimaced as they passed, biting back a smile when David winked at me.

"Oh, hell." I stared at the foyer—a complete and total disaster after my battle with my untimely zombie friend. "No, no, no," I said. "This isn't good. I have people coming in exactly"—I consulted my watch—"two hours and thirteen minutes. A messy house is simply *not* part of my game plan."

David and Allie shared a look. "She overreacts sometimes," my loyal daughter said.

"I know," he assured her.

"Overreacts?" I repeated, indicating the mess. "Excuse me?"

"It's a knocked-over table, Mom. I think we can handle it."

"Maybe," I said grudgingly. "But the living room still needs to be vacuumed and dusted, and the dining room table needs to be set. Not to mention the food that needs to be prepared—"

"I thought you went to Gelson's," David put in.

I shot him a look through narrowed eyes. "It still needs preparation," I said, and he held up his hands in surrender.

"What do you say, troops?" he asked, jostling Timmy. "Shall we help Mommy not have a nervous breakdown?"

"Yeah, yeah!" Timmy said.

"I guess," said Allie.

"Hell no," said Eddie. "I didn't make the mess. I'm gonna go watch *Cops*."

"Gramps is like that," Allie announced to Eric. "But I guess you already knew that if he's your great-grandfather, right?"

"It's amazing what I don't know about my own family," David said, without missing a beat. I made a mental note to later ask him if I'd ever bothered to tell him I'd set Eddie up as his curmudgeonly great-grandpa. The lie might not hold, but now wasn't the time to confess all.

"Foyer," I said, pointing to David. "See if you can get the drawer back in the table, and if you can't, turn it so the gaping hole faces the wall and shove everything from the drawer into the hall closet."

"Aye-aye, Captain," he said, saluting and making Allie laugh.

"You," I said, pointing to her. "Pledge and a dustrag."

She saluted as well and went to work in the living room. I gave Timmy the Swiffer mop and let him dust the hardwood floor. Miraculously, no one complained. I should invite David over to do housework more often.

"It's a stupid prophecy," Allie announced, after she'd tackled most of the wooden surfaces in the living area. "If Abaddon thinks you can kill him, then all he has to do is never become corporeal."

I had to smile. Never in all her younger years had I anticipated a conversation with my daughter about the corporeal or noncorporeal nature of a demon. "Of if he does," she continues, "he should stay away from you. Like go to Alaska or something."

"The truth is, though, that we haven't heard the actual

prophecy," I pointed out. "If we ever manage to track that down, maybe we'll have a better understanding."

"Maybe," she said, sounding dubious. She looked around the living room, then held up her dustrag. "So what now?"

"Actually, it's looking pretty good," I admitted, amazed we'd pulled the room together so fast.

"So we're done?" Allie asked.

"I think so."

"Why doesn't Allie come home with me," David said, ignoring the way I turned and gaped openmouthed at him. "That way she'll be out of your hair for the party, but you'll know she's safe."

"*Yes!*" Allie screamed, jumping into one of her cheerleader routines. "I am *so* there!"

She turned and raced up the stairs, her little brother following at her heels. I waited until her footsteps faded and then grabbed David's elbow and tugged him closer. "What are you doing?" I asked. "We talked about this. Twice, in fact."

"I'm sorry, I'm sorry. We can call her back down and tell her no."

I started to say that we absolutely would do that, but I couldn't get the words out. "I can't do that now," I said. "The cat's out of the bag. Tell her no now, and she'll be morbidly depressed for the next century."

"I really am sorry," he said, but his expression didn't match the words. "I didn't think."

"No," I agreed. "You didn't." I drew in a breath, forcing myself to calm down. It was only fair that Eric got to spend time with Allie and vice versa. I knew it, and I wanted it. Truly.

What I *didn't* want was the situation thrust on me when I was unprepared. Too late for that now, though, and as long as I had an explanation made up by the time Stuart go home, I supposed I'd survive.

Surviving, after all, was what I did best.

Eighteen

With Eddie asleep in the recliner and Timmy plugged in to *Curious George*, I dove into party prep mode, my intensity fueled in large part by my frustration level.

Trust.

David knew I hadn't made a decision about Allie staying with him, and yet he'd deliberately raised the issue in front of her. Yes, I understood he desperately wanted to spend time with his daughter, but he'd blindsided me. And it wasn't the first time.

Irritated, I crunched up a wad of foil and hurled it across the room, then screamed when I saw it whiz past Stuart's face.

"Oh my God!" I pressed my hand over my thudding heart. "You scared me to death." And not just because I'd almost nailed him in the face with a tinfoil projectile. What if he'd been here half an hour earlier? Seen David? Overheard any of our conversations? "What are you doing here, anyway? Shouldn't you still be in the air?"

"Rough day?" he asked, coming closer and sliding his arms around my waist.

"You could say that," I said, melting against him. "Yeah, I think that *rough* definitely sums it up." I tilted my head back and squinted at him. "Seriously, why are you here? Your plane isn't supposed to have even landed yet."

"Would you believe me if I said I moved heaven and earth to get to you?"

I cocked my head, looking into his eyes as I considered the question. "Yeah," I finally said. "I think I would."

"Then that's what I did," he said, kissing the tip of my nose. He pulled back and glanced around the kitchen, still in a state of organized disarray. "So what do you need?"

I considered the question, suddenly feeling more grounded and in control than I had all day. "Not a thing," I said. "Right now, the only thing I need is you."

Since Stuart first got the public office itch, I'd gone to innumerable cocktail parties hosted at various homes and other venues around the county. And, yes, I'd hosted a few of my own. My first had been a disaster. In addition to having one too few wineglasses (thanks to a last-minute need to use the stem of one to take out an uninvited demon), I'd made a fool of myself by trying to drench with holy water a judge that Stuart was trying to impress. On top of that, I'd almost forgotten the cocktail napkins and I'd come *this* close to burning the pasta sauce.

Most important, I'd been an absolute space case in the kitchen.

To say that I'd improved dramatically would be what we in the mommy business like to call a fib, and what we grown-ups call an out-and-out lie. But I had improved a tiny bit, and as I efficiently pulled cocktail napkins and frilly toothpicks from their designated place in the sideboard, I couldn't help but mentally applaud my social togetherness. I wasn't Rachael Ray, but at least I was a step up from Lucy Ricardo. For me, that was saying a lot.

After a quick shower, I changed into one of the cocktail

dresses that had been filling my closet ever since my husband turned politico. I did what I could with makeup and hair, considering I lacked the cosmetics gene, then hurried back downstairs.

As I ran around fluffing cushions and picking lint off the backs of chairs and trying to look like I'd actually cooked the meal rather than simply unpacked it, Stuart took Timmy upstairs and settled the little dude in for the night. Not that the kid was happy about a six forty-five bedtime, but sometimes you have to make sacrifices for the good of the family, and I'm sure Stuart was making a point to drive that lesson home to our little man.

I also took advantage of the fact that there was half a house between us to call David. I told myself I was being responsible and maternal rather than paranoid and freaked, but either way, my fingers were dialing. Unfortunately, no one was answering, a little fact that didn't do my nerves one bit of good.

"Calling Laura for backup?" Stuart said, sneaking back into the kitchen.

"You're rather light-footed today," I said, frowning at him. I had enough critters creeping around the house; I didn't need my husband added to the mix.

"I wanted to surprise you," he said. He made a twirling motion with his finger, then eased up beside me and kissed the back of my neck. "Hold up your hair," he murmured, then slipped a chain around my neck. "I know you wear your crucifix," he said, "so I got a longer chain on this one. The lady at the store said it's very fashionable to wear two necklaces at a time."

"Did she?" I asked, my fingers caressing the two intertwined strips of gold, coming together to form an abstract heart. "It's beautiful."

"It's supposed to represent love. Togetherness. Life intertwined and all that mushy stuff."

I hung my arms over his shoulder and raised my face to his. "I like that mushy stuff," I said. "And I love you."

"That's what I like to hear," he said, then kissed me, soft and gentle and yet somehow demanding, too. As if the necklace were a commitment, and he'd just sealed a promise with his kiss.

The doorbell rang as we broke from the embrace, and I watched as Stuart's face shifted from the man I loved to the man of the people. He turned and took my arm, and together we went to the foyer. "You're going to win, you know," I said. "How could anyone resist you?"

He turned to me, and I saw a shadow in his eyes. "You may be right," he said. "At least all our pollsters are saying the same thing."

A little tingle of alarm sang out, making me uncomfortable for reasons I didn't understand. "You disagree?"

He lifted a shoulder even as his grin revealed a single dimple. "Let's just say that I acknowledge the election is mine to lose."

Now I'm a veritable connoisseur of cryptic comments, and as those things go, that one ranked way up there. But I didn't have time to inquire because Stuart pulled open the door and I was thrust into über-hostess mode, greeting and serving and making the kind of inane chitchat that I'd actually become somewhat proficient at over the last few months. To be honest, I don't even mind it that much, which was not a statement I'd ever thought I'd make when Stuart first told me he was running for office.

Then, my instinct had been to hide under the bed until after the election.

Today, though the timing was inconvenient, the party really wasn't much trouble at all. I circulated, paying special attention to Stuart's boss and mentor, Clark Curtis. Then I said hello to everyone who actually worked on Stuart's campaign, then did the schmoozing thing with the newbies—everyone Stuart was trying to win over.

I've never taken an exit poll, but as far as I can tell, nobody has met me at one of these parties and then run away screaming, swearing never to vote for Stuart. In the land of politics, my understanding is that makes the party a raging success.

For the first thirty minutes or so, the cocktails flowed freely, the guests mingled, and I checked occasionally on dinner. I'd made the mistake of buying a meal that had to be reheated—a decision that wasn't a mistake until I hid a zombie in the oven. But I swear I checked the oven completely for stray fingers and toes and found nothing.

Besides, it's like what I tell Timmy if he finds a gnat in his yogurt. Extra protein.

Not that I was seriously concerned. The body was off with David—wherever *he* might be—and I needed the oven for party central.

I'd met Martina Brentwood at a party a few weeks earlier, and she popped into the kitchen to give me a hand as I was tossing the salad. Because I was happy for the help, I let her circulate, wrangling everyone to the table with the announcement that the meal was ready.

The first course passed without incident, which is good considering salad really shouldn't cause all that much trouble.

The main dish, though . . .

I divided the dish onto two platters, and Martina carried one in as I carried the other, assuring Stuart that he should attend to his guests at the table and not worry about the food.

We were in our rarely used dining room, and I squeezed behind five chairs to get to the end of the table nearest the window. I put my platter down in front of Stuart right as Martina set hers down at the opposite end. As she did, she let out a howl that could have shattered glass.

"Oh my Lord," she cried, even as I grabbed for the nearest knife. "What the devil is that?"

I followed her finger, then gasped along with everyone else at the table as a hand scurried across the doorway and into the living area, dragging a wrist and part of an arm behind it. Apparently, I'd missed a part.

Oops.

"Good God," Stuart said. "What the—"

"Halloween," I said, hurrying back from the far end of the table.

"In March?" Clark said.

I shot him my best hostess smile. "I, um, have a friend who makes prototype toys. He sent me this for Timmy. To, you know, play with." I cringed, certain everyone at the table would see through my big fat lie.

"In Italy?" Stuart asked. "Kate lived overseas for years."

"Right," I said, because having an Italian toy-making friend seemed much more lie-compatible than a California toy-making friend.

Raymond Jones, a newbie from whom Stuart was gunning for contributions, pushed back from the table. "We always do Halloween up big, and that looks like the perfect thing to have creeping down the hallway toward the trick-or-treaters. Can I take a closer look?"

"Oh," I said. "Uh." I looked at Stuart, who looked back, clearly baffled as to why I wouldn't immediately offer to let our guest examine the disgusting body part. "Yeah," I said, wondering if this was the night my secret identity ended up being not so secret after all. "Um, sure thing."

I pushed my chair back about as slowly as humanly possible, then headed into the living room, our guests trailing after me like little goslings.

"There it is," I said, pointing under the couch. "It, um, has a really good motor."

Stuart started to bend down to get it, but I beat him to it, certain I was raising a few eyebrows by lying flat on the floor in a dress. What choice did I have, though? If he let those fingers close around his wrist, Stuart would be wearing permanent zombie. At least until I got out the pruning shears again.

I clutched it around the wrist and tugged it out, cringing as the fingernails dug into the finish on our wooden floor. *Great.*

"So, um, here it is," I said, holding it out for inspection. "I'd rather you didn't touch it," I said. "My friend, uh, he's paranoid about his patent. And there are some bugs. The fingers," I said, snatching it away from Martina, who was reaching in that direction. "The, um, spring is too strong. You can get quite a nasty bruise if the hand closes on you."

They all leaned in, peering close to the Halloween toy.

"It's so lifelike," Martina said.

"Amazing detail," Clark added.

"It really is remarkable," I agreed, holding the thing far enough away that the wiggling fingers couldn't grab on to anything. "To be honest," I said, aiming a bright hostess smile at the crowd, "it's about as realistic as you can get."

Despite roaming body parts, the party was a huge success, and the fact that Stuart helped clean up afterward added that extra little bit of sparkle to the evening. That was about all the sparkle I got, though, as my husband was completely exhausted from traveling and playing politico.

So while I swept the kitchen and living room floors, he went upstairs to crash. Not a particularly romantic way to celebrate a successful party, but I confess I didn't mind. It's hard to be romantic with one husband when your mind is focused on the other—where he was, why he wasn't answering his phone, and whether he was watching out for your daughter.

I knew, of course that he was. But the first two questions were driving me nuts. Where were they? And why wasn't David answering his cell phone? Isn't that the point of mobile phones? To be, you know, *mobile?* The only time I ever turned my phone off was when I was patrolling, and—

Oh, shit.

No. I shook my head, holding the Swiffer handle firmly and resisting the urge to flail out with it and break something, just to satisfy that one initial burst of anger.

Instead, I let the handle fall to the ground, clattering

against the hardwood floor as I sprinted toward the stairs and Allie's room, fear growing in the pit of my stomach.

I wasn't sure what I was looking for, but when I saw the newspaper half-buried under a pile of books on Allie's bed, my stomach did a little tumble, and I tried to think back to whether I'd read the morning paper.

I hadn't.

But neither had I seen it sitting on the kitchen table where Stuart usually left it.

I frowned, realizing that Stuart had left that morning before the paper arrived. Allie must have gone outside and gotten it, taking it straight up to her room. But why?

There was only one answer I could think of, and it didn't involve a social studies project.

I shoved the books off and pulled out the paper, noticing immediately that the local metro section had been opened, read, and hastily shoved back together. I followed suit, my eyes skimming the text until I saw a small article tucked above an ad for a new art gallery—a nasty car wreck on one of the local canyon roads had resulted in two dead. The third passenger in the car—Colby Shelton—walked away with only minor scrapes and bruises.

A lump filled my throat. Surely she and David hadn't—

But, somehow, I knew that they had.

Damn, damn, damn.

I left a note for Stuart that I was heading for Laura's to discuss a recent date gone bad, and then I called Laura from my car and left a message telling her not to call my house because I was supposedly at hers. A very high school approach to handling my life, but under the circumstances, melodrama, sneaking around, and covert operations seemed completely apropos.

My main problem, of course, was that I didn't have a clue where to go. Demons often head back to the place of their making, but in this case, I was dubious. Tyle Canyon Road was a narrow, two-lane stretch with no shoulder and a nonexistent pedestrian population. What would be the point?

More likely, the demon had already been recruited into the Abaddon fold and was off on a mission (in which case I might do well to simply wait at home for him to find me, as I seemed to be at the apex of all recent demonic plans). Either that, or the demon was trying to assimilate himself into his body's former life. In which case he might merely go home.

I tried David's first—on the faint hope that I was wrong and the more practical hope that if I was right, David would have done some research on where to find Colby Shelton . . . and would have left his findings lying conveniently on his kitchen table.

Unfortunately, a quick review of David's apartment suggested he wasn't as organized as all that. A rather nasty turn of events from my perspective, leaving me with absolutely no idea where to find my daughter—or the husband I intended to kill the moment I laid eyes on him.

I'd pretty much decided that Tyle Canyon Road was my only option after all, weak though it might be, and I was heading back out the door to go there when my cell phone rang.

I snatched it up, sagging with relief when I saw that the call came from Allie.

"Where are you?" I demanded without preamble.

"At the carnival," she whispered, terror in her voice. "Oh, God, Mom," she said. "Please, hurry!"

And then my daughter screamed.

Nineteen

David's apartment was on the beach, and reasonably close to the boardwalk. Even so, I'm pretty sure I broke the sound barrier, arriving there in what had to be record time.

I've recently started keeping a hunting vest in the car, supplied with knives, holy water, crucifixes, and other handy demon-hunting tools. I pulled it out from under my seat as I drove, then managed get both arms through the sleeve holes without injuring any pedestrians or property in the process.

I drove the van up on the sidewalk, barreling through the narrow walkways until I slammed on the brakes half a block from the gypsy's tent. I piled out of the van, then raced toward the tent, hoping to arrive unseen and unheard.

I managed, but I wasn't sure what good my anonymity would do me. Not in light of the scenario played out in front of me.

Colby Shelton (at least, I assume it was him) lay dead on the floor alongside the gypsy woman. Dukkar held a gun to David's head, a rather effective method of keeping him still.

And my precious Allie cowered in a corner, her eyes wide and terrified.

Not the kind of scene I liked walking into, and I couldn't help but wonder how they'd gotten themselves into that kind of mess in the first place.

Not something I worried about for long, though.

"Vile beast," Dukkar said, pulling back the hammer.

"*No*," Allie shouted, her scream enough to distract and buy me time.

I wasn't crazy about fighting with a gun in the equation, but I didn't see that I had a choice. I leaped forward, then managed a spinning crescent kick that caught Dukkar in the jaw.

David—thank God—saw me' coming and pulled his body down hard even as Dukkar's head snapped back.

I kicked again, this time sending the gun clattering across the floor. Allie scrambled forward and grabbed it, holding it tight in two unsteady hands.

"I'll take that," I said, reaching for the gun as David twisted Dukkar around, pinning his arms behind his back.

"I should kill you," David said, his voice low and dangerous. "Give me one reason why I shouldn't kill you right now."

"David," I said, a warning in my voice

"I am not like you. My heart, it is pure."

David shoved him away, disgusted by either Dukkar or his words. "What is it?" he shouted. He pointed at the demon carcass. "Didn't I kill that thing before it could kill you? *Didn't I?*"

Dukkar stared into the face of David's rage, stubbornly silent.

"What the hell is it that you think you know about me?"

But Dukkar wasn't telling. Instead he looked from me to David and then back to me again. Then he turned on his heel and raced from the tent. David moved to follow, but I grabbed him back.

"No," I said. "Let him go." Right then, I truly didn't trust David not to kill him.

"Bastard," David spat, even as Allie climbed to her feet and ran forward, catching both of us in her arms.

"What the hell do the two of you think you were doing?" I asked. "Do you have any idea how scared I was?"

"We figured out where Shelton would be," Allie said, her voice small.

"Did you?" I asked, my voice cutting close to sarcastic. "Come on." I started heading toward the rental, the two of them following close behind.

"We didn't get here in time to save the lady," Allie said. "But Daddy took out the demon. Doesn't that count for something?"

"It counts for a lot," I said. "Too bad all those bonus points get erased by the fact that you weren't supposed to be out here in the first place."

I closed my mouth, grinding my teeth together. "You know what? Just get in the car." Allie's issue was sneaking out. David's was much larger, at least from my perspective. Best not to combine the two.

"But—"

"In."

She hung her head and climbed inside without further argument. I doubted I'd have as easy a time of it with David.

"I didn't—" he began, but once again, I cut him off.

"You know what? I don't even want to hear it." I shook my head, anger heating to the boiling point. "I trusted you," I said, my voice low and dangerous. "I trusted you because I always have. Because I know you. Because I know you would never—*ever*—put our daughter in danger. At least that's what I thought. I guess I was wrong." I drew in a breath and looked him in the eye. "So don't ask me again, okay? Don't ask me if I trust you. Because the answer has changed. From now on, the answer is no."

He closed his eyes, flinching as if I'd slapped him. I guess in a way I had.

I turned and headed for the driver's side of the car.

"Kate, please . . ."

But I kept on walking, not turning around. I couldn't.

Stop now and I'd either cry or kick, and neither option was a good one. Better I get some distance. For that matter, I wondered if love had been clouding my judgment all along. *He is Eric Crowe*, the old woman had said. *And the blackness clings to him like night.*

Was that what I was seeing? The blackness of which the old woman spoke?

I thought of Dukkar's face, so horribly pummeled, not to mention the other little hints of temper I'd seen. And, of course, the lying. Taking risks with Allie's life.

Did it all add up to something dark? Something dangerous?

Even more, I realized, this wasn't the first time he'd encouraged Allie to keep secrets from me. I should have seen it before, but now it made sense. Her exhaustion Monday morning. Allie and Eric's covert whispers at the carnival on Sunday. Not to mention Allie's knowledge about the demise of my scuzzy demon attacker.

They'd gone out patrolling that night, keeping their actions a secret from me.

Was he damaged? And if so, was I the one who'd damaged him?

I slid into the van and clenched the steering wheel tight with both hands. Beside me, Allie sat buckled in, her body scooted as far away from me as possible. Smart kid.

"The demon wasn't working for Abaddon," she said, breaking the silence as I pulled back onto the highway.

That caught my attention. "What are you talking about?"

"Daddy said something when they were fighting about how when he got back to the ether he should tell Abaddon nice try, but better luck next time."

I stifled a smile. That was a very Eric thing to say. "And?"

"The demon sneered, all hoity-toity-like. And then he said that he was not subservient to Abaddon. At least not until he became The One. What do you think it means?"

"I'm not sure," I said. "But it definitely sounds like Abaddon's trying for another invincibility gig. Maybe this demon's going to be loyal only when he has to be."

"Maybe," Allie said dubiously.

"I do know one thing for certain, though."

"You do?"

"You're grounded," I said. "This time for real."

"Yeah," she said. "I figured that one out all on my own."

Wednesday morning, I dropped Timmy at Fran's for a play date with Elena, but instead of heading home, my car steered itself automatically toward Laura's.

I shifted into park in front of her house, debating. It was early, but I knew she wouldn't mind. Laura wasn't simply an early riser, she was an early baker, and odds were good that my arrival would be greeted with a smile and a gigantic blueberry muffin. Frankly, I could use both.

Decided, I got out and marched to the front door. Still locked, and although I had a key, I rang the doorbell. She'd had a date last night, after all. Probably best not to barge in.

"Hey," she said, pulling the door open and frowning at me. "Why didn't you let yourself in?"

"Date night," I said, leaning around her to seek out signs of male life. "Wishful thinking?"

"I don't know about him," she said, "but *I'm* wishing." She cocked her head toward the kitchen. "Come on in. I'm making muffins."

My mood ratcheted up a notch toward sunny. "Blueberry?"

She scrunched up her face. "Lemon poppyseed," she said. "Sorry! If I'd known you were coming . . ."

"It's okay," I said, helping myself to a cup of coffee and mourning the loss of my blueberry fix. "You're not my personal baker."

"No, but—" She stopped. "Kate, what is it? What happened? This isn't about lemon poppyseed muffins."

I sniffed, then realized that my cheeks were wet. "Sorry," I said. "I'm a little overwhelmed these days."

She pulled off the oven mitts and crossed her arms over her chest, looking at me. "I guess you would be," she said gently. "Want to talk about it?"

"Yeah," I said, realizing that was why my car had driven itself over here. "I guess I do."

I sat down at the table, absently eating a lemon poppyseed muffin—a testament to how upset I was—and told her about Allie's sneaking out. "To go patrolling with David." I pressed my lips together, as if that could hold back the ill words I wanted to spew about the man I'd loved for so many years. But I was on a roll, and though I might regret them later, I couldn't hold back. I drew in a breath and gave voice to what I'd so far only thought about. "What if the gypsy woman was right? What if Eric's soul really is black? He flat-out lied to me. Or, at least, he lied by omission." And my real worry—the one that truly terrified. "What if because of him, Allie gets hurt? Or killed?"

"Oh, Kate. I'm so sorry. But I don't think—" She cut herself off, standing up to go busy herself with loading the dishwasher. An obvious ploy to avoid looking directly at me.

"What?" I pressed. "You don't think what?"

"Well, *why* would Eric's soul be mucked up? The jumping-into-David thing, right?" she asked, and because I hadn't told her about using the Lazarus Bones, I didn't correct her.

"But we've been around him for a while now, and he seems perfectly normal," she continued. "He's helped you hunt demons, he's been a gentleman more or less about the fact that you're sleeping with another man. He even told Nadia to take a hike," she added, referring to an extremely hot, extremely aggressive Hunter who'd had designs on Eric recently. "All he wants is you. And if that means his soul is black, then you have some problems with Stuart, too."

I couldn't help but smile, even if I didn't fully agree. Laura, after all, didn't have all the facts. "Maybe," I said.

"And Allie's almost fifteen, Kate," Laura said gently. "Part of me thinks you're looking for the easy excuse."

I tilted my head, brow furrowed in question. "What are you talking about?"

"She's a teenager. More than that, she's a teenager who's just had some major life upheaval. Couple that with raging hormones and it's really not a pretty picture. Trust me. I know of what I speak."

I looked at her, the hint of sadness under the strong lines of her face. She wasn't at odds with Mindy, not really. But they'd lost serious ground over the last few months. I didn't want that to happen to me and Allie, and yet I couldn't help but fear that the train was already pulling out of the station with Eric as engineer stoking the engine.

I brushed away a tear. "Speaking of hormonal," I said with a wry smile. "I . . . I guess I feel like I've changed everyone in my life who's close to me. Allie. You. David."

"How have you changed David?"

"Oh." I hesitated. "*Change* probably isn't the right word. I only meant that he's no longer my husband, even though in his memory he is."

"Fair enough," she said, and she nodded so earnestly that I felt guilty for the lie.

"Laura, I—" I closed my mouth, wanting to pull the words back in.

"What?" She peered at my face. "Kate, you're scaring me."

I drew in a shuddering breath, then lifted my face to meet her eyes. "He died, Laura," I said, my voice barely a whisper. "He died at the cemetery that night. And I—I brought him back."

"Oh." She dropped into the seat next to me, her hands clasping her coffee mug so tight I thought it might break. "But—*how?*"

"The Lazarus Bones."

Her eyes widened with understanding, and as they did, I poured out the story along with my fears and frustrations. "And now I don't know. What if I did something to him? To me? What if I really did change him? What if I damaged him?"

"Oh, Kate, I wish you'd told me. I mean, it's not like I could have done anything, but—"

"I know." I exhaled, actually feeling a little better for having told her. "I wish I'd told you, too."

"So you think the gypsy lady is right?"

"I don't know," I said. "No. Maybe. I don't know."

"You need to talk to someone other than me, you know. If you're worried about David's soul—if you're worried about your own—you need to talk to a priest."

I nodded, then took a long sip of coffee, knowing she was right. There was only one way I could truly find peace. As the saying goes, confession is good for the soul.

"I'm glad you're back," I said, sitting across from Father Ben in his office. "I was afraid you wouldn't be." I was playing with the hem of my T-shirt, taking a loose thread and wrapping it around my thumb until the end turned purple.

"Careful, Kate. People will think you have something on your mind."

"Huh?"

He nodded at my lap, where I held my tortured thumb.

"Oh. Right." I unraveled the thread, feeling a bit like a schoolgirl sent to the principal's office. A ridiculous feeling, especially considering I'd come here of my own free will.

"I'm sorry I haven't had a chance to look for—"

"That's not why I'm here," I said hurriedly. "Not *Forza* business, I mean." I frowned. "Well, not really." I drew in a breath. "I need to talk about something, Father. Something personal."

I saw the subtle shift in his face, as Father Ben moved from the role of mentor to priest. "Would you feel more comfortable moving to a confessional?"

I shook my head. "No. But this is eating at me, and I need . . . well, I guess I need a priest."

"You came to the right place," he said with an encouraging smile.

I drew in a breath, said a silent prayer, and confessed what I'd done. "I played God," I concluded. "I had a tiny bit of dust from the Lazarus Bones, and I wasn't strong enough to resist. I should have—I know that—but I didn't." I licked my lips, ashamed. "I couldn't."

"Oh, Kate. What woman couldn't? He was the man you loved, only recently returned to you. Your actions reflect nothing more than your nature."

"What's that? Vile and untrustworthy?"

"Hardly," he said. "Try human."

I managed a halfhearted nod, fearing he was only trying to placate me. "I think I did something horrible, though. More than playing God, I mean. I think the results—" I cut myself off, hating to give voice to my fears, but knowing I had to. "I think I did something to David. Something bad."

His brow furrowed as he considered me. "You're serious?"

I nodded, tears in my eyes. "Could a demon have come in with Eric's soul? After I used the Lazarus Bones?"

"I don't know the answer to that, but what has he done to make you think this?"

I sank down in my chair, my fears seeming vague and abstract. "His temper, for one. It's on edge. And it's violent, too. And everything with Allie," I added, taking a quick detour to explain everything that had happened recently. "Not only did he flat-out break a promise to me, he deliberately put her in harm's way. He could have gotten her killed."

"Anything else?"

"He's spending a lot of time away," I said, my voice small. "And then there's all that stuff about the blackness within that the old lady from the carnival spouted." I pulled my knees up to my chest and hugged them, wishing I'd grilled the woman more in the beginning. Now I would never have the chance.

"That's pretty much everything, and I know you're going

to say I'm paranoid, but Father, I really think there's something there."

"I do, too," he said, gently.

I looked up, surprised. "You do?"

"Guilt. Fear. A lot of emotions that make up a curtain through which you're viewing David now."

I tilted my head to the side, silently looking at him.

"I've met David, Kate," Father Ben said. "Before and after you used the Lazarus Bones. He's a good man. He comes to mass, helps out at the church."

"Yes, but—"

"Kate, there's nothing you've told me that's not completely understandable. David—*Eric*—has been through a lot. And while we all strive to be calm and rationale, we are at the same time human. And humans can only bear so much."

"His temper," I said.

Father Ben inclined his head. "Under the circumstances, I don't think a bit of temper is unusual. In fact, it's probably to be expected."

"But Allie—"

"He's her father, and he's been usurped from an authoritarian role. Even more than that, he has no real idea how to parent a teenager. His only point of reference is his youth. Your youth, too. So tell me, Kate. Are the things he has done with Allie so different from his experience as a teenager?"

"No, but—"

"I don't think this is a demon issue, Kate. I think it's a marital one."

"Marital?"

He lifted his hands. "Granted, not the typical marriage, but some of the underlying issues are the same. Parenting. Boundaries." He regarded me seriously. "Perhaps I can assist not as your *alimentatore*, but as your priest and counselor."

Okay, this was really not the response I'd expected. "You're talking *marriage* counseling? With David?"

"We could even start informally today. He left only a few

minutes before you arrived. If we call him, I'm sure he'd be happy to turn around and come back."

"He was here? Why?"

"Research," Father Ben said. "He's been spending some time in the archives lately."

That was news to me, and despite Father's attempts to soothe me, David's surreptitious research and trips to Los Angeles were simply making me more nervous.

"Should I call him back?"

"No," I said, standing up, and forcing myself to give due weight to Father Ben's theory. "I'm overreacting."

He looked at me, as if he weren't quite sure he believed me. I wasn't sure I believed me, either. Part of me wanted desperately to take Father Ben's words to heart. Another part of me feared the worst.

"I have one more idea," he said. "May I discuss this with Father Corletti? Perhaps he can reassure you in ways that I cannot."

"Of course," I said, pausing in the doorway. "I'm glad you're here, you know. You're a great *alimentatore* and a terrific priest," I said. "Most of all, you're a wonderful friend."

I could see his answering smile in his eyes. "Thank you, Kate. That means a lot."

"So you really don't think my soul is in jeopardy?"

"For using the bones to raise David?"

I nodded, lips pressed tight together.

"As many times as you have saved us from Satan's work, I tend to think that God will grant you at least one free pass. Okay?"

"Sure. Thanks." I drew in a breath and stepped out of his office. I knew he was trying to make me feel better, but the fact that I needed God's pass meant that I'd been right all along.

Someone was following me.

I'd left Father Ben's office, then cut through the courtyard between the bishop's hall and the cathedral. I'd been all alone. Now I heard footsteps behind me, and I whipped around, my hand in my purse, my fingers tight around the hilt of my knife.

Behind me, Dukkar raised his hands, a huge duffel bag hanging from one shoulder, his eyes wide. "Please, I do not mean to startle you."

"What the hell do you want?"

"I give you this," he said, dropping the duffel. He unzipped it, then reached in and pulled out a mass of filthy cloth, which he proceeded to unroll in the shadow of the Virgin Mary's statue.

"The Sword of Caelum," he said, his head inclined as he backed away. I looked down, then let out a little gasp of awe as I saw the beautifully forged blade and intricately jeweled hilt.

"It's amazing. This is really it?"

"It is," he said. "And it is to be wielded only by you. *The Hunter whose body and soul shall nurture and give life to the generation to come. That Hunter shall wield the sword and strike down the Decimator, sending him to hell and death for all eternity.* There is more," he continued. "A mathematical component of which I do not know the details, but which our people have discerned to be this place. This town."

He took a step back, waving his hand to encompass the duffel and the sword. "That," he said, "is the nature of the prophecy. That," he said, nodding toward the sword, "is for you."

"The Decimator?" I repeated. "Goramesh? That's who the sword will kill?"

"That is the demon for whom it was forged, yes."

"Not Abaddon?"

He looked curiously at me. "No. Not Abaddon."

I licked my lips, trying to make sense of this shift in information. "The old lady said she didn't know anything about a prophecy or about a sword."

"She hesitated to trust you," he said. "I hesitate, too."

"Why?"

"Because of *him*. He has the demon within."

I trembled, not liking the sound of that. "And me?"

"You? You are not unmarked. But you are clean."

Didn't *that* sound great? "So you trust me with this?"

He hesitated, then nodded. "If the demon is to die, it would seem we have no choice." He took a step back, inclining his head a bit as if I were newfound royalty. "I do not know that you are our best hope. But you are most assuredly our only hope."

I cringed. Not exactly a rousing vote of confidence. But apparently the most that I could hope for.

Twenty

The Hunter whose body and soul shall nurture and give life to the generation to come.

Pretty damn clear, all things considered. If Dukkar was right and the mathematical portion of the prophecy really did point to a geographical location in San Diablo, then I was the only Hunter here giving birth to anyone. Which meant two things—I was destined to strike down Goramesh with this sword, or die trying. And my daughter truly was the next generation of Hunter.

"Or Timmy," Laura said, when I ran my reasoning past her.

We were sitting on the back porch, and now I looked sideways at her and scowled, not because her comment was foolish, but because she was right. Timmy didn't have the genes of two Hunters, but that was hardly a strike against him. Most Hunters were recruited from normal families. Orphans like me who were trained by *Forza*.

"And the wheel keeps on spinning," I said. "First I lose my daughter, and then I'm going to lose my son."

"You haven't lost Allie," she said. "A long way from it, I'm betting."

"I haven't seen her since last night," I retorted. "She's locked in her bedroom, pissed at me for grounding her—"

"And pissed at herself for deserving it," Laura finished.

"Do you really think so?"

"Kate, she saw a bloodbath. And she's not a stupid girl. She has to know your rules were to protect her. She blew it. She almost got killed. Yeah, I think she's hiding in her room licking her wounds. It's not you she's mad at, it's herself. And maybe David, too."

"That makes two of us," I said.

"Go tell her what you've learned. I mean, this Goramesh thing is huge, right? Abaddon is all over the place, but the prophecy applies to Goramesh. Do demons work together a lot?"

"No," I said. "They don't. That's what has me worried."

"So let her help. Tell her what Dukkar told you. Show her the sword. Let her be involved the way you want her to be. With books and the computer and weapons training until she really is ready."

"You're a good friend, you know?"

"Hell, yes."

I laughed. "And modest, too."

She cocked her head toward the back door. "Go ahead. I'll go home and do the same. Maybe this is the break we need. An intersection between Abaddon and Goramesh. I can't imagine what, but maybe something will spring out if we all start looking for it."

She was right, of course, and as she headed back to her house, I headed inside to talk to my daughter.

I was sidetracked by the ringing phone. I considered ignoring it, but when I checked the Caller ID and saw that the call originated in Italy, I answered.

"Father Ben must have called you," I said, after Father Corletti and I went through the usual greetings.

"He is worried about you," Father said. "As am I. My child, why did you not confide in me?"

I sank down onto the couch and hugged a pillow, feeling

all of seven years old again. "I was ashamed, I guess. I didn't want you to know I was so weak. I mean, he was dead. And by every law of nature, he should have stayed that way."

"You were weak, Katherine, I will not deny that. But that weakness does not stain you any more than being human does."

"Really?"

"I promise I speak the truth."

"But what about Eric? I didn't harm myself, but what about him? I opened the same door the demons use, and—"

"And he used the same portal. It is not common, I will grant you that, but it is not unheard of, either. Eric himself had done it before, yes? Moving into David's body?"

"Yeah," I said, hesitantly.

"You simply opened a portal to allow that to happen again. And because it was the Lazarus Bones, the injuries to the body healed. But Katherine, the key is that you *allowed* it. You did not force it. Whether he remembers it or not, Eric ultimately made the choice to come back. And he returned for the same reason you used the bones."

"Love."

"It is a powerful magic in and of itself, is it not?"

I nodded, unable to speak.

"Eric is no different than he was before. If anything, he is stronger for having your love to lift him up. Do not take that away from him. If anything, he will need your strength now more than ever."

"What do you mean?"

He paused, but I pressed. "Father, what do you mean?"

"Only that there are difficult times ahead for Eric. For David. He is the same man, and yet he is also different. He must learn who he is, and to do that, he will need a rock to hold him in place. You've always been that rock, Katherine. Can you still be there for him?"

"I think so." I ran Father's words back through my head. "So Father Ben was right? Eric's temper and the risks he's taken with Allie—those are just him trying to work it all out? To deal with what's happened to him and to figure out how to be the father to a Hunter-in-training?"

"You didn't harm Eric, Kate. Trust yourself. For that matter, trust your instincts."

I smiled, because now he sounded like he was giving me a *Forza* 101 lecture. But my instincts were still tingling.

"Fair enough, but my instincts say you're not telling me something."

"There is one other thing," Father Corletti admitted. "With the Lazarus Bones, the strength of the raiser imbues the raised, and they are forevermore connected, both in spirit and in some ways in body."

"Which means?"

"Katherine, it means that David's fate is now tied to your own. If you die, then David dies, too."

"Dear God," I murmured.

"I debated whether to tell you," he admitted. "But you have the right to know. And, truly, does this knowledge change anything?"

"You're kidding, right?"

"I am not," he said. "Katherine, child, I have seen you and Eric together, and even now I hear the love in your voice when you speak of him. Is your life not already intertwined with his? Are you not forever linked with Eric, body and soul?"

I swallowed, closing my eyes as the truth of his words washed over me. "Father," I said. "Sometimes, I think you see too much."

"Goramesh?" Allie said, after I relayed what Dukkar had told me in the cathedral courtyard. "Wow." She made a face, probably remembering the last time she'd been up close and personal with Goramesh and his minions. Not exactly the best summer on record for either her or for Timmy.

"I wanted to bring you up to speed," I said, which wasn't entirely accurate since I'd mentioned nothing to her about my conversation with Father Corletti. "You need all the information you can get if you're going to burn through the research and help me find answers."

"You're still going to let me help?" she asked, her voice small.

"Do you want to?"

"Uh-huh."

"Then yeah," I said. "You can help. Maybe you can figure out why Abaddon's minions are worried about the sword when it's Goramesh who can be struck down by it."

She took the sword off the bed where I'd laid it and hefted it in two hands. "Doesn't look like anything special," she said.

"Mystical things often don't."

"Right," she said. "Okay, so let's think." She crossed to her desk and came back with a spiral notebook filled with pink paper. "Clues," she said, then started writing and talking at the same time.

I tucked my leg under me and looked over her shoulder as she wrote.

"Vengeance meets revenge," she said.

"Goramesh and Abaddon," I said, the reference clear now that we knew that these two high demons were hanging around San Diablo.

"So what is The One?"

"A higher demon they're trying to conjure?" I suggested.

"Like a trapped demon they're trying to release?" Allie said, obviously calling on her own practical demon-hunting experience.

"Maybe," I said. To be honest, I really wasn't sure.

"At any rate, it's a clue. So it stays on the sheet."

"The thing the gypsy lady said," I continued. "'In the shadow of the Lord.'"

"Right," Allie said, dutifully writing it down. "And the bit about the hallowed eve when the sanctified blood flowed. Oh! And the nighttime. What was it? When day turns into night?"

"'Falls into,'" I corrected. "'And one shall augment the other,'" I said, closing my eyes to aid my memory. "'And the prophecy shall be no more.'"

"What does *that* mean? You can't kill Goramesh after all?"

"Or maybe it means that's when I do kill him."

She looked at me, eyes eager. "I like that idea."

"Honestly, so do I."

"So can you think of anything else?"

I shook my head. "I think you've got it covered." I slid off the bed and headed for her door.

"Mom?"

"What, baby?"

"I'm sorry." She licked her lips, then looked down at her feet. "I knew I shouldn't go—not just to Daddy's, but patrolling and all that, too. But I really wanted—"

"Your dad," I finished. "I know, baby. You're not the only one who's sorry. I should have moved heaven and earth to get you guys time together. Forgive me?"

Her eyes widened a little with surprise. "Sure."

"Good."

"I love you, Mom. You really are the best, you know?"

I smiled, my throat tickly with tears. "I don't know about that," I said. "But I try." Right then, in fact, I was going to try a little harder.

I blew her a kiss and left her to her research. Then I went downstairs, drew in a breath, and picked up the phone. David answered on the first ring, not with a hello, but with an apology.

"No," I said. "That's my line. I should have listened from the beginning and let you and Allie have your time together. I don't know why I didn't. Maybe I was afraid and making excuses for pulling away. But I can't. I'll never be able to pull away from you. We have to figure out a way to make this work."

"You were afraid?" he repeated. "Of me?"

"Yes. Maybe. I don't know." I tilted my head back, trying

to order my thoughts. "Of us. Of my life. Of what was going to happen to it now that you're back. But I ended up hurting you and Allie, and I'm sorry."

"I should never have taken her out," he said.

"Well, I'm not going to argue about *that*," I said, and when he laughed, I knew we were back on track. "More's happened," I said, then filled him in on my visit from Dukkar at the cathedral.

"You have the sword now?"

"Yup." I'd left it in Allie's room, but I figured it was safe up there. At the very least, Stuart wouldn't find it, as he considered her room a public health hazard and only entered in full hazmat gear. "And apparently it's Goramesh I'm destined to bring down. Not Abaddon."

He whistled. "Do you think Goramesh knew about this before? When he came to San Diablo for the Lazarus Bones?"

"I'm thinking not," I said. "I ran into my share of minions then, and none mentioned a sword."

"That could be a good research angle, then," he said, slipping into academic mode. "It's only been a few months. Research where Goramesh has turned up since you defeated him, and maybe we can find a clue as to what he's up to. And see if his whereabouts intersect Abaddon's."

"That's the best plan I've heard so far," I said. "You game for playing research dude?"

"Absolutely."

I waited a beat, thinking about my words before saying them. "And do you want overnight company to help you out?"

"Love it, but wouldn't Stuart be a little irritated if you spent the night with another man?"

"Not me," I said. "Allie."

Silence.

"Eric? Did you hear me?"

"Yeah," he said softly. "Yeah, I'd love some overnight help."

"We'll be over in an hour," I said. "I'll tell Stuart she's staying over at a friend's. And David? Let's forgo the patrolling, okay?"

"Lesson learned," he said. "This is an inside visit only. And Kate?" he added, his voice filled with both relief and sadness. "Thank you."

With Allie at Mindy's that night (or so the story went), Stuart and I spent the evening cuddled on the couch with our little boy, indulging him with a bowl of popcorn and the full-length *Curious George* movie. A toddler's idea of heaven. And, I have to admit, being curled up in my husband's arms wasn't bad, either.

"Bernie and I are going to talk to a few lenders next week about financing the house," he said at one point, drawing a dirty look from Timmy. "You're still okay with it?" he finished, in a much-lower voice.

"I trust you," I assured him. "If you tell me we can make it work, then I'm all for giving it a shot."

"Financially, I think we'll be okay. Can we handle the rest of it? You and me, I mean," he said, examining my face. "Real estate isn't exactly a low-stress hobby."

"We'll muddle through," I assured him.

"I love you, you know," he said.

"I know." I snuggled closer. "I love you, too." I drew in a breath, remembering my assurance to Laura that I was going to tell Stuart everything on Wednesday night. And here Wednesday was, and I wasn't talking.

I needed to open my mouth and confess. I knew that. But somehow, the words wouldn't come. It had been—to put it mildly—one hell of a week, and everywhere I turned, I saw demons. Everywhere, that is, except Stuart. With him, I saw only my life and my house and a normal evening in suburbia.

Sue me, but I didn't want to give that up.

Tomorrow pressed down on me, demanding confessions and truths. But right then . . .

Right then, I wanted the fantasy.

So I spent the evening with two of the men in my life, snuggling and being silly, even while my mind whirred, wondering how all the clues fit together, fearing another demon would burst in to try and take the sword, and feeling an utter sense of helplessness because I had no idea what Goramesh and Abaddon were up to. Or, for that matter, when.

I kept the worries and fears hidden in the night, but they came out to haunt me in restless dreams, and I tossed and turned so much that Stuart woke me twice to pull me close and murmur soft words.

I woke up in the morning to a relatively empty house—me and Timmy and a note from Eddie that he was catching a lift from Stuart to the library. A rare treat in my world, but today the silence weighed on me, reminding me of the answers I didn't have and the anger that was still approaching.

I called David, and felt a little lump form in my throat when both he and Allie thanked me for arranging the overnighter. They hadn't found any answers yet, but Father Ben had messengered them over a box of books, and they were settling down in front of the table right then.

"I can send Allie home if you want," David said. "Or I can keep her here today and drop her by after dinner. I'll even drop her at Laura's if that will make your cover story more plausible."

"Sure," I said, feeling foolishly left out, but not really knowing what to do about that. We weren't a threesome anymore, and no matter how sad that made me, I had my trade-offs.

"Like you," I said to Timmy as I scooped him up and carried him outside. I watched him play like a wild thing, even throwing a ball for him to kick and chase, and getting down on hands and knees with him to draw giant chalk pictures on the back patio.

"I love you, Mommy," he said at one point, tossing his chubby arms around my neck.

I pulled him close, smothering him with hugs and kisses. "I love you, too, buddy." And more than anything, I wanted to keep him safe. I didn't know how, though, and answers weren't coming my way, even with my team of crack researchers burning up the books and the Internet.

There I was—a big fat prophecy hanging around my neck—and I didn't have a single idea what to do about that.

Not one of my more stellar moments.

"Have you talked to Father Ben today?" Laura asked me when she came over for coffee and Easter egg stuffing after lunch.

"I talked to him yesterday," I admitted, "after I left your place. But we didn't talk about research. I tried to reach him today, but no answer. I'm wondering if he had to go back out to the desert to help Holy Trinity with their Easter preparations. His cell never seems to work when he's out there."

"Maybe," Laura said. "But it probably means you can't count on him for much in the way of research."

"During Holy Week, there wasn't much he could do anyway. He was pretty booked twenty-four-seven. Besides, isn't that why I've got you and Allie and David?"

She tilted her head looking at me. "Father Ben helped, huh?"

"Good call," I admitted. "Thanks."

"It's been a hell of a week for you, hasn't it?"

"The roughest in memory," I admitted.

"In that case, I think we should uncork a bottle of merlot. We deserve it." She looked at the tabletop littered with confetti, tissue, and hollowed-out eggshells. "We *definitely* deserve it."

She got up and grabbed a bottle from our wine rack. "I'll uncork it, since you're at a disadvantage with your grievous injury."

"Actually, it's kind of handy," I admitted, waggling the

splinted finger. "I could imbed a small knife in there and it could be part of my standard patrol kit. Maybe even fix a hose with a bottle of water strapped under my arm. Squeeze my armpit and squirt holy water on my victim."

From there, we elaborated on practical demon-hunting gear. Water balloons filled with holy water. Stilettos hidden in Victoria's Secret underwires. The possibilities were endless.

By the time Stuart came home we'd filled four dozen egg cartons and discussed everything from the impending demise of San Diablo to how the fashionable Demon Hunter dresses for success.

I looked up, smiling at my husband, and realizing that my mood was better than it had been in days.

"You look chipper."

"Hanging out with my best friend and my little boy," I said. "What's not to love?"

As Laura said good-bye and headed out, Timmy ran in and gave his Daddy a hug, decked out only in his underpants. Stuart swung him around, then clutched him tight, these two men who shared the bond of family. Of blood.

I smiled, still feeling a little sappy and sentimental.

"Shouldn't he be dressed by now?" Stuart asked, bursting my bubble of sentimentality. "For that matter, shouldn't you?"

"For what?" I asked.

"Mass," he said. He tapped his watch. "In less than thirty minutes. It's already past five." I looked up and realized how dark the sky was getting.

"Today? But it's Wednesday."

"It's Thursday, Kate. Holy Thursday."

Even as he spoke the words, I realized. *When the sanctified blood has flowed.*

Christ. The eve of the crucifixion.

Today.

Whatever the demons had planned, it was happening at nightfall today.

I shoved back my chair, toppling it over. "Oh, God, Stuart. I'm so sorry. I can't stay. I have to hurry. I have to go."

"**Dammit, David!** Pick up the phone!" I raced through the San Diablo streets, my cell phone clutched to my ear. "Dammit, where could he be?" I drew in a breath. "I'm on my way. I've already left a message on your cell. Put Allie in a taxi. Wait for me outside. I'll explain when I get there."

I hoped he got the message, because I needed his help.

Prophecy or not, I wasn't keen on facing either Goramesh or Abaddon. Worse, I still didn't know where to go.

I called Laura and filled her in.

"Good God," she said, "what did Stuart say?"

Stuart had gaped at me, particularly when I'd raced up to Allie's room and come down with a sword and some bullshit story about how I had to return it to the museum as part of some committee program I'd forgotten about. Now, however, wasn't the time to relay all that to Laura.

"I'll tell you later," I said. "Right now, I have to figure out where to go. *In the shadow of the Lord.* That's what the gypsy lady said. Can you see what you can figure out? If I'm right, whatever's going down is happening at sunset."

"I'm on it," she said, then clicked off.

My phone beeped, signaling an incoming voice mail. I pressed the button, put the phone on speaker, and listened as I whipped the car through a red light and stomped on the gas.

"Got your message," David said. "Taxi's on the way, and I'll wait for you on the front step."

Good.

One less logistical nightmare to worry about. Now all I had to do was figure out where to go once David piled into the car.

I had to wait at a light before I could turn onto David's street, and I kept one foot on the brake and one on the gas, revving the engine impatiently until traffic slowed and

I could jump the light, almost getting sideswiped in the process.

I whipped into a no-parking zone even as Allie and David were climbing down the steps. Sure enough, a taxi was waiting, and I opened my door, planning to jump out of the car to hug my daughter and hurry David along.

I watched as David brushed her hair out of her eyes, and even from here, I could see the love on his face, along with a sadness that could only stem from the years he'd missed watching her grow up. She leaned in, taking the duffel he passed to her and then planting an affectionate kiss on his cheek.

That's when all hell broke loose. And I don't mean the demonic kind.

"What the hell do you think you're doing, you son of a bitch?" a familiar voice screamed. And then—as my fuzzy brain processed reality—Stuart burst out of the Infiniti and raced forward. I could see Timmy strapped in his car seat in the back, watching the spectacle as his daddy rushed forward and landed such a solid punch to David's jaw that he knocked him backwards.

I sprinted from the car, even as Allie bent down, grabbing Stuart's arms from behind before he could launch himself at David, who was back on his feet, his face a mask of pure rage.

"Calm down, calm down," I said, grabbing David before he could pummel my husband. "Think about how it looked from Stuart's perspective."

"*Kate?*" Stuart looked at me with total disbelief. "What in heaven's name is going on here?"

"Trust me. It's not what you think."

"Not what I think? I think I saw the high school chemistry teacher behaving inappropriately with a minor. *That's* what I think." He shook Allie off him, then put his arm protectively around her, stepping in front of her as if afraid David were going to reach out, grab her, and run like hell.

I kept a tight hold on David's arms, fearing he'd turn Stuart into a replica of Dukkar. At the same time, I couldn't seem to stop moving. The sun was rapidly descending, and we needed to get moving if we had any chance of stopping Abaddon. I might not know exactly what he was up to, but I knew it had to be bad.

"Please. Stuart, you deserve the full explanation. And I'm going to give it to you. I swear. But the sun is about to set, and we really have to go."

"You're leaving? With him?"

"Not now. Stuart. Please. Take Allie home and we'll talk about it later."

"Kate—"

"Dammit, Stuart. Do you trust me or not?"

For a moment, I wasn't sure what he was going to say. Then he turned and steered Allie by the elbow to his car. "This isn't over," he said, not to me but to David.

"I know," David said. "Believe me, I know."

"The key is *augment,"* David said as I pulled out of his neighborhood and got back on PCH. "Allie figured it out right before you called. *One shall augment the other and the prophecy shall be no more,*" he quoted.

"Not understanding it any more than I did the first time," I admitted.

"The first time, we only knew about Abaddon," David explained. "Now that we know Goramesh is poking around here, too, it started to make sense."

"Augment," I said. "They're making each other better?"

"Joining together," he said. "At least, that's our best guess."

I took my eyes off the road long enough to look incredulously at him. "They can do that?"

"Apparently. Allie found some references in an ancient text," he added, his voice full of paternal pride.

"But, why? What's the point?"

"Didn't get that far," he admitted. "You called, and here we are."

"Right," I said grimly. "But where do we need to be?"

"That's the big question," he said. "Could be anywhere."

My cell phone rang, and David reached down, pushing the button to answer in speaker mode.

"No luck," Laura said. "I'm not finding anything. All I can figure is that with all the religious references, whatever's going to happen will happen near a church."

"In the shadow of the Lord," David said.

"We go to the cathedral, then."

"It's not the only church in town," Laura said.

"No," I agreed. "But it is the oldest. And we know it's been the focal point of demon activity before."

Since no one else had a better idea, that's where I headed. Laura promised to keep looking, and David clicked off as I kept my hands firmly on the wheel and drove like a maniac.

"Will Allie be okay?" David asked. "With Stuart, I mean."

I shot him a sideways glance. "She'll be fine," I said. "I've got some serious explaining to do, though. Things I should have said a long time ago."

"I'm sorry. I never meant for—"

"Not now," I said, more sharply than I intended. I took a breath, softening. "I can't worry about it right now. Not if we're going to figure this out. Not if we're going to stop these demons from joining—or whatever the hell they're doing."

Perched on the top of one of San Diablo's cliffs, the cathedral was reached by climbing a narrow, winding road that the city was forever promising to widen. I took it at a dangerous pace, the engine in the rental straining as I gunned it around a slow-moving truck and David held on tight.

"Sorry."

"Don't apologize," he said. "Just get us there."

I floored it, and we raced the rest of the way up the hill. The parking lot was full—parishioners attending mass on Holy Thursday—so I swung into a handicapped spot and we both jumped out of the car.

"Where?" I said, reaching back in for the Sword of Caelum. I wasn't exactly going to blend in at the church, but at the moment, subtlety wasn't my priority.

"Check the church," David ordered. "I'll look around the grounds."

I peered inside, but mass seemed to be progressing as mass always did. The bishop was reading his homily, and I shut the door quietly before anyone could notice me.

I met David back outside. "No luck," he said, and I relayed the same message.

"It wouldn't be in the church anyway," I said. "Unless part of the ritual requires the demon to suffer." A demon can't walk on holy ground, not without suffering intense, unbearable pain. But though that might rule out a church as the ritual location, that also meant we had no good ideas left.

"Near the church, though," David said. "That has to be what the 'in the shadow of' language means."

I tended to agree. Right then, though, there were no shadows. The sun had already set, and the day had been overcast anyway.

"That's west," I said. "Which means if this is happening at sunset"—I shot him a grim look, as we were at least ten minutes past that marker—"then the shadows would be falling to the east."

We both turned, looking past the parking lot at the treetops, visible as the hill curved down.

"*The park*," I said, flashing on my conversation with the bishop on Sunday.

"What park?" he asked, following me because I was already heading in that direction, the sword tight in my hands.

"There's a clearing down there," I explained, my voice low in case anyone was listening to our approach. "An old park where some of the kids play after church. But it doesn't belong to the church. There's nothing holy about the ground."

"Sounds promising," he said, reaching out to grab a tree root for balance.

"We have to be right," I said. "The bishop told me it's an

archaeological site now. Apparently some animal remains were found, and the initial hypothesis is that the animals were used in rituals."

"A sacrifice to the demon," David said.

"Might tie in to the 'sanctified blood' part of the gypsy's message."

"It better," David said grimly. "We're out of time."

The path curved sharply and bent down the hill, and we tried to move quietly and quickly, hoping not to advertise our approach. Didn't matter. Because when we finally burst through the clearing it was clear that there were no demons present.

Instead, we saw Father Ben, nailed to a portion of the wooden playscape with his arms spread wide and blood dripping from his hands, his feet, and the multiple stab wounds in his chest.

Twenty-one

"*Ben!*" I rushed forward, David at my side, desperate to get him down.

"Kate." His voice was low, singsong. "They are still . . . here."

"Hold on, Father," I said. "I'm going to get you off this." He'd been crucified, nails through the wrists and ankles. Giant, railroad-style nails that were now embedded deep and refusing to budge.

"Dammit!" I cried, my eyes swimming as I tried to pry one up using the blade of the sword and David worked on another with a much smaller knife.

"Too . . . late," Ben said. "The joining. Will make them stronger. Invincible. That is . . ." He swallowed, his eyes rolling up into his head as he fought for strength.

No, no, no!

"Stick with me, Father. We'll get you down. You'll be okay." I said the words, but I didn't believe them. Not really. The life was slipping from him, and I was hollow inside.

"The reason," he said. "The joining. Don't let it happen. Would be . . . the beginning . . . of the . . . end."

His head lolled forward, and I clapped my hand over my mouth, looking frantically at David, even though there was nothing he could do, anymore than I could.

Ben was dead, and the demons who'd done this to him were nowhere to be found.

"David—" I stumbled over my words, unable to get my head around the situation. I'd lost friends before, but this was different. This was *now*. And so far, I'd managed to keep my corner of the world safe. The demons had moved in, but I'd always gotten there in the nick of time.

I looked at David through tear-filled eyes and realized that wasn't entirely true. The demons had won with David, killing him in a cemetery mere miles from here. He was only standing with me because I hadn't played by the rules.

Today, though, there was nothing I could do.

"Oh, God," I whispered. "Ben, I'm so sorry."

"We'll avenge him," David said, picking up a rock and hurling it. It crashed through the thick brush in front of us at the same time a sharp scream rang out behind us.

"Nooooooooooo."

I turned to find Allie racing toward me, Stuart at her heels with Timmy on his hip.

"My God, Kate," Stuart said, even as the ground beneath Ben started to shake, the blood-soaked earth bubbling and rising.

I looked at David. This wasn't over. In fact, it was just beginning.

"Get out of here," I shouted to Stuart. "Do you want to get killed?"

"Monster!" Timmy screamed as a scaly, clawed hand shot out of the blood-soaked muck. I lashed around, leading with the sword, but it was no use. The demon shot out of the ground at superhuman speed, then crouched at the top of the playscape, scales cracking and wings trembling with delight as it looked down at Father Ben.

"Just like your little friend Cami," the demon said, its voice low and croaky. "How I have longed for this day. For my revenge."

"Abaddon," I said, holding the sword at the ready and moving slowly toward my daughter.

The demon hissed, then smiled, its parched skin cracking with the effort.

"Allie," I said, my voice low and urgent. "Get out of here. Get you and Stuart and Timmy out of here right now, or I swear you're grounded for life."

"Kate," Stuart said, his voice shaky with fear. "What the fu—"

"*Now*," I screamed. "Do you want to die? Do you want Timmy to die? Get out of here now!"

"Come on, come on," Allie said, ushering them up the hill as the demon cackled.

"Don't even think about it," David said. "Your battle is with us."

"Battle?" Abaddon said. "You mean massacre." He turned to sneer at David. "I have waited a long time for my revenge. You brought cardinal fire into my lair and thrust me back into hell. Eviscerated my followers. Destroyed my plans. I have much to avenge."

"Good luck with that," David said, his voice hard.

"You burned in the fire, too, did you not?" the demon continued. "Burned, burned, even as your walls came tumbling down. So dangerous," he sneered, "for children to play with fire."

As if to illustrate the point, the blood-soaked soil burst into flame, then burped forth another demon, this one to land naked on two feet in front of me, his scaly body an amalgamation of goat and man, his arms webbed as if to form wings.

A long, thin claw reached out to me. "You," he said. "You foiled my army once. You will not defeat me again."

"Goramesh," I said, the word as heavy on my lips as the sword in my hand. I lashed out, aiming to drive the blade through the bastard's heart, but getting him only in the gut. Shouldn't matter, though. I had the sword, and this was all over.

"You shouldn't have come," I sneered. "Or didn't you hear the prophecy?"

He crumpled to the ground, wings covering his back like an injured insect.

"I think I like this sword," I said, to nobody in particular. "Your turn," I said then to Abaddon as David and I moved in tandem to attack the demon.

"No," he said, wings stretched wide as he soared into the sky. "I don't think so."

A rumble sounded behind us and I turned to find Goramesh rising, his cackling laughter echoing through the trees and filling the night sky with cawing crows.

I stared, dumbfounded, my hand clenched tight around the apparently useless Sword of Caelum.

"*Fool*," the demon hissed, then rose into the air. The two demons circled each other, and then, as David and I watched helplessly, they each nose-dived toward the playscape, colliding with and being sucked into the body of Father Ben.

As I watched, horrified, the body rumbled and stretched, as if a battle were going on inside.

"The sword, Kate," David cried. "Stab him with the sword."

I lunged to do that, cringing even as I hurled the sword blade over hilt to land deep in Ben's midsection.

The wound opened, and out poured a black, oily goo.

I left the sword embedded in Ben's body, and David rushed forward to pull it out, stopping in the act of tossing it back to me as he watched the goo shimmy and shake, then take solid form, a single demon rising, at least eight feet tall with a wingspan of equal breadth.

I pulled out a spare knife and stood ready for battle, but it didn't matter. The demon was no longer interested in playing, and in a split second, it took off, disappearing into the night sky. A demon, corporeal in its true form.

And, if Father Ben's dying words were true, invincible.

"Ben," I whispered, tears streaming down my face as I clutched Ben's body, now removed from the posts. "I'm sorry. I'm so, so sorry."

"Shhh," David said, loosening my grip on Ben and pulling me close to him.

I buried my face in his chest, taking what comfort I could from his arms, tight and strong around me. "I messed up," I said. "He's dead because of me."

"He's dead because of evil," David said. "No other reason."

"I should have saved him. That's my job. That's what I do. And he's my *alimentatore*. I should have——"

He pressed a finger to my lips. "Hush now," he said, and though my mind kept whirring, thoughts lost in a foggy haze of pain and regret, my lips stayed silent.

We stayed that way for an eternity, David holding me close. Me trying to pull strength from him, finding comfort in his touch, if not absolution. I'd lost people before—friends, fellow Hunters. But the loss of Ben, with his death so vile, and mere minutes before we'd arrived, seemed to rip my soul in two.

When I finally felt strong enough, I pulled back, then noticed the sword on the ground beside us. I reached for it in anger and frustration, prepared to hurl the thing into the bushes.

"No," David said, stilling my hand. "You might get another opportunity."

"The damn thing doesn't work, anyway," I said. "We never even had a chance."

"Maybe there is no prophecy. Maybe that's not the right sword," David said. "But maybe it is and we're just missing a piece. Don't throw away the one bit of hope we have, Kate."

"Hope," I repeated harshly as Ben's body lay lifeless beside us. "I don't even remember what that is."

A sad smile touched David's lips, and he stroked my hair, his own eyes reflecting the hope I desperately needed to find. "It's time, Kate," he said. "You need to go home."

Stuart.

Another shock of loss rippled through me, and I was certain I didn't have the strength to face my husband now.

"You can do this," David said, reading my thoughts. "It's time for you to go."

"I can't," I protested. "I can't leave him here. Not like this."

"I'll take care of it," he promised. "I'll call *Forza*. I'll handle it."

"But—"

"I'll handle it," he repeated gently. I knew that he would. Though San Diablo might not have a disposal team, they still existed for emergencies. And covering up the death of a priest definitely qualified.

"I should be the one," I said, my voice small. "I should—"

"You should go home to your family," David said firmly. "I'll take good care of him. But now, sweetheart, it's time for you to go."

It was well after midnight when I walked through the front door to find the house dark. My breath caught in my throat, and for a moment I had the horrible feeling that the place was empty. That Stuart had left and wasn't coming back.

I swallowed a strangled cry, determined not to lose it.

"Ben?"

Stuart's low voice ripped through the dark, sending shock waves of relief through me. *I hadn't lost him.* Not yet, anyway.

"Dead," I said, moving into the living room.

I found him sitting on the couch in the dark. A bit of moonlight filtered in through the back door, casting him in shadows, his expression unreadable.

"Stuart," I began. "I'm—"

"I almost quit the campaign," he said, his voice calm, his words startling.

"What?"

"I've been thinking about it for weeks. I thought I'd quit, and we'd be close again. Because for the last few months we haven't been. Something has been driving us apart. Not completely. Not horribly. But it's been there, like a wedge, threatening to break apart everything."

I nodded, knowing exactly the wedge of which he spoke.

"I thought it was me," he continued in that calm, collected politician's voice. "I thought I would quit. I thought I'd fix it." He lifted his head, and I could see a glimmer of the whites of his eyes. "But it wasn't me, was it, Kate?"

"No." I drew in a breath. "No, it wasn't."

"Right," he said, his voice monotone.

I wanted to shake him. To scream that he should be raging at me, furious and demanding explanations. Breaking furniture and swearing. But he wasn't. He was calm. And somehow that steady, stable voice scared me more than any of his raging ever could.

"What's going on, Kate? Allie's too broken up about what she saw to tell me a damn thing. So *you* tell. What was that? What did I see? And what the hell was Allie doing with that man?"

I started to sit on the couch next to him, then changed my mind and moved to a chair. I drew in a breath and faced him. "That man is her father," I said, biting the bullet and jumping straight into the fire.

"David Long?" he said, the suggestion in his voice clear. "You and David Long? And you never once told me?"

"Not David Long," I said. "I didn't meet David until a few months ago."

"Then, what?"

"It's David's body," I explained. "But Eric's soul."

"Dammit, Kate," he said, his voice finally edging toward fury. He stood up and ran his fingers through his hair. "You think this is some kind of a joke? Some asshole teacher is taking advantage of our daughter and—"

"Not an asshole teacher," I said. "Her father. I swear to God, Stuart." I crossed myself. "As God as my witness, I'm telling the truth."

"This had better be good," he said, his voice harsher than I'd ever heard. "Talk. Now."

And so I did. Starting all the way back with my childhood. "That's all I knew," I said, reaching my teenage years. "I'd grown up in the *Forza* dorms, studying, training. And when I was old enough, I started hunting, too."

"And Eric?"

"My partner," I said. "At first. Then my husband. And we wanted a family, but life expectancy for Demon Hunters isn't off the charts, so we retired in L.A. And then when I got pregnant, we moved to San Diablo."

"And the story about Eric being mugged? Dying in San Francisco?"

"True," I said. "Or, at least, I thought it was at the time. It turns out it's more complicated than that. But I swear to you, when we met, I was out of the demon-hunting business."

"This is a lot to take in, Kate."

"I know," I said. "I'm sorry. I've been looking for a way to tell you, but—"

"Maybe you should have looked harder," he said.

"Yeah," I agreed. "Maybe I should have."

"Does Allie know?" he asked, then immediately answered himself. "I guess she better. Otherwise she thinks he's just the chemistry teacher."

"She knows," I said. "But she's only known a few months."

I backtracked then, explaining how I'd first encountered Goramesh, how I'd been sucked back into demon hunting in order to keep my family safe.

"Doesn't sound all that safe to me," Stuart said. "Timmy and Allie were in that graveyard," he said, referring to a huge battle at the end of last summer. Stuart hadn't known I'd battled a demon; he'd only known the kids had been thrust into danger.

"It's not just about us," I said. "It's the whole world. It's good and evil. Life and death. Stuart, you saw that thing tonight. That's a demon, and now he's walking the earth, with nothing but death and destruction as a goal. And I'm one of the few people on this earth trained to stop him."

"And here I was impressed when you managed to make a cake that didn't sag in the middle."

I managed a small smile. "I can take out a demon," I said. "Doesn't mean I can bake a cake."

He sat down again, his expression pensive. "The Halloween toy," he said. "Not from an Italian friend, I take it?"

"Not exactly."

"Mmm."

"Stuart?" I dragged my teeth over my lower lip. "What are you thinking?"

"That all this is a bit much to take in. That you should have told me everything ages ago. And—dammit, Kate—I'm jealous as hell that you've been spending time with Eric." He cocked his head. "*Only* spending time. Working with him. On all this demon stuff. Right?"

"Yes. Of course. How can you even ask that? You're my husband."

"But so is he," Stuart countered.

"I would never be unfaithful to you," I said. "I would have hoped you knew me well enough to know that."

"Exactly what I would have hoped," he said, his voice sharp.

Score one for Stuart.

"What are you going to do?" I asked.

"I don't know," he said. "I came home planning to pack a bag for me and Timmy and go to a hotel. I'm not really sure why I didn't. Maybe I wanted the explanation. Maybe I wanted to believe you when you said you'd explain everything."

"I did explain," I said, swallowing a throat full of tears.

"You did," he said. "And I appreciate that. But my God, Kate. Zombies in our house. Demons in our yard. Our children in danger. I'm not sure if I didn't have the right idea in the first place, albeit for different reasons."

A tear trickled down my cheek. "I see."

"Will you give it up? Can you walk away and tell this *Forza* thing that you've had enough?"

"No," I said, then saw him wince at the harshness of my answer. "I don't have a choice. When Eric and I retired here, we thought we could walk away from *Forza*, from being Hunters. But it's not a job, Stuart. It's my life. And life finds you, you know? I made a choice a long time ago to be a Hunter," I said, though in truth the choice had been made for me. Raised in the *Forza* dorms, I had known no other life. "And if I had to do it all over again, I'd make the same choice. Because this is important stuff. I'm fighting evil, Stuart. Can you understand that? The world needs people who can fight the good fight."

I licked my lips, watching his face, but unable to read it. "This life has made me the woman I am. The woman you love. Who loves you. So it's up to you now, Stuart. Can you live with that? Can you love the woman I am?"

"Oh, Kate . . ."

"Please," I said, fighting tears. "Please tell me you'll stay."

"I love you, too," he said. "It's a lot to make work."

"I know it is. But we can do it. Please, Stuart. Please try."

He stood there, his usually expressive eyes unreadable, then turned and went to the back door. I saw him hesitate, then open it and go outside. I waited, not sure if I should follow, but after five minutes I couldn't take it any longer.

I found him on the swing, and his eyes cut toward me as I stepped through the threshold.

"Stuart?" I asked my voice small.

A beat, and then he held out his hand, reaching for me. I went to him, hope and relief vying for space in my heart. He settled me on his lap and pulled me close, tears brimming in his eyes, too. "It's going to be hard, isn't it?"

"Everything worthwhile is," I said. "Are we worth it?"

A silence that seemed to last forever filled the room. Then he nodded. "Yeah," he said. "We are."

I woke up feeling warm and loved and relieved. The night had been sheer hell, but in the end it had been worth it. Stuart knew the truth, and yet he'd chosen to stay with me, his body as much as his words assuring me that he loved me.

The bedcovers were horribly rumpled, but Stuart wasn't buried in the pile. I checked the clock, and saw that it was after ten. I sat up with a start, realizing that Stuart was long gone for the office. My purse was by the bed, and I reached into it, fumbling for my cell phone to call David. I needed to know that Ben had been taken care of. He deserved the best; surely more than he'd gotten.

I found a voice mail waiting for me. David, assuring me that he was arranging everything. That *Forza* had been called in, and that Father Ben was in good hands. I closed my eyes, crossed myself, and said a silent prayer.

Then I swung my legs off the bed. I wanted revenge—wanted to find this new demon that Goramesh and Abaddon had merged into—and yet I didn't know where to begin. They were surely gone now. And as much as I'd told Stuart that this was my life now, I couldn't see hauling myself all over the world chasing demons, even if my husband was home holding down the fort.

The truth, though, was that I was secretly glad it was over. I felt ripped apart from the inside. I needed time to decompress. Time to get over losses and assimilate the changes in my life.

I padded into the hallway and checked Timmy's room. Empty, which wasn't too surprising. I was sure Allie had gotten him up, and now I needed to go down and talk with her. I'd checked in on her last night, but she was sound asleep and I couldn't find it in my heart to wake her. Now, though, I needed to see how she was doing after last night's horror.

But it wasn't Allie I found at the kitchen table with my little munchkin. Instead, I found Stuart, a bowl of oatmeal in front of him and a bright blue spoon in his hand.

"Come on, little man," he was saying. "How are you going to get big and strong if you don't eat up?"

"Chocolate!" said Timmy, and Stuart laughed.

"Might make you big," my husband acknowledged, "but

I'm not sure about strong." A flash of melancholy crossed his face, and as I watched, he grabbed Timmy, pulling him from his chair to plunk the boy on his lap and hug him close.

There was nothing unusual about the move. Nothing that should have my antennae twitching. But they were. And when Stuart looked at me over the top of Timmy's head, I knew what was coming.

I held my hand up, desperate to stave off the words, but it didn't work. The gauntlet came down anyway.

"I'm sorry, Kate. I can't do it. I thought I could, but I can't."

I swallowed. "What exactly are you saying?"

"I'm saying I need some time to think. And I need to know that Timmy's safe."

Ice-cold fear shot through me. "You're thinking of taking Timmy away." I stood up straighter, a fighting posture. "I don't think so."

"Kate, be reasonable."

"You talk about taking my son away, and this is as reasonable as I get."

"You can't keep him safe."

"The hell I can't."

"Was he safe last night? Was he safe last summer? And how many other times have there been? Times I haven't even known about when you were keeping him so very safe from the ghosties and ghoulies."

I shook my head, wishing I had words, but knowing I'd never convince him.

"I'd take Allie with me if I could," he said. "But you know damn well I'd win a fight with Timmy at the center." He looked me in the eye, and all I saw was betrayal. "Don't make me fight that battle."

"He's safe," I repeated stupidly, knowing even as I spoke that he wouldn't believe. Knowing it wasn't even really true.

"Did you kill that thing last night?" he asked, and I heard a glimmer of hope in his voice.

I wanted to tell him I had. That I'd done the superhero

thing and taken out the boogeyman, making the neighborhood safe and secure.

I wanted to say that, but I couldn't. Instead, I closed my eyes.

"That's what I thought," he said, standing up. "I love you, Kate. But Timmy and I have to go."

"**Mom?**" **I felt** the bed dip down as Allie sat, the scent of Earl Grey tea wafting near my head. "Mom, you have to get up. It's Good Friday. We need to go to mass."

"I'm taking a pass," I said without opening my eyes. I'd been in a funk since Stuart left, living in my bed for more than a day, sleeping and coming out only when I desperately needed food. Immature and irresponsible, yes, but that kind of behavior fit my mood just fine.

"But Father Ben," she said, her voice catching. "We have to go. We have to say a prayer."

"I've done nothing but pray since last night," I said, my fingers stroking the necklace Stuart had given me. "So far, it's not helping."

"Mom," she said, her voice breaking. I rolled over to face her, feeling like the absolute worst mother in the world. And why not? I was.

"I'm sorry, Al. Yes. We'll go to mass." I glanced at the clock. Two hours until the noon service. Surely I could pull myself together in two hours.

I sat up, expecting her to head to the shower herself. Instead, she stayed on the bed, carefully inspecting each of her fingernails.

I pulled her close and gave her a hug. "I've been wallowing, and it's not fair to you."

"It's all my fault," she said, her chin trembling.

"What? How do you figure?"

"I wanted to see Daddy. And Stuart—and, and—and if he'd just found out some other way. But he insisted on following you, and I couldn't stop him, and—"

"This is *not* your fault," I said firmly. "It's mine. I should have told Stuart a long time ago. There would have been an explosion then, too, but it probably would have been smaller. And maybe we could have survived it."

"Will you guys survive this explosion?"

I hesitated, weighing my possible answers and deciding truth was probably the best option. "I don't know," I said.

She nodded, then straightened her shoulders. "Well, you have to get up now. You're a Demon Hunter, right? And you have a job to do."

"Do I? They'll be gone now. The only reason Goramesh risked being near me despite the prophecy was so that they could have the joining ceremony. Why would he stay now?"

"Well, he's invincible now, right? Wasn't that the point of joining?" Allie asked. "So if he's invincible, why not stay?"

The kid had a point.

"Maybe the sword still works," I said.

"I thought it *didn't* work," she said.

"Yeah, well, there is that. But I can't believe the demons went to all this trouble to keep me from wielding this sword, only to find that it doesn't really have any powers. There's something else going on. Maybe the time of day when the sword has to be used. Maybe the blade has to be coated in blood. Something."

"I'll figure it out," she said. "I swear."

I pulled her forward and kissed her forehead. "I bet you will, too."

"Except who cares now?" she asked. "The prophecy said you'd kill Goramesh. But he's not around to kill anymore."

"Maybe he is," I said. "Maybe it still works now that he's joined with Abaddon."

"Get Gora-don with the sword and kill them both?" Allie asked. "That would be cool."

"Gora-don?"

"Well, what would you call them?"

"Touché. But, yeah, that's pretty much what I was getting at. But, again, why stay in San Diablo?"

She sighed, shoulders sagging. "I guess you're right," she said, pushing off the bed. "If there's even a chance you could take him out, he's going to be long gone."

"Unless there's some other reason for him to stay here." What that reason could be, though, I didn't know.

"I'll go get dressed for mass," Allie said. "Want me to check on Tim—*Oh.* God, Mom. I'm sorry."

I managed a smile. "It's okay, baby. They'll both be back. Stuart just needs some time."

The bishop didn't mention Father Ben once during mass, which wasn't too surprising, as no one at the cathedral would have yet realized he'd gone missing. Even so, I said my own quiet prayers for him, and also for Stuart and Timmy, pleading with God to bring my family back together. To give me the chance to make it right.

After mass, Allie raced upstairs, ready to hit the books. As for me, I'd barely had time to make a cup of coffee when the doorbell rang. I raced for it, almost careening into Allie in the living room. "Stuart," I cried as I ripped the door open. A guess that, in retrospect, was ridiculous because he has a key and is perfectly capable of using it.

"Not Stuart," David said. He looked at me, long and hard. "I hope you're not too disappointed."

"Oh, God, Eric." Seeing him brought everything back, and as I tugged him inside I felt the tears well up again.

"Should I have stayed gone?" he asked, one arm pulling Allie close.

"No," she answered immediately, as I echoed the sentiment.

"I came to talk to Stuart," he confessed. "I get the impression it's a little late for that."

"He's gone," I said, my voice not really cooperating. "He

took Timmy with him." I wiped away a tear, hating the fact that I kept losing it in front of my teenage daughter.

Perceptive kid that she is, she looked between the two of us, then took a step back. "I was doing some research," she said, hooking a thumb toward the upstairs. "I'm gonna get back to it, okay?" She pointed to David. "Don't you dare leave without saying good-bye."

He promised, and she disappeared, taking some of the weight of parental responsibility with her.

I led David into the kitchen, then passed him a cup of the coffee I'd just brewed. "I'm sorry about Stuart and Timmy," he said.

I cocked my head. "Are you really?"

He shrugged. "About Timmy, yes. About Stuart . . . Honestly, I'm tempted to try to move in on his territory. And I'd be lying if I didn't say that I'm fighting the urge to tell you it's for the best."

"Keep fighting," I said dryly. "That's not what I need to hear. Not today."

"I am sorry about what this is doing to you."

"Ripping me apart? Yeah, that part pretty much sucks." I drew in a breath, regarding him. "Do you really? Think it's for the best, I mean?"

To Eric's credit, he seemed to genuinely consider the question. "All I know," he finally said, "is that you're my wife. Everything else is white noise."

I waited a moment, letting his words wash over me. Then I held out my hand. He took it, and we stood there, lost in the past with the present a blur and the future a mystery.

"Kate," Eric said, his voice husky. "I'm sorry."

I looked at him, instinctively knowing this was an apology, not a condolence. "About what?"

"This," he said. "I promised I wouldn't do this." He pulled me close then, holding me tight even as his mouth took mine, so gentle and yet so firm.

I dissolved into the kiss, my head telling me to push him away and my heart craving everything that Eric had to offer.

I lost myself in it, finally coming back to my senses and pushing him gently away.

"You said you wouldn't," I accused.

"What can I say? I'm human. I'm flawed."

"Eric . . ."

"He walked out on you, Kate. I want you to think about that. He walked out on *you*." He tilted my chin up so that I had no choice but to look at him. "I never left you willingly, never stayed away. And I've done everything in my power and more to come back to you. Think about that these nights when your bed is empty."

I closed my eyes, trying to block out his words, not wanting the emotional maelstrom right now. Not at all sure I could handle it.

My rescue came in the form of the shrill ring of the telephone. I grabbed it up, then heard Father Corletti's soft voice on the other line.

"Father," I said, my voice carrying the depth of my grief.

"I know, child," he said. "And I mourn with you. But I do not call now in remembrance of our friend and colleague. Something has happened."

I crooked a finger, urging David to come over and listen with me as Father Corletti continued.

"The unthinkable has happened," he began. "The Lazarus Bones have been stolen."

Twenty-two

"So what does this mean for us?" Laura asked, putting a gentle hand on my shoulder even as she slipped a steaming cup of hot cocoa in front of me. I smiled up at her, grateful. I'd run her through the hell that was my life, and in true best friend mode, she'd turned the coddling up full blast.

Father Corletti hadn't been able to give us much information, but he did tell us that the mark of Abaddon was found in the vault that held the bones. And the priest who guarded the vaults uttered a single word—*Decimator*—before slipping into a coma.

The High Demon Goramesh was known throughout heaven and hell as the Decimator.

"For one thing," Eddie said, "it means there's some damned unsavory sorts in *Forza*." He looked at me. "And don't go sticking up for them," he said. "I'm not saying every last one of them's corrupt. But you know damn good and well that no one—not even some invincible mongo-all-in-one-super-dude demon—was getting into the Vatican vaults and pulling out the Lazarus Bones. Not without some inside help."

I didn't argue, primarily because he was right.

"How they got the bones isn't the issue," David said. "The question is, what do we do now?"

"Assuming there's even something for us to do," I said. "Unless Gora-don is coming back to San Diablo, it's not really our problem."

"We can make it our problem," he said. "Head after him. Chase him down and destroy the bastard before he does any more harm in the world. I think Ben deserves that, don't you?"

"Of course," I said, starting to feel a bit battered. "But I can't pack up and gallivant around the globe. I have a home here. A family. Roots."

"Still?" he asked, as Laura, Allie, and Eddie turned sharply to gape at him.

I wanted to lash back at him, to reach out and slap this man I truly did love with all my heart. He'd crossed the line just now. Because he wasn't the only man I loved, and he damn well knew it.

"Kate," Laura said, apparently reading me right. She made a motion with her hand, the kind of gesture moms use to remind their toddlers to sit down and be good.

I sat, scowling and wondering if I'd get a cookie for behaving.

"Daddy's right," Allie said. "It wouldn't have to be like we're leaving for good. But if we have a lead, shouldn't we follow it? For Father Ben?" she added, with a catch in her voice.

"Oh, baby," I said, melting a little bit. "Believe me, I want to nail them to the wall as much as you do. But it's a moot point, isn't it? We *don't* have a lead. We don't have anything."

"So we patrol tonight," David said. "Might not find anything. But if we run across a demon, we may also run across some buzz about where the Big Bad has gone."

"Can I come?" Allie asked, looking between me and David before putting her hands together as if in prayer. "Please? I'll be good. I'll be careful."

I caught David's eye, saw that his face was passive, regretful. This was my decision, I knew; David wasn't going to countermand me again.

"Yeah," I said, taking a deep breath. "You can come."

"Yes!" She gave a little whoop and started dancing around the kitchen, and despite myself, I had to smile.

"Do you really think you'll learn anything?" Laura asked. "I mean, why come back here? There's a whole big world of cemeteries out there. Lots of potential bodies to raise."

"But there must be a reason to come here," Allie said. "This is where they came in the first place."

"But that's because the Lazarus Bones were hidden here," I said.

"Then why didn't he just take the bones and leave?" she asked. "Why hang out here to try to raise the dead? I mean, by that time you were pretty on to Goramesh. He knew it was going to be a battle. Why not take the easy way out?"

Why not indeed?

"Kid's got a good point," Eddie said. "Is there something about San Diablo that makes it a better place for raising the undead?"

"I don't know why it would be," I said. "But with this town," I had to admit, "anything is possible."

"The more I think about it, the more I think Allie's right," I said, later that evening as we walked along the boardwalk.

"Yay, me!" she said, keeping up the pace between me and David. "What am I right about?"

"That Goramesh tried to use the Lazarus Bones here for a reason. And that means that Gora-don will be back, too."

"What reason?" David asked.

"I'm not sure," I admitted. "But think about it. Goramesh made a big deal out of raising an army of the dead. But it's not like we had barrels full of the Lazarus Bones. How many bodies can one little bag animate?"

"How much did it take you to raise me?"

"Not much," I admitted. I frowned. "Maybe that's it. He was planning on raising as many corpses as he could until the dust ran out. But I don't think so. I think there's something about our cemetery that lets the bones work exponentially."

"Like a spider web," Allie said. "One body connects to another and to another until all the dead bodies rise and do their zombie thing."

"Pretty much, yeah."

"But we can't prove it," Allie said. "It's not like we have any of the dust left."

"And we were in the cemetery when you raised me," David said. "Nobody else came back to life."

"True. But you weren't buried."

We all looked at each other and shrugged. It was a good theory—as sci-fi television plotlines go—but hard to prove out in practice.

"So do we post a sentry at the cemetery?" Allie said. "Regular patrols?"

"We'll have to beef up patrols," I said. "But it won't be difficult for them to simply pick a time when we're not around. We leave, Gora-don comes, and a few hours later— *poof!*—an army of the undead."

"Yuck," Allie said. "I'm not sure I'm really liking that scenario."

"Me, neither," I admitted.

"We don't even know if it *is* the scenario," David said. "And the truth is that we're not going find the answer tonight. For that matter, I'm not sure we're going to find *anything* out tonight. As far as I can tell, the Elvis demons have left the building."

He grinned down at Allie, who rolled her eyes. "*Dad*-dy."

"Couldn't resist," he said. He moved between us and swung

an arm around her shoulder. "Shall we call it a night? Say we're officially off duty?"

"Might as well," I said.

"Good." He took my hand. "In that case, you can relax your stance, Hunter."

He squeezed my hand, and I squeezed back, feeling warm and safe and loved. And the truth was, I desperately wanted what he was offering me. A closeness. A togetherness.

A family.

The only problem was, we three weren't my family. Not anymore.

And as soon as I got home and into bed, I pulled my knees up to my chest and cried. I loved Eric desperately, but I missed Timmy. I missed Stuart.

So help me, I missed my life.

Saturday morning I decided to start the process to canonize Laura. I'm not entirely sure a non-Catholic could become a saint, but I intended to do everything in my power to raise her to that lofty order. After all, as I looked around our neighborhood park, filled with moonwalks, food tables, a petting zoo, and lots of game booths for the kids, I knew the true measure of friendship—taking on a horrible committee-head role when your best friend is so preoccupied by demons and husbands that she becomes more or less dysfunctional in the domestic world.

Not that I was all that in the domestic world before the husband and demon woes, but it was nice to know Laura had my back.

"Not a bad party, huh?" Laura said, passing me one of the ice cream sandwiches the committee had pulled together in my kitchen.

"It's really amazing what I can accomplish when I put my mind to it," I said.

"Mommy! Mommy!"

I looked up, and my heart did a little flipping number as

I saw Timmy skipping and running toward me. I scooped him up, swinging him around and around as he squealed and giggled. "Hey, Big Guy! You having fun hanging with Daddy?"

"No monkey," he said, with a pout, a comment that didn't make much sense until I realized that Stuart must have moved into a corporate apartment without cable. My poor guys, roughing it like that.

Speaking of my poor guys, the elder of the two came forward clad all in gray. Fluffy gray, that is, with ears and a cotton tail.

I pressed my hand over my mouth and made a concerted effort not to let my laughter show in my eyes.

"If the opposition gets a picture of you in that," I said seriously, "the election is all over."

"Thanks. Thanks a lot."

I cocked my head, looking at him. "Seriously, thanks for doing this. The kids would be really disappointed without an Easter Bunny."

"Not a problem," he said. He cleared his throat. "So. Any more demons? Are you still, what? On active duty?"

"Nothing much is happening," I admitted. "But I'm keeping my eyes open." I hesitated, not sure this was the time or the place. "I'm not going to stop, Stuart. You understand that, right? It's important, what I do. You saw what we're up against. It's an ongoing battle, and I'm on the front lines."

"I know," he said. "And believe it or not, I respect that. I'm even pretty damn impressed, even if I may not look it," he said, indicating his bunny suit. "You're doing an amazing thing. Unbelievable, but amazing."

"Thanks," I said, more moved by his words than I would have expected. "So, um, anything new with you?"

He laughed, a genuine laugh that brought a smile to my lips.

"What?" I asked.

"It's only been a little more than twenty-four hours, Kate."

"Oh. Well, it feels like more."

"Yeah? I think I'm glad to hear that," he said, so intently that even though he was wearing a bunny suit, I felt my face heat with a blush.

"Actually, something has changed," he said, as I set Timmy down to go chase Elena, who was waving at him like a wild thing.

"Really? What?"

"Found out more about the house."

"The mansion, you mean? What happened?"

"Turns out Theophilus Monroe actually lived there for a while," he said, referring to the famous descendant of the town's founder.

"He *lived* there?" I asked, my ears pricking up because Theophilus was famous for both his family tree and his obsession with the black arts. "In the Greatwater mansion?"

"Apparently he dated one of the Greatwater daughters back around nineteen twenty-four. He even designed the whole back balcony. Apparently it's an add-on after the original was cracked in an earthquake." He grinned like a man who's won the lottery. "With that kind of notoriety, though, the house has a unique appeal. Bernie and I both think it will be snatched up the second we put it on the market."

My heart started beating faster as I considered what all this could mean. "Did he design that spiral staircase?"

"Down to the cemetery? I don't know," Stuart said, his brow furrowing. "Probably. It fits the stories about Theophilus. Thumbing his nose at his family's piety."

"The family funded most of the original renovations on the cathedral, didn't they?" Originally part of the mission trail, the cathedral had undergone a series of renovations over the years, the most current of which was ongoing.

"I think so," Stuart said. "Why? You have that look in your eye."

"Do I?" Frankly, I probably did. I leaned forward and kissed him hard on the mouth. "Part of that's for Timmy," I said. "I want you to share."

"You're leaving?"

"Thanks to you," I said, "I've got some work to do."

"I may be completely off base," I told David. "But it's too perfect. Theophilus dabbled in the black arts. That's common knowledge."

"And he designed a balcony that led down to the cemetery," David put in.

"A cemetery," I stressed, "that seems to be the perfect place for raising an army of the undead."

"I'm with you all the way," David said. "But what are we doing at the cathedral?"

"Research," I said, killing the engine and opening my door. "I'm sure I've seen boxes of Monroe archives down there. If we're lucky, maybe there are some of Theophilus's notes on the remodel."

"I'm not sure we've been that lucky in a while," David said.

I shot him a sideways glance. "Then we're due."

"No argument from me," he said.

The archives are accessed through the sanctuary, and as we passed through the nave, we stopped and lit a candle, each of us saying a silent prayer for Father Ben.

"Are you okay?" I asked, noticing that David looked a little green.

"Fine," he said. "Tired. A little under the weather, but basically fine." He nodded toward the heavy metal door. "Let's go."

I hurried forward, pushing the door open, then treading carefully down the stone stairs to the cavernous room in which I'd spent more time than I liked to remember. "Those four," I said, pointing to a row of large banker's boxes along the far wall. "And I bet they're all completely filled with bugs."

"We'll see," David said, hauling the first one up to a tabletop and pulling off the lid. Sure enough, as soon as light hit the innards, I could hear things scurrying. *This* was why I'd fallen behind on my archival volunteering. Bugs. Yuck.

He brought another box up for me, equally infested, and we both settled in for the long haul. This is the part of demon hunting that I find boring, mostly because it *is* boring. And so far, nothing I was finding in the documents proved me wrong.

David, on the other hand, was obviously fascinated, spending way too much time skimming over each page before he flipped it and moved on to the next.

"This isn't a rare-books evaluation for a collector," I said. "We're trying to find an answer. You want to pick up the pace?"

"Sorry," he said. "Old habits."

"Sounds like you're reverting back a lot lately, actually."

He frowned. "What do you mean?"

"Father Ben said you've been coming down here," I said. "Do you want to tell me why?"

He looked at me, his smile enigmatic. "Honestly, Kate, I don't. Not now."

I nodded, unreasonably hurt. "More secrets," I said.

He sighed, pushing aside the papers he was examining. "I'm not going to get into it now," he said. "We have enough to deal with. But if I tell you it doesn't relate to any of this, that it can wait, and that I will tell you down the road, will you believe me?"

"I don't think I have a choice," I said. Then, because the truth was he didn't owe me his secrets anymore, "Yes. I'm sorry. Yes, I'll believe you."

"I'm not trying to hurt you or keep things from you, Katie," he said, his eyes soft, his attention only on me. "Let it go for now, okay?"

I nodded, then focused again on my papers. He was right. We had work to do.

Work that—unfortunately—we were still doing at half past five the next morning.

I reached over for the hamburger David had gone out for an hour earlier. "I feel like we're in college," I said. "Cramming for a final exam."

"You never went to college," he said, smiling at me.

"No, but you did." He'd managed to squeeze school in even while we hunted, finishing out his degree after we'd retired in Los Angeles. "I watched and realized I much preferred sleeping at night."

"Too late now," he said, tapping his watch. "It's morning. Should we pack it in?"

"Hardly," I said. "We made it this far. There's only one box left. We split it."

He managed one deep, put-upon sigh, but it was for show only. Then he reached in and pulled out a pile of documents, our hands brushing as I did the same.

"Gotta admit it's cozy," he said.

I tapped his pile. "Work."

Ten minutes later, he looked up. "I think I found something. Come here."

I went around, reading over his shoulder from a small spiral-bound notebook filled with cramped, penciled cursive. "I can't read it. Can you?"

"I skimmed through the earlier pages," he said. "It's Theophilus's notebook, and he was definitely dabbling in magic, looking for a way to infuse the dark arts through the whole of the town."

I grimaced. "Maybe that explains why we're such a demon magnet after all, despite the cathedral."

"It could," he said seriously. "It sounds like he made some real progress. Right here, see?" He tapped the page.

"*Filum veneficum*," I read. "Uh, my Latin's a little rusty here. Wanna help me out?"

"An enchanted thread," he said. "And in this part of the notebook, he's discussing the cemetery."

"So we've found it," I said.

"I think maybe we have. But that's not all. I've seen that term before. It's a term of art in black magic circles."

"Meaning what?"

"Not sure," he said. "I remember seeing it, but that doesn't mean I've studied it."

"So what should we do? Head to your apartment and see if we can find it?"

"I think I can manage one better," he said. "Come on."

He pocketed the notebook, then led the way upstairs. Outside, I saw that the sky had begun to fill with color from the impending sunrise, and the birds were filling the sky with morning song. David pulled out his cell phone and dialed. A pause, and then he rattled off a request in Italian to speak to Father Corletti. A few seconds later, and Father was on the line.

David looked around to confirm no one else was around, clicked the phone to speaker, then explained to Father what we had learned.

"You are right to have recalled the term," Father said. "*Filum veneficum* is the theory through which we believe that demons in their incorporeal state communicate. They are individual, and yet they are all connected."

"What does that have to do with the cemetery?" I asked.

"It appears that your Mr. Monroe was attempting an interconnection of his own. That, at least, would be my guess."

"At the cemetery," I said. "And Goramesh apparently thought he'd managed it. That's why he wanted to use the Lazarus Bones here the first time. Raise one body, and he'd end up raising them all."

"That would be my best guess," Father Corletti said. "What time is it there?" he asked, his tone suggesting he wasn't merely making chitchat.

"About six fifteen, why?"

"Because black magic is always strongest before the dawn of a holy day. A Satanist's way of thumbing his nose at God, you see."

"Today is Easter." I breathed, facing east and watching the light stream over the horizon. "I can't believe we're too late again."

"We're not too late until it's over," David said, slamming his phone shut and tugging me to the car.

"Call Eddie," I said, shoving my key into the ignition. "Tell him to bring weapons. And get Laura to stay with Allie. If you can't reach her, call Stuart. I don't want her alone. Not now. Not when an army of the undead may be rising just a few miles from our house."

Without a better idea of where exactly to go, I steered the car toward the center of the graveyard, near the angel statue where Goramesh had tried to raise his army so many months ago.

As guesses went, it seemed reasonable enough. The statue was a stone's throw from the Monroe mausoleum and tucked in under the cliff upon which the Greatwater Mansion perched.

"This better be right," I said, the van bumping along the caliche-covered roadway. "It's a big cemetery, and I don't have another idea."

"It's right," David said, his voice all business. "Look."

I turned to follow his finger, then gasped in surprise. Even though I'd been expecting it—even though I feared it—the sight of dozens and dozens of bodies clawing their way out of the ground shocked me. And, yes, it terrified me, too. Two against hundreds—with an invincible demon thrown in to the mix. It didn't sound like a battle we'd walk away from.

"*There,*" David said. "Cut across the grass and mow down as many as you can."

"Right," I said, forcing myself to think positively. We couldn't fail. Fail, and my children were in danger. Fail, and the whole world fell.

I gunned it, steering the car right over a line of five demons clawing their way out of the ground—and managing to take off a few heads in the process.

"That is about the grossest thing ever," I said.

"No argument from me. That way," David said.

I followed his finger and realized we were coming up on the rear of the angel statue.

"If they've already risen," I said, "will Gora-don still be here?"

"I don't know," David said grimly. "But my guess is yes."

"Because he needs to be nearby to control the zombies?"

"They're not zombies, Kate. Not any more than I am."

I flinched. "Right." I knew that. This was the Lazarus Bones we were dealing with. Dead bodies returned to their original state. Portals opened. Demons diving inside. "Then why?"

"To oversee the victory, for one thing," David said. "And why leave? He's invincible now, isn't he?"

"I'm rather hoping not," I said, hitting the brake as I took a wide curve.

"He's going to think so," David said. "But most of all, I think he'll be here because he knows we'll come. And we're the two people he wants dead more than anyone else in the world."

"Nice to be loved," I said, as we rounded the statue and—true to David's theory—saw Gora-don perched on the back of a grave marker, black eyes peering in our direction.

"Party time," David said, pushing open his door.

I grabbed my hunting vest and the sword, then followed him. Or I tried to, anyway. A crowd of five demons had gathered at my door. I scurried to David's side of the car, jumped out, then jammed my splinted finger forward to get an approaching demon with a solid poke through the eye.

"You cannot win," Gora-don said. "Look around you. My army walks, and today, I shall have my revenge upon you two."

"I wouldn't be so sure," I said, though I confess the impact was probably lost as midway through the sentence a demon pounced on me, knocking me to the ground and landing a punch so solid in my gut it knocked the wind out of me.

"Kate!" David yelled, slicing his cane through the air and slamming hard against the demon. He wobbled and let go of me, and I used my handy-dandy sword to slice off the creature's head, then stabbed the beast through the eye for good measure. No sense having any more headless demons roaming around.

"Rise, children, rise!" Gora-don called, wings splayed wide as he stretched out his haunches, balancing on the grave. "Rise, and do my bidding!"

All around us, graves split open, bodies emerging, covered with dirt and dust. From the far edges of the graveyard, more demons marched, slowly and methodically, as if they knew there was no hurry. We were screwed, after all. Didn't matter if we went down now or five minutes from now.

"*No*," I said, pulling out the water gun filled with holy water that I kept in the vest. It sliced and burned through the flesh of the demons, slowing them down enough so that I could whip around and slice through two more demons.

I needed to keep thinking positively. I had the Sword of Caelum, and although it had failed me last time, this time my faith would see us through. Somehow, we'd find a way to win. Gora-don couldn't be invincible. Because that meant we'd already lost. And that was a result I simply couldn't accept.

"Fools!" the demon hissed. One wing lifted to the sky. "*Now, my children. End this now.*"

The demons who'd been moving slowly now speeded up, surrounding us, moving in for the kill.

"Gora-don," I said. "We have to go after him. Kill the maker and we'll kill all of these guys."

"You're sure?"

I remembered what Father Corletti had told me. About how David and I were connected now. "Yeah," I said. "I'm sure."

"Easier said than done," David said. "Especially as rumor has it he's invincible."

"There has to be a way," I said, tossing my now-empty water gun aside, then lunging forward. I nailed a demon through the eye with my splinted finger even as I kicked backwards to loose the one who'd grabbed hold of my ankle. "Got any tricks up your sleeve this time?"

"Fresh out of cardinal fire," he said, as we both kicked and chopped and slashed our way through our seemingly endless horde of attackers. "Sorry."

"And it would have been so perfect," I quipped.

"This time, I think it would have its downside," he said, then shoved the point of his cane through the eye of an old lady barreling down on him.

I grimaced as the throng in front of me parted, making way for one single demon rushing toward me, the sound of Gora-don's cackle lifting all the way up to heaven. I gasped, stunned by what I saw.

Eric. Fresh from the grave, his body restored courtesy of the Lazarus Bones.

"No!" I cried, my eyes on Eric's body even as Gora-don swooped through the sky, landing in front of David with wings spread.

"What's the matter, Katie?" Eric's body said. "Aren't you happy to see me?"

"Kill him, Katie," David shouted, but I hesitated. So help me, I hesitated, and in that split second of indecision, he grabbed me, yanking me toward him and catching me around the neck. Fifteen yards away, David was holding his own against Gora-don, and no help to me. If I was going to survive this, I was going to do it on my own.

"Time to die, sweetheart," Eric said, the words ending in a howl, low and guttural as a stream of holy water hit him in the face.

"Get your hands off her, you filthy swine," Stuart called—his voice filling me with both joy and relief.

I twisted out of the Eric-demon's reach, then saw Stuart and Eddie rushing forward, armed with super-squirters, knives, and crossbows.

"Easier than arguing with him," Eddie said. "And you sounded like you needed the help."

"You will all die now," Eric said, standing back up and rushing toward Stuart.

Eddie got him with another blast of holy water, then screamed at me to go help David. "I'll watch this one," he said with a nod toward Stuart, who was actually managing to hold his own. "You take that sword and put it to good use."

Since that was an idea I was more than happy to get behind, I raced toward where David and Gora-don sparred, David lunging with the saber from his cane even as the demon seemed to effortlessly parry.

"Weakling," it hissed. "Do you really think you can win against me? You cannot. Do not even try. Join me instead. Join me, and serve at my right hand."

"I'm thinking no," David said, even as I rushed forward to thrust the Sword of Caelum right where the demon's heart would be.

Gora-don only laughed. "You see?" he said. "Thank you, Kate darling, for participating in my little demonstration. I am invincible, and even though Goramesh resides within, he is no more himself. The prophecy," he said, spreading his wings and lifting himself tall to the sky, "is no more."

"No," I said, shaking my head. "There has to be a way."

"Fool," the demon hissed. "Little fool."

"Kate!" Stuart called. "*Kate.*"

I turned, then blanched as I saw Stuart barely fending off three demons in full attack mode. Eddie was nearby, trying to fight his way toward my husband, but he wasn't managing; the crush of demons was too thick, and it was all he could do to defend himself.

"Hang on, Stuart! I'm coming!" I turned to race that way, but a swarm of demons blocked my path as well, and though I cut them down with the sword, they just kept coming.

No, I screamed in my head. This couldn't be the end. We couldn't die here. Evil could not be allowed to win.

But it *was* winning. Even as I held the sword that could supposedly bring us victory, we were losing.

We had failed. The sword had failed us.

Or had it?

I shivered, my thoughts turning dark.

Perhaps the sword hadn't failed at all. Perhaps we'd been wrong about who was prophesized to wield it.

I whipped around, slicing a demon in two at the waist as I did so. Behind me, Gora-don still toyed with David, now battered and bleeding from fending off the demon's claws.

It was, I realized, a game to the demon now. He believed himself to be invincible, and he was going to play with David and me in turn, tormenting us until he'd achieved his revenge, then tossing us aside to die.

I gritted my teeth. Not if I had anything to say about it.

Stuart's cries ripped through the air, and I knew we were almost out of time.

"David!" I called, then hurled the sword toward him. He watched, perplexed, as it spun hilt over handle through the sky. "Use it. Use it *now.*"

"What are you—?"

"Do you trust me?" I asked.

He didn't answer, simply steeled his face and lunged forward, planting the sword up to the hilt in Gora-don's gut.

At first, nothing happened. Then a flood of purple light seemed to consume the demon, whose disbelieving expression was almost comical.

"What?" the demon cried. "How?"

But he never got an answer. The purple light consumed him, and the demon disappeared in a puff. And as he did, the army of demons dropped to the ground, the demonic essence sucked out of each of their bodies.

I looked around at the cemetery, now looking much like a battlefield, and had to wonder what the authorities were going to think.

"What happened?" Stuart called from where he lay on the ground, his voice soft but strong.

"We won," I said, drawing in deep breaths of sweet air.

"Damn straight we did," Eddie said.

Only David said nothing. He simply looked at me, asking *how* without speaking a word.

"I wasn't the one in the prophecy," I said, simply. That was the short version of the answer. The long version was how I realized. So many hints and clues coming together. Eric's bloody palm opening Abaddon's chamber so many years ago. His temper. The blackness in his eyes. Abaddon's cryptic comments here and earlier with Ben, references to cardinal fire and the breaking down of walls.

The prophecy didn't refer to my giving birth to a child who would grow up to be a Demon Hunter.

It referred to Eric, in whose soul was brought forth a new kind of Hunter. A demonic Hunter, once trapped, but set free by the very cardinal fire that had once saved us from Abaddon's wrath.

I didn't know how. I didn't know why.

But Gora-don's death proved out that I was right.

Eric was part demon . . . and he'd been fighting his nature for years.

"Kate—" he said, and I realized that he understood. More than that, he knew about this secret inside of him.

"It's okay," I said, brushing my hand over his cheek, touching the face of a man I'd thought I knew so well, and was only beginning to understand that I didn't really know him at all.

"Kate," he said. "I love you. It's not what you—"

I held up a hand, stopping him. "I love you, too," I said. "I don't think anything could change that." I closed my eyes and took a deep breath, realizing exactly how broad a category *anything* was. But I'd spoken the truth and I wasn't inclined to take back the words.

"I don't understand everything," I continued. "But I trust you, David. I trust you to explain everything to me in time." I took a breath, then kissed him on the cheek. "Right now, though, I have to go check on my husband."

"Kate," Stuart said as I knelt down beside him. "Exciting life you lead."

"It has its moments," I said. "Are you okay?"

"A little shaky, but I'm alive."

"So am I," I said. "Thanks for saving me back there. I think I owe you big time."

"I know what I want my reward to be."

"You do?" I asked, amused.

"You," he said simply, his eyes cutting to David. "There's more going on here than I realize. More between you and David than I understand. But I'm going to fight for you," he said, his voice strong.

He looked at me, his eyes filled with both love and determination.

"And Kate," he added, his words cutting deep into my soul, "I'm not going to lose."